PULASKI
The Forgotten Hero

OF TWO WORLDS

By Joan and Mel Gordon

EL PORTAL PRESS
Savannah, Georgia
2017

PULASKI
THE FORGOTTEN HERO

OF TWO WORLDS

Consultant: J.R. Roseberry
Cover illustration: © Oksana Gruszka www.oksanaart.com
Interior book design and layout: Dianna Little

Published by El Portal Press
P.O. Box 10024, Savannah GA 31412

Hardcover ISBN: 978-1-945343-04-9
Paperback ISBN: 978-1-945343-05-6

Printed in the United States
First Edition, October 2017

To those who fight for freedom and all who seek enlightenment.

ACKNOWLEDGEMENTS

We appreciate all who continued to offer us encouragement, support, advice, and their time throughout this major undertaking.

We give posthumous tribute and gratitude to three people:

Raymond S. Gordon who passed his passion to write a book to his youngest son.

Louis A. Wilson, MD who encouraged Joan to always reach higher and whose medical research and caring for those society shunned served as the role model for Dr. Borloff.

Alan Gibson, a great friend and person, who hosted a lively discussion group where ideas were generated, voiced and debated. The mental exercise stimulated the creative juices.

They made us better people and we miss them and many other loved ones.

J.R. Roseberry encouraged our idea of writing a book about Casimir Pulaski, spent hundreds of hours editing our voluminous first and second drafts, guided us to others who were helpful, was on call to meet with us, and improved the title.

Johnny Gordon loaned us his mother's (Olive Gordon's) family Bible in which the reference to General Pulaski being the father of a distant relative was found along with correspondence written by great aunt Letta Bell Smart trying to verify or refute her grandmother's claim.

Aunt Ruth Atkinson, a special lady, gave us her love, support, and encouragement.

Dr. Douglas Shores' book, *Casimir Pulaski, General of Two Nations*, was a reference source we used frequently. His research is the most thorough we have found. We are grateful for his diligence in separating fact from myth in many areas of General Pulaski's life and death.

Richard Thompson, Henry Hamilton, Eloise Gordon, Benedicte Hatchette, and Laure de saint priest provided idyllic retreats where we could write, research, and refuel.

Paul Wolff put his personal priorities on hold to be our "Grammar Nazi". He saw that we needed him, and was tenacious in making our book better

Tony Morris of Armstrong University conducted excellent writing seminars on Ossabaw Island, Georgia where we met Dave Poyer and Lenore Hart, two great writers who were generous in giving us their time. They watched us and the book grow and advised us how to write better, spin a story to keep it interesting, and "show rather than tell" the action.

Frank Green, a renowned editor, gave us a much-needed dose of reality about how much farther we had to travel.

Chris Scott, Dave and Dottie Kennedy, Maria Boling, and Mary Ellen Johnson encouraged fledgling authors like us by creating and hosting writers' groups. All of the members gave us good, honest, and constructive feedback on our work.

Lynn Turner's creative criticisms helped make our work "better than we thought it could be."

Patty Patterson read the manuscript and gave us much needed encouragement.

Special thanks go to The Poles in America Foundation leaders, Dr. Jack Pinkowski and Peter Obst who contributed significant information about General Pulaski. Peter was our "go-to" person when we had a question about Poland, Polish traditions, or Pulaski myths.

Edward Pinkowski, a scholar, researcher and writer has devoted much of his life to the study of Poles in America, especially Casimir Pulaski. We are greatly indebted to him for the trails he has helped clear about General Pulaski's death, burial, and physical attributes through his generous donations.

The Savannah Committee for General Pulaski members, particularly Janina and Glenn Ball, also gave us insight into Polish history and customs as well as details about our heroic hero. Edward Krolikowlski, the former chairperson, was an invaluable source of information.

Iwona Stefaniak, Director of the Casimir Pulaski Polish-American Museum in Pulaski's hometown of Warka, Poland was most generous with her time and support, giving us private tours of the museums and information about Pulaski's infancy and childhood.

Warka Mayor Darius Gizka, was also very welcoming and supportive of our efforts.

Mary Landers, of the Savannah Morning News, Dan Poole with the Pickens County Progress, and Kathleen Williams of the Darien News added support through providing information and printing our articles about General Pulaski.

Marie Labarre invited us to speak to the Association France Etats-Unis to an enthusiastic audience.

Duane Rowan dog-sat, and took care of all the troublesome minor and major emergencies that erupted on the home front while we were away researching and writing.

Phil O'Dell was the first person we turned to when a need arose we could not handle. And he always filled it.

Christine Millar was our art model, assistant, house sitter, and on-the-job support person. We owe her much.

Oksana Hormuche used her considerable artistic genius to design and paint our front cover of General Pulaski on his horse. She also helped with the translation of Polish words.

Of course, our editor and publisher Frank J. Mendelson, praised, pushed, and prodded us in a professional and courteous manner to meet our self-imposed deadline.

Finally, the biggest "thank you" goes to our family members, present and past, who gave us life, love, guidance, moral compasses, and determination.

INTRODUCTION

We began writing this book when we found a yellowed letter in an old family Bible. In it, written in graying lead pencil, a far-distant grandmother claimed she was the illegitimate daughter of Revolutionary War hero, General Casimir Pulaski.

Was this true? Or was it a convenient creation to hide a family secret in the folds of a national hero's cloak; a national hero killed on a battlefield in Savannah. One who could not refute the claim? The question begged for an answer.

Hoping to solve this mystery, we began researching General Pulaski's life. Along the way, we encountered General George Washington, U.S. Minister Benjamin Franklin, Catherine the Great (not so great in Pulaski's opinion), Frenchman Marquis de Lafayette, the famed Winged Hussars of Poland, the ferocious Tatar warriors, and of course, General Pulaski himself. We also discovered a little-known fact about his sexuality that had been a closely guarded secret for more than two hundred years.

As we learned more, our admiration and interest grew. The more we dug, the richer the soil. Brave, honorable, and loyal, he was a natural leader who focused his life on military strategy and fighting for freedom of the individual in both the old world, and the new. He became a general on two continents, gaining fame by saving one of the most sacred religious sites in Europe, and later General Washington's life.

But he had human frailties. He was proud, arrogant, headstrong, and impulsive. And there was his darkest secret, one hidden from the moment of his birth—he had been born with a sexual abnormality. Amazingly, he overcame it and accomplished extraordinary feats in a mere thirty-four years of life.

From his early childhood, Pulaski loved horses. He became a horseman without equal. Pulaski perfected the hit-and-run tactics that were used by the American military long after his death. The cavalry he created was invaluable in America's fight against the British in both the Revolutionary War and the War of 1812 and against other adversaries in every war America fought through World War I.

The cavalry became a crucial element in the vast expansion across the continent, protecting American settlers who migrated into new territories.

General Pulaski helped save General Washington's life at the Battle of Brandywine. History proclaimed George Washington the Father of our Country and General Pulaski the Father of the American Cavalry. Rightfully so.

Even though many places bear the name Pulaski, his great contributions to America are little known. Surprisingly, this is also true in his beloved Polish homeland where he fought valiantly against the Russian invaders. It is suspected that almost two hundred years after his consistent wins against Muscovite forces that were often five times larger than his own, the Russian Communists removed his name from Polish history books.

Our desire to correct this injustice to a great Polish-American hero became a driving force for us to elevate General Pulaski to his rightful place in history, even as we endeavored to trace his influence on, and possible kinship to, our family.

We combined historical fact with much fiction to tell his story in human terms. In this novel, you will meet characters we believe could have helped or hindered him along the way. Our research took us to the battlefields, and towns of Poland and America where he lived and fought. We have spent hours in museums and libraries, and studying the research of Pulaski scholars. There are disputes and discrepancies in the texts we read and the tales we heard, confirming that all recorded history is subject to the historian's interpretation at the time of its writing. In this historical novel, we tried to remain true to the man we came to know and admire, and to the principles that guided him throughout his life.

Most of the battles described did take place, including the Battle of Brandywine where Pulaski helped save General Washington. Although this book is not purely factual, it does include many details gleaned from aging church records and the archives of libraries in Europe and the United States. It is a collection of real and fictionalized characters and stories, woven together to offer the reader a rich appreciation of this brave man. Back to the letter in our family bible, and a distant great grandmother. Was her claim valid? We invite you to join us on our journey along the many historic roads we traveled to find that answer.

One thing, however, is quite certain. General Casimir Pulaski is a kinsman of all who struggle for freedom from dictatorship, and those who have a love for horses.

We hope he will receive the recognition and appreciation he so rightly deserves — Pulaski is one of history's greatest heroes and horseman.

Joan and Mel Gordon
Savanah, Georgia 2017

CHARACTERS

They seized center stage in the sea-change that swept across continents, creating the world we live in today.

CASIMIR PULASKI, a child with very special physiological and intellectual attributes, was born to Josef and Marianna Pulaski in Warsaw, Poland. He met and fell in love with a duke's wife and defended Poland against Russian invaders. He brought his horseback military tactics to America and became the Father of the American Cavalry.

GEORGE WASHINGTON served as a colonel in the British Army, then defeated the British in America's fight for freedom and became the Father of his Country.

SOFIA AUGUSTE overthrew her husband, Peter, and ascended to the Russian throne as Empress Catherine the Great.

STANISLAW AUGUSTUS PONIATOWSKI, one of Catherine's lovers, became king of Poland.

LEAH MCELVEEN, granddaughter of an Irish gambler and an Indian Princess, learned the Indian ways and language in frontier America.

By 1777, the lives of this diverse ensemble were eternally intertwined. They were brilliant, tragic, and all too human.

THE INFLUENCE OF THE TATAR

olish General Casimir Pulaski, like his ancestors, bore a strong resemblance to the small but formidable Tatar warriors in size, strength, fearlessness and drive to win. He was as strong, determined, and fierce on the battlefield as any Tatar. And like their conqueror, Genghis Khan, he had the ability to quickly analyze his enemy's strengths and weaknesses and plot new strategies, all while on horseback in the heat of battle.

The Tatar were fearless warriors who swept down like wind-blown prairie fire during the 12th century from the steppes of Russia and China. They conquered, slaughtered, and sold into slavery anyone unfortunate enough to be in their path.

They were feared far beyond their borders, but then they had no borders to call their own. Horses were their lifeblood. They shared their area of origin, a remote section of Mongolia, with the horses which had been domesticated in that region hundreds of years earlier. A combination of evolution and heredity made the Tatars and their horses small in stature but explosive in action. Other, larger, Asians and Europeans had to bow to their ferocity and virtual invincibility in battle.

A mid-13th century church chronicle reports that when Flemish Franciscan Friar Jack of Rubruck set out on a three-year journey to explore the land of the Tatars, he was advised prior to his departure from Kiev to leave his European-bred horses behind, because Tatars had neither straw nor hay nor fodder, and his horses would perish. He found both the four-legged equestrian beasts and their two legged beastly masters sturdy and resilient, having learned to live off the land.

Along with horses were the similarly diminutive yaks, the long-haired bovine ancestors of the much larger and later developing American bison. The yaks and horses were key to the Tatars' survival. The horses provided transportation, while the yaks gave them milk—which they drank raw, fermented to make a sweet odiferous wine, and dried and pounded into a hard, nutrient rich tack, which, while bitter to the taste, was easy to carry across the frigid mountains and hot deserts—all of which they travelled in search of new towns and villages to conquer and plunder.

An ancient myth described the Tatars as riding the wind, drinking the dew, and having hearts of iron and whips for swords.

They showed no fear of death. Like angry ants spilling out of a demolished dirt mound, they poured down the mountainsides and across the plains devouring or destroying everything, killing and leaving no one alive to regroup, resist, or seek revenge.

It took the mighty Genghis Khan, who established the legendary Mongol Empire in 1206, to subdue the terrible Tatars.

In retaliation for their bloodthirsty rampage, the powerful Khan exacted a revenge worthy of the defeated Tatar hordes. He forced them to line up against giant cart wheels, then methodically slaughtered every man, woman, and child who stood taller than the hub on the wheels. The smaller ones were trained as warriors to follow his battle plans. Although Genghis Khan eliminated most of the pure Tatar tribes, their genes were carried across vast conquered areas in the bellies of raped and widowed women. While the Tatar bloodline became diluted, their progeny of mixed races shared a common trait with the warriors of old. They were always ready to fight and willing to accept nothing short of victory.

Like the Tatars, Pulaski believed himself invincible and proved himself in bloody battles against the Russians in Poland and the British in America. Americans and Poles are fortunate that for a few glorious, and trying years, he was indeed invincible and invaluable to their cause.

This is his story. This is the story of Casimir Pulaski, Polish and American patriot, Father of the American Cavalry.

CHAPTER ONE

A NEW WORLD

Le Croisic, France
June 1777

The battle-seasoned, yet apprehensive thirty-two year old Casimir Pulaski was preparing for his greatest adventure and adrenalin rushed through his veins. He was leaving for America, a distant and strange land. He had heard it was a wild place with godless savages, cut throats, and ruffians ruling by brute force. He would arrive knowing no one, without his troops, unable to speak the language, and unfamiliar with its customs. But he had overcome worse and he was more confident of his future than at any time since leaving his homeland, Poland. He would succeed in America. He had to, he could not return home.

Jaw locked in determination, he stood arrow straight at the edge of the wharf resplendent in the carefully tailored, gold braided, blue and white uniform of a high ranking Polish officer. He watched the white-capped indigo waves rush in to mingle with a teal green surf, crawl up the shell strewn beach, and retreat into the deep blue water again.

He had never seen the ocean and was awed by the vastness of the Atlantic and both surprised and relieved to see the calm beauty before him. He expected the water to be dark green and murky; churning into monstrous rolling waves driven by vio-

1

lent storms. He remembered a painting showing such a scene and stories he had heard that the sea was a treacherous place, swallowing large ships and their passengers. He didn't expect such tranquility.

Despite his regal bearing, Casimir's dark hair, ebony eyes, black moustache, and short, thin muscular body were clear indications that his heart pumped the blood of his fierce Tatar ancestors. He had the arrogant air of one who knew he was tougher and smarter than most. He knew it because he had commanded thousands of troops in battle against the Russian invaders who vastly outnumbered his forces and still, he usually won. He was rarely defeated and he was thinking only about victory in America. His greatest glory was yet to come. Woji, the old gypsy soothsayer, had predicted it.

Always alert and vigilant, as if he were preparing for an attack, he surveyed his surroundings. His gaze followed a hill that rose from the seaport and was abloom with brightly painted shutters and doors decorating the stone and brick homes of sea captains, merchants and their families. Casimir thought, *perhaps the bright colors help the wives, sons and daughters endure the long separations from husband and father that a seaman's life requires.*

At the foot of the hill, brusque and burly workers crowded the dock, rolling barrels of wine and rum, carrying sacks of dried jerky, hardtack, bread and bacon, and pushing carts loaded with hay across the pier to the loading ramp. Casimir briefly wondered, *why hay,* but soon forgot about it as he watched the bustling scene.

From the many grunts and curses they uttered, he guessed the dock laborers were from different regions — Africa, Spain, France, and Holland. Aside from their belches, farts, and coarse gestures, the common thread among them seemed to be a diet rich in gin, rum, garlic, and onions. They fell back to allow him to pass but not far enough for him to avoid inhaling their foul smells. He hurried along the opening they made, taking in their slovenliness and gave them a disdainful look.

Breaking free of the throng of workmen, he paused to again admire the emerald water at the shoreline. His thoughts turned to Franciszka. It was the color of her eyes. Eyes that, depending on her mood, could show warmth, humor, wisdom, or love. And love was what Franciszka was to Casimir, he had no other experience of romance and love and wanted none. Their hearts would always be together regardless of the distance that might separate them.

A web of mixed feelings tormented him. *Would she come to see him off? Could she, even if she wanted to?* He desperately wanted to see her once more, for what could be the last time. *Still he knew parting again, this time perhaps forever, would wound them both. And there was still, the unavoidable fact that Franciszka was married.*

His thoughts returned to the voyage. He knew little of America beyond what he had heard from Bazarek, the Turkish mercenary who had served with him. According to Bazarek, it was full of belligerent and illiterate criminals banished from their home countries. But for that matter, he too was banished from his homeland and he reasoned America must also have brave and civilized men like the U.S. Minister Benjamin Franklin, who was so gracious to him at Versailles, and the revered General George Washington. He admired brave and intelligent men and he was especially looking forward to meeting Washington, who like him, had repeatedly united and inspired untrained men to fight against a far larger and more disciplined army. Now here was a man and a cause he was more than willing to join. If only he could once again have troops of his own to command.

He continued to reflect on his future in America and his past in Poland. *America will be so new and strange, so different from my Poland. But I can't turn back. I have no place to go. I must prove myself and restore my family's name. What will it be like not to un-*

derstand the language? How will I communicate? If only Father were here to advise me.

The memory of his father dying alone in a Turkish prison, perhaps even killed by the Turkish guards, and the fact that he could not bring his body home for a proper Catholic burial haunted him. *Father deserved an honored spot at Jasna Gora Monastery or the church at Warka, not on Turkish soil.*

Casimir who adored his brother Frank almost as much as his father, knew he had tried. Frank had negotiated the release of their father's body and started home with it. But he had encountered enemy forces at the Polish border. Alone, without troops, he couldn't break through and was forced to bury their devout Catholic father in an unmarked grave in a Muslim land.

His torment continued as he thought how Frank died rushing to protect him, *I couldn't save him! And the location of our father's grave died with him.*

A large wave broke ashore, interrupting the calm and his reflections of the past and Poland. His thoughts returned to his future in America. *I have no family and no friends in America, not even a reliable horse. Oh, I had such fine horses in Poland, and how I miss them. Without a great mount, how can I prove myself?*

I have so many challenges confronting me. I will probably never see Franciszka again, he thought sadly. *She is more than the love of my life. She mentored me in the arts and history at Courland, helped me reconcile with the Bar Confederate leaders, counselled me to build diplomatic relationships with European monarchs, and was my comforter after the slaughter of so many innocents at Jasna Gora. She has helped me in happy and harsh times. I will be lost without her.*

And how will I keep my secret? In childhood, I believed it made me special — smarter and stronger. When boys laughed at me, I proved I was superior by throwing them to the ground and pummeling them until they begged for mercy. He remembered how con-

4

vincing others that his body gave him extraordinary strength and intellect ended abruptly in a French prison. A hellhole.

Even though I am tougher and more agile than most, neither I nor even Hercules could have subdued the eight brutes who stripped and ridiculed me. If America is the rough place I've heard, I must be discreet. He had heard that not so long ago, people in New England thought to be different were accused of being the Devil's disciples and were burned at the stake or drowned. *What if my anatomy is judged to be the curse of Satan? What would they do to me?* He knew it would be especially difficult on board the ship, but he was confident he would find a way to conceal his secret, just as he'd done most of his life.

Soon, I will be totally alone for the first time in my life, he realized. *Even in prison and during exile I had some of my officers with me. But, there is nothing left for me in Poland or even Europe.* His experience in France certainly was not kind. He could still smell the stench of the overflowing privy buckets and taste the maggot-filled gruel he and rapists and murderers fought over. He heard their guffaws and felt their rough hands as they stripped him, and violated his officers. *No,* he thought, *my future is in America.*

He turned into the wind and the ocean breeze felt gentle and warm. But it didn't relax him. He had heard far too many stories of violent storms tearing ships apart or driving them onto rocky shores, drowning all on board. On his way from Versailles, he had stopped to pray in the great cathedrals at Nantes and Le Croisic. Both held special prayer services for the sailors and fishermen of the parish. Tiny wooden sailing ships hung on each side of the altar as a reminder of how small any vessel is on the vast ocean. And the stormy scene in the painting lingered.

A sense of foreboding came over him and he thought, *As I step off these planks spanning from firm land to tossing ship, I will be stepping from the world I know to one completely foreign. I have no assurance that I will survive the crossing to reach that distant shore, or be any more welcome there than I was in Turkey and France following my exile from Poland.*

As he was having these misgivings he saw his lifelong friend Paul Dobrachek striding toward him and his spirits rose. They had shared so many thrilling and often dangerous moments since childhood. Casimir thought, *if only Paul could sail with me.*

Paul walked confidently down the street to the pier, smiling and waving to Casimir. A gust of wind blew his brown hair across his bronzed forehead, the afternoon sun turned it and his hazel eyes to gold. The breeze caught his redlined silk cape and lifted it away from his white trousers, blue and white vest, and blue jacket fastened with gold buttons. His self-assurance showed in the way he thrust out his chest and stepped in a victor's cadence. He and Casimir were a perfect team on and off the battlefield. They were too arrogant to fail, too disciplined to weaken their resolve, and too well-trained to let others lead. Casimir's spirits rose.

They met at the edge of the pier where they clasped forearms in the special way they had developed in childhood. Feathery white clouds floated across a cobalt sky accentuating their Polish uniforms of blue and white.

They were a striking pair. Paul was four inches taller and two years older than Casimir and had the square shoulders and sun-speckled eyes of the Polish nobility. The two were once again as invincible as they had been on the battlefields of Poland.

They were manly and magnetic, a colorful contrast to the laborers, farmers, merchants and adventurers hoping to find instant riches in the new world. Some were running from creditors, others from the fallen women they had tripped, a few from years of servitude, and most from dull futures.

Casimir had a higher purpose in going to America. After they had exchanged greetings, he turned to Paul boasting, "I will

6

help General Washington defeat the British. I will reclaim my reputation and restore my family's name that the whore, Catherine, slandered with lies. How absurd that she is now called Catherine the Great of Russia."

Paul cocked his head, rolled his eyes, grinned, and said, "Oh the poor British. How I pity them when you arrive."

They walked together as tall and straight as a ship's mast, with chests puffed out like wind-filled sails. Those on the pier parted to let them pass, most even tipped their hats or made a slight deferential bow.

"Is Maurice coming to see me off?" Casimir asked.

"No, I am sorry, to say. His mother is dying and he will be by her side until the end."

Casimir nodded. "This is sad news. I never met her but I heard she was a good woman who suffered much misfortune. Please give him my deepest sympathy.

"I understand why he can't be here and your need to stay in Poland. I look forward to the three of us fighting together again, in America. But before you join me, will you take care of matters at the prison?"

Paul's face broke into a crooked smile, "It's done," he said, "But not exactly as you planned. The money you sent for Captain Monski's release was used instead to buy a knife from a sentry. He stabbed a guard and slit Boshka's throat. He told the jailors that Boshka and the guard got into a fight and killed each other. Monski still has the knife and is in control. Everyone is too frightened to contradict him or to say anything about what happened to you and your men while in prison. Our friends are securing the money for Captain Monski's and your other officers' releases.

"All the men are grateful for the promotions you gave them as you were leaving the prison. As you said, it will help them secure higher-ranking positions in another army."

"Good, justice has been served," Casimir said, and desperate for news, asked, "Have you seen my mother and sisters? How are they?"

"Yes, your mother sent this," Paul replied as he removed a package from underneath his cape. "I suspect by the smell of my jacket it's those sausages you like so much. She and your sisters enjoy good health. Joanna has entered the convent at Jasna Gora and plans to become a Sister of Charity. Your brother, Antonin, seems to receive special privileges from his Russian captors while in jail. He writes your mother frequently that he is well and not that unhappy to be a guest of the Russians."

"What! Not unhappy to be in a Russian prison? How can that be? Still, it comforts me to know he is well and able to write to Mother."

"Now, what of your father, how is he?" Casimir inquired.

Paul's smile disappeared.

"Ah, that is the reason I must stay. I need to protect the family estate from the Russians. He was totally devastated by your father's capture and death. You know they were as close as you and me for more than forty years. My father, like yours, fought hard against the partition of Poland. He argued in front of the Sejm, every day for six weeks, trying to convince the Parliament members to stand up against the greedy Russians, Prussians, and Austrians who moved against us. Of course, Catherine's henchmen got to the members, in particular the Marshalls Radiziwill and Poninski, with bribes and threats. They cast the deciding votes for dividing the country. Father was heartbroken and worn out. His health was gone, he was the same age your father would have been, seventy years old.

"He came home to us with a burning fever and we lost him three days later. Thank God he died before the actual division of Poland took place."

"Paul, I am so sorry," Casimir said as he laid a hand on Paul's shoulder. "I truly feel your loss, for it is also my loss."

"Thank you Kas, you know he loved you like a son," Paul replied in a strained voice calling Casimir by his childhood nickname.

Casimir nodded.

"My dear friend, my business here is finished. Now, I go to help the Americans. When you go to Jasna Gora, please give my regards to the Paulite monks."

"Of course, I will, the brothers will be happy to hear of your good health. And I will join you as soon as I can settle my family business. I must make sure our interests are protected from the usurper, Catherine. I know it will be impossible to leave Maurice behind, so expect both of us to join you. We will show the Americans how tough Poles fight."

"Thank you, Paul. I have missed the excitement of command."

"Yes," Paul said. "We all have. I know it was horrible for you Kas, to be exiled from the country you loved and fought for, but it wasn't easy for us to stay in Poland under Russian subjugation. Maurice and I are anxious to join you in America and fight again." Then, he snapped his fingers and said,

"Oh, I almost forgot. When people heard you were sailing to America, I received several requests to give you letters and documents to deliver. One is from the Marquis De LaFayette's wife. I understand he is fighting with General Washington. He may be able to help persuade the general to fund your cavalry. I didn't promise anyone that you would distribute their correspondence. It's up to you whether to assume the responsibility."

"Paul, of course, you know I will be happy to do whatever I can to help loved ones stay in touch," he said, secretly hoping Paul understood *his* need to stay in touch with those he loved.

Paul handed the leather fringed pouch hanging from his shoulder to Casimir.

"I heard Monsieur Franklin set up some sort of post service in America. Perhaps you can use it and relieve yourself of the burden of delivering each letter."

"Be assured Paul, I will see to it that everyone gets his or her letter."

Paul hesitated a moment, glanced back over his shoulder and said, "Oh, one other thing I nearly forgot, a friend wants to accompany you, I hope you don't mind."

"What? A friend? Who? I would welcome the company of a friend. It would make the crossing more bearable. Does he speak English? Who is it?"

Paul chuckled at the mention of English and turned his head toward the mainland before saying, "English? Eh, I don't think so. He has spent his entire life in Poland."

Casimir looked out toward the dock and saw a beautiful white stallion with a blue and gold saddle blanket prancing on the road just as proudly as he and Paul had strutted down the walkway. Visner! Pushka's and Pearlina's colt!

Jan, his former trainer, now an old man, led the horse toward him. Casimir's joy burst from his face, eyes, and arms that automatically reached out to them. He missed Pushka during all of the dark days since his escape from Poland. He knew his equine friend had died by now. But, oh, how wonderful it was to see his offspring. The young stallion was an exact duplicate of Pushka. Casimir hugged Paul and dashed down the pier to greet Jan and Visner.

Gray and white seagulls flew by, salt spray brushed his lips and tongue, and Visner's nostrils breathed warmth against his neck. For a moment, it was his seventh birthday again and he was back at his home in Warka, Poland. His father had led him to the barn where Jan held the reins to his birthday gift, Pushka, the beautiful white stallion of his childhood dreams.

His father made him promise to take full care of the horse. He had to muck the stall, feed, and brush him every day. It was an easy promise for a boy receiving such a beautiful horse to keep. But now he realized that it would be more difficult, actually impossible, to care for an equally magnificent horse on a ship. Suddenly the joy Visner's appearance gave him was replaced by the harsh reality of his situation.

"Paul, this is so kind of you, but the Captain will not allow him aboard, there are no provisions for a horse."

"Everything has been arranged. He may not be as comfortable as he would be at home, but he will have everything he needs."

Casimir remembered the hay being loaded as he waited on the pier. "Thank you, thank you, thank you," he said over and over to Paul and Jan.

Afraid his voice would crack if he tried to say more, he hugged them both, grabbed the gold braided lead rope from Jan's hand, turned and strode quickly to the ramp.

With one backward glance, Casimir scanned the hill to see if Franciszka had come to say farewell. A good thing, she hadn't, he decided. If he saw tears on her porcelain cheeks he would crumble.

A deck hand tried to lead Visner onboard the ship where he would have to hang in a sling a good part of the seven weeks it would take to make the crossing. The horse planted his forelegs on the swaying loading ramp and pulled back against the rope. But Jan and Pushka had trained him well in Casimir's absence. When Casimir took the rope and ordered "Visner! Forward!" the horse followed his master's commands.

Visner was the one living connection to his family and home he would take with him to America. The horse was a reminder of happier times with his father. It was his father who knew when it was time for Pushka to stop fighting and training, and instead start siring colts like Visner. Casimir needed Visner, and he gave special thanks for Paul's wisdom and love in making it possible for him to bring the horse with him.

He ran his hand down Visner's side, trying to calm him before leading him back to the railing for their last glimpse of Europe and a goodbye wave to his friends. He thought the blue green water of the Bay of Biscay was the most beautiful sight he had seen since leaving the Pulaski Estate in Warka. What a long time ago that was. Nine of his thirty-two years were spent fighting and in exile. Years of glory won and lost, love and death, hardship and loneliness, and now, finally, an opportunity for a fresh start in a new land.

He snapped a sharp salute to Paul, waved to Jan and turned to lead Visner below decks when his gaze was drawn up the hillside to stone walls and steps leading up to its summit. A woman stood at the top waving a white-gloved hand to capture his attention. The wind whipped the wide sleeves of the blouse she wore under a blue satin vest, and threatened to dislodge her white hat with the blue plume. It was Franciszka wearing the same outfit she wore the first time they rode together. She knew it was wise to keep her distance, but she was compelled to see him off. She saw that he recognized her and waved to him again, this time with a slower and gentler sway to her arm. He realized she, not Paul, arranged Visner's delivery to him as well as the hay and other provisions for the horse being on board. It was her message of love and hope for a safe journey and it could not have been clearer or stronger, or more deeply felt.

He wrapped his arms around Visner's neck to show his gratitude before waving goodbye. The deckhands began casting off the lines. Another long look, and she disappeared. His throat swelled and tightened. He was on his way to America to a new world and a new life.

The jolting of the ship as it moved out into the waves brought Casimir back to the moment, although he didn't want to leave Franciszka or his pleasant childhood memories of Pushka. He turned to Pushka's offspring, Visner, and led the trembling horse below decks where he began a brushing to calm him. The horse seemed more comfortable in his new surroundings after Casimir finished the brushing and gave him a little grain.

Grooming Visner soothed Casimir. He sat down on a stool next to the horse and pulled out the package from his mother. Paul was right. It was sausages, and a slice of Sarah's wonderful cheese cake, but the package also held two books—his father's diary and one of Doctor Borloff's journals.

A note was tucked inside the diary.

CHAPTER TWO

A SPECIAL CHILD IS BORN

Warsaw, Poland
March 1745

Casimir, my prayers go with you. I received your father's diary along with Frank's belongings sent by the monks who buried him. Father would have wanted it passed to you. He kept a detailed account of your development and accomplishments, as did your good friend, Dr. Borloff. I'm also including the doctor's journal.

These two books give the most accurate record of your birth, childhood, and young adult years. Both men were extremely proud of you, and the love each held for you was boundless. Your 'specialness' as your father lovingly called it, inspired Dr. Borloff to research many other cases of sexual ambiguity and to similarly document those children's many accomplishments. Both believed, as I do, that you and others like you are able to draw upon the strengths of both men and women, making you stronger and smarter — just like your father always told you.

We shall be together again, either in this world or the next. God Bless my son,
Your Loving Mother

He was stunned. Casimir immediately began reading the journals and was amazed to discover the details of his birth. Combined with his own memories, the chronicles of his life showed an infancy and childhood immersed in an incredible love and devotion showered on him by his parents and Dr. Borloff. What others considered an abnormality was really an amazing blessing only he and his family would understand and appreciate.

He turned the pages slowly, taking in the story of his birth and infancy:

Josef barely got back to the family's massive stone home in Warsaw in time for Casimir's birth, with Dr. Thaddeus Borloff following in his private carriage. Josef went directly to his study, where he unlocked the glass cabinet door and took out a handful of his finest Turkish cigars, cigars that were saved only for very special occasions. He placed them on a silver tray next to a decanter of fine French cognac and nodded in satisfaction thinking he and Dr. Borloff would celebrate the ensuing birth later that evening. Just as he sat down to await the latest Pulaski arrival he heard the now familiar first cry of a newborn infant.

A woman screamed. The pride and love that had swelled within him quickly changed to alarm. He called, "Marianna?"

No, it wasn't her voice. He raced to the bedroom door just as Dr. Borloff flung it open and yelled at the maid,

"Get out, out of here, and no more of your silliness! Do something useful for God's sake. Fix some soup and tea. And keep your mouth shut."

Josef pushed past the doctor into the familiar bedroom. The day was the kind of cold that only comes in early spring after winter has already grayed and whitened the countryside. Seeping through windows and under doors, it numbed the senses into believing the warmth of summer might never return. Heavy velvet drapes the color of chestnuts were drawn across the floor to ceiling windows. They kept out some of the cold, and all of the light. A stone fireplace filled half of the opposite wall. The red coals, a large candle chandelier, and other candles flickering in wall sconces provided a dull light mixed with willowy shadows. Stale air scented with days of accumulated ashes, candle wax, and unbathed humans was trapped by the drapes and closed doors.

He could see Marianna knotted into a tight ball trembling under a mound of thick green and gold brocade duvets. She was sobbing. No one tended the cradle near the bed. No sound came from it. Had the baby died? He looked at Dr. Borloff for help.

"Is the baby . . . the baby . . . alright?"

He nodded his head slowly. "Yes, the baby is fine and very healthy from all appearances."

"Then why is Marianna sobbing so? Is she ill?" he asked, as he rushed to the bed, lifted her into his arms and pressed her against his chest.

"My Darling why do you take on so when we have a healthy child? Let me look . . . do we have a son or a daughter? I forgot to ask when I saw you so distraught. And why did your maid scream? Now, hush darling, let me see our child."

Marianna, struggled to keep him away from the cradle as he said, "Darling let me see our child. Why do you stop me? Do we have a new son or a beautiful daughter?"

Irritation crept into his voice when Marianna didn't answer. She had a hollow stare as if she were in a trance. She began whimpering and an almost imperceptible rocking back and forth that grew into a frenzied, tormented twisting, turning, and thrashing. She began a loud, plaintive, moan like that of a lone wolf grieving for a mate.

Josef was confused and upset. Marianna had not acted this way at the birth of their other children. With a frightened look on his face, he turned to Dr. Borloff.

"Doctor, please tell me, what is wrong? Was the birth too difficult for her?"

"No, she is understandably distressed but will be fine in a few days."

"Why? Why is she so upset? Tell me. Tell me what's happening. Is something wrong? Why will neither of you tell me if I have a son or a daughter? I want to know! Now."

"As I said earlier Josef, the baby appears to be healthy," Dr. Borloff spoke calmly, softly, "and Marianna is as well. You have a lot to be thankful for. But there is an abnormality."

"Abnormality? What abnormality are you talking about Doctor?" Josef asked, his voice choking in disbelief.

"There is uncertainty, uncertainty at this time as to whether it's a boy or a girl."

"What? What are you saying? It doesn't make sense, you are wrong," Josef shouted, teetering on a thin wire of disbelief upon which he had to stay balanced or plunge headlong into insanity.

"Josef, my friend, I wish it were not so. Perhaps at a later age, the child will develop more in one direction than the other. But whether your child is raised as a son or a daughter will be up to you and Marianna. For now, it could be either way. Whatever future you choose for this child there is no reason it can't result in a strong, healthy, and intelligent person who will make you proud. I am sorry. It is rare but not unheard of, and I have seen it before. I believe Church doctrine describes it as *'cause weakness'* when a child is born and such confusion exists."

"No!" Josef shouted. "I am a devout Catholic and I've never heard of this cause weakness. I don't believe it. This is a mistake. The baby was injured during childbirth and will heal to be normal. Marianna, isn't that what happened?" Josef clutched at a possible explanation as the fragile wire began to disintegrate. He moved to the cradle and picked up the bundle that began squirming and kicking in his arms. A hopeful smile spread across his face. The baby acted perfectly normal. Then he began turning back the yellow crocheted blanket.

The wire snapped.

"Oh God, no. A freak. My child is a freak! This can't be real. It's impossible. What made this happen? How do we fix it?"

At the baby's cry, Marianna recovered enough to take the bundle from Josef. She looked at Josef and the doctor and shouted, "Stop! Both of you stop! This is my fault. I missed Sunday mass twice in the last year and didn't confess my sins of vanity and pride. God is punishing me for my disobedience to Him."

Her anguish was relentless as she relived the months prior to the birth over and over, wondering what else she had done wrong. She began rocking back and forth.

Josef put his torment aside for the sake of Marianna. He forced himself to control his emotions. Taking her again in his arms and holding her close to his chest he whispered, "Marianna darling, you did nothing wrong. It is God's will to give us this choice, to let us decide what our child will be. It is our duty to procreate, and I believe also to guide, train, nurture, and develop our children to their full potential. This baby will simply require a bit more from us. Doctor Borloff said the child may change, and grow into one or the other. That is what will happen. We will soon have a normal girl or boy and this will be forgotten. I'm sure of it."

But in truth he wasn't sure of anything except his guilt and therefore this punishment. He whispered to himself, "No, Oh God no! This is my fault, it is because of what I did. It was wrong, so very wrong. That is why we are being punished."

Marianna tucked the baby in the cradle, and returned to bed exhausted and fell asleep. Josef, slouched forward, with his head bowed and his arms and hands dangling limply between his knees. He was racked with thoughts of his terrible sin that brought such a catastrophe upon his family.

Dr. Borloff moved quietly to a soft, heavily cushioned arm chair in the shadows of the far corner of the bedroom. He needed rest and he didn't want to disturb either Marianna or Josef by rising and leaving the room. Long ago, he had learned to catch short naps whenever and wherever he could. He nestled deeper into the chair and dozed off.

The doctor awakened forty minutes later reflecting on his own life. Few people lived to have a seventieth birthday and fewer still continued working at such an advanced age. But he felt an obligation to counsel and heal the sick. When he couldn't save a patient, he was the first person the family turned to for solace. His aching joints slowed his pace, and setting broken bones or saving fools wounded in duels no longer gave him the satisfaction it once did.

Still, the miracle of birth lifted him, especially in a case like Josef Pulaski's where he was delivering the child of a child he had helped birth forty years earlier. He considered such people his second family.

He had seen or heard of almost every human ailment and condition, even a birth such as this, although only twice. He rubbed his gray bushy brow with a hand stiffened by arthritis and freckled with brown age spots. His eyes were clouded by cataracts, and he showed the wear caused by decades of traveling uneven rocky roads by horse and on foot to reach those in need. And now he had a new burden, to console parents with an abnormal baby.

He cleared his throat and made a small coughing noise to bring Josef back to the present. Marianna had slept fitfully, and was awake, softly weeping while cradling the baby in her arms. Josef took the child from her and numbly pulled the blanket back again. The dreadful reality of what he saw showed on his face.

Dr. Borloff saw their pain and tried to soften it. "Marianna, my dear, your husband is right. Although it is rare I have seen this before. You are blessed with a healthy child who, with the right upbringing and environment, can lead a near normal life and become a successful member of society. And time may correct the situation.

"It's late and I must be on my way. You and the baby are fine and don't need me. I have less fortunate patients to call on tonight. And, just one final word," he said pausing to look first at Marianna and then Josef. "Do not let this deter you from having more children. I can practically guarantee this will not happen again. You are good Catholics, fine citizens, and caring people. The world needs more of your offspring."

Josef resolutely straightened his shoulders. He looked lovingly at Marianna, nodded his head up and down and said, "Thank you doctor. We will let God guide us. Now forgive us for keeping you from seriously ill people who need you much more than we do. I will see you to the door."

Josef paused and placed a hand on the doctor's arm in the foyer stopping him before he stepped out into the chilly March air and said, "Thank you Dr. Borloff. Knowing that you have seen this before, gives us some comfort. Will you advise us on how to best structure the right home life and training for the baby? What did other parents do?"

The doctor dropped his gaze from Josef's face to the floor and said quietly, "In truth, I have personally witnessed only one other case. The parents could not accept the situation. At that time neither I nor anyone I knew had seen such an abnormality. The parents thought it was a curse of Satan. They were ashamed and rid themselves of the baby. It was given to a peasant family in a remote area and raised as a boy who was worked in the field like an ox. I followed the case out of curiosity. He excelled at a very early age, easily learning tasks assigned to him and outworking much larger children. Unfortunately, he died from an injury before reaching maturity when he might have put his physical strength to good use at the shipyards, coal mines, or even in the military.

"I have heard of only one other. I met a doctor in Paris who witnessed such a child's birth. I am sorry to say that ending was not good either. The parents had the means to raise the child at home. They chose to raise it as a girl, but shut her away from the rest of the family and all contact with the outside world. She became a lonely, tormented young woman.

"In their paranoia that others would think the family was cursed, they built a fence that completely encircled the house. No visitors were allowed to enter the gate, much less the house. The rest of the family were as captive as the poor girl closeted upstairs. They lived like hermits in fear and shame that their secret would be discovered.

"When she was sixteen the poor creature jumped from her third-floor room. She landed on the fence and was impaled. It took six painful days for her to die from the internal bleeding and infections.

"The French doctor who treated her said the family later found diaries she had written in Latin. Can you believe it? Apparently, she had an exceptional mind and taught herself several languages as well as reading and writing from the books she was allowed to have while confined in her lonely room.

"Perhaps you have heard of Queen Christina, who was raised as a boy until she was five years old and afterwards as a girl. Even though she became Queen of Sweden, she had a troubled life and seemed to be uncertain about her gender. She had a brilliant mind, but shocked her countrymen by dressing as a man, switching from Lutheran, the Swedish state religion, to Catholicism, and having romantic liaisons with other women. She was driven from her throne and banished from her country.

"I am sorry to tell you all this, but you asked and you need to know. As you can see, I can be of little help to you other than to tell you that this child may be exceptional and deserves thoughtful understanding and as much love, if not more, than your other children."

Josef hesitated. "What . . . what about . . . is it possible doctor, for this child to have children, to give me grandchildren to carry on the Pulaski line and if so, would they be normal grandchildren?"

The doctor's eyes were full of empathy for the distraught Josef, and he answered the only way he could. "Perhaps, perhaps not, there is no record either way. Again, I am so sorry I cannot give you better answers. I wish I had more knowledge to share with you, but I know of no literature or research."

The blood drained from Josef's face and his lower lip began to tremble. He dropped all formalities and pleaded, "Thaddeus, please tell me. You've been a family friend, no a family member, as well as our physician. Please tell me, could the first family have been partially right? Could a parent have done something so wrong that God's wrath descended on the family and the poor innocent child?

Doctor Borloff was weary, hungry, and worried about a man ten miles away who was dying of pneumonia. He had little patience left and used formality to reinforce his position as a physician. "Monsieur Pulaski, you are distraught or you would not ask such a foolish question. You are far too educated to believe in such superstitions."

"You are right. I am ashamed that I was more concerned about why this happened than the welfare of the baby. Forgive me doctor. Of course, I know our child is not cursed, or lesser than any other child on this earth. It will be a son—MY son. He will be strong. And he will know that he is a joy and a blessing to this family. Like the poor children you described, he will excel at all he attempts. The difference is, I will dedicate my life to giving him the love, attention, and training to help him become a remarkable man. I assure you, he will be loved."

The doctor clasped Josef's hand saying, "God Bless you, Josef. You are an enlightened man and this child is more fortunate than normal children to have you as a father."

Doctor Borloff stepped out into the frosty night air and shuffled back to his waiting carriage. The wind whipped his gray hair and he tightened his long black coat around his thin, bent shoulders. He quickened his pace under the light of a bright but cold new moon and stars twinkling in an onyx sky. The dark smoke from the coal stove that heated the servants' quarters floated above the white birch trees where it was joined by wood smoke from the fireplaces. The scent of the coal smoke was like its texture, heavy and dark. It stung his nostrils causing him to cough and reach for his handkerchief. The smell of the wood smoke was lighter and more inviting. He breathed it in and thought how pleasant it would be to sit in front of his own fireplace enjoying the warmth and smell of seasoned apple and cherry logs from his orchard.

As he climbed into his carriage he reflected on how both wood and coal fires serve a purpose, one for ambiance and cooking the other for heating large areas quickly, although both could be used for either purpose. *Like people,* he thought. *Some give warmth and light like wood and see all the good in life. Others are darker, like coal, quicker to heat in anger. But like wood and coal they all contribute to the world, making it interesting.* His thoughts turned to the new Pulaski baby and he mentally predicted that with Josef's and Marianna's guidance, he will be different. *He will be neither fully male nor female initially, but a bit of both. Like the fires that spring from lightning and burn the grasslands to make them more fertile, he will be a special force. And, I have a hunch, given Josef Pulaski's vow to dedicate himself to the child's upbringing, he will make the world richer.*

The driver moved the carriage onto the graveled driveway and the tired doctor was asleep before the carriage exited the main gate at the Pulaski Estate.

Josef walked back to the bedroom where Marianna was nursing the new baby, tears streaming down her face. In a loud and forceful voice, he said, "My darling, we have a SON, a son who will be strong, smart, and a joy to us. We will name him Casimir, after Casimir the Great, because he will be a great man."

Marianna gave him a weak smile, nodded, and pulled the baby closer to her breast. "See, he is already a joy, a precious boy."

When the doctor arrived at his next destination, there was little he could do for the poor man with pneumonia. He had often said that pneumonia is an old man's friend, because it ends the pain and suffering of sick elderly people. By the time he arrived at his own home it was past midnight, yet his faithful housekeeper, Maria, was still waiting up for him.

The doctor had lost his wife, Irena, ten years earlier. Because his profession was healing the sick and because he loved her so, it was agony for him to watch the tumors consume her body. He was helpless when she needed him most. He was unable even to ease her pain without drugging her with opiates. Perhaps that was one of the reasons he now had more interest in research that could lead to cures, rather than treating the symptoms of diseases.

He knew, Peter, his only son, considered him eccentric for continuing to work, and resented the time he spent doctoring other people's children rather than visiting his own grandchildren. In retaliation, his son claimed to be too busy with his work and family to spend time with his Father, and he rarely brought the children for a visit. Thaddeus Borloff was thankful for his work. It kept the loneliness at bay, at least most of the time.

When Maria lost her husband of forty years, she applied for the job as Dr. Borloff's cook, even though ministers' widows were provided for by the local parish church and she didn't need income.

The doctor thought the reason was that she wanted to ease the boredom of her own life and to feel useful again. Now she was much more than a cook to him, she ran the entire household. She had prepared a lamb stew earlier in the day, and when she heard the doctor's carriage approaching, she quickly reheated it on the kitchen stove. She also had a warm fire blazing in the library fireplace and his pipe and a decanter of brandy on the table next to his large leather chair.

"Ah Maria, what would I do without you? This is perfect. Everything a cold old man needs at this hour," Thaddeus sighed as he eased himself into the chair.

"You work too hard. You should rest more and enjoy your son and grandchildren instead of chasing through the snow to help pampered people with their petty complaints who do not appreciate you," she scolded while placing a plate of piping hot stew on the table.

"Well, sometimes that is the case, but it certainly wasn't to-night," he said, as he blew on a spoonful of stew to cool it. "I delivered a baby tonight, and bringing a new life into this world is worth traveling through a little snow. It was even more so in this instance. The baby is a special child and it is for moments such as this that I continue to work. I'm sorry I can't tell you the family name. You may understand why later, and you can stop your fretting about my traveling rough roads so much.

"I still marvel at the differences in people, especially parents with their children. When everything is not as they think it should be, they turn to me in desperation and ask for answers I can't give them. What do they think normalcy is? Every person is different in some way. Why should one difference be acceptable and another not? This baby is healthy. Why bemoan something about its body that doesn't fit their idea of normalcy?"

Dr. Borloff shook his head in exasperation and took a large helping of stew, then, laying the spoon aside, continued,

"I have cared for many families and watched their young grow into adulthood, have their own children, and eventually grandchildren. The nieces, nephews, and cousins usually bear some family resemblance but are different in other ways. Some have high morals, are successful, dedicated and studious, while others are lazy, immoral, stupid, and dependent failures.

"What makes the difference? They all belong to the same family. Is it the family environment, the type of discipline, experiences of the parents and grandparents, or some other influence? I have some ideas. I think this child born tonight will be an interesting study in the influence of family and upbringing on helping a child become a successful adult regardless of obstacles at birth. I have no doubt that, unlike the others I know of, this infant will be nurtured and loved.

"Who knows how strong and exceptional it might become with the proper upbringing? I do know I plan to stay in close contact with the family and watch the child's development.

"In the future, I plan to practice medicine less and focus more on research while recording and distributing my observations regarding unusual cases. If, as I suspect this child excels mentally and physically, such a report could prevent parents from hiding or harming such children. They would recognize the potential for their children even when their bodies are not considered normal."

After finishing the stew, he fell into a pensive state. Removing the empty plate Maria replied, "Doctor, I could not follow all that you were describing about the child, but I am sure you were and will continue to be, a great comfort to the family.

"But, for your sake and the sake of your patients, please try to get some rest. Don't stay up the rest of the night working on your medical journals."

He smiled at her and nodded, "I will, I promise, Maria. Now leave me with the fire and my brandy as I contemplate what I saw today, and other unusual cases I have witnessed. Good night."

CHAPTER THREE

PENITENCE AND THE SISTERS OF CHARITY

Warsaw, Poland
1745

onfused and guilt-laden, Josef turned to the only source of comfort and relief he knew, the Church. He entered the rectory to pray for forgiveness for himself, and mercy for his newborn son. He stopped to kneel before the statue of the Virgin Mary, and bowing slowly moved into the confessional where Father John waited.

"Father John, please help me," Josef said, with tears in his eyes. "I have sinned and my innocent child has been punished. I broke my marriage vows and fathered a child out of wedlock. Now my new son was born with . . . the doctor calls it 'confused sex'. He is neither a boy nor a girl. It is so awful!"

Tears dampened Josef's cheeks as he buried his face in his hands. The anguish of this most faithful man of his parish was plain to Father John. "My son," he intoned somberly. "You are doing the right thing by having come to share your torment with me. I have watched you pray and have seen the pain on your face. I know your heart is full of love for your wife and family. But what of the other mother and child? Do you provide for them?"

"Yes, of course Father. She is a good woman and deserved none of the hardship I brought upon her. I am despicable and I am stupid."

"My son, you have sinned by violating your sacred vows. But I hear such confessions often, and usually both the man and the woman are guilty. It is rare that one or the other is totally to blame. Tell me, has she confessed? Is she repentant?"

"Father, she is as innocent as a lamb lost in the wilderness. Two years ago, one of my former clients arranged for her husband's murder in order to steal their estate and to leave her alone and vulnerable. When he attempted to take advantage of her, she refused his advances and he savagely beat her. Then he raped her.

"She came to me, seeking legal justice. Sex with me or any other man was the last thing on her mind. How can I explain. Over the course of several months of meetings with her about her case, and the subsequent trial, I went from feeling sympathy, to becoming emotionally entangled and finally physically weak, and oh so stupid.

"I knew I shouldn't have tried to help her. The man had been my client. To prosecute him was unethical, and I soon lost other clients because they feared I might turn against them in similar situations. I jeopardized my career and my family's welfare because I convinced myself I was doing the right thing. I started out thinking I was being noble, but I soon succumbed to her beauty, and the weakness of my flesh. Then Father, I lost the case.

"That was the beginning of my punishment. I later learned that this powerful and cruel scoundrel had bribed and threatened the judge and jury until they ruled in his favor. Now I am forced to tolerate his arrogance when I encounter him on the street. He even rides around the plaza on the prized Arabian stallion he received when he foreclosed on her estate.

"This injustice was a terrible blow to both of us, and drew us even closer together, extending the affair that would otherwise have ended soon after it began. But, it lasted long enough to produce a child—a healthy, *normal* son! I've done everything I could to repair the damage. I have provided her a decent home and have taken care of all expenses since the foreclosure. Her son will go to good schools, receive training equal to my other children and be well fed, clothed, and housed, just as she is. I will continue to spend time with him when I can, because every boy needs the influence of a father. But I will have no private contact with her or any other woman, and have vowed to be doubly attentive to Marianna and our children. Still this awful thing has happened. Now, with the birth of an abnormal child, I have brought a curse upon our house.

"Father, I deserve punishment for my wrongs, and so does that miserable excuse of a man who attacked her. If it were not a sin, I would gladly end my life to make things right. But my poor innocent baby and wife did nothing to warrant God's wrath. What can I do to help them? How can I help my family? My guilt is unbearable."

"Josef, surely you know God would not punish a child for a parent's sin. You must continue to repent, and you must continue to defend our faith which is so threatened in these times of turmoil and unrest.

"You should also make a pilgrimage and beg forgiveness from the Black Madonna in the Jasna Gora Monastery. You need not worry, your son will be brought up in the Church and may prove a blessing to you, not a curse.

"If you wish, I will christen your child in the privacy of your home, away from public view, but endowed with God's love and understanding. You are doing the right thing by bringing him into the faith."

Josef sobbed, "Oh Father, I don't deserve this kindness but Marianna and Casimir certainly do. Should I tell her of my infidelity?"

"No Josef, not for your sake, but for hers, you must suffer silently. To do otherwise will only deepen the pain and cause grief between you."

"Thank you, Father, I will do everything you suggest. We will be forever grateful to you for performing the service privately."

When Josef returned home, he found Doctor Borloff with Marianna and the baby. She was exhausted but calm and even smiled faintly.

The doctor's presence worried Josef, "Doctor it is good to see you, is there a problem?"

"No, no, Josef, everything is fine. I was just checking on our newest Pulaski. I plan to continue to visit, if that is acceptable to you."

"Of course, we are most grateful for your concern."

"It is more of an interest than a concern Josef. May we share a cup of tea while we talk more?"

"Yes, forgive me, I should have offered you some refreshment earlier, but wouldn't you prefer a glass of wine?"

"No, I have work to do at home. Tea is fine and perhaps we can have it in the front parlor, closer to the door. I don't want to get too comfortable or I might accept that wine and stay longer than I should."

Leaving Marianna to rest, they walked into the smaller parlor that was used to receive overseers and others who wanted to discuss matters regarding the estate. It was plainly furnished with a roll-top oak desk and chair centered in front of two book cases filled with almanacs, and journals about horses and farming. Two straight back chairs faced the desk which was covered with dark leather-bound ledgers containing transactions regarding the estate.

Against the opposite wall, two tufted green velvet chairs flanked each side of a small fireplace. A gold-leafed serving table stood between them. Josef motioned for the doctor to take one of the chairs, as he pulled on a braided cord hidden behind matching green velvet drapes. He moved to the other chair as Robert, one of his footmen, appeared. Josef asked him to bring two cups of tea and some cake from the kitchen. Soon Robert returned with a tray containing tea service and a small applesauce cake which he placed on the table between them.

Josef cut the cake and offered Dr. Borloff a slice. He accepted before saying, "I hope you don't mind, Josef, but I suggested something to Marianna without discussing it with you first."

"What is it Doctor?" Josef asked as he poured the tea.

"Well, I didn't give her all the details, I merely mentioned I located some Sisters of Charity who are willing to help with the baby. I suspect, under the circumstances, she will attempt to do all the changing, bathing and other personal care herself. It would be a huge burden, with the other children and household matters she must manage.

"That is thoughtful of you, doctor. Thank you. But I am not sure it is a good idea to have anyone other than our immediate family care for him, even sisters of the Church for . . . for . . . obvious reasons."

"I understand Josef, but this particular order of the Sisters care for soldiers wounded on the battlefield. Some of the wounds are disfiguring and debilitating and many times their genitals are severed, or mutilated. These women attend to disfigurements that they do not discuss with anyone, not even amongst themselves. They know that to disclose such things would make it harder for the patient. They are very discreet. Little Casimir will need a lot of personal training and guidance from both of you. These nurses will allow Marianna time to care for the rest of the family and focus on Casimir's emotional needs rather than his daily physical requirements."

Josef sighed wearily realizing that Marianna certainly needed the help. She was already growing pale from her worry and work. "Yes, you are right, doctor, this is truly a wonderful offer. How can we ever repay you for your kindness?" *It's so much more than I deserve,* Josef thought.

"I mentioned my interest in the baby earlier," replied the doctor. "I would like to follow his progress and record my observations in medical reports. I am sure he will receive special nurturing from you and his mother that will become a positive influence. It is that influence I want to observe and record. Based on the cases I've heard about, I think these special children are far more gifted than others. They seem smarter and sometimes stronger than the children we refer to as normal. I wonder if that is because they strive so hard to be like other children, or if it is due to some inherent strength that comes from having a sexual duality. I believe I can prove that when raised in the right environment these children will excel at anything they attempt. I also believe this condition may not be as rare as we think. The two sets of parents I know about hid or got rid of their babies. I believe many such cases exist that are never revealed. I hope my work will convince people faced with this situation that their babies are gifted and special, not abnormal And, through the proper nurturing, they can reach their true potential, exceeding the accomplishments of an average child. If my work persuades others that they are truly exceptional, then rather than being considered cursed and cast aside by their parents and society, these children could flourish.

"As far as repaying me for any kindness I have shown your family, you can allow me to visit often to conduct my research. I will not use names, or in any way disclose who my subjects are, for I intend to try to find others, as many as possible, through a network of doctors who may have encountered similar cases."

Josef, exhausted from trying to soothe Marianna and deal with his own guilt, nodded slowly. "This is a lot to consider at one time, Thaddeus. Allowing outsiders to care for the baby, and studying him might subject him to unnecessary exposure when all we want to do is to protect him from ridicule and prejudice. As you said, we want him to excel, but at the same time we want him to have as normal a childhood and life as possible."

"Josef, my friend. The past week has been hard for you and Marianna, but I give you my word I will never do anything to diminish or harm this child or this family. He is already very dear to me."

If my child can help others receive love rather than fear and abandonment from their parents the risk may be worth it, Josef thought, and then became confident about what his decision had to be.

"Yes, Thaddeus. Yes, for the sake of this child's health and development and for the sake of the others your work may help. I say yes, to both the Sisters and your research. We are blessed to have someone so kind and so wise as part of our extended family."

Josef and the doctor rose from their chairs and shook hands, to acknowledge their friendship and their agreement that Casimir would be part of Dr. Borloff's research.

"Thank you, Josef. Now I must be off. I checked the baby and he is doing well as I knew he would. I'll arrange for one of the sisters to visit tomorrow to talk about the care they will provide for Marianna and our little Casimir."

After seeing Doctor Borloff to the door, Josef moved the tea aside, poured himself a glass of wine, and began contemplating Casimir's future. *I must keep him away from public places where his secret might be discovered by people who would not understand and denounce him. Home tutoring or private schools with private rooms and privies will be best for him and not unusual for the son of a noble family. I will encourage him to participate in sports, rugged sports like wrestling, that require physical strength but do not involve teams with boys changing clothes together. And I will guide him toward a career in the military. God knows our country needs a real army that can defend our faith and our lands. Casimir may live up to his namesake, Casimir the Great, and become a great leader one day.*

His weariness was gone and he continued to think of the remarkable man his son could become. His mind moved into a fast-paced planning stage.

I will tell him the truth: that he is special. I know he is. I will guide him toward a man's career, the military. I will tell him that his body is different from other boys, not in any way less, but maybe better. And, in fact he will be stronger and smarter than other boys. Yet others might not understand his 'specialness' so he should not reveal it. Marianna and I simply must decide the best environment, education, and training to assure as normal, happy, and productive life for him as possible. Regardless of whether my sin is to blame I will make sure he becomes exceptional, succeeding at everything he does. He will have all the personal attention and love a father can give a son.

Joseph whispered under his breath, "I love all my children, but Casimir and I shall have a special bond."

He moved from the chair and hurriedly walked to the bedroom to share his vision for their son with Marianna.

CHAPTER FOUR

HORSES

As two-year old Casimir slept, Josef watched his small arms and legs flail as his little hands, already toughened by grasping the reins of his hobby horse, groped handfuls of air as if he were climbing a giant ladder to the sky. Casimir later told his father that he dreamt of horses, white horses, as far back as he could remember. In his most frequent dream, he was thrown from a great white stallion and rolled between its hoofs, before he regained his perch by climbing up its braided tail.

Josef was proud of his exceptional son who already displayed the defiance and competitiveness that would bring him respect and ridicule, glory and grief, honor and hardship throughout his life. Now, as he looked down on him, Josef foresaw that Casimir would become a strong leader and knew he had made the right decision at his birth. Casimir was all boy, a son any father would be proud of, and the upbringing he was receiving would assure his future success.

He ruffled the boy's silken hair while urging, "Wake up son. The new day has started and cook Sarah has prepared kanapkis of rye bread, ham and cheese for you. Today there is blood pudding, the food of the Tatars for strong warriors like you. Mother will join us for breakfast and then it's off to Graden where you can ride your wooden pony and wave your toy sword to drive away all those mean Russian soldiers. Your friend Paul

Dobrachek will be there, and I expect you to best him in every battle you fight, as you always do."

Josef was leaning over the crib as the small boy yawned, grinned at his father's smiling face, and tried to reach the corner of the waxed black moustache that curled upward at each side of his thin lips. The two had a special bond, and Josef could see that Casimir loved and wanted to please him. He seemed to already understand what was expected of him, and what he could accomplish. Josef cherished these moments with his son and felt his heart would burst with the love that swelled within him.

He let Casimir's fingers brush the edge of the moustache before pulling away, scooping him up onto his shoulders, and beginning a military march into the dining alcove the family used for informal meals.

Marianna was sitting at the table nursing Casimir's younger sister, Paulina. Josef thought she looked positively beautiful. "Josef, you are spoiling him beyond redemption," she scolded, still looking down at her daughter. "You have other children you know."

"Yes, my Sweet, and you know I love them all. Just as I know that this little tiger has also captured your heart."

"Where does he get such a strong, dominant personality at this early age? You are a strong woman, but your refined background doesn't lend itself to such a forceful child nor does my intellectual interests. It's like Casimir has inherited the determination and fierceness of his namesake, Casimir the Great. I hope he will also exhibit the wisdom and compassion of our great King Casimir. Do you think he may already know what is expected of one named for such a powerful Polish ruler?"

"I don't know, Josef, but after watching Casimir's older brother and his sisters grow up, I have seen that boys are more active than girls but they usually have more illnesses, and do not grow as fast or learn to walk and talk as quickly. His sisters seemed less distracted by physical games than Frank and they learned faster."

"But Casimir is different. He walked at an earlier age and is healthier than other boys. He also seems to have a greater ability to focus on and pursue things that interest him, whether pretending to be a soldier or drawing crude pictures of the horses he loves."

Josef considered what Marianna said, while thinking that her soft beauty masked a solid core of moral fortitude. She would tackle anyone or anything that threatened her children, husband, or religion. *And my intellect doesn't lessen my determination to fight for what I believe to be right. Could Casimir have inherited our strengths along with the best attributes of both boys and girls without the weaknesses*, he wondered.

He returned to the moment saying, "Don't worry my sweet, you can't spoil a tough guy like this. Now, where are those chess pieces he likes so much? You know, the knights on horses. He loves to play with those horses."

Sarah placed a large tapestry covered cushion in a "grown up" chair where Josef sat Casimir so he could reach the top of the table.

Marianna, pretending to be exasperated, let out a dramatic sigh before pointing across the room and said, "You'll find them where you put them after breakfast yesterday morning in the drawer of that table next to his chair. I don't like him having them so early, because he gets so excited that he forgets to eat."

"He will eat, I will see to it," Josef assured her. "Warriors have to eat to be strong."

He opened the table drawer, reached in and closed one hand over a black knight, and the other over a white one. Stretching out his right hand toward Casimir he opened it revealing the black knight. Casimir reached for it, and giggled when Josef gave it to him. He clamped his tiny fingers around the chess piece and turned back to his father for more, squealing "Horse, Horse" until Josef opened his left hand to show him the white knight.

Josef winked at Marianna, "Such a smart boy. He already knows there are more knights in the chess set and he wants another one!" He teased Casimir for a moment, keeping the white knight just out of his reach. Casimir pounded the table with the black knight repeating, "Horse, Horse" until Josef gave it to him. Casimir grabbed it and started moving both horses around the top of the table as far as his short arms could reach. Josef smiled and nodded to Marianna as they watched the white knight repeatedly crash into and knock over the black knight. "Our boy really will be successful someday. I know it."

But even his proud father could not foresee that Casimir would become one of the world's greatest heroes, courageously fighting for the freedom of two nations, in spite of, or perhaps because of his sexual duality. What Josef did know was that his son already had the heart of a true fighter.

Josef turned and looked out the bay windows at the Winiary Estate garden decorated with birdbaths, birch trees, and gravel paths where the family dogs chased rabbits and an occasional fox among the hedges. Misty sun beams streamed through the trees stringing sparkling diamonds on mulberry leaves laden with dew while the delicate scent of lilacs sweetened the air.

At the edge of the garden, young chestnut trees grew atop the steep river bank. They concealed and shaded the fortifications used a hundred years earlier to repel the invading Swedes with cannons. It was a commanding spot above the Pilicia River at a point where the water was forced to split around a little raised, grassy island. It was a good place for invaders to cross and a good place for defenders to ambush them. This was a lesson that Casimir would learn at an early age.

Josef quietly chuckled remembering that Frank, Casimir's older brother, had promised Casimir he would take him to the island to ride horses when he was older. The two-year-old Casimir had replied, "Now! Now!"

Josef was proud of the fortune he had amassed. His law practice provided a good income which he had wisely invested, buying large blocks of land, including towns and villages. The production of cattle, horses, hay, apples, and vegetables funded additional acquisitions. His father had died fighting the Russians, while he was still young, and Josef had worked hard studying law and later building a law practice. By the time Casimir was born, Josef's elderly mother had died as had both Marianna's parents, so Casimir didn't have the benefit of loving grandparents. Josef vowed to fill the void by spending all his free time with his sons. He hoped to pass his hard-earned holdings to his children, but feared the greed of the Russians who wanted to sack Poland for its treasures during their drive to capture a warm water seaport.

Josef turned from the idyllic scene outside the window, smiling at his rambunctious little boy, still pounding knights on the table. Reluctantly, he prepared to leave for his office in the nearby town of Warka. Although he had an unassuming, almost dull appearance that led people to believe him slow-witted, he was the most successful lawyer in the region. His drab suits draped over slumped shoulders, and a high forehead above bulging eyes gave him the appearance of a plodding turtle. He cultivated this image by asking questions in court that bored the jury, judge and, unfortunately for them, the opposing attorneys. But his mind was quick and agile, more akin to that of a fox than a turtle. Too late, the challenging teams of lawyers would realize the significance of his seemingly pointless questions and find themselves trapped in the crushing jaws of a snapping turtle.

He prayed that he could keep his holdings and that their lives could always be so tranquil, but he feared the worst from Russia and other border countries that wanted to overrun Poland. They were like hyenas waiting for Poland to weaken enough for them to move in for the kill and then cackle over their prize. Poland needed a strong army, but Josef, so persuasive in the courtroom, could not convince his wealthy friends to fund one. He feared what the future would bring for Poland and his children, especially Casimir whom he was grooming to lead armies.

CHAPTER FIVE

SEVENTH BIRTHDAY

Winiary Estate, Warka, Poland
March 1752

asimir vividly recalled his seventh birthday when he first met Pushka, his favorite horse. The journals gave him insight into the events leading up to that wonderful day.

As children, Paul and Casimir played together every day. Two years older than Casimir, Paul was allowed to ride the three miles from the apple orchards on the eastern side of Warka to the Pulaski grounds at the Winiary Estate by himself, where the boys spent their days fighting imaginary enemies.

One Saturday Paul's father, Tomas Dobrachek, rode with him. The two fathers were friends who usually saw each other in the evenings to discuss politics over brandy. Although Josef was surprised to see Tomas during the day, he greeted him warmly. "Tomas, my friend, please come in for tea and cake."

"Ah Josef, I thought I would find you at home on such a nice Saturday tending to more pleasant matters than legal briefs. Unfortunately, I don't have time to stay and visit but I came by to share some information that may be of interest to you."

"What is it? Not more bad news about Russia's moves, I hope."

"No, it's about that scoundrel, Potocki. It seems he got drunk before the big horse race at Krakow. He bet more than he could

42

afford on that white stallion he acquired when he foreclosed on your client, the Widow Wolsky's estate. While running the race, the horse broke stride as he dodged a small child who had darted out into his path. Then the poor stallion lost by a nose to a gelding from the Zielinski farm."

"Being Potocki, he didn't care about the child or the reason the horse lost. Instead, he went into a rage and beat the horse with a fence post. His jockey tried to intervene but Potocki knocked him to the ground with the same stave, ripping a gash in his face. When he started beating the horse again, the jockey swung his legs against Potocki's knees throwing him off balance. Potocki fell beneath the frightened horse and was trampled when it ran to escape further beating. He's paralyzed now from the waist down and can't walk. Never again will he rape another woman."

Stunned Josef asked, "But, what about the jockey and the horse?"

"Well, both required stitches but will be fine. When he got home, Potocki wanted to shoot the horse. But no one would give him a gun and he couldn't get out of bed to get one."

"He ordered that no food or water be given to the stallion. After a week, Zielinski who saw the horse's race performance, offered Potocki a decent price for the stallion hoping to save him. Due to his losses at the track and the doctor's bills, Potocki couldn't refuse.

The horse is now at the Zielinski farm. I hear he's for sale if you are interested."

"I just might be, Thomas," Josef replied, "You know that Casimir has a birthday soon. I'll go to Zielinski's on Monday and take a look at the stallion. If the beating hasn't crippled him or made him mean, he might be the perfect gift for a boy who wants to ride fast horses."

Dr. Borloff, affectionately called Uncle Thaddeus by Casimir, was watching one of Casimir's training sessions when he heard him ask Jan, his trainer, "Jan will you get me a bigger horse from the stable? I am a fighter! I need a big horse. Please, please!"

"Why don't you wait awhile for a bigger horse. Don't you have a birthday coming soon?" Jan asked. He glanced at Dr. Borloff with an apologetic look on his face. Casimir's gift of a spirited stallion was supposed to be a secret.

"Am I getting a horse, a big horse for my birthday? Oh boy, my very own big horse," Casimir said as he jumped up and down with joy.

Then he stopped jumping, his chin dropped down on his chest and he mumbled, "Oh no. I always get Frank's used toys when he gets tired of them. I'll get Bertha, his big, lazy, chestnut mare. She is huge, but she's a plodder. Father likes her because she clomps around the stable yard slow enough for the younger children to ride her. Not me. When I said big, I didn't mean big and slow. I need a real horse."

Jan looked relieved that Casimir had not guessed correctly.

On his birthday, Sarah made Casimir's favorite sernik cake with a local cheese curd, twarog, and drizzled raspberry sauce over the top. It was a treat that he loved.

This year he was allowed to cut the slices himself. As he handed the first piece to his Uncle Thaddeus, the doctor bent down and said, "You know Casimir it is a day of sevens. I have two sevens, I am seventy-seven, and you have one seven. I think that makes this a good time to tell you I am delighted that my prediction at your birth came true. You are an amazing boy and I am so happy I got to watch you grow into such a strong, smart young man. Happy Birthday my dear Casimir. It is an honor to be included in your celebration."

Casimir smiled, gave the doctor a big hug and went back to his cake, passing slices to the doctor, his father, then his mother, his three sisters, and his brothers, Frank and Antonin. Finally, the last piece was his. Somehow that last piece was a large corner, much bigger than the others and it had lots of raspberry sauce running down each side. His father looked at him with a pretend frown shaking his head in mock admonition.

After everyone finished their cake and milk, Josef said, "Casimir come to the stable with me, I may need your help." He winked at the rest of the group and said, "All of you may come as well, in case he is not big enough or strong enough to help with this task."

The spring thaw had not yet started but the March days were growing longer, and the nights were not as cold. Casimir was small, and struggled to keep up with his father's and Frank's long strides through the crusted snow. But he was so excited and determined to prove himself, he managed to stay within a meter of them. Dr. Borloff, slowed by his age, walked next to him. The women followed along trying to keep the hems of their coats and skirts from dragging in the snow. Anna, his older sister carried Antonin on her hip.

As they entered the stable, two of the hunting dogs were fighting. Teeth bared, lips curled, growling, tearing and lunging toward one another's throats they shoved, rolled, and dragged themselves beneath the belly of a mystical-looking white stallion. The horse did not move or shy away from the noisy dogs, but rather stood regally, statue-still, with head lifted and his long white mane flowing down from his neck to his withers. It was obvious he was no ordinary horse. He was strong, proud, and unafraid, the perfect horse for a boy with the same traits. When the dogs rolled out from under him, a stable worker whacked both of them on the head with a heavy rope, abruptly ending the fight. The horse didn't budge.

Casimir's eyes widened, he couldn't believe that this horse would be his, "Oh Father for me — my own horse?" Josef bent down to him saying, "Yes, my son, a magnificent horse for my warrior to ride."

Casimir threw his arms around his father's neck and said solemnly, "Father, I love you so much. He is the horse in my dreams, the one that I told you about. We will run like the wind, no one will catch us, and we will fight and win many battles."

Josef laughed, "Well, you know, it is said your ancestors, the Tatars, rode on the wind. I want you to understand the responsibility of caring for him is yours also. That means feeding, watering, exercising, and brushing as well as mucking the stalls each day to keep his feet clean and dry. A horse without good feet is no horse at all. Will you do it *every* day?"

"Oh yes, I will take good care of him, Father. May I ride him now, please Father! Please."

"Yes, but I must teach you one important lesson about horses first. Breathe deeply into his nostrils to let him know your scent and who you are. He will know you are a friend and be forever loyal."

Casimir walked to the great white stallion, stroked his nose, cupped his hands under the horse's mouth and breathed into his nostril.

"Yes, good job. Now you may go for a ride. What will you call him?" Josef asked with obvious pride.

Casimir did not hesitate. "He is Pushka, he will be my secret weapon, my kin, and my horse-brother."

"Okay, my son. Have fun with your brother Pushka, but be careful of his right flank, he got tangled in some wire and it's still healing."

Casimir walked to Pushka's side, looked into his eyes, and very slowly and gently stroked around the wound. Pushka whinnied low and turned to nuzzle Casimir's shoulder.

Thus began the special bond between a horse and rider that few experience. They were together every day. They communicated without speaking and knew each other completely. In cold weather, Casimir leaned forward and wrapped his arms around the big stallion's neck and they shared their body warmth. When one was sick, hurt, or troubled, the other knew and would help make the pain go away.

CHAPTER SIX

TWELFTH BIRTHDAY

Warka, Poland
March 1757

Doctor Borloff visited several times a month, keeping a precise record of Casimir's progress. He became more confident in his theory that children like Casimir were truly gifted, as he saw the amazing feats Casimir accomplished.

At ten, Casimir begged Jan, "Give me something harder to do. Make it a real challenge." Jan was astonished at the ease with which Casimir succeeded at riding, and the combat tests he was given. Adult men usually failed them. Casimir learned to ride bare back and mastered the ability to slide off on the left side, and still holding the mane, bounce up and over the horse's back and in a run remount from the opposite side, then climb into a standing position, throw a hatchet at a target and hit it—every time.

Only Paul Dobrachek could keep up. He was a worthy opponent with whom Casimir could spar or wrestle. They were best friends and together almost daily. Josef dissuaded Casimir from having other friends, saying he needed to focus on his training rather than playing games with other children.

One day he and Paul went swimming and decided to drop their swim suits to see if it made them faster swimmers. Paul pointed to Casimir's groin area. "Kas, look, you are different from me," he said pointing to his own penis and testicles.

Casimir smiled. "Yes, Father says I am special. He said I am smarter and stronger than anyone else. Well he didn't say *anyone* else but I believe that is true. He said I have the strength of men and the sensibility of women without the weaknesses of either. Except for you, I must not let anyone see me. They cannot know how special I am because they will misunderstand and will be jealous."

Then, they sprang into the air and jumped into the pond, where they swam and romped in water cold enough to take a grown man's breath away. His secret was safe with Paul.

Over time, Dr. Borloff's visits became less frequent. Casimir's tenth birthday party was the last time he visited the Pulaski estate. His body could no longer endure the carriage rides, but his mind remained agile and he remained dedicated to his work. He was fascinated by research on children with what were considered abnormalities. He took careful notes, and was even more precise when writing the results of his own investigations. He neither overrated nor understated the challenges and accomplishments of the children.

His intuition proved correct. There were many more cases than had been reported. As long as he was able, he attended every conference within a week's ride, and distinguished himself by bringing up the subject of 'cause weakness' and spoke as an informed expert. He was sought by doctors who had witnessed or heard of similar cases. When he could no longer travel, he maintained an energetic correspondence with them, as they too began to document the accomplishments of their patients.

The doctor learned of three cases in Sweden, four in France, five in Spain, and seven in Italy. The real surprise was in Russia, where fifty-one cases had been reported. These were the cases revealed to doctors. He guessed only one out of ten such children were accepted by their parents and given the benefit of medical care. The number of these children, some now adults, must be much larger, he surmised.

For a while he wondered about the high number of cases in Russia. The size of the country alone did not explain the disparity in the numbers, especially in view of the vast rural areas where there were no trained physicians.

A Russian doctor replied to an inquiry Dr. Borloff had made, explaining, "During his reign, Peter the Great outlawed the suffocation of abnormal infants. The punishment for violating the law was exile to Siberia for both parents. The Russian Czar traveled thousands of miles, usually incognito, and saw the strength and intellect of two such children. He thought Russia could benefit from these children and the adults they would become. Their greater intellect and appreciation of fine art fit into his plans for an enlightened Russia."

When Dr. Borloff read the letter, he shouted to Maria, "See, more confirmation that these young people are gifted." She didn't know what he was talking about, but she could tell from his tone that the doctor had received news supporting the work he had dedicated himself to for the past several years. "Thaddeus" she smiled and said, "it's time for your medicine. I will leave you to your work until dinner time."

His findings were meticulously written and bound in leather journals. They were arranged by case numbers for which only he knew the code, and placed on shelves that grew from the floor to the ceiling of his office. Honoring his promise to Josef, he never used names, and tried to avoid locations. At first there were few cases reported by other doctors. The information provided about the upbringing and progress of these children was limited. Some of the early cases had only a page or two. But as Dr. Borloff's network of participating doctors expanded, so did the journals.

He met a few of the children and found them to be bright, interesting, and energetic. But his favorite case was that of Casimir Pulaski, and his was by far the largest journal. The doctor was convinced that Casimir would out perform *all* the others. He suspected that during adolescence these children were not easily distracted and could focus on developing their bodies and their minds. He began to think of them as exceptional and Casimir helped prove the thesis. His ability to focus totally on horsemanship and military strategies led Dr. Borloff to conclude that he did not suffer from the diversions most young men his age experienced.

The doctor's early instincts about Casimir's strengths were also correct. Casimir was almost twelve and he was applauded as the champion of everything he attempted, yet he had a love and kindness few boys or girls exhibited. He loved Dr. Borloff and was always courteous and gracious to his Uncle Thaddeus. And while he loved his Father above all else, he also loved his family, Paul, Jan, and of course, Pushka.

For his twelfth birthday, he asked that his party be held at Dr. Borloff's home so the doctor could attend as he had in the past. Doctor Borloff and Maria were delighted. Sarah prepared two sernik cakes—a large one that Casimir sliced and served to the others, and a smaller one for himself.

It was a special day, warmer and sunnier than on any of his earlier birthdays. Everyone's smile was bright and easy with the warmth of a loving family. Casimir's special present was a magnificent sword that had belonged to his great grandfather. It had rested on a gold-tasseled pillow of red velvet in a glass case in his father's library for as long as Casimir could remember. He had longed to hold it, but did not dare to ask for such an honor. It was one of the swords carried by the great King Jan Sobieski when he led the famed Polish Hussars into battle. Their heroic efforts had stopped the Muslin invaders at Vienna, thereby saving Christianity in Western Europe. The sword, made of gold, silver, and hardened steel, featured a hilt with the curved head of a cobra. Inscribed on the blade were the words, *"God of one glory."* Josef looked lovingly at Casimir, slowly brought it forward, and presented the hilt to him.

"Oh Father, it surely cannot be for me. It is so beautiful and special. Can it really be for me?"

"Yes, my son it is for you. It is certainly special, just as you are, and you must treat it as such. Never lose it, and always treat it with respect. It will always protect you."

"Yes father, I will. I'll keep it in a safe place, away from harm. I will not get it dirty and I will oil and clean it often, just as I have seen you do."

Chuckling, Josef replied, "You may certainly get it dirty. A fine sword like this was built to fight. Just as the great Jan Sobieski used it to lead Polish men, I expect you to do the same."

Casimir treasured it almost as much as he did Pushka. It became the sword he carried into battle and the one his men followed when he raised it over his head and urged them forward, shouting "Do przodu, do przodu."

Paul and Casimir spent the afternoon on their horses sparing with swords. Casimir could not yet bring himself to use the revered Sobieski sword but he still bested Paul several times even though his friend was older and much larger.

Doctor Borloff sat in a large wooden chair with wide arms in the warmth of the bright sun under a leafless linden tree. He was smiling and nodding. Josef came over to stand next to him, also beaming. "Josef, your child is amazing. He is the perfect model of all the children I have heard of or read about who excel. You must be so proud of him. I know Casimir will be famous one day. I know it. He is already bold and brave, there is no doubt, but I wonder if either Casimir or you will be courageous enough to reveal his physical features to others. It would help so many like him if the world could see such a wonderful example of how extraordinary these children are. Honestly, I doubt the world is ready. But I hope in Casimir's time it will be, and that my work can speed the process."

Josef did not answer. He remained silent, simply smiling at the doctor whom the entire family adored. He walked away with the doctor's plea for disclosure hanging in the spring air.

Later in the day as the sun lost its warmth and the sky became pink on the horizon, Josef said it was time to leave. When the family turned to go they saw Dr. Borloff asleep in his chair. The late afternoon had turned cold, and the old man had no coat or sweater. Josef noticed he wore loose-fitting slippers without stockings.

"Quickly, Casimir go in the house and ask Maria for a wrap for Uncle Thaddeus. Then come back and help me get him inside."

When Casimir told her what he needed for Dr. Borloff, Maria ran to a trunk, pulled out a brown sable lined sleigh blanket and dashed outside with him. "Hurry, wrap him in this", she cried. "He should not be out in this cold evening air."

Josef, Maria, and Casimir tried to wake the doctor but he was groggy. Casimir and Josef lifted him from the chair and after Maria wrapped the blanket around him, they carried him inside to his bedroom where they eased him down on the edge of his bed. As Maria removed his slippers and turned back the covers so he could lie down, Casimir moved quietly to the bed and kissed his Uncle Thaddeus on his hot forehead before going back outside.

Josef nodded to Maria and followed Casimir out of the house. Casimir jumped on Pushka's back and started home as Josef helped Marianna into their carriage. Maria suddenly burst through the door. "Mr. Pulaski, the Doctor is asking for you," she shouted, "Please come back! He is burning up and very agitated about something."

Josef instructed his driver to take Marianna home and return for him. He followed Maria into the bedroom where the Doctor was thrashing about. He calmed down when he saw Josef but his voice was urgent, "Josef, please come sit. It is important, please listen to what I have to say."

"Of course, my dear Thaddeus anything you want. What can I do for you? What can I get for you? You're burning up, would you like something cool to drink?"

"No, no, Josef, this is very important. You have my will at your office. I want to add something to it. Will you write an addendum for me now? Maria can be my witness."

"Yes of course, my friend, but let me come by tomorrow when you are more rested."

"Tomorrow may be too late," the doctor warned, raising his trembling hand to clasp Josef's arm.

"Nonsense," Josef tried to assure him, "you have outlived most men and have many more productive years ahead of you."

"Josef, sometimes it is a curse to be a doctor. When someone you love cannot be helped or when it is your own time, your years of training are only useful in letting you know the end is at hand. I know my time is very soon. Now please get pen and paper."

" I will do as you ask if you promise to rest afterward," said Josef before instructing Maria to bring pen and paper.

Fear gripped Josef, as he awaited her return. How would they all live without this man who had become doctor, friend, and one they considered a beloved family member? He was particularly worried about Casimir who had benefitted so much from the doctor's interest and love.

When Maria returned, the doctor began dictating, "In addition to the stipulations in my existing will, I want my volumes of research to be donated to the library at the Medical and Research Schools of St Petersburg State University."

Josef interrupted. "To Russia! Thaddeus, you cannot do such a thing! Russia! Our enemy!"

"I understand your feelings. Militarily you are correct. But Russia is far ahead of the rest of the world in recognizing gifted children. This school was founded by a decree from Peter the Great, the same man who forbade the killing of children like Casimir, and all the others I have studied."

His voice was getting weaker as he continued. "I further instruct that Maria organize my correspondence by country and the doctors within that country who contributed to the research. They are to be notified of the distribution of my work upon my death so they may go to St. Petersburg to study if they so desire. It is my hope that the monks at Jasna Gora or elsewhere can be enlisted to go to St. Petersburg and make a precise copy of the volumes. Once a full copy is completed it should be taken to a printer so the information will be available in areas that are closer to researchers who may want to continue my work."

"I know this sounds prideful, but I believe it is important work that can change opinions all over the world, making people more tolerant of those who are not like them. If that were the case, the world would be a much better place."

These words seemed to take the doctor's last bit of energy and Josef said, "Thaddeus it is written as you directed. Let me lift you so that you may sign it here with Maria as your witness. I will attach it to your will tomorrow and then come by to check on you."

The old man nodded, took the pen from Josef, and signed with a trembling hand after being propped up with pillows into a sitting position.

Speaking in almost a whisper, he said, "Thank you Josef. Take good care of Casimir and give him my blessing and love. Tell him not to fret. As I have said often, pneumonia is a friend of old men. I am thankful to have lived long enough to watch him grow into an amazing person."

Then the Doctor sank back into the pillow as the pen dropped from his hand. The signed document fell to the floor. Josef checked the doctor's pulse and nodded in reassurance to

Maria, whose face reflected her fear and concern. Josef retrieved the codicil to the will, signed it, and passed it to Maria who also signed as tears streamed down her face.

"I will see you tomorrow Thaddeus," said Josef, patting Dr. Borloff on the shoulder before leaving, silently hoping a good-night's sleep would revive the doctor.

The next morning, he pretended to leave for his office as usual but instead hurried to Dr. Borloff's home where Maria's red eyes and tears told him everything.

"When?" he asked.

"About two o'clock this morning. He said he would not die on Casimir's birthday. He wanted that day to always be a happy one for him. I sent the driver to his son's house with the news. Now maybe he will have a little time for his father, at least enough to attend the funeral and listen to the will being read. How angry he will be to learn the doctor's most valuable possessions were his journals, which he left to a university, and the house, which he left to me." She shook her head sadly, lifting a corner of her apron to wipe away the tears from her eyes before returning to prepare casseroles and other dishes to feed the people who would come to pay their respects. It was a nice gesture, but Josef suspected that she was cooking because she needed to stay busy. She had aged along with Dr. Borloff to whom she had been devoted for many years. He knew that with Thaddeus gone, her future was uncertain.

When Josef returned home, Casimir met him at the door, and saw that his father looked drawn. Had he done something wrong? Had he displeased his father? Had he not trained hard enough? Was he not a good enough rider? Or was it those dreaded music lessons? He tried, but his fingers were meant for gripping lances and horse reins, not stroking piano keys or violin strings. Was that it? It must be really bad for his father to return home at ten in the morning and ask him to come to the library.

"Father, I am sorry about the music . . . "

"Hush Kas, my dear son. You have done nothing wrong. I must give you some very bad news. I wanted you to be the first to hear it."

"Is it Pushka? Something has happened to Pushka? I just fed him, he seemed eager to train."

"No Casimir, it is about another dear friend of yours. Dr. Borloff, your Uncle Thaddeus, whom you love so much, died early this morning."

Casimir's found it hard to speak. No one close to him had ever died. His world was stable, full of loving people. Uncle Thaddeus had always been with him.

"No father. That can't be. Remember, he was at my birthday party yesterday. He was fine. Who told you this? They are mistaken. It is someone else who has died. I am sure of it."

But he really wasn't sure of it, and as he looked at his father's face he knew the truth. His throat tightened and burned. He couldn't speak. Breathing was hard and he couldn't swallow. He remembered all the birthday parties with Dr. Borloff smiling at him, and the times they had gone for walks, "*to talk about how you are doing Casimir with your studies and your military training.*" He remembered the times the doctor watched him train with Jan, or lead sieges on imaginary castles with Paul. He was always rewarded with a smile that said, 'Well done'. At three Casimir began to call him Uncle Thaddeus, and no real uncle could have shown more love. The doctor was quite proud of the family title Casimir bestowed upon him, and took his role as uncle seriously.

Casimir looked away from Josef. He could not remember ever crying. Strong boys and warriors did not cry. In fact, his father said he had cried only once, and never whimpered, or sulked like most children do. It was because he wanted to be placed on the back of a horse before he could walk. He had a real tantrum when he was not lifted and placed into the saddle.

He didn't want his father to see him cry now, but he couldn't conceal his shaking shoulders as the sobs rose and were forced back. How could this happen? How could someone who loved him so much and seemed to know all his troubles and doubts have celebrated his birthday yesterday and be gone today? He thought his Uncle Thaddeus would be with him forever. Now he was gone. Did that mean he could lose others? His mother, sisters, brothers and, worst of all his Father?

For all his display of bravado, confidence, and arrogance, today he was simply a small boy of twelve who missed his Uncle Thaddeus.

"Son, please turn and look at me," said his father. "There is no shame in crying for those we love. It is not weakness but strength that allows us to care for and love others.

"And it is important for you to understand two things: The first is that almost everyone is loved by someone. The people you will meet on the battlefield, some of whom you will kill, are loved by sisters, brothers, mothers, fathers and wives. But remember this, they are the enemy and must be overcome for us to remain free as we fight for what is right. But as men, family men, they deserve our respect and must be treated respectfully. That means their bodies must not be mutilated and if they are taken prisoner, they must be treated fairly. You have yet to learn that war is a hell beyond description that men create for themselves. It is not a game like you now play.

"My second point is that love is not limited to a few people. Just as the roses in your mother's garden grow three or four new branches from the stem where an older branch is cut back, you will find more and more people to love as you grow older. Very special people like our Dr. Borloff, must eventually give themselves up to the pruning shears so that new growth can enter our lives and give us more love and beauty."

The tightness and burning in Casimir's throat lessened. He welcomed his father's open arms and allowed himself a loud sob as he nestled his head into Josef's chest.

The things he learned that day about loss, love, and respect for others remained with him all of his life. The lesson was like a final parting gift from the man who had shown him so much love, his dear Uncle Thaddeus.

CHAPTER SEVEN

FRANCISZKA

Winiary Estate and Warka

He was fourteen, she seventeen, and she was an entirely new experience for him. She lived near the town of Warka, where his father had his law office and served as mayor. Josef Pulaski managed legal matters for her father, Edward Kransinki. One day she accompanied her father to Josef's office while Casimir was there to help him review maps of some newly purchased land.

Josef greeted them warmly and Mr. Kransinki addressed his daughter, "Franciszka, you know Monsieur Pulaski and, I presume, you are the young Casimir Pulaski I've heard so much about. Am I correct sir?"

Casimir was awestruck. She was the most beautiful girl he had ever seen, and her father was expecting something from him. What? All he could manage to say was, "Yes, sir. I am Casimir."

"Ah Casimir, I am happy to finally meet you. Your father is quite proud of you," said Monsieur Kransinki, stretching out his hand to Casimir who recovered enough to shake it.

"Casimir, this is my daughter, Franciszka."

Startled, Casimir didn't know how to act. What should he do? Should he take her hand and kiss it like his father and Frank did when they were introduced to women?

The thought of touching such a beautiful girl frightened him and he stepped backwards, almost toppling over a stool. He suddenly lost confidence as the heat began rising to his face. This shouldn't be happening. He was always in command of every situation. He was the invincible Casimir Pulaski! But, this was totally different. What to do?

"Pleased, pleased, to meet you," he stammered, unable to look at her. He suddenly found the pine knots in the table next to him interesting, as he dug at them with his fingers and turned his gaze away from hers.

His panic turned to terror as she walked over to him and held out *her* hand. Mercifully, she noticed his discomfiture and turned toward the table, pointing to some idle doodling on a scrap of paper. It was a pencil sketch he'd made of himself, dressed in an intricate uniform of braids, buttons, epaulets, and wide-cuffed sleeves sitting astride Pushka with the Sobieski sword raised over his head.

"What's this Casimir?" she asked.

He couldn't form words to respond, let alone explain that he planned to be a great mounted warrior, and replied haltingly, "Noth . . . nothing, just some . . . something I did while father was busy with a surveyor."

"It looks very much like you, is it?"

Casimir's face grew even hotter as a blush spread up his neck and across his cheeks. His mouth went dry.

Her father nudged Josef and winked as they looked at the young couple. Both smiled broadly.

"Why it is you, isn't it?" she teased, "How dashing you are."

"I, I, I guess it could be," Casimir replied, his gaze now scanning the floorboards between them.

"Well, it is a beautiful likeness of both you and a horse. Is he yours?"

"Yes, his name is Pushka."

"He's so regal. Is he fun to ride? And the uniform you're wearing is beautiful. Did you see it in a book?"

"Oh yes," he exclaimed, forgetting his fear as the talk turned to riding horses. "Pushka is wonderful. I designed the uniform myself."

"It is stunning, very fashionable. You seem to have a talent for designing clothes."

Casimir did have a talent for designing clothes, especially colorful uniforms, an ability few boys possessed. He had a good eye for hues and tones that blended well together, and his sisters often consulted him about which dress, hat, and gloves to wear to a party—but he found it impossible to form the words to answer her.

"Well, maybe I could ride Pushka someday?" she said, demurely dropping her long lashes over the brightest green eyes Casimir had ever seen. "I would wear my prettiest riding outfit to be presentable next to you in your dashing uniform."

He was terrified by the thought of being alone with her and of having to carry on a conversation, and decided he could never do it.

"Uh, uh, no, I don't think that's a good idea." he said, finding his voice, "He doesn't like to be ridden by anyone but me."

"Casimir, what are you talking about?" Josef interrupted. "All your sisters ride Pushka. You're being foolish and rude to our guest. Of course, you will take Franciszka riding whenever she wants to go."

"Oh, I forgot about my sisters. Well I guess it would be alright—when it's not raining of course, or too hot, or too cold, or too early in the morning . . . "

"Casimir! I cannot believe how you're acting. ANYTIME she wants to ride you will take her!"

"Yes, of course, father," he agreed, then asked her, "Would Friday be convenient for you Franciszka?

"It would be perfect Mr. Pulaski. I will come early so we can have a full day of riding." Was she taunting him? A full day, how could he ever be with her and talk with her for a full day? And he had called her by her first name, rather than Miss Kransinki, something considered very rude. Oh, why was he being subjected to such torture?

Josef shook his head, exchanging a knowing look with her father as they chuckled under their breaths.

Casimir was still finding it hard to breathe. He felt trapped in a terrifying yet beautiful dream and was torn between disappointment and relief when she and her father finally left.

For the next several days, he alternated between dread and eager anticipation of Friday when she would come to ride Pushka. He could think of little else. This was a strange new experience for him. The only females he had spent time with were his mother and sisters. His father did not encourage him to meet girls, and, until now, he had little interest. He hated going to parties, especially when that meant dancing. He had no time for such foolishness. Suddenly, he could not understand how a girl could so distract him from his training.

When finally, the day arrived, he was waiting on the top step of the entrance to the Winiary mansion. The Kransinki family carriage pulled up the driveway between two rows of linden trees. It was July, and the trees said to be favored by the Blessed Mother, were in full fragrant bloom.

Just as he had practiced over and over, Casimir strode to the carriage door and helped Franciszka step down onto the graveled driveway. He took her outstretched hand in his, bowed deeply from the waist, and brushed his lips against it, just as Frank, amused by his younger brother's sudden interest in proper etiquette with girls, had taught him to do.

True to her word, Franciszka was dressed splendidly in a blue satin riding skirt and matching vest. Under the vest she wore a white embroidered blouse with wide sleeves and two pink pearl buttons at each of her small wrists. The sun glistened on a gold coin dangling from a chain around her neck. A jaunty white hat, with a blue plume near the upturned rim completed the outfit.

"Mademoiselle Kransinki, welcome to Winiary," Casimir greeted her, straightening his back to give her a full view of his newly designed uniform, with white trousers, high-rise brown leather boots, gold-braided blue jacket with red epaulets that matched the lining of his cape and the fez sitting at a rakish angle atop his black, well-oiled hair.

"Dzien Dobry, Monsieur Pulaski" she replied, wishing him a good day.

Ceremoniously crooking his elbow to be a proper escort, he led her to the stable. When Jan saw them he almost laughed. They looked more like they were going to a costume ball than a day of riding.

He met them with Pushka and Bertha, Frank's gentle, old horse. Pushka pranced and whinnied his good morning greeting to Casimir. When Jan started to hand Pushka's reins to Casimir, he stepped aside and turned his head toward Franciszka.

Casimir took Franciszka's white gloved hand to help her onto Pushka after she placed her riding boot into the stirrup. The scent of her perfume drifted through the air. It was a combination of the exotic spices Sarah used while cooking her Christmas feasts, mingled with spring roses, and freshly mowed hay. Casimir breathed deeply to inhale the pleasant fragrance. It made him light headed and a bit dizzy.

Once mounted, Casimir could immediately see that she was an experienced rider, and was grateful that she laughed and smiled more than she talked. It was obvious she shared his love of horses and he soon relaxed. Knowing he was a superb horseman helped his confidence grow. Because he was on Frank's old horse, Bertha, it was harder to demonstrate his skills. Bertha was big, slow and unspectacular.

After about an hour of riding in silence, they paused under the shade of a giant oak where Casimir said with a somewhat cocky air, "If you will change horses with me, I will show you tricks I have taught Pushka."

"Of course, Casimir, I would love to see the performance," she responded, stressing the word 'performance' knowing Casimir was getting ready to show off.

After they dismounted he walked over to Pushka and started to mount. He took the reins in his left hand and leapt so hard and fast that he catapulted himself over Pushka's back so far that he almost tumbled off on the opposite side. Frantically he made a mid-air correction and landed off center in the saddle with a loud plop. Franciszka stifled a giggle.

To cover his embarrassment, he quickly began the 'performance' with the order, "Pushka, pray." Pushka bent his knee lowering his head as he knelt forward.

"Pushka, rise and attack the enemy soldiers." He commanded. The horse rose on his hind legs and furiously pawed the air with his front hooves.

"Don't let them get away!" Again, he followed Casimir's orders, stomping the ground as he came down and turned in a semi-circle.

"Pushka, behind us." The massive hooves struck out into the air behind them.

"Now Pushka let everyone see us ride into battle." The horse rose skyward and Casimir waved an imaginary sword high in the air.

"Oh, Oh, that was wonderful," Franciszka gasped, clapping her hands together.

Now emboldened, Casimir said, "Before we go back, would you mind riding double for a while? Pushka needs the training of having two people on his back. If you hold onto me—I mean for safety—you won't have to worry about him throwing you off.

"Oh, yes! I would love to," Franciszka replied, so excited she was already looking for a place to tie Bertha's reins.

"It's alright, Bertha will follow us. She is trained to find her way home if we get separated," Casimir said, with a shake of his head showing disdain for the gentle horse's plodding nature. He pulled Franciszka up with his hand as she slipped her foot into the empty stirrup and easily maneuvered her skirts to slide sideways onto Pushka's back behind him.

"Please put your arm around me, for safety," he said. "You're not astride his back like me so you could slip off if he suddenly bolts." She complied slipping one arm around his waist even though both knew Pushka was too well trained to suddenly bolt, and she was too good a rider to 'slip off'.

It was obvious to him that Franciszka admired his riding skills and once they were on Pushka, he expanded his chest several inches and straightened his torso until he was leaning backwards. He was almost against her face where he caught the scent of her hair. It was different from her perfume. It was her own delicate and appealing scent. He knew his mother, each of his sisters, and even Sarah had their own special aroma. All were pleasant but each slightly different. He wondered if this were true of all women. But it didn't matter, no fragrance could match the wonderful, delicate, and most pleasing scent of Franciszka. It was lighter than lilacs, softer than the morning mist, and sweeter than fresh honey.

Just as he thought what a delightful day it had become, Pushka began to misbehave. Seemingly, the horse had had enough and was jealous of the attention his master was paying to the other rider.

After only traveling a short distance, Pushka started loudly passing gas. Casimir tried to cover the sound by talking about the weather. He rambled about how the wind blew, the shape of the clouds, the lack of rain and on and on, desperately hoping Pushka would stop making those embarrassing sounds. But, the louder and the longer he talked, the more noise Pushka's gastronomical gyrations produced. It was endless. When he ran out of conversation about the weather, Pushka was still passing gas. Streams of sweat ran down Casimir's red face. This was horrible. How could Pushka do this? He had always behaved perfectly.

Franciszka tried to pretend not to hear the explosions escaping from under Pushka's tail, directly underneath her, but it was just too much to ignore and it had offered many opportunities for her to tease Casimir.

She giggled, "You have taught him well Casimir. I'm sure that this would chase more enemy soldiers away than his kicking hooves."

"I did not, I certainly did not, teach him to do that. I am so sorry. We will dismount now. I have no idea why he acted this way. I am so sorry, I really am."

She laughed to ease his embarrassment and said, "Well, fortunately, our Polish grass is sweet and mostly odor free."

Casimir was humiliated by Pushka's unseemly behavior but Franciszka's laughter and words saved the day and somehow he found the nerve to say at the end of the ride, "I hope Pushka's antics did not ruin things for you and you will come to ride with us again. We would both like to see you, and he does need the exercise."

To his delight, she impishly replied, "I liked riding Pushka— well, most of the time. Yes, I'll be happy to come again. Is day after tomorrow a good time?"

"Oh, yes! Yes, it is. I'll see you then."

Jan told Josef that Casimir missed six training sessions over the following two weeks. He used the excuse that he needed the experience of teaching others to ride in preparation for when he would train troops. Of course, he was teaching the same person, Franciszka, each day.

Much later Casimir learned that rather than being angry, his father had been pleased and Josef then told him the reason.

"You see, Casimir, the Kransinki family is wealthy with land holdings almost as vast as ours. I thought a marriage between you two could result in a merger into one of the largest estates in Poland. And I am genuinely fond of Franciszka. She is smart and funny as well as pretty. As I saw that light moustache form on your upper lip, I thought perhaps marriage and children were possible for you. I began thinking of Franciszka as my future daughter-in-law so I talked to her father about a marriage between the two of you."

Edward Kransinki came into my office a month after you and Franciszka began riding together." His father continued with the story.

'Monsieur Pulaski, I have come to ask you to update my will,' he said.

"Of course, I will take care of it for you right away, but before you change it, I have something to discuss with you that might impact what you want to do."

'What is it my trusted counsellor?'

"You remember the exchange between your daughter and my son when they met here last month?" I asked.

'Well yes, it was rather humorous to watch the young Casimir's infatuation with her.' He laughed.

"Well that infatuation has grown, and they are spending a great deal of time with each other. They ride together almost every day."

'I see, Josef, but what does that have to do with changing my will?'

"You and I have worked well together, and we are both successful in not only raising beautiful and handsome children but also in amassing large tracts of land. I want above all else for my son to be happy and to choose wisely when it comes to finding a wife. I have observed Franciszka over the years. More recently I have watched affection grow between Casimir and her. I believe a marriage between them would be a very wise choice of a wife for Casimir and would make him most happy. I know I would consider her the same as one of my own daughters."

"And my friend," I continued, "it could result in our mutual families controlling a huge estate that would wield a great deal of influence at parliament and at the castle."

Mr. Kransinki's brow wrinkled as he responded slowly, 'Josef, I am truly sorry. You have presented a compelling case as you always do.

'It appears I may have influence at the castle from another source. The reason I wanted to change my will is because Franciszka is to be betrothed to Duke Karl. He will likely become King and she will have no need of an inheritance from me. I mean to leave my entire estate to my wife and son.'

"I was shocked. I asked how it came about, since she was obviously enjoying your company. Although you weren't old enough to love her as a husband, you were definitely smitten. I had no doubt you would be successful in a military role, surely successful enough to provide her with a good life, and I would have made sure of that."

'The problem is that Duke Karl met her at a ball in Warsaw last fall.' Edward replied. 'He is as taken with her as your Casimir. It is an opportunity for her and our family that will never come again. As you know, Duke Karl is the king designate. There is no choice but to accept. He is old enough to know his heart better than someone as young as Casimir.'

"Yes, of course you must accept," I acknowledged. "I pray Franciszka will be happy. I will revise the will as you wish. Under the circumstances, I think it's best if their riding together stops, although I hope they remain friends. I know Casimir will be disappointed, but he is young and will recover."

Graciously he extended his hand to me and said, 'She will be told tonight of the course her future must take, and that there will be no more riding with Casimir. Thank you for understanding.'

Casimir put the diary and journal aside. It seemed happiness was a permanent resident in his life until Dr. Borloff died and after that only an occasional visitor who taunted and teased him into hoping for a return to the bright and beautiful days of his youth.

Oh, if fate had not intervened. His heart cried out. If Franciszka and I were married how different life might have been. What a tragedy. Duke Karl never became king, I never married, and father's fortune is gone. So many plans and hopes destroyed by one Russian empress.

Saddened, he returned to his memories and his father's diary where the early happy times were recorded.

CHAPTER EIGHT

SEVENTEENTH BIRTHDAY

Wolny Winiary Estate, Warka
March 1762

osef and Marianna sat by the library fireplace where six-foot logs burned slowly, giving off warmth and scents of apple and beech wood. They were both thinking of Doctor Borloff and all he had contributed to their lives. Marianna broke their silent remembrances.

"I am glad Maria agreed to live with us. She helps me a great deal with the younger children and she is a blessing to Sarah in the kitchen."

"I think your offer to have her here was a blessing to her my dear. She was lost in that empty house after Thaddeus died," Josef replied.

"But there is a different matter I've been waiting to talk to you about, something I wish Thaddeus was here to help us analyze."

"What is it Josef? Is it about one of the children?"

"Yes, my love, indirectly it is.

"A couple of weeks ago, I was at the horse market in Radom where I saw an unusual thing. It was a young horse driven to frenzy for no apparent reason. He was a charging beauty. He had a long flowing mane and tail, a muscular body, and a glistening black coat with a white blaze and a snip on his face, three white

71

stockings and a sock. He was in a corral by himself and ran the perimeter non-stop, as fast as lightning. He didn't stop the entire time I was there. I thought he would surely drop from fatigue, but he just kept running and running back and forth around the corral.

"I asked to meet the owner, a Mr. Closky, to find out why the horse acted in this way. He told me the horse was for sale at a very low price. He said he would take less money than he paid for him because he was untrainable and should be butchered. He had already killed one rider with his wild and crazed running. He asked if I had noticed the notched ear. I said no and asked him what that meant. He told me that when a horse kills someone it must be marked for life with a notched ear.

"According to Mr. Closky, after he bought the horse he discovered that what he thought was a gelding was probably a rig, a horse whose testicles haven't dropped making it appear that he was born without testicles."

Marianna gasped and started to rise from her chair. "Josef, why are you telling me this? What are you trying to say?"

"Wait, my love. The owner said he believes that the testicles never dropped, and simply got trapped inside the horse where they became overactive, offering him relief only through ferocious non-stop exercise. This horse has more stamina and physical strength than ten normal horses."

Marianna, looked at Josef with a mixture of revelation and disbelief.

"Casimir! Casimir is already more driven and stronger than most larger boys. Can it be true that he is the strong male you predicted at his birth even with the female-like features?"

"I believe it is possible. At the very least he is more male than female and has acquired the best traits of both sexes. I believe our little Casimir will become a giant among men through his fierce determination to win."

Josef realized then that his guilt and uncertainty were gone. He did not have an abnormal son; he had an exceptional son who was independent, intelligent, and a natural leader. Other boys were already looking up to him. Like the other children Dr. Borloff had studied, he was above average both physically and mentally.

Finally, Marianna and Josef found peace, realizing they were not cursed but unusually blessed to have Casimir.

Josef did not tell Marianna he bought the rig horse, thinking that the horse and Casimir were similar with both having hidden testicles concealing their maleness.

With warnings that no one should attempt to ride the horse, Josef left him with Farmer Luckow, who worked some of the Pulaski lands. *If he can be trained, what a warhorse he will make,* Josef thought.

Casimir continued to win all contests and challenges and clear each hurdle in his way. His consistent wins in battles with Paul and other older boys made him fearless and somewhat arrogant.

"I am unbeatable," he proclaimed. "When I fall from my horse I get back on with a leap and charge forward while others stay on the ground moaning from some minor injury. I am quicker, stronger, and smarter than any man I have ever met. I cannot fail at anything I do."

Casimir overcame sprained ankles, broken bones, cuts and gashes on most of his body by the time he was fifteen, and none of it slowed him down. It was as if he felt no pain.

But deep within he had doubts. He was small, standing just above five feet tall, and the mark on the stable door that his father used to measure each child's growth had stopped moving a year ago. Would the brave, tough men he needed to build his father's army follow one so small? Would he be able to find a wife worthy of the Pulaski name who would love him as his mother loved his father, and would she be a helpmate for life, raising

73

their children, managing their home, and supporting his career? Would he be able to have children? He knew his father, who he worshipped, was disappointed because he didn't excel in some of his studies. Would he lose his father's love?

Casimir hid such concerns by filling his days with audacity, action and adventure. He acted much like the Tatars, and was far too impatient to sit still and listen to tutors. He had little interest in his studies, politics, girls, or almost anything other than military tactics and leading men into battle on horseback. He spent the precious hours he had away from his teachers riding horses and training with Jan and Paul or arranging and rearranging the pewter soldiers his father had given him into battle formations. Josef started inviting battle-hardened soldiers, many of them wounded, to visit Casimir. He wanted Casimir to learn military tactics and the consequences of commanders making the wrong decisions. Casimir repeated the tactics of the generals on his pewter battlefield and then rearranged the soldiers in the ways he would have fought the same battles. He was sure his ways were better.

Casimir's seventeenth birthday was celebrated in the usual way, with the family gathering for Sarah's sernik cake. Casimir glanced at the chair where Uncle Thaddeus had sat during his earlier birthday parties, still missing him.

After dinner, Josef asked Casimir to walk to the stables with him. On the way, he asked. "How is Pushka's training coming along?"

Casimir grew nervous, wondering why his father was asking such a question.

"Pushka does well at everything I teach him Father," he finally said, "Why do you ask?"

"Well I thought you might want to try a horse that is a bit more of a challenge now that Pushka is trained."

"Oh, really Father? I love Pushka and always want to ride him, but a tougher horse to train would be wonderful."

"Tomorrow I will take you to see a horse that is said to be untrainable. Somehow I believe you might disprove that."

Casimir was excited to train a new horse so tough no one else could train him. He couldn't wait to show his father what he could do.

The next day, Josef, Jan and Casimir visited Farmer Luckow to see the rig horse.

Casimir immediately identified with the animal. There was not an ounce of fat on him, he was pure muscle. He recognized the anxiousness of the horse, its obsession with activity, and its need to be in control. The horse reared up as soon as they approached and made a loud, high-pitched squeal instead of a snort to warn them away. Casimir didn't flinch even though he was small next to the large horse on the other side of the fence.

Josef wondered if this was a good idea. He wanted Casimir to continue to hone his horsemanship skills but not at the risk of his life.

The horse spun, came down hard and began to run the perimeter. Around and around he went, bucking, kicking, and snorting while tossing his head; neither slowing nor breathing hard. Casimir's eyes never left him and he knew the horse was watching him as well.

"Father," he said, "he is wild and beautiful. I know how he feels. He is different from other horses. He is special like me. He has more stamina and is tougher than other horses."

Josef said, "I think you're right Casimir, but at the same time he is very dangerous. He has killed a man and he doesn't know you. He will see you as an enemy trying to take away his freedom. You must train him only when Jan and other men are with you. I don't want you hurt. Do you understand me and promise to have help around at all times?"

"Yes, father. I promise until you see he is no longer a threat to me."

"Mr. Pulaski, this is crazy," cried Luckow when Josef instructed him to prepare the horse for their departure. "It took five men to get a halter on him. He will kill your boy the first day he tries to work with him. Please listen to me. This horse should be destroyed. I'm willing to do it if you can't."

"Mr. Luckow, the horse belongs to me and I will do with him as I see fit. Now please have your men put a lead rope on him so we can take him home."

It was a rough trip back to the Pulaski estate. Both Jan and Josef rode beside the big rig, each holding a rope that extended around its forelock and muzzle stretched tight on each side. Casimir rode on Pushka in back with a taut third rope around his neck. Whenever he attempted to charge forward, Pushka first stood firm, and then at Casimir's order, backed up tightening the rope. This showed the rig that Casimir was his master. Nonetheless, the horse reared, kicked, screamed and bucked the entire ten miles home.

Marianna was aghast when she saw them coming down the road with the horse awash in its own white sweat and slobber. From its frenzied behavior, she knew immediately that he was the rig Josef had told her about. It was one of the few times during their marriage she was furious with her husband. She turned and went inside, slamming the door behind her and angrily muttering, "Casimir will kill himself trying to train this beast and it will be his father's fault."

Weeks later, she had to admit that Josef's intuition was good. Casimir was engrossed in working with the horse he had named, Wolny[1]. He used Pushka as an example, even tying Wolny to Pushka's saddle, dragging him around the barnyard, and trying to get him to do the things Pushka did. Casimir began sleeping in the stable between the two gates that led into their stalls. Wol-

---

1   Strong

ny was so smart that he knew what Casimir wanted, but he was unwilling to do it, resisting even the simplest training. He knew he was special and different from other horses and he sensed the same thing in the young man. He began trusting Casimir long before he showed it.

One day Casimir, exasperated, told the stable man to put a saddle on Wolny. Three men approached the horse with a 'twitch', a stick with a rope through the end of it. One grabbed Wolny's ear and twisted it while another clinched his upper lip through the loop in the rope, then twisted the stick to tighten it until the horse froze in pain and stood perfectly still, trembling in anguish.

"Stop that! Stop it now," Casimir yelled when he saw what they were doing. "Twitches are forbidden in this stable. Let him loose. Now!" The men did as he ordered, then scrambled up the sides of the wooden stall to get out of the horse's way. The one who twisted the stick wasn't fast enough and Wolny tore away the seat of his pants with his teeth. The man was all too glad to give up the pants rather to have his bottom chewed. Then Casimir climbed onto the railing of the stall, sprang onto Wolny's back, and shouted, "Open the gate."

Wolny charged through the door and began gyrating. He zigged, zagged, bucked, jumped, and kicked with all the fury of a wounded mountain lion. Casimir realized for the first time in his life that he may have taken on too much. The horse was going to win this one and he would end up on the ground. He tried his best to pull Wolny toward a stack of hay, but the horse headed outside. Casimir's hand sustained severe rope burns from having gripped the halter rope so tight. To his credit, he held on for a few seconds while the stable hands, still perched in fear on top of the stall, could do nothing to slow or stop the horse.

Wolny bucked so high and fast that Casimir was catapulted more than twenty feet through the air, landing on the hardened earth that surrounded the barn.

He had his breath knocked out of him, and when he didn't jump to his feet as he usually did, it was Pushka's turn to go wild. With his mighty chest, he knocked the stall door open and rushed to the rig, attacking Wolny with raised front hoofs coming down on his back and sliding down his side. Wolny whirled around and tore a chunk out of Pushka's left flank. Pushka's scream brought Casimir to consciousness in time to see the horses kicking, biting, and banging against each other.

"Stop them, stop them," he screamed to the men who were scrambling out of harm's way. "Bring a torch. Bring it now, hurry, put it in Wolny's face."

When Wolny retreated from the fire, he yelled, "Pushka, back, back boy, back up." Pushka did as commanded, favoring his left leg.

When Josef heard what happened he came to the barn with a gun, ready to shoot Wolny, but stopped in his tracks when he saw Casimir rubbing Wolny's nose. Casimir looked at him, saying "Pushka will be okay, Jan treated him with some healing balm. It was just a skin tear, no muscle damage. He will need to rest for a few days. I'll ride Wolny until he recovers."

"Casimir, what happened here? I heard Wolny almost killed you and Pushka."

"Wolny needs to be strong, independent and the one in charge, kinda' like you and me, Father. He didn't want anyone to ride him. He threw me off his back as if I was a barn fly, then Pushka tried to defend me, just as he would in battle.

"It was a terrible fight between the two of them. Pushka would have died for me. It took whips and fire to stop them. But I think it made Wolny understand the bond between Pushka and me. Being so driven all the time is not easy Father, and it can be very lonely. I believe Wolny wants to bond with me like Pushka has. Of course, we tended to Pushka's injury first. Wolny was forgotten in all the excitement and was left untethered in the barnyard. When

I realized I needed to find him, I saw him standing at the barn door looking at me. Apparently, he had watched me tend to Push-ka and he realized we would do anything for each other. Then he walked to me and stood quietly until I started stroking him."

Josef, shook his head in disbelief. "I never doubted you would train him son, but the way it happened is not only baffling but a lot more dangerous than I thought."

Soon Wolny turned and ran into the corral where he started running non-stop again, this time without the crazed look in his eyes.

Josef realized the way Casimir handled the fighting horses and tamed Wolny was typical of a mature man, not that of a teenager. He walked back to the house where a worried Marian-na met him at the door.

"All is well my dear, our son is wise beyond his years, espe-cially when it comes to training horses."

CHAPTER NINE

FRANCISZKA

Warka, Poland and Courland Estate, Poland
1762-1763

osef made it a point to retain the Kransinki family as clients and friends over the years. With Edward Kransinki's ties to the now Duke Karl, and his wife Duchess Franciszka of Courland, Josef saw an opportunity for Casimir and the family.

Edward liked Casimir, who was showing a maturity beyond his years. He also admired Josef for his business acumen and the gracious way he handled the news of Franciszka's betrothal to Prince Karl.

He visited Josef often when he was in Warka, and through him Josef kept up-to-date on life at the Courland Estate, where Franciszka was happily managing the Duke's household.

To those who didn't know him, Josef appeared to be a quiet, polite, dull man without high aspirations, while in reality, he was always looking for ways to help his children, particularly his sons, to achieve a higher status for themselves and the family. If they could influence Poland's national policies, perhaps his dream of having an independent Poland defended by a strong army could be realized.

One day he and Edward Kransinki talked over tea heated on a coal-fired stove in the corner of his law office. Earlier that morning Josef had picked up some punchkins at the little bakery shop and they now enjoyed the sticky, glazed pastries with their tea and conversation.

The aroma of the tea and the warmth of the cups were soothing, and the treats put both men in a good mood. It was cool outside, but the fire in the coal stove took the chill away. Both men were content. They had good families, sizeable fortunes, and the future looked bright, especially for the Kransinkis.

Josef thought this was a good time to broach the subject on his mind. "Edward, I know this could be a bit awkward, but do you think the duke would consider taking Casimir on as one of his pages? He has pretty well forgotten his infatuation with your daughter and is completely devoted to horses and military tactics, too completely in my mind, although I guess I am somewhat at fault. It's time he learned the protocols of court, the manners of a gentleman and the basics of literature, music, and history. These refinements will help him as much or more than battle strategies in life, and service in the court will give him exposure to them."

Edward stroked his graying goatee with a slender and heavily veined hand and, after some thought said, "Franciszka occasionally refers to how much she enjoyed riding with Casimir but she is also now preoccupied with other matters. Running a household for a future king who likes to throw parties is no easy job. I think they are both different, more mature people, with new interests now, so I don't think the situation would be awkward at all. She and the duke are hosting a hunting party next week and I'm invited. I will inquire for you. I believe one or two of the pages will be returning home soon, and perhaps Casimir could fill one of their posts."

"Thank you, Edward, I appreciate it very much as will Casimir—one day. Giving up his riding, fencing, and shooting won't be easy for him, even for a few months."

"Quite a son you have Josef. Your pride in him is warranted. You have raised him right. I'll let you know what Duke Karl says as soon as I return."

So, it was arranged without consultation with either Casimir or Franciszka. Josef thought it was perfect for Casimir. If he impressed the duke, and the duke became king, both Casimir and the Pulaski family would benefit. Even if Duke Karl did not become king, Casimir would have expanded his education and training in the service of a royal family.

Sharing a glass of sherry with his wife the next evening, Josef disclosed his plan.

"Marianna, I plan to send Casimir to Duke Karl's court to learn protocol and the manners of a noble gentleman. It seems inevitable the duke will become king. The Courland-Semigallia Region is huge and is proving to be the perfect training ground for him to learn the intricacies of governing. When he secured the appointment to the region from Empress Elizabeth some of the Protestant aristocracy feared he would impose Catholicism on them and many resisted the appointment. But he cleverly resolved that problem by inviting the nobles who will vote for the next king to his grand parties and the country hunts he holds at the Mitau Schloss Palace. They now give him their full support. His winning personality, royal blood, Polish heritage and beautiful wife make him kingly in their eyes. Casimir could learn much about politics from such an astute man."

"But Josef, you know his wife is the former Franciszka Kransinki. Now that Casimir is older and growing manlier each day it could be a disaster to send him near her."

"I don't think so my dear. Casimir quickly returned to perfecting his riding skills and military strategies after she left for Courland. He will know how to conduct himself. Besides, he may have an opportunity to watch the Russian Cossacks in training while there. No woman could compete with the Cossacks for Casimir's attention."

"Well you are probably right about that dear. I pray the Cossacks keep him occupied on their side of the border and never cross over to ours."

When Josef entered the gym, Casimir was on top of Stephen, a big eighteen-year old with bulging muscles. Casimir was delighted to see the veins begin to swell in the lad's neck and forehead. He had him pinned face down on the mat with his right arm twisted up under his shoulder blade and was waiting for Stephen to cry 'enough', so there was a look of total capitulation and gratitude on Stephen's face when Josef said, "Casimir, release Stephen and come over here to talk with me for a moment please."

Several thoughts flashed through Casimir's mind. *Just when I was about to win. Next, I was going to challenge that giant Olaf. No one has beaten him, but I'll change that. Too bad father showed up. I wonder why he came to the gym. Am I in trouble? Surely he saw how well I wrestled Stephen and will praise me.*

Josef was not surprised by Casimir's prowess since he won every contest he entered. But he wondered how he had done it so easily, seemingly without much effort.

"Casimir, how were you able to get Stephen to the mat with that arm lock? It looked so easy for you."

"Well it was pretty easy Father. You see I go in knowing that I can win. Stephen thinks he can win because he's bigger than me. But I know I will win because I'm smarter, quicker, and more agile. A big person can't move as fast as me, and they wear out sooner. I simply keep coming at them, ducking their blows and dodging their attacks when they come back at me. When they think I'm on the defensive, I run back in, give them a couple of quick punches to the belly and dance away again. Eventually they become so tired they start making mistakes. They let their guard down and I find an opportunity to attack their ankles for a takedown."

"Well that seems to work very well Casimir. Now, I have some news for you that doesn't involve fighting.

"The duke of Courland has graciously accepted my request that you spend time as a page in his estate. That's where you will learn the correct way to conduct yourself at court, at dinner parties, in homes of the noble families, and on the dance floor with beautiful young women. Hopefully, you'll gain an appreciation for art, music, and literature as well. These are basics that any gentleman needs to conduct his business and social life properly. One day you will help manage the Pulaski Estate and will need these skills."

Casimir's heart sank. He had no interest in such trivial things. He had work to do preparing an army for the Russian invasion that his father was certain would come. Dancing. Dining at elegant tables. Bowing and wearing powdered wigs. Reading poems or looking at paintings of naked women. How pointless. But he must always honor his father's wishes.

"Father, I appreciate your concern for me and I will do whatever you want, but it is really a bad time to interrupt my training. I have developed a new strategy for horsemen that will make us victorious when we are invaded. I need to stay here and perfect it. That is far more important than learning how to waltz fine ladies around a dance floor."

"Oh, and what is this grand new strategy that will change how wars are fought?"

"It starts by not ordering men on both sides of a battlefield to march straight into bayonets and cannon fire. That is old. It's barbaric and usually not successful. Men should be on horseback, rushing in fast, killing, pushing the enemy back, and then, if necessary, retreating to the safety of woods or forts, as I do in wrestling. They will be saved to fight again the next day and the days that follow until the enemy has been defeated."

"Well it sounds to me like you already have it perfected," said his father. "I know you have the horse part. You and Wolny are fearsome, I'll give you that, but it is important that you gain skills in etiquette, and learn how to conduct yourself in places other than stables and battlefields."

"Oh Father, you know I went to the Theatyni Collegium Nobilum School last year to study drama and I played Julius Caesar. Isn't that enough?"

Josef laughed. "If I recall correctly, the drama you studied had more to do with acting out battle scenes and death than it did with learning about the great playwrights, just as your art class turned into a horse drawing exercise. No, my son, it is time for your sake and for the future of your family that you gain some culture."

"But Father . . . "

"Casimir, surely you know battles and wars are won in places other than the battlefield. Diplomacy, perception of strength and intellect, along with outsmarting the enemy is far better than a lot of senseless killing.

"If needed, you have the fighting skills to win many battles. Now it is time to build a personal arsenal of weapons that most do not have: strength of character and belief in your cause, wisdom, calmness in the face of death, diplomacy, communication skills, and political know how.

"You already have the character and a great deal of wisdom for your years, but you need to acquire the nuances of diplomacy, effective communication, and politics by observing Duke Karl and the noblemen who visit him.

"And one other thing, my young warrior, your strategy to fight from horseback is neither new nor infallible."

For once he thought his father was wrong and blurted out: "Yes, father, it really is unbeatable. It has to do with surprise, doing the unexpected and keeping the enemy confused. My new horseback strategies will win every time. I am sure of it."

"Really? Well fighting from horseback is not as novel as you think young man. Many, many years ago, the Polish Winged Hussars were undefeated due to *both* their horsemanship *and* their intellect. It took both to conquer their enemies. Training horses to do maneuvers in battle and being able to ride well were not their most important weapons."

"Well, what else did they do that made them so victorious? I know they had a great leader in King Sobieski, but I will be just as great, especially now that I have his sword. But what were their special weapons? Did they have better swords, stronger horses, or poison arrows?"

"Listen carefully and I will tell you, Casimir.

"When I served in the army under General Drusky he insisted that all of his direct subordinates study the history of warfare. My favorite part was learning about the tactics of our great King Jan Sobieski and his winged Hussars. They were undefeated. The enemy's horses turned and ran from them. And both the horses and men they faced were competent fighters. But, you see Casimir, they used their minds and their knowledge of horses to win.

The Muslim principle of Jihad—a war against non-believers—was embraced by hundreds of thousands of Muslims and mercenaries who fought and defeated armies in country after country until Jan Sobieski took to the battlefield with his winged Polish Hussars. He stopped the Muslim invaders at the walls of Vienna before they could extinguish the light of Christianity."

"How Father? How did they do that after so many others had fallen?" Casimir asked, wide-eyed in anticipation.

"They designed and wore big wooden hooped wings with bird feathers that fit onto their backs." Josef explained, "The

86

wings protected them from arrows while the feathers flapped and looked like large wild attacking birds. They designed longer and lighter lances that were hollow and easy to carry. They could thrust them into men and horses while still so far away that the enemy's shorter lances couldn't reach them.

"When they appeared in front of their adversaries, their horses walked in step to a slow drumbeat. As they drew closer to their enemies, the drumbeat quickened to signal a slow trot, then the Hussars moved closer together until the pace of the drums became faster and the horses moved tighter into a full canter. The Hussars closed their ranks until they were riding stirrup to stirrup. The ground shook from the hooves of so many horses running so close together It sounded like thunder. Their wings flapped in the wind, and to the poor enemy's horses they looked like a flock of giant vultures coming in to rip them apart.

Then, King Jan's Hussars began yelling and riding faster to a wild, drum beat while the wind moved even faster over and under the wooden wings creating a loud, eerie screeching sound. The Muslim invaders' horses went into a frenzy. They began to spin and turn, trying to run away from what they thought were monsters coming to devour them.

"Then some of the Polish Hussars wearing skins of wild animals raced to the front smelling like leopards, tigers, and lions. The terrified horses became even more crazed as they caught the scent from the pelts of their ancestral predators.

That's when the long lances the Hussars had designed caught them, downing them and their riders. In their panic, the enemy's own mounts threw and injured or killed many of them. Our Polish Hussars masterfully used their knowledge of the horse, including the evolution of horses, to defeat much larger forces. And they used their minds to plan their weaponry and their battlefield tactics."

"At one time, the Polish Hussars had command of any battlefield they entered and the other countries of Europe came to Poland's door begging them for help and assistance. Oh how I wish that were true today."

"Father that is amazing. I wish I could have seen them, but I would have thought of something to do from horseback, like . . . like . . . throwing fireballs onto their wooden wings."

"Believe me my dear son, that was tried. You still have much to learn even though you think you are invincible. I am sure you will use your time well at Courland coming back to us much better prepared to deal with adversaries on and off the battlefield.

"Oh, by the way Casimir, I forgot to mention, I heard the Russian Cossacks are in training near the Courland Estate."

"Really Father? Do you think I'll get to see them? Now, I might be able to learn something from them."

"Well, son, I can't be sure, but remember King Sobieski and his Hussars defeated the Russian Cossacks and the Muslim Infidels. What I am sure of is that you will make your mother and me proud with whatever you learn at Courland. When you return I will throw a big party with musicians playing beautiful waltzes and invite all the fine young ladies so you can twirl them around the ballroom floor with your new dance steps.

"And one final thing, Kas. This will be painful I know, but neither Wolny nor Pushka may go with you.

"Oh no Father, I will need them, especially Pushka. We are together every day, he will miss me too much. And I him. Please at least allow Pushka to go."

"I'm sorry Casimir. Wolny may not go for obvious reasons. He's too dangerous around people who do not know his temperament. And if Pushka goes, I fear the two of you will be off riding at every opportunity you have. You may have escaped your tutors at home to go riding, but I intend for you to have as few distractions as possible at Courland. Besides, Pushka is getting older and needs some rest from your demanding routines. I'm thinking he will be ready soon for a different job and a Pushka colt might make a good back up for Wolny."

Although Casimir was excited by the idea of a Pushka colt, he knew that being in a strange place without him would be lonely. Casimir groaned, embraced his father and sadly walked outside to ride Pushka home.

The events that occurred during his six month stay with the Duke of Courland influenced Casimir's life forever. He became reacquainted with the lovely Franciszka, now Duchess of Courland, he studied the famed Russian Cossacks in training, and learned that retreat is sometimes necessary.

Franciszka was leading a storybook life. When Duke Karl met her, he fell madly in love, not only with her physical beauty but also her quick mind. She had an insatiable appetite for history, art, literature, and music, and she could quickly grasp the heart of a problem, then just as quickly find a solution. She was a good conversationalist on any subject from astrology to philosophy. Karl's royal upbringing required him to have a good education, particularly in history and government, and it was refreshing to find a woman who could match and occasionally surpass him in these and many other subjects, although he would never admit it. She was also graceful, charming, and an elegant hostess. He knew she would be the perfect queen, but because she was not of royal blood his father did not approve their marriage.

Against the wishes of his father, King Stanislaus Augustus III, Duke Karl and Franciszka were secretly married in Warsaw. By Polish law, because she was not a member of royalty or a high ranking noble family, neither she nor any children she bore could receive royal titles. The marriage must have been a bittersweet victory for her, while she had all the trappings and privileges of royalty, not having a title was a daily reminder that she was not of the royal class. The Duke shielded her as best he could by introducing her as Duchess Courland and insisting that she be referred to as "The Duchess". Her popularity made it easy for everyone from servants to nobles to comply.

Franciszka read every book she could find, but history was her favorite subject. She studied Genghis Khan, Caesar, Cleopatra, Alexander the Great and his father, Phillip. Her beauty, along with her appreciation of the arts and her knowledge of history and geography, made her fascinating to men of all ages and social positions. She had received several offers of marriage before she turned sixteen. But Duke Karl was irresistible. He was nine years her senior, the heir apparent to the Polish throne, and the most sought-after bachelor in Poland. What she found especially appealing were his wide brow, long delicate nose, and thin lips which reminded her of the countenances on the Greek statues she had seen in her history books. Her parents were jubilant because they knew the marriage would elevate their status.

She did not forget Casimir, but marrying the future king of Poland made him a distant memory, that is, until the day he arrived at the Courland Castle, Mitau Schloss, to be her husband's page.

When Duke Karl walked into the sitting room of the palace with Josef and Casimir to introduce his new page she could see how much Casimir had matured. He projected a deeper, wiser persona by the way he carried himself, and through his dark eyes that seemed to extend into his soul. He walked straight and proud next to his father. Franciszka suddenly realized she had missed him. She wished she could still go horseback riding with him, but knew a Duchess, even a Duchess in name only, could not be seen riding with her husband's page.

"My dear, I believe you know Monsieur Pulaski and his son, Casimir."

"Oh yes," she smiled, and embraced Josef. She missed her father and was delighted to see his old friend again. "How are you? Have you seen my father recently? Oh, but I am being rude and thoughtless. Please forgive me."

She turned from Josef to Casimir and with a formal demeanor said, "Monsieur Pulaski, welcome to Mitau Schloss. I hope you will be very happy here."

She held out her hand to him and Casimir took it, bowed low, and touched his lips to it just as he had when they first met on the Pulaski estate. Franciszka was even more beautiful than he remembered.

"Duchess, it is an honor to be accepted as a member of the Courland staff. I am indebted to the both of you," he replied, looking from the Duchess to the Duke. He had heard many good things about Duke Karl, and over the past several days his remorse about leaving his training lessened as he realized how much he could learn in the Duke's service.

Josef smiled while giving Franciszka a fatherly look, and thinking about what a wonderful daughter-in-law she would have been.

"My dear Duchess your father is quite well," Josef said. "We shared lunch together just a few days ago. He sends his love and promises to come see you soon.

"But now I wish to personally thank both of you for allowing Casimir to train on some of the niceties of life here at Courland. We both deeply appreciate the opportunity you are providing. I'm proud of his military abilities, and I am sure at the end of his time with you I will be equally proud of the social skills he will develop here as a page.

"And to you Duke Karl, it is my hope Casimir will distinguish himself in your service. Please do not hesitate to assign him as many duties and tasks as you like. He is stronger than most men, and does not tire easily. He can assist with your hunting parties, and with a little instruction he might serve as a valet, or even helping the Duchess with her entertaining. I want him to be useful. Please keep him as busy as possible."

Josef turned to make sure Casimir was listening, before saying, "Now, I have a long ride home, so I will beg my leave of you."

"Oh, no," Franciszka protested. "You must stay for dinner and enjoy the evening with us. You can start on your journey tomorrow morning when you are fresh."

"It is certainly most tempting my dear, but as the mayor of Warka I have many things to attend to.

"Now Casimir, I will leave Bertha with you and I will ride Pushka back home as we agreed." The mischievous twinkle in his eye was not missed by Franciszka, who remembered Casimir's disdain for the large gentle horse as she suppressed a smile.

Josef turned and thanked the Duke again, bowed to Franciszka, and gave Casimir a look that said both, "Behave — and I love you."

He followed the butler to the door thinking it would be best if Casimir immediately became immersed in life at the palace, without a father in the way.

Casimir regretted his father's decision to leave. He wanted his assurance, calmness and guidance to quiet his trepidations. The Pulaski homes in Warsaw and Warka were elegant, but neither compared to a palace like Mitau Schloss. And he would be relegated to the status of an underling for the first time in his life. At the Pulaski homes he was part of the family and was catered to. That would not be the case here.

The gleaming marble floors, glistening crystal chandeliers, and handwoven tapestries that covered the walls between priceless paintings and gold-framed mirrors were intimidating enough; but then there were the footmen, doormen, valets, butlers, under-butlers, lady's maids, musicians, courtiers, cooks, stable hands, gardeners, and, of course, pages. He didn't know how to act in such an environment—how should he address people?

He suspected there was some sort of ranking among the servants with some being addressed more informally than others. Where did a page fit in the order of things?

And one glance into the dining room filled him with anxiety. There were sixteen pieces of silverware next to each plate and a formal dinner was not planned. Was it this way only for the family? How would he ever learn it all? Why had his father offered his services for anywhere he was needed, even at entertaining.

Then he realized why. It was just such ignorance of fine manners that motivated his father to enroll him at Courland as a page. But, understanding did not bring relief. He would do his best, though he still longed for Pushka and the stables at Winiary. There was no such need for fancy manners in the stables.

Casimir was given greater access to the Duke and Duchess than the other pages because of Josef's friendship with Franciszka's father and his past friendship with her. While at Courland, Casimir and Franciszka spent many evenings together, engaged in discussions of history, a favorite subject of both.

Casimir was even more mesmerized by Franciszka's beauty than when they first met. While he did not think much about girls or women, her exquisite appearance and carriage captured his attention more completely than a thousand Winged Hussars, and he surrendered his heart to her without question.

Franciszka had her mother's refined features with thick dark hair falling into cascading ringlets around her delicate pink porcelain face as it escaped from the pearl hairpins she used to hold it atop her head. Having an eye for fashion, he noted she frequently wore pearls, in necklaces, earrings, and even as buttons on her clothes. The gold medallion she wore when they first went riding was always around her neck, sometimes dangling from a pearl necklace. Her hands had long delicate fingers which were nimble on the harp and piano. Her eyes were the green of alpine grass in spring projecting both wisdom and mirth. She carried her four foot ten-inch frame so gracefully she seemed to float across any floor, especially the dance floor, and she had a way of raising her right eyebrow in a flirtatious, almost provocative, manner that forced his heart so far into his throat he feared he might strangle in her presence. The aroma of Christmas spices, fresh mown hay, and spring roses still made him dizzy whenever she came near.

He had less interest than she in poetry and paintings. But when they talked of the great battles of Phillip, Alexander, Caesar, and Xerxes, the Persian conqueror, he was intensely interested and engrossed in every detail she could recall from her historical studies. He was particularly interested in stories of Caesar and Cleopatra as he had played Julius Caesar at the Theatyni Collegium Nobilum School. He identified with, and admired the Great Caesar who was powerful, charismatic, and arrogant. Cleopatra was not mentioned in the texts he studied at the school and now that he heard their full story, he thought it was absurd that a great general like Caesar was distracted and possibly ruined by such a woman.

He second-guessed the revered war heroes of the past, questioning if they had followed a different strategy than the one they implemented would the victory have come sooner with fewer losses. Or, conversely if their enemy had been on horseback leading their legions what would the outcome have been. He was surprised and flattered that she could follow his talk of different strategies and battle tactics.

He saw that Franciszka was a wonderful complement to the Duke and ran his multiple large households with efficiency, grace, and charm. And, just as Casimir's mother did for his father, she helped the Duke entertain important guests, handled all the details of running a large household full of servants with various shortcomings, and undoubtedly would raise their children to be ladies and gentlemen when that time came. Casimir idolized her.

He was deeply in love, and his feelings confused him. The thought of her married to a man he so admired made him feel guilty. He often thought of her as a fragile goddess to be adored, revered, and protected. Some evenings as she played the harp, he thought that the angels must be guiding her fingers, for the music was so sweet and serene . Just being in her presence made his heart race, his breath quicken, and his cheeks flush. He was tortured, not knowing how to deal with these new feelings.

He needed help and thought, *If only Father were here, I could ask him if his throat burned and he had trouble breathing each time he saw mother when they first met.*

Of course, mother was not married to a Duke. I fear being with the Duchess for what I might do or say to make her unhappy with me.

An older woman of twenty and married, Franciszka was well aware of the effect she was having on this seventeen-year-old caught somewhere between adolescence and manhood. She was fond of him, and enjoyed his obvious obsession. She fueled the flames by looking deeply into his eyes as she played the piano or harp and gave him a smile that seemed to be saved for him alone. When she added the flirtatious raised brow, he melted like butter left in the sun on a hot summer day.

She often increased his joy and his discomfort with a slight shake of her head that freed more ringlets from the pearl hairpins and a giggle saying, "Monsieur, Pulaski, my warrior, will you dance with me?"

She would then have the palace musicians begin a waltz as she lifted her hand to his and stepped inside his arms to be twirled around the grand ballroom. She was the perfect size for a small man and her touch turned his veins into coursing rivulets of hot lava. It took all his strength to keep his hand against her back making it as immobile as the hand on one of the cold marble statues that lined the palace hallways. He was terrified of following his desires and moving it to her rib cage where he could touch the base of her breast. It was a miracle he could stay on his feet at all under such stress much less execute a complex waltz step that he was just learning.

As the evenings came to a close and he was drunk with desire, she would tease him with a coquettish smile and say, "If you really do like my amateurish music, and are not too busy with your work and studies perhaps you will allow me to play for you again? Your dancing is becoming quite good."

"Oh no. Oh yes, I mean. I meant, I meant, no your music is not amateurish it is divine and yes, I would love to hear you play again. Would tomorrow be too soon?"

"Of course not, Monsieur Pulaski, I will look forward to playing again tomorrow in the evening," she replied as she left the room making sure the edge of her skirt brushed against his leg as she exited. An older, more experienced man would have known that her reference to 'playing' had nothing to do with music and everything to do with teasing him.

When he retired to his bedchamber late at night his mind would not let him rest. He could think only of how it would feel not to be restrained by the dance steps but to really hold her. His greatest desire was to wrap his arms around her and to protect her from all harm. He was as fervently devoted to her as the knights of old were to their pristine ladies. He saw her as totally pure, and he would always be her defender and guardian. His fantasies did not go beyond touching, holding, and protecting her.

In truth, he knew of nothing beyond that. His father was waiting to see if he showed any interest in sex before discussing it with him. Paul told him about the dreams and fantasies that excited him so much, especially at night. He confided that the pressure was too much to bear unless he regularly relieved himself.

It was all lost on Casimir. It had nothing to do with horses or battle strategies and he thought Paul was too distracted by it. He felt none or those urges, or at least he had not yet.

He knew from being with Paul, Antonin, and Frank that his body was different. When he studied art at the Collegium he saw paintings of both nude males and females, but none that looked like him. How would Franciszka, or any woman react to his anatomy? It was a question that never bothered him. His father said he was special because of his physical attributes and he had proven that many times by being a champion at anything he tried. Someone as sensitive and smart as Franciszka would understand his specialness.

Alas, he had to admit that, like Caesar, he was now very distracted by a woman. It was difficult for one who had built a life of discipline and regimentation to be so sidetracked. But it was a path he was happy to follow. Now he had a stronger reason to defend Poland and her citizenry. Franciszka. She must never come to harm.

He admired the Duke for his regal bearing, his camaraderie with other nobles, vast knowledge of Polish history, and hospitality to him. In the mornings when he met the Duke and Duchess on their way to breakfast he would feel the hot blush returning to his face and found it hard to meet the Duke's eyes. But he still hungered to see Franciszka again as soon as possible.

Franciszka was having her own sleepless nights. The Duke was already showing signs of growing tired of her. He hardly noticed the evenings she was spending with Casimir, preferring to drink brandy and play cards with friends or meet with the game warden to discuss the best areas to take his next hunting party.

Casimir was a boy when she rode with him at Warka. She enjoyed riding with him and found him mature beyond his years but his obsession with horses and battle plans did not intrigue her. Now this dashing young man with his interest in history and music had her fascinated. He was so attentive, and obviously so attracted to her that she could not help but be flattered. She soon felt a sensual pull that she knew he felt as well. But she also knew his motives toward her were kind, loving, and protective. He wanted nothing from her but to share her company. How many women were that fortunate?

She did think the musical interest was an excuse to spend time with her, but he was a good student, and was mastering the waltz and other dances under her tutelage. Instinctively she knew he was destined for greatness and she could also help him execute the dance steps of diplomacy and negotiation, and when the time came, victory waltzes. Without a word on the subject they had both dedicated themselves to the success and protection of the other. It turned out to be the most important partnership in Casimir's life.

The Courland palace was near the Russian border. One evening Franciszka suggested Casimir ride out and watch the Russian Cossacks train. He couldn't believe his luck. He would be able to observe the famed Russian Cossacks doing their maneuvers.

At daybreak the next morning, he rode out to the small hill to which she had directed him. He dismounted and climbed up an old fort rock wall and pulled out a spyglass, and spent most of the day watching and analyzing their movements.

Casimir developed an early distaste for the Russians from his father. Josef told Casimir, "When I was a young boy the Russians killed my father at the Battle of Kalisz. They were brutal and showed no mercy to our brave men on the battlefield. I never knew my father but I was told they violated his body, hung him from a tree and threw lances at him for target practice while he was still alive. Someday we will have our justice."

That and the threat of a Polish invasion by the Russians created within him a desire for revenge. But despite his feelings, Casimir had to admire the daring Russian Cossacks in training.

In the evenings, he was so animated by what he saw during the day that his uneasiness in front of Franciszka temporarily left, and he would tell Duke Karl and her about the Cossacks' maneuvers.

"They show no fear. Russian Cossacks jump astride their horses waving swords and charging ahead as if the possibility of retreat or death does not exist. They ride like they are part of their horses. They have different weapons for fighting from horseback and on the ground. They are great horsemen, but do not have the trust of their horses like I do and cannot rely on their mounts to help them in the heat of battle. They are tough, agile, and fearless, but not so smart. They would make a formidable enemy but I am a better strategist and fighter than the Cossacks. I wish I could have but one battle with them and show them how we Poles fight not only with weapons but also with our heads and our hearts."

But secretly he feared that if sufficiently outnumbered he could be captured by the Russians. The nightmares began shortly after he started watching the Cossacks train. He remembered his father's story about the mutilation of his grandfather's body by Russians. In the dream he was captured, separated from his officers and men, and tortured. The physical torture was easily endured, but other indignities were almost unbearable. In the nightmares, he was stripped naked, his physical distortions revealed, talked about and ridiculed. Ignorant ruffians pointed and guffawed at his genitals. He, the champion, was humiliated, degraded and vilified. Thus began the fear of capture and exposure that became a lifelong paranoia. Death rather than capture became his goal.

The Duke's voice brought Casimir out of his reverie about Russian Cossacks and capture. "Don't be ridiculous. Stop talking nonsense about fighting the Cossacks, they are too many for us," the Duke interjected as he excused himself, leaving Casimir and Franciszka completely alone. The court musicians were not summoned and the servants were having their dinner in the kitchen.

His daily prayers were answered, and at long last he was alone with her. But his joy was short lived. He became more distraught than he believed possible when he saw a tear glistening in the corner of her eye. He rushed to her side, and unthinkingly took her hand in his. "Franciszka, my Duchess what did I do? Did I create your sorrow?" He then implored again. "What did I do, what did I say to hurt you? Tell me how to restore a smile to your face and I will do it no matter the cost."

She lifted her hand from his and said, "My fearless young warrior, I could not bear to have you killed or injured by the Cossacks. Such talk of fighting them frightens me." Then she placed her hand back in his.

If he had snatched a handful of lightning from the sky the jolt could not have equaled the shock and heat that her touch sent through his body. He saw her breasts rising and falling rapidly and he knew, knew in his heart that she felt the same heat, the same longing, the same magnet drawing her to him. Now he understood what Paul had been talking about. He imagined what ecstasy it would be to kiss and caress her, to hold her, tell her of his love, and to possess her. He was a virgin and had never felt sexual desire before meeting her. He was shaken by the experience, but his training in duty and responsibility saved him.

No, no, his disciplined mind screamed. *She is married to the future king.* He turned from her and with quick frantic strides rushed from the room without looking back.

Yet he found he was trembling from emotion and passion. He was joyous that she felt the same, but knew this union could not happen.

He respected and liked the Duke, and he remembered his vow to his father. He was sent to Duke Karl to enhance the family's prestige, not to dishonor it. An affair with the Duke's wife was unthinkable no matter how much he desired her.

Passion was new to him, but controllable. He would avoid it in the future. He had read that the Roman gladiators believed sex weakened them, and he could see how women distracted young men from more important matters — just look at Caesar. He would not be weakened. He would deal with it.

He was careful not to be alone with her again. When they were together with others in the room, she noticed that he had changed. His youthful infatuation had matured, he was no longer shy or awkward around her; but more mature with a decidedly determined step and sharpness of shoulder. She knew he loved her, and that the denial of that love had strengthened him. She resolved that their relationship would be one of devoted friendship. It became an honorable solution that left them with dignity and respect for each other.

The distractions of court protocol and watching the Cossacks train helped him through the days and nights that followed.

Then, after only six months at Courland, he had to leave.

In spite of all his gracious and winning ways, Duke Karl could not avoid conflict with the Russians. The reasons were simple. He owned huge land masses worked by thousands of serfs near the Russian border, and he had a legitimate claim to the Polish throne.

His former supporter, Empress Elizabeth had died. Catherine was now the Russian Empress, and she wanted to weaken him. Catherine had devoted her life to becoming Empress of Russia.

She had done everything Elizabeth asked and more. Coming to court as an eleven-year-old from Prussia, she gave up her native language and church to speak Russian and join the Russian Orthodox Church. She even married Elizabeth's nephew, the imbecilic, slobbering Peter.

Her one disobedience was to reject Peter in the marriage bed. Having to submit to a ridiculous, deformed, giggling idiot was just too demeaning. Instead, she took lovers and then endured the agony of having her babies snatched from her arms to be sent to work as serfs on lands Elizabeth owned. Yes, she had sacrificed everything to become Russia's Empress and she was going to be the greatest Empress—no, the greatest ruler that Russia would ever have. That meant she had to have a warm water port, and expand Russia's control to neighboring countries. Most specifically, Poland.

She was ready to begin. Duke Karl's Courland Estate and Palace would be the first stepping stone into Poland, and she had her own plans for a King of Poland, plans that did not include him.

She reinstated Ernst Johann von Biron's title as Duke of Courland. Empress Elizabeth's predecessor, Anna, had withdrawn the title and exiled him to Siberia. He was very happy to be in Catherine's good graces and would gladly do her bidding if he could get Courland back.

Next, Catherine told her ambassador, Prince Repnin, to go to Courland and subdue Duke Karl, "as you see fit". Once on the scene, far from Court, he acted as if he had as much power as the Empress. He forced local decisions to his own will. He contacted Von Biron and encouraged him to take Courland back supplying him with 5,000 Russian troops.

Von Biron didn't hesitate. He sent word to Duke Karl that he would take Courland by force if it was not surrendered within three days. The Duke had only 1,200 trained men at the estate and some forty personal guards. He dispatched a messenger to his father, the king, seeking help. But King Augustus III was ailing, exhausted by his age and the toll of fighting the Seven Years' War. He did not have the strength or will to take on the Russians.

His reply was disappointing to both Duke Karl and Casimir:

"My son, leave the estate to the Russians. If you resist they will only bring in thousands more and you will be thrown into a Russian prison for ransom from me, or worse, killed. Leave immediately, take your family with you and send your courtiers home. You will join my court in Warsaw and will have no need for them. Do this for me and for Poland."

Casimir protested and pleaded with Duke Karl when he received the news of the order to surrender.

"No! No Duke Karl! We must not submit to the Russians. We must fight to the death if necessary. I can lead your troops to victory if you will put me in command. I guarantee it."

The idea of an untested youth asking for command of his troops would have amused the Duke had he not been so frustrated by the news. Yet he could not allow that frustration to show. He must remain calm and seem in control as he organized the surrender and evacuation of Courland. He had no choice but to obey his father, the King. And he was not in a mood to debate the issue with a seventeen-year-old page to whom he had obviously given too much leeway. A mere page should never question a Duke, especially one carrying out the orders of a king.

"Page Pulaski! Stop this foolishness now. I have orders from the King to follow and you have my instructions. Now go help the staff pack what the Duchess will need to take with her to Warsaw. And do not speak to me again of this matter."

I have no choice but to return home, Casimir thought. *But if Russia moves soldiers deeper into Poland, I will be ready to meet and defeat them. I will chase them back into that frozen wasteland. I am capable of raising and training an army that will surprise our enemies with new strategies. I will have future opportunities to defend Poland and shall.*

Empress Catherine would supply him those opportunities. She was plotting and preparing. Taking Courland was her first move to gain control of Poland, and there would be many more. She was as determined to have Poland as Josef and Casimir were to save it.

He dreaded leaving Courland and Franciszka. He left on one of those bright, clean, blue-sky-cool days of early spring. The crisp air held both the lingering cold bite of winter and the warm kiss of spring. He watched a pair of storks preparing a nest with small branches and dried grasses atop a tall birch tree. They reminded him of the young storks at Winiary that hatched each year in the old elm. While it would be good to see his father and family, and of course, Pushka, he was bitterly disappointed that he could not fight.

The river running through the Courland Estate was full and frothy from the melting of the winter snow. It would soon flood the flat plains around it, depositing rich soil from upstream.

The air was aromatic with the smell of fresh turned earth as the laborers prepared the soil on higher ground near the house for cabbage, potatoes and other vegetables. Robins pulled earthworms from the fresh upturned soil. A screech owl watched from the hollow of a nearby tree waiting for the night when he would feed on field mice and baby rabbits. The serfs were not told of the impending departure of the Duke and his Court. They would be left to the Russians and their merciless ways.

A bright spring day would normally have lifted Casmir's spirits signaling to him that greatness was ahead for him and the Duke and Duchess. But the reality that he could not fight the Cossacks and that he had to leave Franciszka erased the pleasantries of the day. For him, the world was still cloaked in the cold grayness of a bitter Polish winter. Being caught in the power struggle between two monarchs and subjected to their politics and royal protocols was new, unfamiliar, and in his mind, unfair.

But then his sunshine arrived. She met him at the curved driveway in front of the palace. She smiled warmly at him as he dismounted and cautiously kissed her outstretched hand. He said, "My Duchess I wish you much health, happiness, and joy all the days of your life." She nodded and clasped his hand a bit tighter.

He saw that a fine coach to transport her to safety waited. The Duke would remain an additional day to destroy or pack sensitive documents that could not fall into Russian hands. On the side panel of the carriage was an emblem of deer, lions, and green olive branches. It was the Courland Crest, emblazoned in gold against a blue lapis background. It represented the innocence and purity of deer, the strength of lions, and the peace of the olive branch. The rest of the carriage was royal red with white scrolls highlighted in gold leaf decorating its sides, front, and back. Ten horsemen in blue and gold uniforms, blue and white tri-cornered hats, and miniatures of the Courland Crest embroidered on their epaulets sat astride perfectly matched black prancing horses near the coach.

The grandeur and symbolism were not lost on him. He decided that the legions he led would be dressed splendidly, ride tall on strong horses, and be considered the most elite and strongest force ever created. They would proudly carry the Pulaski coat of arms depicting the blind raven with its many noble and protective powers as they rode straight and defiant in their saddles. They would be as strong as lions when their homeland was threatened but they would also be deer-gentle, never looting or ravaging conquered lands and people. They would be quick to raise the sword of defense but just as quick to raise the olive branch for an equitable peace. They would be honorable men led by an honorable man, fighting for freedom.

Franciszka and he still stood together and she had not released his hand. She said, "I am so sorry things are this way. I thought I would have many happy years here at Courland and you would come often to visit. I am disappointed for you that you could not confront the Cossacks, but I am also relieved that you will not be in danger."

"My dear Duchess, I long for nothing more than to protect you and defend what is rightfully yours. I am disappointed that the king has ordered otherwise. It is a great sorrow for me that I cannot fight for you and for Poland."

"Yes, dear Casimir. It is sad for all of us. But in many ways most sad for you to be restrained from battle after all your preparations and training to fight." She let her hand linger in his for a moment longer then slowly released his hand and smiled at him. "I have a gift for you. I hope it will cheer you and remind you of Courland and our time here together."

A stable man walked down the driveway toward them leading a magnificent white Arabian mare. Casimir immediately sensed that she not only looked like Pushka but her temperament, intelligence, and strength matched his as well.

His spirits jumped and Franciszka saw the light on his face. "I am pleased that my intuition in selecting this horse as a gift for you, was a good one, Monsieur Pulaski."

He strode over to the horse, took the reins, and rubbed his face against her warm nose and breathed into her nostril. She whinnied in the low happy way of horses as he led her back to Franciszka.

"Your father wrote that you would be spending your birthday away from your family for the first time and I wanted to give you something special", Franciszka said. "Little did I know when I bought the mare she would be both a birthday and a good-bye gift."

He was astounded that he actually had forgotten his birthday. With all the excitement of the threat of attack and disappointment over not being able to fight the Russian Cossacks, he completely forgot about what had always been the most important day of the year for him.

"I am overwhelmed by your kindness and your knowledge of my heart. Thank you, my dear, dear Duchess. What is her name?"

Franciszka shook her head. "Things happened so quickly with the Russian threat and preparations for evacuations after she arrived last week, I don't think anyone named her. What would you like to call her, Casimir?"

"Pearlina," he said, without hesitation.

She smiled broadly and then wiped a tear from the corner of her eye. She knew her love of pearls prompted him to give the horse the name. She said, "I know this is not a forever parting, we shall see each other again and have many fine adventures to share. We are forever friends and I will always help you anyway I can."

"And I will always protect our homeland and cherish the memory of our time together," he promised.

There was a telltale twitch at the corner of her mouth as she tried to maintain the reassuring smile. He swung himself up onto the beautiful Arabian mare in a quick, easy motion. He knew Bertha would follow. At least he wouldn't be seen riding "Miss Plodder" out the gates of Courland.

One of the coachmen helped Franciszka into the carriage. They would be going in opposite directions. He waved good-by as he turned the mare toward the Winiary Estate and home.

She leaned out the carriage window for a final backward glance of her declared protector thinking how splendid he looked. The brown leather saddle she had chosen for the mare perfectly matched the soft leather of his long riding boots. The Sobieski sword glistened in the sun at his side and Pearlina pranced along as if she knew how special she and her new master were.

As he was riding home, Casimir was again frustrated that he was denied the chance to fight the Russians. His mind would not let go of what might have been.

I have always won, every contest, every challenge given me. I would have won against the Russian Cossacks too, if only I had been given the chance. And Franciszka doesn't know what I can do. She didn't see my brilliant strategy or my strength. It seems lady fate has turned her eyes away from me.

I have now watched the loss of a part of the Poland I grew to know and love. A part that belonged to our future king and to Franciszka.

In deep thought for hours, he tried to figure out how he could have changed the Duke's decision.

He had no way of knowing that someone even more famous than Duke Karl on another continent in a different time, would give him the chance to make such a daring rescue.

The monotonous squeaking of the saddle and rhythmic clomping of the hooves added its own sad music to accompany his melancholy. Then Pearlina let out a neigh.

Coming back into the real world, he realized he wasn't far from home. Pearlina's pace quickened as she sensed the presence of other animals. He let her have her head, and trot up a small rise. At the top, he could see faint lights in the distance much like flickering fire flies. It was the lights of home. As the mare's pace turned to a trot, a new energy within him surged, and he realized how fortunate he was to have a friend like Franciszka to give him such a fine horse. He again vowed to be her protector and to fight for his Poland.

Arriving on the family grounds at Winiary, he felt a rush of warmth and belonging. As he opened the door to the stables he saw a proud white head with large dancing hazel eyes staring at him. A deep rumbling sound was coming from Pushka's throat, he was welcoming his companion and friend home.

"Pushka, look what Franciszka sent you," he called. Pushka started a little dance to display his pleasure. The movement was not lost on the mare for her neighs and soft squeals said it all. As Casimir removed her tack, she and Pushka talked. He soon moved her to a nearby stall. He fed and brushed both horses relishing the reunion with his friend, Pushka. For the moment, Courland and the Russians were all but forgotten. He was home and it felt good. He was tired and anxious to get into his own bed for a good night's sleep.

CHAPTER TEN

SEA ADVENTURES WITH SHARKS AND SULTANS

Atlantic Ocean
1777

What a life I've led, Casimir thought, as he took a break from reading about his childhood to walk around the deck and reflect on his good fortune.

Why, before Peter the Great put a stop to it, children like me were smothered at birth. Mother and Father could never do such a heinous thing, but many parents would have closed me off from the world. But instead of thinking of my abnormality as a deformity, Father saw me as special and dedicated his life to helping me achieve my goals. With his support, I became a great military leader winning fame and glory, but oh, with such loss and suffering. It's been a life full of adventure, yet I feel that just as the gypsy woman foretold, my greatest glory is still ahead. I will find my place in America with General Washington and become a hero once more.

Strolling on the deck, he hoped to meet members of the crew and get their help learning English on the long voyage. Unfortunately, most of them signed on in Nantes, France and spoke only French. Casimir was relieved that he could at least communicate with them in French, a language he was fluent in. He would not give up trying to learn English and would listen carefully to the captain and the few English-speaking passengers aboard. He decided to also study navigation, a subject he knew little about.

He was afforded certain benefits due to his well-dressed aristocratic appearance and because he was traveling to meet General George Washington, and one benefit was a cabin on deck. While it was barely large enough for his trunk and a hammock, it was away from the squalor and stench of the lower decks where people were crammed together eating, fighting, and answering the calls of nature in close quarters. His tiny space on deck was a godsend because he was not forced to use the public privy buckets in the hold.

When he went below deck to spend time with Visner, he found fresh bodies of wharf rats, killed in fights, and could smell their excrement. *But at least the rats died fighting for a scrap of food or sip of foul water*, he mused. Such crowded spaces brought out the worst in men and fighting frequently erupted between the drunken louts over a card or dice game, a ration of wine, or even a perceived slight of one's heritage. And there were deaths along the way. Some stemming from slit throats and beatings, others from tuberculosis, pneumonia and even childbirth. It required a strong constitution to survive seven weeks of unhealthy air, food, water, and the cutthroats below deck.

Battlefields strewn with rotting corpses were something Casimir was accustomed to. They were part of the price people paid for fighting for a cause. The fallen men were heroes to their families and comrades. But he was not familiar with the sea and he thought of the sharks, whales, and large fish that followed the ship as gigantic water monsters. They trailed the boat relentlessly, waiting for the next human carcass to be tossed overboard. There was nothing noble about having your body ripped to pieces by these creatures after dying in the crowded, stinking belly of a ship. The memory of flesh being torn from bones in the water stayed with him for the rest of his life. So did the voice of his dream in Woja's cave, *"Water will threaten you."* What did it mean and how could he avoid being drowned or eaten in the water," he wondered.

Trying not to dwell on the sea burials, he focused on learning about seamanship. Casimir heard that the British navy was the greatest threat to the colonies. He thought John Adams' recommendation to Washington to establish a small navy and augment it with commercial vessels, known as privateers who were granted permission to fire on British ships, was brilliant. He admired General Washington for taking the risk of following Adams' suggestion and couldn't wait to meet this man who conducted a war on land and on sea with a volunteer army.

Casimir was aboard such a privateer, the Massachusetts. It was scheduled to dock at Marblehead, Massachusetts, a safe port, thanks to Washington's Navy. He knew his record of defeating much larger Russian armies with small bands of troops had impressed Benjamin Franklin, whose letter to General Washington was clear on that point. It seemed logical that if he acquired navigational knowledge, the general, who commanded both the Army and Navy, would appreciate his accomplishments and initiative. He was convinced that winning General Washington's support was the way to obtain the authority and funding to create his own American cavalry.

He enjoyed watching the stars at night and the crew taught him how to navigate by the constellations. They also instructed him in how to predict the weather by watching sunsets and sunrises repeating the rhyme, *'red sky at night, sailor's delight; red sky in the morning, sailor take warning.'* It was uncanny how often that phrase proved true.

"Such knowledge will be useful on land as well as on sea," he mused.

Captain Fisk took notice of the little man with European flair soon after he boarded his ship. Members of the crew reported that he had an avid interest in learning about ships, navigation, America, and especially General George Washington. Most of them had never been to America, and knew nothing of the general so they could only teach him about ships and how to sail them. When the captain learned he could not speak English, but knew French, he invited Casimir to his table for dinner one evening which included Monsieur DeClerq, a fancy Frenchman, who liked to play cards with the other passengers.

It was a festive evening. The captain could speak only a few words of French but DeClerq knew enough English to give Casimir a general idea of what he said. Casimir struggled to remember the English words but they were too confusing. The captain spoke rapidly, making it difficult for Casimir to study individual words and DeClerq spoke poor, heavily French-accented English.

After cigars, DeClerq rose and said, "I must leave this pleasant company, friends have asked me to play cards. Perhaps you will join us Monsieur Pulaski?"

"I do enjoy the game," Casimir replied. "Please ask me again. The captain has a fine chess set made of jade and bone and he suggested a game. It has been so long since I've played, I want to see if I can still remember how. Chess has its own language, so I won't need an interpreter. Thank you for your help interpreting during dinner and please enjoy your evening, Monsieur DeClerq."

DeClerq bowed to both men and left. Captain Fisk motioned for Casimir to take a seat at the chess table. From his demeanor, Casimir guessed that the captain prided himself on being a good player and was welcoming an opportunity to show off his skill. Casimir's own interest in the game began when he was two. Captain Fisk's wide eyes and open mouth showed his surprise when early in the game Casimir maneuvered one of his bishops into position and captured the captain's rook.

Minutes later, he took the captain's queen and, for all practical purposes, the game was over. The Captain's face hardened and turned red, but soon softened again as he smiled and reached across the table to shake hands with Casimir to congratulate him on his victory.

Casimir knew it was bad form to beat his host, but he could never willingly lose at anything. The captain begrudgingly admired such tenacity, and something told him that this determined young man would let neither form nor force stand between him and victory, whether at the chess table or on the battlefield. He bid Casimir good night and retired to make the day's entry in his ship's log where he noted that George Washington might be getting just the help he needed.

DeClerq sought Casimir's company and Casimir was grateful for the opportunity to converse with an apparent aristocrat, even though something about the man did not seem trustworthy. When DeClerq again invited Casimir for a game of cards, he accepted. He enjoyed cards as much as he did chess and was usually successful at both.

A tall black man approached Casimir immediately after he saw DeClerq walk away. In a low, conspiratorial voice, he addressed Casimir in Polish.

"Monsieur, be careful. No one wins more than a hand or two at cards with that man. He is like the sharks in the water. He shows no mercy to the weak. His money bag is heavier since he came on board while those of others are lighter."

He was one of the biggest men Casimir had ever seen and his black face glistened in stark contrast to the white turban atop his head. A long black braid of hair hung down his back.

"Thank you, my friend, I shall be careful— but you are not Polish," responded Casimir. "Where did you learn to speak my language and how did you know I am Polish?"

"You wear the Polish cavalry uniform and I heard your friend and you speaking on the dock. You thought I was one of the dock workers and paid me no notice."

Casimir, visibly embarrassed, said, "I apologize for that. You are obviously a learned gentleman. Perhaps we can talk more. It is good to hear the language of my homeland. Where did you learn it?"

"It was during my travels, where I learned most languages. I am from Morocco, a land of goat farmers and seamen, but I am neither. I am a mercenary, mapmaker, merchant, and trader. I am good with the cutlass and the quill and I have used both in ports around the world. By the way, I am called 'Sultan' for obvious reasons," he said, pointing to his turban. His wide smile showed teeth as white as freshly fallen snow sparkling in the sun before he turned and quickly walked away. Casimir thought he moved with the stealth of a panther and indeed, his gold flecked eyes were similar to those of that powerful black cat. *He has the muscles of a gladiator with the mannerisms of an aristocrat.* Casimir noted and then remembered, *'Sultan' did not share his real name with me, I wonder why.*

Casimir was sure that Sultan's mind was far too quick for DeClerq, or most other men.

He and Sultan began spending evenings together swapping stories of battles fought, political intrigues, and great men. Sultan was captivated by the stories Casimir told him about Jan Sobieski and his winged Polish Hussars. And Casimir was enthralled by the Sultan's tales of traveling the great Silk Road to China and vowed he would travel it himself one day.

As Sultan predicted, Casimir won an occasional hand at the beginning of the card game, but as the evening wore on DeClerq won far more often. He knew DeClerq was cheating but not openly enough for Casimir to challenge him in front of the group. But one man did. He was a farmer who lost all the money he had saved to buy a plot of land in America and, utterly distraught, he jumped up from the table and shouted at DeClerq, "you cheatin' dandy. Give me back my money!"

DeClerq slowly withdrew a pearl-handled pistol from his belt, laid it on the table, and said quite calmly, "If you cannot afford to lose, do not play," and the forlorn farmer had to back away and leave.

Casimir's analytical mind and excellent memory enabled him to keep track of cards dealt, played, and discarded, and he knew that luck alone could not explain the number of times DeClerq came up with the exact card he needed to win. He reasoned that DeClerq must have cards concealed in his clothing to retrieve during the frequent use of his handkerchief to blow his nose, or after a coughing spasm. Perhaps it was when he picked up a dropped coin from the floor, or adjusted the cuff on his jacket. DeClerq was good, and catching him in the act would be difficult. Casimir decided to wait for the right opportunity.

When Casimir avoided his card games for several days, De-Clerq sought him out and became friendlier. "Monsieur Pulaski, why are you going to such an uncivilized place as America? You are obviously from wealth, no? Why would you leave the sophistication of European courts to live like a commoner? Ah, perhaps you go to meet someone, or invest in land or other ventures in the New World? Do you have family or friends travelling with you?"

"Monsieur, my reasons for going to America are many, too many to bore you with. How about yourself? Why are you on such a long journey?" Casimir answered with as little real information as possible. He suspected DeClerq was trying to determine if he had money to steal. Casimir was too smart to continue playing cards with him, but to deter him, and to try to catch him cheating, Casimir agreed to another game. The result was the same, Casimir lost more than he won and DeClerq was the big winner.

Casimir left the card table early to spend several hours on deck enjoying the evening breezes and stars. He watched and marveled at the sailors working and climbing to the tops of the masts with only starlight to guide them. It was near dawn when he went below deck to give Visner oats and a good brushing. The horse showed his appreciation by rubbing his face against Casimir's arm.

He returned to his small cabin and found his trunk broken open, the leather pouch containing the letters he was to deliver in America tossed on the floor, and both his father's diary and Dr. Borloff's journal missing. Terror gripped him. He thought DeClerq was responsible, but to confront him would bring attention to the missing books and possibly the exposure of their content. He thought DeClerq might try to blackmail him, extracting a price to get them back. Or worse, reveal the contents, in which case Casimir could be seen as an agent of Satan because of his unusual anatomy and be thrown overboard to the sharks.

Sleep evaded him and he spent the next day trying to devise a way to kill DeClerq without being discovered. *If I could only catch him publicly cheating at cards and draw him into a duel. That might work but it still wouldn't get the journals back, and what if someone else took them?*

He stayed in his cramped cabin all day, depressed and too afraid of what others on the ship might know, to venture out. Finally, after nightfall, he decided to go on deck and inhale the sea breeze to clear his mind. No one seemed interested in him, which he thought was a good sign meaning no one knew what was in the journals. There was a warm breeze blowing wisps of clouds, the sailors called mare's tails, across the moon and stars. From what the sailors had taught him about the constellations, he could tell they were sailing on a course due west and he wondered how far it was to Massachusetts. Would he make it there safely, and if not, what would happen to Visner? Would his secret journals be publicized?

A long shadow fell across the deck and he turned, expecting to see the smirking face of DeClerq. Instead it was Sultan, who had something dangling from his right hand. He wondered what Sultan knew and whether DeClerq had talked.

"Monsieur, I believe these belong to you," Sultan said as he raised his right hand revealing the large silk handkerchief De-Clerq used during card games. It was tightly wrapped and tied around something large and bulky.

Casimir took the package and started untying the knot, wondering what was inside and what Sultan was doing with it. When the corners of the handkerchief were turned back, he saw the precious journals. He was astounded and turned to face Sultan who explained,

"DeClerq has wanted me to play cards with him since we sailed. I would not because I know he cheats but tonight I agreed after I saw him leave your cabin early this morning while you were with your horse. When you didn't appear all day, not even to brush and water the horse, I knew you had trouble and he was responsible. During tonight's game, he dropped a coin to the floor and while picking it up took an ace from his boot. I bent down at the same time and seized his arm while the card was still in his hand. Everyone saw it and demanded their money back. I promised to get it if they would give me a few minutes alone with him. They wanted to kill him, but I told them I knew how to make him suffer enough to give up the money, and if they killed him he could not show me where it was hidden. They withdrew to wait for me to return with their money.

"I made him take me to his cache. It was in the root balls of the apple trees the farmer is taking to America. I found these books in it as well as money, dice, decks of cards, and pistols. He insisted that most of the money was from his wife's fortune and that he brought it to stake his games. He begged me to let him keep it and the pistols for protection. I had no way of knowing how much money was his, and how much he took from others by cheating, so, I claimed it all and the pistols as well. Don't you think the pearl handles were made to match my cutlass?" Sultan grinned as he patted the pistol handles in his belt.

Casimir chuckled in relief and amusement at Sultan's arrogance. But was the crisis over? He flipped the pages of the journals making sure they were all there, and was reminded afresh of the secret they contained.

Sultan saw the worry return to Casimir's brow and said, "Don't worry, he reads no Polish. I saw only enough to know they belong to you. Any secret they tell is safe, including the bounty on your head."

At this last disclosure, Casimir's head jerked up. Seeing the startled look on his face, Sultan said, "Yes, I heard in France and Germany the songs about the Polish horseman who embarrassed the Russian generals so often. Perhaps that was you?"

Casimir was overwhelmed with gratitude and when he had thanked Sultan for the fourth time asked, "But what of DeClerq?"

"He is now unarmed on a ship full of enemies. I divided the money evenly between everyone who lost to him. Even that did not satisfy all of them, since some had lost more than others. Several suggested he might take a swim," Sultan said, holding Casimir's gaze. Casimir nodded slowly, knowing DeClerq deserved punishment, but shuddering at the thought of sea monsters eating anyone, especially someone still alive.

CHAPTER ELEVEN

ELECTION OF A KING

Lwów, Warka, and Radom, Poland
March 1763-1768

ultan and Casimir began to spend their evenings together, telling stories about their own lives and those of people they knew or had heard about. One evening Sultan said, "It is adventuresome to travel to new places alone, but it is also lonely. Do you have relatives or friends who will join you in America? If they speak English, they could be a great help to you."

"I hope my good friends, Paul Dobrachek and Maurice Benowski will join me when they settle family business in Poland. They fought with me in several battles and we're a powerful team when we ride together."

"I am sure you are Casimir. But what about family. Do you have a wife? Children?"

"No wife or children, but my mother, and three sisters are still in Poland. I also have a brother, but he is a guest of the Russian prisons. They're the only family I have left."

Sultan heard the sadness in his voice and thought Casimir must have lost loved ones. There must have been a father, and perhaps a wife or girlfriend as well.

"And what of your family," Casimir asked Sultan.

"My entire family was killed in a tsunami near Tangiers where we were washed ashore. We were on a boat fleeing from the Bar-

bary pirates who had pursued us from Rabat. I was told the boat was broken apart, but I was in a wicker basket that floated free. Someone found me and took me to the local orphanage which was overflowing with children who somehow survived when their parents did not. I remained there until I was twelve," he sighed.

"A rich merchant adopted me and took me on his buying trips to the Orient. That's where I learned how to trade, negotiate, and understand several languages. He also taught me how to keep records and logs and how to protect myself. When he died, I inherited his business, along with his cutlass, spyglass, and lust for travel. So, you see, it is easy for me to travel the world. I have no attachments.

"And your father, Casimir? Tell me, do you still have him?"

Casimir could see there was no intent beyond interest in a friend and boredom from the voyage that prompted Sultan's questions, so he responded in detail.

"My father was a gentle and peaceful man who loved his family. He was also a successful lawyer and businessman who was quite brilliant. He could see and understand things that others could not. He knew Poland had lost its former glory and was weak, having no real standing army; and knew that Russia hungered for a warm water port. Austria and Prussia wanted to take Poland for their own, and he saw the danger of two or more of those countries forming an alliance and invading Poland. He tried for years to persuade the rich landowners to fund a real army, warning them that without a strong military force they could lose all their wealth if an invasion occurred.

"But instead of donating money for an army to protect their interests, they squandered it on lavish parties, multiple mistresses, and country hunts. It sickened my father that they had no sense of pride in their homeland and no will to understand the dangers threatening it. Your country had to deal with pirates. We had the pillaging Russians.

Father's fears became reality when our former King Augustus died and it was time to elect a new one. That was when the physical invasion of Poland began, it was the reason father and other like-minded Poles formed the Bar Confederation to expel the Russians.

Scratching his neck, Sultan interrupted. "I'm not following you Casimir. How was this election of a king an invasion? And you mentioned brothers. How many did you have?"

"I had two brothers. Frank, who was older than me, and Antonin, who is younger. Frank was killed fighting the Russians, and Antonin was captured. He's still in a Russian prison. And father," he hesitated, choked with emotion at the memory of all he had lost, "he died in a Turkish prison."

"My dear man, I am so sorry to hear of your loss. It is very different from mine. You had years of love that were suddenly taken away. I never knew the family I lost. You were lucky to have had those years, but I am sure it was quite painful when they ended. If it's not too hurtful, please tell me how all this happened."

Casimir welcomed the therapeutic release of telling someone about all he had fought for, suffered, and lost.

"Sultan, my story is long, but if you are truly interested I will tell you. I do enjoy hearing my language especially when I'm the one speaking it."

"Oh yes I would like to hear your tale." Sultan laughed. "My ears also like Polish or any other language that tells a good story."

"Very well then. Stop me when you have heard enough," Casimir said before he began his long story of victories and defeat.

"You see, I served as a page at the Court of Duke Karl at Courland. Perhaps in your travels you have heard of him. He was the son of Augustus III and heir apparent to the Polish crown.

Sultan shook his head, indicating he did not know this part of Polish history. Casimir continued.

"When King Augustus III died, the Russian Empress Catherine wanted her own man on the throne, one she could use to subjugate Poland. Augustus, who was weakened by sickness long before his death, was not a strong ruler, yet he had refused to bend to her. When he died, she made her move.

"She was busy with her many lovers and playing the enlightened ruler of Russia, so she appointed Nikolai Repnin, an egotistical maniac hungry for power, as her ambassador to Poland. She planned to use him to take control and ultimately overrun our country.

"Catherine summoned Ambassador Repnin and assigned him the job of making Stanislaw Poniatowski, a Pole and one of her former lovers, king of Poland. But first, of course, Duke Karl had to be eliminated as a candidate.

"The ambitious Repnin was all too happy to follow her orders. He openly bragged about how wealthy and powerful he was going to be when he was controlling Poland. He was overheard whispering to one of the court ladies in her boudoir, 'Catherine may control Poniatowski from a distance but I will be the hand in Poland pulling the puppet's strings. He will do things my way.'

"But Casimir, if Duke Karl was the son of the old king, how was Poniatowski elected?" Sultan asked.

"By intimidation, bribery, and murder," said Casimir, who snarled with contempt.

"Duke Karl was at the home of my father's friend, Count Garrau, in Germany when word of his father's death reached him. According to Count Garrau, the news left him cold. Karl was not close to King Augustus III, and after he left the Polish Royal Court he did not communicate with his father. He resented, as did I at the time, the king's decision to relinquish his Courland estate to the Russians.

"The Duke was drinking and eating too much, had become lazy and overweight, and confided to Garrau that he didn't think he had the energy to return to Poland and wage an aggressive campaign for the throne.

"But regaining the power and prestige of a royal court was tempting. While still pondering whether he should return to Poland Ambassador Repnin's messenger arrived with a note for Duke Karl which was menacing, although cleverly worded so that it could also be interpreted as cordial. It said, 'Come to Poland. I will meet you with a force of 20,000 men. — N. Repnin'

"Karl had no troops and little hope of raising any outside Poland. It was the same bitter medicine he had tasted before at Courland, but he had to swallow it seeing Repnin's message for what it was — a threat, and a very real one.

"Of course, my father and I were disappointed that Duke Karl didn't return to Poland to seek the throne. Since we were unaware of Repnin's message we couldn't understand why he didn't want to be king. Had we known of Repnin's threat, we would have raised more than enough troops to give Karl an escort back to Poland. This left only one candidate, Stanislaw Poniatowski. Yes, a Pole, but one that had been absent from the country for more than twenty years, a good part of that time spent in Catherine's bed. He was a despicable person to be king of Poland."

"This can be a little confusing to one not involved, are you following all of this Sultan?"

"Yes, yes, the politics of the European monarchs have always fascinated me. Please go on."

"Well, election day finally came. We left for Lwów, to a field outside Warsaw where the election was being held. Father was a member of the electorate and even though Poniatowski had no opponent, Father insisted on going, if only to show his objection to Catherine's attempt to rule Poland. My brothers Frank, Antonin, and I accompanied him.

"I remember it was a pleasant day, without a hint of the ugliness we were about to encounter. It was late fall and the air was light and dry. The fields of wheat, oats, and alfalfa had been mowed for the last time. The smell of drying hay teased our horses' nostrils as we rode through the countryside. Dragonflies with peacock-colored wings danced around us, while golden-breasted, ring-necked pheasants called to each other as they searched for grain in the stubble of the fields.

"Frank, always the thinker, asked our father why we bothered going to the election since there was no candidate but Poniatowski, and it might look as if we supported him by being present."

"Ah, I was wondering the same thing," Sultan interrupted.

"Yes, but here is the key, Sultan. He was not elected unanimously, not without coercion anyway. In answer to Frank's question, father looked sternly at each of us and said:

'I do not go to vote for Poniatowski, but to publicly withhold my vote from him. He will win, but he will not have the unanimous vote of the electorate. If others join my lead, he may not get enough votes for a majority. We might have a chance at another candidate. Perhaps Duke Karl will reconsider and come forward.'

"Ah, I can see that your father was a clever man indeed, and brave to oppose an empress and a soon-to-be king."

"Yes, in that moment I was prouder of him than ever. I recognized what he had tried to teach me — that politics can win over wars.

"We arrived at Lwów in late afternoon. We were shocked when we rode up to the large square courtyard that had been hurriedly constructed for the election. It had a hard-packed earth floor surrounded by three-foot-high walls which were covered with green canvas to make them look like hedges. More than 20,000 Russian troops stood in formation outside the walls — 5,000 on each side. Two pass-through openings in the "hedges" were visible at opposite ends of the courtyard.

"Placing my hand on my sword I moved closer to father to ask what he thought this show of force meant.

'I don't know Kas, but I believe they may try to force a unanimous vote,' he speculated.

'You won't do it, will you?' I asked.

"He said, 'I'll try not to, but I won't throw away the lives of my sons to make a statement that will not change the outcome. Take your hand away from your sword. Now is not the time.'

"We had no choice but to ride through one of the openings, and once inside, we saw about 10,000 of the electorate. I remember thinking that there were enough of us to overcome the Russians if the spineless cowards would fight. Who knew, maybe these self-indulgent fools would finally see what father had warned them about for years.

"As evening came, campfires were lit, the tea was brewed, and groups of men gathered to discuss their dilemma. Those who supported Poniatowski argued for a unanimous vote, but even they were shaken by the obvious threat from Russia. Some acted unconcerned and we all wondered why. Soon I knew.

"Men from Gdansk sat around a campfire, and as I walked by I overheard one say, 'Yes, hold out for more. They will pay handsomely for your support. They want Poniatowski to get every single vote cast. There's plenty of gold to go around. Didn't you see the wagons? Catherine has more than she can count and she is more concerned about who she'll sleep with tonight than how much her men paid for a vote. If she gets her way, she'll be using Gdansk and our ships to transport everything from sable furs to soldiers around the world. She would have to pay handsomely for the port and our ships but with this election she gets it all. Just go in the small building at the back of the courtyard and make your deal, but hurry before the line starts forming tomorrow morning.' I walked away thinking that they were disgusting, greedy traitors, selling out their country for a hand full of gold.

"The first vote was to be held the afternoon of the next day, and it would take perhaps a full day for so many men to answer with an "Aye" or "Nay".

"Just before the voting started, two large cannons were moved into the opening at the south end of the square, while two wagons loaded with gold bars were pulled into the opening at the north end. The meaning was obvious: vote for Poniatowski and receive gold—resist and receive a cannonball.

"Casimir, where did so much gold come from?" asked Sultan. "It must have been many fortunes!"

"Catherine had wagon loads of gold stolen from Poland to buy the voters she couldn't intimidate with the twenty thousand Russian 'escort' troops. The wealth of the Russian czars seems endless and comes from their vast land holdings that are worked by millions of serfs. She also plunders churches, castles, and homes in pillaged lands like Poland and Lithuania.

"When we arrived, negotiations had been going on for days between members of the electorate and Repnin's men to determine how much money would be paid for a vote. The men around the campfire were correct. Those who held out for more, usually got it, as long as they didn't hold out too long. In the end, very few rejected either Poniatowski or the money. Father was the exception.

The vote began and each time a courageous person voted "Nay" he was dragged away by Russian troops. Those still waiting to vote could hear the screams from the beatings that followed each 'nay' vote.

"Finally, 'Josef Pulaski of Warka, how vote you?' rang out.

"Father looked at us and shouted at the top of his voice, 'Abstain'.

"The Russian officers turned to each other in bewilderment. An 'Aye' meant they did nothing other than pay the bribe money. A 'Nay' meant that they would beat the offending person. But they had no instruction for someone who decided to abstain.

"Four Russians decided to use their own judgment and approached father. I immediately moved to his side and pulled my sword from its sheaf. Frank and Antonin did the same. The soldiers hesitated.

'Leave him for now. His time will come,' one soldier said to the other three. They looked at their commander who nodded for them to retreat. He didn't want to risk an uprising.

"At the end of the election process, Poniatowski had enough votes to win, but it was not unanimous. Thirteen men died for voting against Poniatowski that day. Father survived by abstaining, and after he set the precedent, many other men also found the courage to abstain.

"The next morning the abstainers, including father found their horses slaughtered and gutted. The warning was undeniable. It was their horses now, but the men and their companions would be next.

"At ten o'clock it was announced that the vote records were lost and the election would be held again. We grieved the loss of Bertha, our trusted family horse, but Frank, Antonin, and I were far more precious to father. The horse could be replaced. We could not.

"Father did what was necessary to protect us, knowing that if he survived he could fight again. His wisdom overcame his defiance. When his name was called again, he shouted 'Aye' and most of the other abstainers from the day before did the same. The two brave men who refused to change their vote were never seen or heard from again.

"When we left, father and I rode double on my horse, Pushka, but it was not an ignoble exit. The crowd cheered as we rode back through the hedge. We had shown the defiance many felt. The ones who were shamed were those who sold their vote and their country for a pocket full of gold. We Pulaskis rode tall and proud and said prayers for the two brave souls who refused to change their vote.

"The Russian officers took note of this and reported to Repnin that we had gained the support of many in the crowd and would be trouble in the future.

"I must not go on my friend, I fear I am boring you."

"Oh no, please do. Your stories of kings and queens are far more fascinating than my pirate tales. What happened next? Did the Russians attack you on the way home?"

"Well, no they didn't because they didn't have a chance. You see Frank and I became responsible for checking on father's land holdings at an early age. We grew up riding across the entire country several times a year so we knew the back roads, bridle paths, and short cuts through the woods to reach home. We convinced father to take a route that few Poles, not even he, let alone Russians, knew about. We arrived home safely.

"Later, our informant at the Russian court reported that Repnin was furious when his men failed to ambush us on the road back to Warka. But his fury paled in comparison to Catherine's when he told her what happened at the election. Even though father eventually voted her way, the fact that 'that little worm', as she called him, dared defy her and encouraged others to do the same, had magnified her hatred for us. She had lusted after our land, villages, and wealth for years. Now she was determined to destroy us and our name as well.

'I will see the entire Pulaski nest of snakes dead after they are disgraced' she ranted. 'They will not get away with challenging the Empress of Russia.' And she almost made good on her threat except that this Pulaski snake survived and I will not rest until the Pulaski name is revered again."

Sultan did not understand what Casimir meant about the Pulaski name but said, "Now I see where you got your daring and determination, Casimir. Your father was an extraordinary man."

"Thank you, Sultan," Casimir responded, beginning to feel genuine affection for this man who seemed to admire him and his family. "Being compared to my father is a great compliment.

"We were told that Catherine's tirade went on for forty minutes and at the end of it Repnin cowered in a corner, feeling neither powerful nor rich.

"Should I go on?"

"Yes, please do," replied Sultan.

That night, "Repnin told his lover at court, 'I fear I may be banished into exile by Catherine. I have lost her trust because of a Pulaski. I will see them all disgraced and dead.'

"But Repnin was not banished into exile as he feared. Instead, Catherine sent him back to Poland to make the changes she wanted warning, 'And this time you better make it happen or you will beg me to go to Siberia. '

"Repnin immediately dispatched thousands of Russian troops to Poland. The barons, whose lands they occupied, were outraged and convened a parliamentary session in Radom to decide how to get rid of them. Father, Frank, Antonin, and I all attended.

"When Repnin heard about the gathering in Radom, he entered with an escort of soldiers where he threatened the landowners if they refused to disperse. He then vowed to bring 15,000 troops to their next session and force them to vote as he directed.

"Father was so incensed. He shouted, 'One hundred thousand will be too few to subdue a free Polish people!'

"Repnin, who was already full of hatred for father, let his anger erupt and started a shoving match with father, kicking him as they were being pulled apart. 'You, despicable, dull little man, I will bury you,' Repnin yelled back, 'You will not defy me again.'

"Father shook with rage, at being publicly subjected to the insult of being kicked by a Russian, but he stopped Frank, Antonin, and I as we reached for our swords.

'No! Stop where you are.' he said, pointing toward the door for us to depart while Repnin was storming out the opposite side of the building.

"On our ride home he instructed us to never fight in anger. He said, 'It puts you at a deadly disadvantage. There is much time for revenge.'

"But father when do we fight?" I pleaded. 'I watched Russian Cossacks take Courland from Duke Karl. I saw the wrong king forced upon us. Now Repnin has pushed, kicked, and insulted you. We have talked enough. It is time to drive the Russian rats from our Polish soil. The time is now.'

"He was calm. 'My impetuous son, control your tongue and listen,' he replied. 'Wars are not won in one-day battles. You have never killed anyone. War is very different from the games and training you enjoy.

'Yes, you could win against the enemy one-on-one many times. But even you could not fight ten, twenty, or a hundred alone. We could inflict pain on some Russians, but it would be like a hornet sting. They would swat and crush us with their overwhelming numbers and destroy our nest, our homeland. We must be prepared to defend not only our lands but the whole nest and colony of Poland as well.

'Courland was defended by 1,200 good soldiers but the Russians were 5,000 strong.' He went on. 'King Augustus had no choice but to remove his son from danger, just as in the end I had no choice but to vote for Poniatowski for the sake of my sons. A fight there would have wasted many good lives. And as for today's insult? What is an insult compared to our lives? We will be wise, work hard, and be ready when the time comes to get our revenge.

'To win we must carefully prepare and build a mighty army of thousands of men who are trained and dedicated to our cause. We must receive the blessing of the Holy Mother for our mission to free Poland from the Russians and preserve our church and faith. We will wait until we have the strength and wisdom to win a war, not a mere skirmish.

'So, my eager son, save your anger for the important battles ahead. I assure you we will act. After developing a sound plan, we will topple and gut the giant bear.'

"Unbelievable Casimir. What a great man your father was. How I would have loved growing up in your home with such a man. Again, I can see where you get your strength."

"Yes, it was a wonderful childhood and young adulthood. My father devoted his life to me. He guided me in everything and always gave me sound advice. Now, have you heard enough? Am I'm beginning to bore you as well as myself?"

"By all means, no," said Sultan, encouraging him to continue. "Besides what else do we have to do on this ship? I don't think DeClerq will be hosting anymore card games and I want to hear about the battles you fought and won. Please go on."

"I think you're right about DeClerq. But please stop me when you get tired of listening.

"Our ride home to Warka gave us time to reflect on the day. I can still see the sun making its colorful descent, leaving behind a sky of gold-edged clouds. The night air cooled and a new quarter moon rose in the east as stars sparkled and shimmered in the darkened sky.

"My anger turned to excitement as I thought that I would finally get to plan strategy and become the fighter for which I was trained.

"When we pushed open the massive entry gates guarding the entrance to our home, the iron latches scraped and creaked. The dogs charged toward the noise, teeth barred, but when they recognized us, they began wagging their tails, to welcome us home.

"As was typical of my father, he used the scene as a lesson for his sons, especially me.

'Fear and anger can be your best friend stimulating your senses in an emergency or, they can be your worst enemy, causing you to strike out without focus. They will weaken you if you give in to them.

'You see our dogs? First, they were scared and angered at being disturbed. They struck out with no plan of attack. Real intruders would've cut them down one by one with pistols, swords, knives, or even stones. They were not moving together but scattered, striking wildly. That is what we must avoid.

'You saw me let anger almost take control with Repnin. Had I given in to it, I could have been arrested and imprisoned in Russia. What good could I do from there? Now, starting tonight, we must use anger wisely. We will anger the enemy, cause him to lose control, and drive him from the Poland that we deeply love. Tomorrow, after we have gone to church, you three will go to my villages to gather the Polish Cossacks I funded to prepare for just such a time.'

"But father how will any of us sleep tonight?" I asked. "There is too much to think about and do for sleep to come. Can't we start now with fresh horses?"

"He smiled at my eagerness and said with calm and confidence, 'God will bless us and give us sleep and the strength we will need in the days to come'.

"But sleep was still a long time coming that night. I made and remade plans of attack most of the night, remembering what father said, and thought of ways I could make the enemy crazy with anger, operating like a swarm of hornets, hitting them by surprise, stinging them repeatedly and then flying off before they could swat me or even find me.

"Finally, a short rest came. I was up early the next morning, and was the first to arrive for breakfast. Frank, Antonin, and father joined me so full of excitement they hardly touched their food. We were ready to prepare for the fight to come.

"It was a short walk to St. Nicholas Bishop's Church, where our family had attended all of my life. The walk calmed us. It was a sacred moment. Father John, our aging priest, greeted us warmly at the side door of the church.

'Dzien Dobrey, my friends. What brings you to church so early on a Tuesday?'

"Frank, Antonin and I crowded close while father explained our mission to him."

'Father John, as you know, the Russians are occupying portions of Poland, and we have evidence that they plan to overrun the entire country and force us to submit to the whims of Empress Catherine and her henchmen. If they do, they will steal our lands and sack our churches. We are here to swear an oath to the Holy Mother that we will protect our homeland and our faith from these usurpers.'

"Father John motioned us inside. St. Nicholas was no longer a wealthy church and did not have the expensive paintings and tapestries that had formerly decorated the walls. Father's funds paid to heat it for the weekly services. Built when the town of Warka was founded in the early 1300's, it was in grave need of renovation. It did have one treasure, however, a baptismal basin that dated to Casimir the Great's time.

"Father John's life was devoted to his faith and his parishioners. The thought of invaders violating the church was abhorrent to him. For more than four decades, he had baptized, married, and presided over the funerals of the Catholics in Warka. Slowly moving his heavy body, draped in the worn black robes of the priesthood, he walked down the stone floor of the central aisle, and silently counted the steps to the alter. Thirty-nine steps from the east door where he met us to the center of the nave, another forty-seven steps to the alter. Before he lost his sight, he had memorized each detail of the interior of the church with its exact dimensions measured in footsteps.

"Parishioners donated food and fuel to Father John so he could survive the harsh winters in the large, drafty rectory. He rarely turned down a dinner invitation since cooking was difficult and he could not afford a cook. His life was routine and sedate. I think he was gratified to be included in a plan to preserve Poland and have a role in protecting the Holy Catholic Church. Such an important undertaking brought light to the cold, lonely, and, for the most part thankless life he led.

"He asked Frank and I to bring the ancient baptismal basin from a darkened alcove to where he stood. An altar boy appeared with an ornately carved silver chalice that looked out of place in the austere church. He handed it to Father John, who poured holy water from it into the basin.

"We knelt and received communion, and then a special blessing from Father John who anointed each of us with the holy water from the sacred basin.

"After we rose, tranquil and reverent, Father John sent the altar boy for his personal Bible, then asked each of us to place a hand on it. With one hand on the Bible we held each other's free hand, forming a circle of unity while taking the oath knights took so long ago binding them to defend Christianity, homeland, and family. We pledged:

We will be without fear in the face of our enemies,
We will be brave and upright so that God will love us,
We will speak the truth even if it leads to our death,
We will safeguard the helpless and do no wrong.

We swear to:
Defend the one true faith,
Sacrifice so others may live free,
Live with honor,
Defend our homeland and our families to the death.

"We raised our brightly polished swords in unison. The tips and then the hilts were crossed to signify unity and, if required, even death.

"Life was never to be the same again. We saw very little of mother and my sisters or, for that matter, our home at Warka after that morning. We were consumed by making preparations for the conflict ahead and then repelling the Russian invasion. Family gatherings and peaceful moments were rare and all too soon the family grew smaller.

From their position near the main mast, Casimir and Sultan heard a bell and then a voice calling, 'Relieve the Watch,' the signal that the person on watch from midnight to four a.m. was being relieved. They realized that they had talked all night.

Sultan, looking pensive, said, "Thank you Monsieur Pulaski for sharing this part of your life with me. It makes me admire you and your family even more.

"I want to hear about the war you fought with the Russians and the political manipulations of the evil Empress Catherine but I fear even your exciting stories could not keep me awake much longer. Let's talk again soon."

"Good night Sultan," Casimir responded. "Thank you for being a good listener and a good friend."

TWENTY-THIRD BIRTHDAY & WAR

Poland
1768-1771

asimir was nostalgic after talking with Sultan. As daybreak crawled over the ocean, the ship came back to life and sleep was impossible. He unwrapped his journals and started to reminisce about past intrigues and battles.

Just as Ambassador Repnin threatened, his Russian troops entered Poland twenty-nine days after the meeting in Radom and seized several dignitaries and a Polish Bishop, taking them back to a Russian prison. This military act of atrocity against the state and the church sent a message to Polish opposition that Russia, and Repnin in particular, would retaliate if challenged.

Rather than subduing the opposition, however, the abductions of Polish dignitaries and clergy rallied the leaders who later formed the Confederation of Bar.

The outraged Polish Royal Chancellor Andrzej Zamoyski, a respected leader of the opposition, spoke for many when he said, "I will not be part of this travesty and outlandish act by Russia to control us. I now resign to show my disgust at such a move by Russia. I would have no dissatisfaction with the new king had he been properly elected, but with his failure to intercede I have no choice. Long live the opposition! May the King have a short reign."

Due to the uncertain times and preoccupation of the Pulaski men with the ensuing war, Marianna planned a very special joint birthday party for Casimir and his father. They were incredibly close and their birthdays were only weeks apart, so a joint party seemed perfect. For all Casimir's fierce warrior exterior, inside he was still the son who worshiped his father and got excited about birthday parties and Cook Sarah's sernik cake.

His birthday was in early March, while Josef's was in February. Josef would turn sixty-four and Casimir twenty-three. The dual celebration demonstrated how close the two were, and Marianna sensed this birthday party needed to be exceptional. She made sure she served the favorite foods of Josef and all three sons. To accommodate their appetites Sarah made three separate sernik cakes. Sisters Paulina and Joanna played Polish music dating back to the days of Sobieski and Casimir the Great on the piano, flute, and harp, and read their music by the flickering light of candles held in intricately carved silver candelabras.

The family ended the evening by attending a special midnight service. Father John had become too frail to continue his Church duties some weeks earlier. The new priest, Father Stephen, had arranged the service in appreciation of the many gifts and donations the Pulaski family had given the Warka Church and their generosity to Father John. After the family had taken Communion, Josef and his sons knelt at the railing around the altar with arms folded across their breasts indicating they were asking for a special blessing.

Father Stephen was touched, providing blessings and giving each a prayer for a safe return home from their defense of the faith and Poland. The evening ended on a somber but warm note for Casimir. His idol, his father, had shared his birthday with him, and he realized how much love his family had bestowed on him for the entire twenty-three years of his life. He would do anything to defend them and their lifestyle.

And I still would, if only they were all still alive to defend, he thought, as the ship rolled to the right in the early morning waves.

As he looked back on his life, he realized how special the dual celebration in February turned out to be. By the time his birthday arrived in March, he, Frank, Antonin, and Josef were deeply ensconced in the conflict with Russia. He had enjoyed the last family birthday celebration they would have together.

Later in February 1768, Ambassador Repnin coerced, pressured, tricked, and bribed members of the Polish parliament into declaring Poland a protectorate of Russia. Casimir recalled how furious his father was at this overt attempt to place Poland under Russian control. Josef contacted his country's most influential magnates to arrange a meeting in the town of Bar.

At sixty-four, Josef had outlived most men of his time. Casimir knew his father had every right to relax and enjoy his family and the wealth he worked so hard to earn. Yet, because of his high moral standards he took his sons to the town of Bar, to vow again in the grand cathedral there to fight the Russians and serve the Catholic Church.

The forced election of Poniatowski was an invasion without troops and Josef Pulaski was willing to go to war if necessary. But Casimir knew that being a brilliant attorney, his father hoped he could avoid military confrontation by challenging the Poniatowski election peacefully through the courts. When that failed, there were only two options left for Josef. One was to relinquish his fortune, and subjugate his family to the greedy Catherine. The other was to oppose her with military force and fight the fight that had been fermenting since his childhood. Their staunch belief that they must defend what was right, along with the oath the Pulaski men had taken, allowed them no choice but to fight.

Casimir reflected upon what a zealous well-trained warrior, eager to fight for his faith, country, and the family's fortune he was at the time. He was energized and excited. He had honed every detail of his strategy to entrap the enemy. He would charge into their formations, hitting them hard then quickly withdraw when they launched a counterattack at what they thought was a retreating force. Too late, they would see the rest of his men lying in wait to close in around them. It was a strategy that served him well throughout his life.

His training was lacking in only one area. He had never served under, or taken orders from anyone. The very idea of taking orders rather than giving them was abhorrent to him. He saw no need for guidance or input from anyone, except his father whom he relied upon, and the Church.

In his mind, he was an invincible champion ready to send the Russians home in quick order. He had spied on them while at the Courland estate and studied their tactics. He knew them well enough to outmaneuver and outsmart them in battle.

"Father, I am ready, let me fight," he begged, but Josef's answer was, "Not yet my son. I tried to encourage our friends to fight this Russian takeover and they hid from the truth. I agree we need to act quickly, but we are practically alone. We must have an army, one strong enough to stop the Russians. It is important that you and your brothers find young men throughout Poland who are willing to fight. Bring them together and train them to be efficient fighters. For now, that is more important than getting involved in minor skirmishes. We will need horses, ammunition, arms, money, and provisions, as well as men. We must prepare thoughtfully and plan carefully for the good of the country we love and for the faith we cherish and live by, or we all shall perish."

Casimir understood the truth in his father's words. He and his brothers set out to find troops and supplies. Over the weeks and months that followed their saddles seemed to grow to their bodies as the brothers rode through rain and cold. They crossed the country, always seeking men, money, and munitions. They tried to spark the same patriotic fire that burned in their own bellies in those of Josef's former clients and friends.

The magnates were as prissy and cowardly as ever, but their eyes were slowly opening to the dangers around them. The private armies kept solely for parades and parties had limited arsenals of weapons but Casimir knew he could train the men to use them effectively. He and Frank, coached by their father in the art of negotiating, were powerful influencers. They soon secured enough troops and weapons to help defend the Polish borders from Russia. Antonin, trained by the banking families in Italy, was equally persuasive in amassing enough money to buy additional horses and equipment.

The Pulaski men were ready to defend Poland, even though King Poniatowski was unconvinced that Russia, Prussia, and Austria were planning to take his kingdom from him. He refused to do anything to stop Russia, so he had to be opposed. In his mind, Catherine supported his election to become king and he had won by a near unanimous vote. That legitimized his claim to the throne with all of Europe. Why would Catherine or any other monarch try to take Poland from him, he reasoned. It never occurred to him that he was meant to be merely a figurehead for Catherine, who was running the country through her Ambassador Repnin. Of course, the Pulaskis and Bar Confederates saw what he didn't — that he was just a means for Catherine to gain a foothold inside Poland. They planned to force that foot to step back, outside of Poland.

For Casimir and his brothers, it was difficult to consolidate the different fancy just-for-show armies into a cohesive fighting force and present a united front to the Russians. There were many Poniatowski loyalists who fought against the Bar Confederates.

There were wealthy property owners like Joachim Potocki and his cowardly cronies who wanted to retain their titles and be left alone. The common people considered Poniatowski, a Polish noble, to be a rightful heir to the Polish throne. After all, he was elected. Thank goodness, the Pulaski family had dedicated support among the aristocracy and merchants who supplemented the troops and weapons Casimir and Frank secured.

But the internal fighting between Poles who supported King Poniatowski and those who did not was escalating toward Civil War, weakening the resistance against the Russians. Eventually, most realized that a free Poland was critical, that internal differences could be settled later. The Bar Confederates became the recognized leaders of the opposition to Russia.

France sent military advisers to help, along with a promise of arms in the future and Turkey considered declaring war on Russia. In St. Petersburg, Catherine could hear the drum beats and rattling of swords in Poland, causing her concern that her plan to take the country was going awry.

The Bar Confederacy sent Casimir to the front lines to defend Poland's borders. His father journeyed to Turkey to get help from the Turks, and Paul Dobrachek joined Casimir as second in command on the battlefield. Casimir had taught Paul what he learned from the Russian Cossacks and together they formed a formidable force. But at that time, neither had killed a man in battle.

That changed quickly. One day, as they were riding along a sharp crest of a wooded hill that bordered a rocky gorge, they spotted a sizeable Russian force moving along the water's edge below. When the fiery Casimir raised his sword to charge down the hill, cross the river, and attack, Paul put a hand on his arm, saying, "Kas, there are too many, at least three-hundred by my guess. We have only fifty men and one cannon and we couldn't fire it from the water.'

Casimir realized his charge without preparation would be foolhardy. His impulsive move could have cost the battle. As he lowered his sword and looked around, one of his men, a sergeant, moved forward saying, "Sir, I know this area, I visited here in the summers as a child. The river narrows about a kilometer downstream and has boulders that force it into a ravine followed by a deep waterfall."

"Thank you, sergeant, for that helpful information," Casimir replied. He turned to Paul. "I'll take half the men and ride the crest of the hill making sure they spot us and give chase before we reach the ravine. You follow with the other men and the cannon."

Paul nodded in agreement.

Casimir turned to his troops, and yelled "charge, forward, always forward" and nudged Wolny with his left spur, who reared up as trained.

He swung his sword through the air. The Russians spotted them, as Casimir had planned, and began racing down the river, trying to gain ground to attack them. But Casimir and his men had better footing and were about a quarter kilometer ahead of the Muscovites by the time they reached the point above the ravine.

Paul ordered several of his men to set up the cannon and aim it at the river below. He instructed his remaining troops to follow him.

Casimir started Wolny down the hill a few meters upstream from the rocky narrows of the river. When the Russians raced down the opposite side he opened fire and the second man in the Russian column jerked in his saddle, let out a terrible scream and fell from his horse. Casimir thought the fallen Russian's screams would never stop, but they did and the silence was worse.

The Russians turned their horses to go back upstream, away from Casimir and his men's fire, but Paul and the rest of the troops were waiting for them and began shooting. Bloodied bodies began to float toward the rapids and waterfall. Paul, in the excitement of his first battle, led his men down the hillside within range of the Russians who were firing at them.

When Casimir started seeing Polish uniforms among the Russians in the river, he shouted "No, No, No! Get them out of the water."

But there was no way to save those men, and the only way to save the others was to kill the Russians. The hill was too steep to climb quickly, and the Russians who were crossing the river above the ravine were close enough to fire on them.

Casimir looked toward the ridge and yelled, "Fire the cannon. Fire it now!"

The blast was deafening and deadly. Ten of the Russians and twelve of their horses were killed. Body parts of horses and men mingled in the river coloring the water an unnatural reddish brown. The dead, dying, and wounded were dragged by the current toward the rapids and waterfall. The sounds and sights of those suffering the agony of death was unbearable. Wide-eyed horses made human like screams, and the humans who could, begged for God's help while others let out shrieks that did not stop until they disappeared over the waterfall. Some were tossed by the current against the boulders, bones shattered, they begged to be shot.

Casimir leaned over Wolny's neck and retched. It was a scene that would never fade from his memory.

When it was over, the remaining Russians ran for cover in the underbrush along the river bank. Casimir didn't order a pursuit. He had had enough. Now his major concern was Paul and his men. How many had he lost?

The answer was twelve, almost a quarter of his troops. Fourteen horses were killed or had to be shot. Thankfully Paul was okay.

The camp was quiet that night. Sitting by the fire, Casimir turned to Paul and said, "We won, but this is no game."

As they continued defending Poland's borders, they often split the troops between them, simultaneously fighting battles at different points along the front. Both had their share of victories. But when Russian reinforcements arrived and the fiercest fighting began, Casimir and Paul fought together, side by side. They were more fearsome than anything the Russians had seen. They won skirmish after skirmish even though they were almost always outnumbered. Their reputations grew, drawing more young men to join and become part of the fight for glory and the freedom of their homeland.

One of those who joined them was Maurice Beniowski, a handsome young man with dark wavy hair, hazel eyes, and a light complexion. Casimir thought there was something familiar about his round face, high forehead, and pensive expression. He couldn't decide who he looked like, but the more he was around Maurice the more he liked him. He appreciated Maurice's ability to quickly grasp details and assimilate them into an analysis of the overall situation, whether it was on the battlefield or the chess board. Those were rare traits. He and his father shared them, and, incredibly, the Duchess Courland exhibited similar analytical talent. Most people simply trudged on day after day, accepting life as it came without realizing they could change things by being more alert to what was going on around them, and trying to determine why.

Maurice Beniowski became a valuable addition to Casmir's forces that grew to thousands. He was ferocious in battle, but contributed most when he served as Casimir's adviser and consultant.

One day he said, "Now is the time to strike. They are weary and missing their wives and girlfriends. They are on foreign soil that means nothing to them. They don't care about Russia the way we care about Poland. They are weak and will run if we hit them hard."

"How can you know these things?" Casimir challenged.

"I watched them from a hill overlooking their camp through my spyglass," explained Maurice. "They do not clean and check their bayonets and muskets at night. Instead, they sit around the campfires drinking and telling stories. Many are hired mercenaries who sing foreign songs and play cards. They don't shave or bathe. They show no pride in themselves or the country they fight for, little energy, and no stomach for this war. We would not have such men with us. They will run as soon as there is any danger, and they won't stop running until they are behind their women's skirts."

"But they outnumber us four to one, how can you be sure we can overcome such numbers?"

"Actually," Maurice responded, "they outnumber us five to one. I estimate 20,000 men but I'm telling you one Pulaski man is worth ten of those louts. They have no bond with their horses. They do not understand how to direct the animal in battle even though their lives may depend on the horse to carry them away."

"And how do you know how many there are?"

"I count their campfires, ten men to a circle around each one. I count the cook wagons. Each one serves 50 men. I count the horses. Only a fourth of them are on horseback. Finally, I count the whores. Not all men are interested so there is only one for every 100 men, but that's still a lot of whores. I tally the total men for each; campfires, cook wagons, horses, and whores. The total is very close to the same no matter how I add the numbers."

Casimir accepted his analysis. "Okay my friend, then let's plan the attack. I don't want to harm the cooks or whores, they are no threat. We have to hit them quick and hard. I'll lead the first charge of 300 men at daybreak when they are groggy and headed for the latrines. Paul will follow with a second wave of 1,000 men a few minutes later when they have started getting organized and think they have me surrounded. He will help me withdraw. You are to lie in wait in the woods here below the base of the hill and join us with another 2,800 men. Paul and I will retreat through your noose and you will tighten it on the Russians as they chase us. Then we will strangle them."

"But Casimir the risk to you is outrageous. You and your men will be outnumbered more than sixty to one on the first charge. You must take more men with you or make a full-frontal assault with all the men at one time."

Casimir laughed. "Look, you said each Pulaski man is worth ten of theirs. They will be stultified from last night's drinking and whoring. They won't be mounted or have their weapons, and most of them will be lined up at the latrine with their pants unbuttoned and their plciowys in their hands. They will be no match for my Pulaski Legion, and I will be in and out so quickly that I'll be in no danger."

The analytical Maurice was shocked by Casimir's boldness while Paul bragged, "Casimir is somewhat correct, Maurice. When I and my men ride in to rescue him he will be in no danger."

"Oh really? Well you just make sure to take care of yourself so I don't get distracted saving you," Casimir countered.

"No worries about that my friend," said Paul. "We will show the Ruskies that they can't tell us who our king will be and try to over-run our country."

The trio rose at three the next morning and went to their seconds in command, who in turn quietly awakened the sleeping troops. Within an hour, Casimir's three-hundred men were mounted and eager for battle. He rode between the ranks, smiling and nodding at each man—shaking hands with a few, giving others a pat on the shoulder, and stroking the necks of several horses.

Resplendent in his blue and white uniform, sitting tall astride Wolny, his mighty black stallion, he addressed his men, "You make me proud, my brave Pulaski troops. You are worthy of your fine uniforms and the Polish and Pulaski banners you carry. You are an elite group, chosen for your bravery, brains, and loyalty. There are thousands who would trade places with you today if they could only measure up to the standards you set. By this evening, you will be known throughout Poland. Soon you will be legendary. Now ride with me to honor and glory."

His speech magnetized the young glory-seeking men. Their colorful uniforms, prancing horses, and his words of praise made them believe they could do anything without harm. Casimir believed in leading by example. He had designed their uniforms, selected their horses, and was the bravest of them all, leading every charge straight at the enemy—and encouraging his men to do the same. They idolized him and followed wherever he led, no matter the risk.

Casimir patted Wolny's side, then rode to the front of the columns with sword raised, moving into a trot quietly up the hill with 300 men eagerly following. He and the troops easily made it to the top of the rise that concealed the encamped Russians, without being detected. At the crest, Casimir yelled, "Forward, forward" as he charged, still waving the Sobieski sword, which became a beacon for the men to follow, when the first light of dawn caught its golden handle.

He and Maurice were right. The Russian troops were like hibernating Siberian bears. They were addled and lumbered around in the semi-darkness, crashing into each other as they looked for weapons, waiting for orders from their commanders. The officers were little help. They had just begun their day by sitting at breakfast tables drinking tea and talking about the politics of getting promoted, or the riches they would share when they overran and ransacked the castles in Poland.

No one was resisting his charge, and Casimir, remembering what his father told him about the Russians capturing his grandfather; hanging him from a tree, and brutally mutilating his body—began to wreak vengeance on the stunned soldiers.

When the Russians finally regained their senses, regrouped, and started launching a counterattack, several surrounded Casimir and thrust their iron tipped poles at him, trying to dislodge him. One struck Wolny's face. When he reared up to escape, another thrust found Casimir. He was hit in the chest and fell to the ground, his boot catching in the stirrup as he fell. His cape wrapped around his spur, becoming too tangled for him to remount. Soon a huge Russian soldier was standing over him with a menacing grin as he raised his bayonet, clasped in both hands, ready to plunge it into his body. Casimir rolled onto his side, grabbed his pistol from his belt, and fired. The Russian fell dead across his legs. Casimir pushed him aside, untangled his cape, remounted and continued his assault on all Russians within range of his sword or lance.

After Paul fought his way into the thick of the battle, Casimir grinned at him and, over the den of gunfire, squealing horses, and moaning, wounded men, shouted, "It's about time you got here! I thought I was going to have to kill and capture them all by myself."

"And well you should have, as long as you've been here," Paul yelled in response. "I had to fight through the real force to save you from these stumbling oafs."

"Save me? You joke . . . " Casimir's retort was cut short by a barrage of fire from mounted Muscovites coming to the rescue of their comrades.

"Time to leave," Paul yelled.

Casimir nodded, spurring Wolny forward to challenge the Russian reinforcements. He and Paul cut, slashed, hacked, trampled and shot eighty-five Russians between them that morning, while their men followed their lead, levying heavy damage as they pressed forward.

Just as Casimir had planned, the Russians thought the attackers had decided to withdraw, thinking they were too outnumbered. They chased after them only to be encircled by Maurice's 2,800 troops that emerged from their hiding place. The few Russian troops who were able to break through the circle faced the forces of Paul and Casimir who were now riding the perimeter of the ever-tightening ring to mop up any stray Muscovites trying to escape.

Soon, the Russians were in full retreat and, having been defeated by a much smaller force, they reported that Casimir's men were riding under some spell, since they had no fear of death. They decided that Wolny was a Satanic horse who killed more soldiers than any man on the field. The stories continued to grow until they claimed Casimir single handedly killed 200 Russians. Actually, he had killed forty-five of the Russian warriors and wounded another thirty.

But those who saw him that day began thinking of him as unbeatable. Tales of his feats, some colorfully embellished, were told in the taverns and marketplaces all across Poland, prompting more young Polish men to join him.

Casimir and Paul learned in their first battle that war is not glorious. Now they recognized it as a hell of unspeakable cruelty, torture and torment. It was a lesson they relived after each engagement. Of the 300 men who led the charge with Casimir, only 174 returned and many were injured. Paul lost 489 of his 1,000, and Maurice lost twenty percent of his men. The Russians fared far worse. More than 5,000 Muscovites were killed or wounded, hundreds of horses were lost and Casimir captured ten of their cannons.

The battle lasted less than two hours — what carnage between sunrise and mid-morning.

They gained some comfort, knowing the Russian losses were four times greater than their own, but losing friends in battle had a sobering effect that brought home the reality of war to Casimir and Paul. Instead of celebrating the victory, they made sure to care for the bodies of the fallen men. Some who had homes nearby were sent to be buried in their church cemeteries, while others were buried near the battlefield. Maurice found a local priest to administer last rites over the dying and dead men, and consecrate the burial ground.

Casimir wrote letters to the families he knew, praising the bravery of their loved ones and the important contribution made to Poland's freedom, hoping in some small way it would help to ease their grief.

Later that evening, while talking with Casimir, Maurice said, "My God man, you're barely old enough to grow a beard and you are leading thousands of men, many older than you. They followed you without question today, and helped you win against overwhelming numbers. Don't you think that odd?"

"Age has nothing to do with it," replied Casimir. "I have trained longer and harder than any of my men. Some men are meant to lead, others are meant to follow. I must lead."

Still, Paul and Maurice saw the deep pain and sorrow he felt for the men he lost in his dark brooding eyes. Despite all his training, the study of great generals and their military tactics, he had no preparation for dealing with the real cost of war. His only encounter with death prior to the war was the loss of Dr. Borloff. Now, the death of his men was excruciating. They were friends and comrades, and, as his father told him following Dr. Borloff's death, family men who loved and were loved by mothers, fathers, children, sisters, brothers, wives and sweethearts. Worse yet, they entrusted their lives to him. They followed him wherever he led. He felt responsible for their deaths, and the grief spreading through Polish households.

And then there was the agony of the wounded. He was frustrated that there was so little that could be done. Most would die

horrible, pain-filled deaths. The wounded enemy were as pitiful as his own. He always allowed them to be removed from the
field by their comrades. He could have taken them all prisoners,
but his heart wasn't in it, nor was he equipped to care for his
own injured, much less the enemy's.

His ability to amass so many troops and lead them to victory
earned him a place on the Bar Confederation War Council, a rare
accolade for one so young. It also boosted his ego and arrogance
toward the other, less successful, (and to him) less competent
officers. He refused to follow orders from commanders he felt
were inferior, and his confrontations with one of the French advisers almost resulted in the loss of his war council seat.

At the battle of Lanckorona, the Bar Confederates were defeated because Casimir refused to coordinate an attack with
Commander Dumouriez, a French officer he considered incompetent.

While Josef was proud of Casimir's bravery and battlefield
feats, he was embarrassed and exasperated by his son's defiance of authority. He considered court martialing him to teach
him a lesson.

Casimir would always remember his father's words. "How
could you be such an imbecile and bring disgrace on our family
after being so distinguished on the battlefield? You were named
for Casimir the Great, a mighty king who brought glory and new
lands to Poland by working with people and being an effective
diplomat. Your behavior is a disgrace to him and to our family.

"Your arrogance is disgusting. You know you must obey orders from superiors just as you expect your troops to follow your
commands. You must lead by example, not by stupid pride."

Casimir, of course worshiped his father, and his words stung
like a yellow jacket. Though his pride would persist, and he
would often be branded with the crime of arrogance, from that
time forward his sole purpose in life was to bring glory to the

family name. Ultimately, the Bar Confederacy leaders came to appreciate his brilliant leadership and masterful military strategy and tolerated his attitude of superiority.

Maurice's assessments of the enemy's preparedness and Casimir's military genius and superior horsemanship made his gorilla style hit-and-run tactics most effective. His mastery of the horse and ability to escape capture became legendary. He distinguished himself in several small battles by surprising the Russians with his quick and fearless maneuvers. They were terrified by the way his troops followed his lead, and, like him, seemed to have no fear of death. He soon became famous beyond the borders of Poland. But the Russians had limitless resources of men and money for munitions that the Poles lacked. Even with the support of some Turkish troops and French advisers, the numbers became more and more one-sided in Russia's favor. He continued to boldly attack the superior numbers and had some minor wins that pricked the skin of the invaders but defeats grew more common.

Neither King Poniatowski nor Ambassador Repinin held Casimir's father, Josef, in high regard. They knew him as a lawyer, not a soldier and patriot. But the movement of his three sons, particularly Casimir, raised a red flag to the danger that he could create.

Repinin, with Empress Catherine's encouragement, decided to put a stop to the Confederate action. He sent General Krechetnikov and eight thousand soldiers to the front with orders to stop Casimir and his troops. Casimir engaged a detachment of the general's advance guard and after a sharp clash the guards retreated with heavy losses.

Casimir's fame grew. He generated more enthusiasm among his men and the Confederate leaders as well as more hatred among the Russians, particularly the generals he embarrassed on the battlefield. As he earned more trust, he was given orders to occupy and defend the fortress of Berdyczow using the four-teen-hundred men who remained with him. His notoriety came at a cost. He was now the principal Confederate leader whom the Russians vowed to destroy. They believed the 'rebellion' as they called it, would be quickly quashed without him.

Casimir and his men left immediately with no supplies or food to sustain them during the defense of the fort. He was not worried, since he believed he would win the battle in short order and they could live on the food that the Monks and townspeople would provide until Antonin joined them with provisions.

Once they arrived at the fort, Casimir began to organize de-fenses. He seemed to be everywhere at once as he surveyed enemy attack routes, planned ways to repel them, and pointed out weak spots in the walls.

He also gave directions to his key officers.

"Maurice, have your men carry boulders from the hillsides to reinforce these stone walls."

"Paul, have your men take large rocks to the tops of the walls to drop on attackers below. When you have finished there, bring wagons of horse and cow manure inside the gates and move it to the roof where it will freeze and snuff out any burning ar-rows, then dig more trenches outside the walls and plant spikes and sharpened wood posts inside them to impale horses that attempt to cross."

Maurice nodded, and moved to organize his men into teams to dislodge large boulders on the nearby hillsides, using poles from elm and oak saplings for leverage. The stones rolled onto boards they had strapped together, and oxen pulled them to the fortress where other men piled them on each side of the existing walls, making them too thick to breach with either cannonballs or battering rams. Everyone worked hard, and soon a long sec-tion of the reinforced stone wall was complete.

Paul, however, did not move.

Instead, he shook his head in disbelief and said, "Okay, I'll get the rocks to the top of the walls and my men will dig and fortify the trenches but you can carry the horse manure yourself."

Casimir was ready to knock Paul senseless for his insolence, but then saw the humor in Paul's jibe and laughed instead. Of course. It was in his nature to expect just as much from his men as he did of himself. But Paul was not one of his regular troops. He had been a confidant and a trusted adviser almost all of their lives and, like Casimir, he was a member of the Polish nobility. Hauling horse manure was not appropriate for one of his rank.

"Okay, my friend, if you are afraid you will get your nice uniform dirty and the pretty ladies inside the fort will get a whiff of horse dung on you and run away holding their noses, then I'll find someone less sensitive for the job," Casimir teased.

"And you, my friend, will be glad you did when you sit down with me at the chess table tonight and all you can smell is the fine cigar I will be smoking," Paul retorted as they smiled and headed off in different directions to complete their battle preparations.

The only access to the fort was a bridge across the moat. The bridge had a slanted gate designed to resist cannon ball fire and Casimir had long spikes placed strategically along its sides to be used to push mounting ladders to the ground. This was the first obstacle Russian General Kretetnikov faced when he arrived to lay siege with his eight thousand soldiers, cannons, and munitions — but it was by no means the last.

When the Russians approached the bridge, Casimir greeted them with artillery fire, holding them at the gate for days while his short supply of food dwindled and ammunition ran dangerously low. Still, he held the fort while waiting for Antonin to arrive with the supplies they so desperately needed. But Antonin did not come. He had been blocked by a large contingent of the enemy and could not fight his way through.

When Casimir received news that Antonin had been captured and taken to Russia, he felt the deep pain of losing a brother, a younger brother whom he should have protected, and the anguish of not knowing what the Russians would do to him. The loss of supplies could be overcome, but not the loss of his young brother.

After bombarding the fortress day after day with little result, General Kretetnikov announced he would begin an all-out assault the following morning, not knowing this was unnecessary. The garrison was completely out of food and water and he could have simply waited and starved them out.

On the night before the attack, Casimir and his men used lighted torches to cause some of their extra horses to stampede through the Russian stockpile of munitions and cannons. It created complete chaos. Following the panicked horses, Casimir and his troops rode through the confusion, seized several cannons, and took them back into the fort before the Russians could organize a resistance.

Still the Poles were in a precarious position. Their replacements and supplies were cut-off with no way to replenish them. Father Lukowski, one of the Carmelite monks living in the cloister at the fort, approached Casimir as he sat at the table he was using as a desk. Never a person to pay attention to clerical details, Casimir had papers strewn across the top, some of which were threatening to blow away in the evening breeze. His mind darted from identifying which documents to destroy if he were captured, to a more comfortable spot of planning a counterattack. He feared capture above all else, and still suffered with the nightmares that began at Courland about captors who tortured and ridiculed him.

Two weeks after the siege began, Repnin, who was now Commander Repnin, accused General Kretetnikov of wasting ammunition while making no progress against the fort or Casimir, and ordered him to withdraw. Unaware of their discussions, Father Lukowski pleaded with Casimir to negotiate respectable surrender conditions. He lauded Casimir's attempts to save the fort. "My son," he said, "you and your men have fought bravely and held off against far superior numbers longer than anyone expected but you cannot continue to fight without food or ammunition. You must now surrender."

"Surrender?" Casimir shouted. "Pulaskis do not surrender. Casimir Pulaski will never give up. My father would not have a son too weak to fight for what is right. Surrender? Never! Those barbarians have my brother in prison. I will beat them, and demand his freedom in exchange for Kretechnikov's life." The blood rushed to his face as he resisted the wisdom of the priest's words.

His fists were clenched and he wanted to pound them on the table, the monk's chest, or anything else in his reach. He wanted to strike out at the injustice of being trapped for mere want of food and weaponry. Defeat was inevitable, but he could not bring himself to surrender to the Russians. What they would do to him when they discovered his secret anatomy would be far worse than dying with honor in battle.

"Your bravery in battle is unmatched," the priest continued. "But sometimes it takes a deeper courage to think beyond your own interests for the good of others. Your men will follow you to the death. You know that. But is that fair to them and their families? Would it not be better to save them now so they may fight and earn their glory another time? There is no shame in surrendering to an army that is six times larger than yours and is well fed and supplied."

Some of the town's people now cautiously approached the table with their meek, balding mayor who timidly pleaded, "Please General Pulaski, the longer you hold out, the more retribution these killers will inflict on us for sheltering you. I fear the consequences for our village if you fight longer."

While his heroism and determination to win never allowed him to consider surrender, he had to acknowledge the truth and wisdom of what both the monk and the mayor said. Visions of the suffering of wounded men and the mangled bodies of corpses tore at him but it was the images of innocent women, children, and priests lying in pools of blood as a result of his pride, that finally swayed him. He was compelled to lay down his arms and surrender for the sake of others, although he wanted to fight to the death. The citizens of the town were innocent bystanders, and the monks were a part of the faith he was sworn to defend. He could not be responsible for harm coming to them.

With surrender, he would lose the chance to bargain for Antonin's release, but he had no choice. The lives of many innocents were more important than the release of one man, even his own brother. Frustrated, discouraged, and against the protests of his officers, he slowly raised the white flag over the fortress wall and bravely walked across the drawbridge to negotiate surrender terms.

General Kretechnikow, who was preparing for defeat and withdrawal, acted like a school boy who had been handed a bag of candy. He was gleeful as Casimir approached. After a moment, he remembered his position and raised his hand to salute the surrendering hero in honor of his bravery. Until this moment, he had expected to withdraw and forfeit the battle but instead he had captured the legendary Casimir Pulaski.

In a fit of happiness and disbelief at his luck he eagerly agreed to the terms Casimir requested: no punishment of his officers and men, no imprisonment in Russia, and no looting of the church coffers.

But soon after agreeing to Casimir's terms, Kretechnikov began violating them by ordering his men to enter the fort, seize all the weapons, and place the Confederate men and officers under arrest. Then he helped himself to the treasures of the fort and cloister.

Further breaking his vow, Kretechnikov, sent Casimir and several men and officers to a prison camp in Russia where they were starved, stripped naked, and randomly beaten. Maurice was the first to be dragged from his cell into the courtyard. The other prisoners watched as the guards stripped him to his waist, tied him to a whipping post, and began an attack of fifty lashes with a bull whip. Next came Paul who, after struggling, was knocked unconscious and thrown back into his cell. Casimir did not struggle. Instead, he laughed, taunting them, as he walked ahead of the guard holding the whip. He took his shirt off on the way to the courtyard and defiantly wrapped his arms around the post declaring, "go ahead you bastard" as the guard tied his hands.

He was struck so many times he lost count and passed out. The guard sent for water which he splashed on his face to revive him, then poured salt into the cuts and dragged him back to his cell. Although in terrible pain after the beating, Casimir was relieved by the fact that his defiance in walking to the whipping post shirtless saved him from being stripped by the guards. His secret was safe. Paul had known about Casimir's anatomy since they were children and Maurice, their other cellmate, always afforded Casimir privacy for some reason, so the guards never discovered his secret.

Although they opposed him, the Bar Confederate soldiers were Polish citizens who had been seized by another country. King Poniatowski, trying to appear kingly, petitioned Russian Queen Catherine to release his Polish subjects who were captured at Fort Berdyczow since there was no declaration of war between the two countries, only border battles.

Catherine craved recognition and acceptance from European monarchs as an enlightened ruler. Carrying out Peter the Great's wishes to Westernize Russia, she corresponded with Voltaire, Diderot, and Cesare Beccaria, all of whom argued against prison torture and the death penalty. The Polish rebellion was an embarrassment to her, and she thought agreeing to release the prisoners would make her seem an enlightened ruler, who cooperated with other monarchs. She hoped it would also appear that she was being unfairly challenged by a group of irrational rebels so the French would stop supporting them with 'advisers'.

Complying with his request would also help her keep Poniatowski on her string. She agreed to release all the men and officers taken at the fort and held in various prison camps if they would sign a *reces*, a declaration of loyalty to Russia.

Casimir refused, but he encouraged Paul and Maurice to sign and sent word to the other prisoners to also sign.

For whatever reason, King Poniatowski's letter to Catherine specified, 'the men captured at Fort Berdyczow'. Therefore, Catherine saw no reason to offer the same terms to other Polish prisoners of war, including Antonin. She had at least one Pulaski under lock and key and she intended to keep him. And as long as Casimir refused to sign, he would stay in prison and she would not need to worry about the Pulaski brothers causing more trouble.

Casimir continued to refuse to sign the reces, and filed claims of brutality and rape of his men with Catherine and Poniatowski. When the charges were ignored by both, he finally signed the reces. Upon his release, he wrote a lengthy letter to General Krechetnikov stating that he felt no obligation to honor the reces since the general had not honored the terms of his surrender and therefore, he would continue his war against any invader of Poland.

Prince Repnin and Catherine were furious at Casimir and less than happy with King Poniatowski. They plotted to bring the Pulaskis down by slander and there were others who had similar ideas for different reasons. Repnin planned to use common highwaymen to capture King Poniatowski and hold him for ransom while making it appear that Casimir was the kidnapper. Meanwhile a disgruntled and disgraced Bar Confederate leader, Michael Kransinski, planned to bring false charges against Josef Pulaski.

Unaware of these plots, Casimir went to Chochim in Turkey where his father and other Confederate leaders were planning their strategy. Casimir asked Josef's permission to return to Poland to enlist new troops and begin acquiring supplies and ammunition. His father granted the request and soon followed, bringing all his troops back into Poland.

Meanwhile, at a meeting of the Bar Confederacy leaders, Michael Kransinski convinced his brother, Bishop Adam Kransinski, that Josef had acted against the interests of the Confederacy and must be removed from command to prevent him from doing further damage. Believing the Bishop's lies, two Bar commanders conspired with Turkish authorities to have Josef imprisoned in Turkey when he returned there. Then they convinced Josef to return to Turkey to gain more support for the war, which he did, not knowing that once across the Turkish border he would be seized and imprisoned.

Unaware of their father's plight, Casimir and Frank, staged guerilla warfare on the Pulaski lands where they exacted revenge on the invading Russians for their treatment of prisoners of war.

Franciszka's mansion was nearby, and Casimir took the opportunity to visit her. He was a dashing hero of twenty-three, and she found him extremely attractive. Due to her husband's neglect that had grown over the past several years, she was longing for romance and excitement. Her knowledge of warfare and strategy was recognized by Confederate leaders and officers, and she was frequently consulted. Casimir's teenage infatuation for her had not diminished, although it was now the passion of a seasoned soldier and leader of men. Her intellect had become an even greater aphrodisiac than her physical beauty.

Casimir lingered at her home for many days, listening to her advice and drinking in her beauty, charm, and sensuality. Her presence calmed him, gave him release from the tensions of war, and made him think of how pleasant life might be after the Russians left Poland.

Franciszka cautioned him. She pointed out his haughtiness although she knew his brilliance and bravery warranted far more recognition than lesser men were willing to give. She did not know that his arrogance was partially a façade to conceal the pain such slights from others inflicted. She counselled diplomacy, and pleaded with him to cultivate important contacts in the royal courts of other countries. He rejected her advice, claiming he was too busy in battle to get involved in the convoluted politics and intrigues of royal courts.

"I have spies in the Russian court that give me valuable information and that is all I need from such lavish and self-centered places," he argued. He would later regret his rash decision.

Casimir left her without violating his oath to honor her marriage to Duke Karl. He loved her dearly, perhaps more so because he could not have her. She felt the same, and was grateful he made no demands of her for she knew she could not have resisted. He believed if her situation were different, they would be lovers or perhaps even husband and wife—and that she would accept his abnormality.

For now, he needed someone to help him with his relationships with the other Confederate leaders he had alienated with his arrogance and independence. His father's expulsion to Turkey and imprisonment was a terrible blow, and tarnish from the slander against Josef coated him as well, at least in the eyes of fellow officers in the Confederacy. Franciszka was remarkably qualified for the job and he turned to her often. Her counsel helped fill the void left by his father's absence, and gradually through her expert behind-the-scenes diplomacy and negotiation, the Bar leaders again considered him a heroic figure.

One gray afternoon he sat with her, his head in his hands in a mood that matched the weather, and said,

"I must go to the aid of Frank. He is on the Dniester River trying to hold Zwaniec with only 400 men against the 4,000 troops Repinin sent General Izmailov. The general plans to take Zwaniec and then Okopy. Both are Pulaski holdings. Frank can't resist much longer. He has only two cannons. But how can I get through? The Russian Cossacks are between Frank and me. My force is as small as his, only 350 men and six cannons. It is impossible," he lamented, pressing his fists against his right temple where a migraine was starting a methodical slow pounding.

"Nonsense, Casimir," Franciszka responded. "You have let these days of idleness and the weather dull your spirit. I see you pressing your head but the headache you have comes from trying to avoid a decision that you must make. Nothing is impossible. Remember the Greeks who stalled 150,000 Persians with only 7,000 men and the 300 Spartans who fought to the death to save Greece. Those 300 will live forever for what they did because they were patriots, fighting for their native soil, using their superior training, equipment and knowledge of the terrain to fight like a much larger army. They and many other leaders have found ways to stop or overcome much larger armies. You will too. You just need to put your brilliant mind to work on it. Your family owns the land. You know it better than any Russian commander, and your men and horses are the best trained in the world. You can overcome the Cossacks. Now where is my confident and arrogant Casimir? Is he hiding behind numbers? I don't think so. It weakens my heart to see you go, but go you must. And win you will."

Her words inspired him. He had not been deterred before by large forces and he would not be now. He left for Okopy immediately with his 350 men and six cannons.

CHAPTER THIRTEEN

WOJA AND JASNA GORA

Poland
1768-1772

When General Izmailov's 4,000 troops attacked Zwaniec, Frank was forced to fall back and cross the Dniester River with Maurice to join Casimir at Okopy.

They were horribly outnumbered and driven into the fort where they were surrounded and trapped. Unable to leave, they fought valiantly as their situation rapidly deteriorated. With the Russians scaling the fortress walls and ramming the gate, defeat was imminent. They had become separated while retreating into the fort and Casimir could not see Frank, Paul, or Maurice, making it impossible to coordinate a defense. Then destiny intervened. A storm swept over both armies, blanketing them in the blackest of darkness. Through flashes of lightning, Casimir saw shimmering scenes of his desperate men crouching on the wet fortress floor, ready to defend themselves when the storm moved on, and Russians clinging to the outside walls trying to find a foothold to boost themselves over the top and into the fort.

The storm clouds drifted to the west and light from the moon revealed Saga, an old gypsy woman, crouching behind the well. Earlier, she had watched helplessly while Russian soldiers beat and raped her granddaughter, before they slit her throat. Saga was waiting for a chance to take her granddaughter's body, still lying in the courtyard, home.

The gypsy could see that the Poles would soon be overrun, and she signaled to Casimir by pressing a bony finger to her lips as she motioned for him to follow her to the back of the fort. At that point, he had nothing to lose so he let her lead him to the top of a three-hundred-foot high cliff. There was no fort wall there since the sheer drop was defense enough against invaders. At the bottom of the cliff, a river surged from the runoff of the storm water and melting snow. Tree trunks and chunks of ice swirled and tossed like snowflakes in a whirlwind in the water below. Casimir didn't understand. Was she thinking they would commit suicide rather than surrender? *Well, that is a possibility, at least for me*, he thought.

He heard screams from Russian soldiers falling from the rain-slick walls of the fortress, but he knew some would soon make it over the top to open the gate into the fort and trap his troops. Then Saga pointed to a steep, slippery path leading down the cliff to the frigid waters below. Casimir quickly understood. It was their only chance. Even though it was a treacherous undertaking and the horses would surely slip and fall, to remain meant death or worse — another Russian prison.

He rushed to tell Frank and Maurice to spread grain and hay on the icy trail and begin moving the men and horses. To give them extra time, he stayed and fought the Russians who had managed to climb into the fort. He pushed some of them off the wall with his lance, while firing his pistol into the faces of others, and stabbing the last two with his dagger. He could not allow any of them to see the escape route. By killing them, he gave his men a few precious minutes to navigate the treacherous trail, but he could stay no longer since the Russians were now pouring over the wall.

Casimir heard the screams as men and horses plunged over the side of the cliff, sounds that ripped at him like a jagged sword. The loss of such loyal brave men grieved him, but when he saw Frank in the lead and Maurice in the middle encouraging their men to move down the trail, he thanked God they were alive.

A flash of gunfire tore through the darkness. A Russian patrol riding beside the river had heard his men descending, and were firing up the cliff at them. He called to the last man on the path, "Come back here, help me." Together they climbed back to the top of the hill and, with Saga's help, were able to dislodge a large boulder and send it crashing down the mountainside into the Russian patrol. Some heard it coming in time to turn back before others were crushed to death. The Russians scattered. For the time being, they were not a threat to his troops.

"You must come with us," Casimir urged Saga. "The Russians will take revenge on you if you stay."

"No, I go to claim the body of my granddaughter," she replied, turning back into the fort.

General Izmailov rode into the fort after the troops who scaled the wall opened the gate, demanding: "Find the Pulaskis. Bring Casimir to me, now." When no Pulaski troops were found, he stormed, "They are here, they have to be here. Look in the well, bayonet the fodder, overturn the wagons, and don't stop until you find them. I want that slippery Casimir and his brother, Frank, and I want them alive so they can pay for tricking Krechetnikov and defying Ambassador Repinin and me. But I especially want them to know it was General Izmailov who caught them. Krechetnikov's prison was nothing compared to what I will do to them."

When none of the Pulaskis or their men were found, Izmailov's anger smoldered and then flared as his eyes fell on Saga. He screamed, "Bring that old witch to me. Tie her to that post and bring dry wood." Then he began beating her with his riding crop while demanding, "Where are they? Where did they go?"

Saga's aged, bent frame made a pitiful sight. The soldiers had pulled her ragged coat away revealing a thin blouse, skirt, and headscarf that were wet and clinging to her frail, wrinkled body. Sagging breasts and a small bulge in her stomach told of the children she had borne. Yet, she was defiant.

Blood oozed from her nose and she spat a mouthful, along with a rotten tooth on Izmailov's uniform. Angered to madness, he ordered the wood set afire, still screaming: "Where did they go? Save yourself, you stupid old witch!" Then the fire caught, its flames leaping skyward while Saga remained silent, turning a look of hatred toward Izmailov. When the wind caught the flames, driving them toward her, Saga screamed, "Ty Ruska swinia (*Russian pig*) ."

A white owl wheeled overhead, and what Izmailov thought was a stray bullet from a celebrating soldier hit her squarely between the eyes, killing her instantly before the flames reached her flesh. The last thing she saw was a caped figure running across the top of the fort wall stopping to point a pistol directly at her. It was all Casimir could do to help her.

Continuing to run along the wall to the back of the fort, he jumped to a large boulder, slid down to where Wolny stood, then mounted and started down the path. He hesitated. The narrow, icy trail would be dangerous on horseback and difficult to follow alone in the dark now that the others had all descended. The snow owl returned and drifted down the mountainside as if to show him the way. He used his body to guide and balance the horse, and, after reaching the river's edge, he found Frank and Maurice in the midst of chaos. The river was frigid and the mounts were panicked by the sight of bodies of horses that had fallen from above being carried by the swift current into a dam of uprooted trees, branches, and ice blocks. Wild eyed, they balked and strained against their reins as the troops tried to lead them into the water. Flashes of lightning showed the bodies of soldiers who had plunged to their deaths. It was an eerie scene. The men were almost as frightened as their horses.

Neither Casimir nor his well-trained Wolny hesitated. They rode directly into the water up to Wolny's belly. Casimir raised his sword over his head urging his men to swim with their horses. The herd instinct was stronger than the horses' fear, and they began following Wolny. The men clung to their horses' tails as the mounts tried to swim, but ice blocks and driftwood pummeled them. Casimir was continuing to direct his men and horses into the water with his raised sword in his right hand when lightening highlighted him and the famous sword. At that instant, a Russian patrol soldier, who had recovered from being knocked down by tumbling rocks, recognized Casimir, and fired his pistol, hitting his right arm.

Casimir was knocked off Wolny and almost drowned before Paul swam to him, grabbed his cloak, and started to pull him to shore. It was not easy. The river continued to swell from the heavy rain, and the current grew even stronger. Casimir was weighted down with sword, cape, pistol, and boots and Paul struggled to keep him afloat while moving toward the riverbank. Casimir helped as best he could, using his good arm as an oar, while kicking his legs to help propel himself toward land. When they reached shallow water, two men rushed in and carried him ashore.

It was Maurice who saw the crossing was impossible and called the men back. More panic set in when the troops tried to turn their horses in the swirling waters. Entire trees with tangling roots caught them in a deathly embrace. Most made it, but others were knocked unconscious or dragged underwater.

Casimir struggled to stay conscious. He had been in the rain for hours and then freezing water. Paul could see that a stream of blood poured from his arm, and that hypothermia and shock were setting in. He pulled Casimir farther up on shore, wrapped him in his own tunic, then ordered his men to build a makeshift sled from driftwood upon which Casimir could be placed until another attempt was made to ford the river.

It became obvious that they couldn't cross at this spot, or remain where they were since the Russian patrol would soon return with reinforcements.

Casimir managed to rally enough strength to instruct Paul to send men into the water to recover reins from the dead horses and all the rope they could find. Paul followed his orders, though he didn't understand why Casimir was interested in such stuff at this critical moment. He also had his men pull those who had drowned free of the rocks to allow their bodies to float downriver, safe from mutilation by the Russians.

They decided to follow the riverbank downstream where the river would widen and perhaps be calmer, aware that the Russians were upstream. Those who could, mounted their horses while other horses pulled sleds laden with the wounded. It was a cold, sodden, and demoralized band of Pulaski cavalry that started down the river. Retreat was bitter enough for the troops, but the foul weather and the wounding of the leader they had thought was invincible added to their misery.

Casimir suffered more than his men, not so much from his wound as from his failure to fulfill Franciszka's prophecy that he would be victorious. Disappointing her deepened his despondency, and knowing he had lost so many good and brave men that night added to his woefulness.

Paul stayed close to Casimir while Maurice took charge of the men, organizing them into a single file while putting the best marksmen at the front, middle, and back of the column for protection. Then, he rode back and forth among them, providing comfort and encouragement.

After two hours of riding, Bazarek Izman, a Turk who had joined them a few months earlier, began singing a bawdy song about a sultan and his harem to lift their spirits. The men liked Bazarek. They appreciated him for leaving his home to join their cause. Soon they picked up the refrain and joined him. Due to the rain and thunder their voices did not carry more than a few feet so there was little risk of the Russians hearing them.

"Oh the Sultan was a lucky man
A lucky man was he
He had a tent with a harem of ninety-three
He liked them all
Short and tall
Thin and fat
But mostly the twins and the acrobat

Oh the Sultan was a lucky man
A lucky man was he
He had a tent with a harem of ninety-three
He liked them all
The young and old
The shy and the bold
But mostly, the twins and the acrobat

Oh the Sultan was a lucky man
A lucky man was he
He had a tent with a harem of ninety-three
He liked them all
But then came his fall
He had to marry
Old dried up Carrie Lee

Oh the Sultan was a sad man
A sad man was he
Now he had only one
And she was no fun
So he ran off to join
the Pulaski Cavalreee

The men's spirits rose as they added more stanzas to the song.

But Casimir's condition worsened. Fatigue from a sustained battle with limited water and food, along with loss of blood and the cold had weakened him. Paul was afraid they might lose him.

After three hours of riding along the river they came to an area with a flat meadow. The rain stopped and the sky cleared as the few stars that were visible lost their brightness to the beginning light of dawn. A white owl fluttered overhead and landed nearby, seeming to watch their movements.

Maurice and Paul agreed the crossing had to be made soon. Although the river was two kilometers wide, full of floating logs and debris, they had to move or the Russians would catch them. They would be easy targets by daylight. The river and the load it carried moved a little slower here. They had to make the attempt.

Paul now understood why Casimir thought to recover ropes and reins from the river. He had the men strap together driftwood to make rafts. The horses would help pull the rafts, loaded with supplies and the wounded, including Casimir, to the far side.

Only sixty of the 350 men who entered the battle survived, and others might perish in the river. Each man was precious and would be sorely needed in the battles ahead. It was the muscular Bazarek Izman who came to Maurice and Paul with a solution to save as many as possible while crossing the treacherous river.

"I swim Bosphorus many times at low and high tide when full of trash and junk from houses on shore," he said. "No problem for me to swim with rope in teeth to pull raft. Better than skittish horse. I take little general first, then help other wounded. It is good plan?"

They knew little of this man. Prior to today he had not distinguished himself and they weren't comfortable entrusting Casimir to him. But, what he said made sense. They agreed that Bazarek would start swimming across pulling Casimir's raft with his teeth. Paul would ride his seasoned horse close behind the float where he could keep an eye on Bazarek while Maurice followed with the rest of the men.

It was a slow and torturous crossing. Even the giant Bazarek had trouble keeping a straight course, especially when the heavy raft swung downstream in the current. Paul marveled at his mental and physical stamina as he focused on the far shore, ignoring all the dangers around him. Yet, even he began to falter and drift downstream. Then Wolny, swimming beside the raft close to Casimir, instinctively moved in front of Bazarek so he could grab his tail and be pulled across. It took more than an hour to make the crossing, and it was a blessing that Casimir lost consciousness and didn't suffer pain in his broken arm from the jolts taken by the raft.

Maurice held the men back to avoid bumping into the raft carrying Casimir, but within a half hour daylight was breaking and they had to enter the river. The horses, already fatigued, resisted, and had to be spurred on and beaten with crops before they would enter what looked like an endless sea of muddy water. It was a dreadful crossing.

The bodies of soldiers released upstream floated past the men in the murky water, like condemned souls of the underworld. Less trained troops would have panicked. But these were Pulaski men, and as long as their general was still in front they would follow where he led.

When Paul and Bazarek finally reached shore, they found a solid rock floor extending from a ledge into the water. Covered with silt, it was too slick to stand on, much less ride a horse across. Wolny tried to climb up on the rock but fell back, splashing and rocking the raft. Paul grabbed his reins and moved upstream where he and the horse were able to get footing in a sandy area. Bazarek couldn't pull the raft against the current, but wouldn't give up. The exhausted Turk crawled across the rock still gripping the tether to the raft with his teeth and right hand while using his left hand and feet to pull himself and the raft across the slippery surface.

Once ashore, Paul rushed back to help Bazarek pull Casimir the rest of the way across the rocky ledge. He told Bazarek to find cover for Casimir where he would be hidden from the view of Russians on patrol. He then left to find a better landing spot, and re-entered the surging river and motioned for the men to go farther upstream to the place where their horses could find footing.

Frank remained behind to watch for the Russian patrol. He found a dismal scene when he finally caught up with them. Only forty-eight men had survived the night and none fit for battle. They needed warmth, but could not risk a fire. All they could do was drag logs to hide their tracks along the river, concealing the point where they landed, and then limp as best they could into the woods. They needed a place to rest and regroup. A thicket of birch, maple and pine provided a place to hide but allowed little warming sunlight through. It was cover without comfort.

Frank stayed close to Casimir while Paul rode out to scout the countryside for food. The breath of both rider and horse froze in the air as he scoured the strange, barren countryside looking for a cornfield or apple orchard that might have a few ears of corn or frozen apples the farmers had missed. He saw nothing edible except a rabbit and he could not risk the noise of a shot.

Shivering in his wet clothes, and worried that Casimir would die without treatment for his wound, Paul thought the end of the Pulaski Legion was at hand. The men, as strong as they were, could not survive in such harsh conditions without shelter, food, and fire. Then, just when he was at his wit's end, without warning, a waiflike child appeared in front of him. At first, he thought it was an apparition, but then realized it was a barefoot boy in rags who was smiling and waving in a friendly gesture. A white owl was perched on his arm. His body looked seven but the eyes said twelve or older. They were the darkest eyes Paul had ever seen.

Paul nodded to him as the boy said, "You are lost, we can help."

Paul scanned the woods looking for others, in case it was a trap, but saw no one and when the boy motioned for him to follow, Paul once more had to go — he had no better plan.

The boy, named Mishkun, as he would later learn, led him up a small rise where the trees became smaller and eventually gave way to scrub brush. When they came to cliffs at the top of the rise, Paul saw people walking down the hill toward him and wondered where they had come from. Then he saw the cave entrances that dotted the cliff's rock wall. He reached for his sword, but stopped when he saw most of them were women and children or old men. None had weapons beyond knives stuck in belts, and everyone seemed friendly.

The owl flew off as the boy led him to a shrunken old woman to whom Paul nodded and asked, "Can you, will you, help my men? We have been fighting the Russians and we are cold and hungry and some are wounded. My leader is gravely ill."

"I am Woja," she responded in Polish.

"We are Saga's people. We have suffered much at the hands of the Ruskies. We know of your great general, his bravery and the mercy he showed our Saga from the fortress wall. You are all welcome here. Mishkun, take him inside my cave to the fire."

Mishkun led Paul inside the cavern. To Paul's surprise the interior of the cave was dry and warm. Toward the back a fire blazed warm and bright, vented through a hole in the rock ceiling. He learned that Ancients had used the caves for religious ceremonies. Now he was overwhelmed to see stores of grain, roots, dried meats, and barrels of wine. The fortunes of the Pulaski troops could not have taken a better turn. He had to get back to the camp and bring them here before any of them, especially Casimir, died of exposure.

"Thank you, thank you so much. I need to return to my troops and lead them here if you will provide them shelter and food. They are freezing and starving and many are wounded. Will you allow me to bring them here?" Paul asked.

The old woman made a clucking noise with her tongue and replied, "Tok, tok, I know, I see them. We must move quickly."

Not understanding how she had seen them or that she planned to accompany him he asked, "May Mishkin and ten men go with me to help with the wounded?"

"Tok, tok, I will also go to help the wounded, first the brave little General and then the others." She reached behind a rock, pulled out a rabbit skin bag and handed it to him. Grateful beyond words, Paul took the bag and moved to the front of the cave.

It began snowing as they moved outside, and when they found the makeshift camp the men made, Paul saw a scene that tore at his heart. Still unable to start a fire for fear the Russians would spot it, the men were shivering and shaking, especially the wounded who were lying on the frozen ground. He saw Casimir still on the wooden drag, wearing his wet clothes, frozen in places. He appeared delusional from the fever that racked his body. Paul could see that his condition was dire. Casimir floated fitfully in and out of a troubled sleep, crying out for Antonin to run, then ranting about Kretechnikov's false promises, and calling for the beatings and rape of his officers in the Russian prison to stop. He tried to raise his wounded right arm as if to lead a charge against the immoral general.

Paul knelt by his side and could see that each time he regained consciousness he suffered excruciating pain. He thought Casimir was too ill to move but knew he would die, if they didn't get him to warmth.

"Thank God, you are still alive and have returned with help," Maurice cried, as he rushed up to Paul. "We saw the Russians ride along the other side of the river. They will circle back when they don't find us farther downstream. We must move quickly, but I fear the jostling may kill Casimir." Paul merely nodded in resolute agreement. They were facing grave circumstances.

Woja moved silently between them like a floating spirit and reaching for the bag hanging from Paul's horse, withdrew a small vial, and pressed it to Casimir's lips, forcing him to swallow a few drops. From another small pouch, she sprinkled a few grains of white powder into his wound and Casimir became quiet and fell into a peaceful slumber almost instantly.

She ordered him stripped of the cold soggy clothes and wrapped in the skin of a mountain goat that she had also placed on Paul's horse. Paul stepped forward and said, "I will do it, please give us a moment" and Woja turned away, acknowledging his need for privacy. Once he was wrapped in the goat skin and Woja was satisfied that he was comfortable, she told Paul that Casimir could soon be moved to the warmth of the caves. Then she started moving among the other injured men. Each received the same treatment as Casimir, a sip of liquid from her pouch and a sprinkle of the white powder on his wound. The effects were magical. Their pain subsided and some of the men started to rise from the ground and to look for their weapons and horses.

When Maurice ordered those able to mount their horses to do so and Paul began attaching the reins of his horse to the pallet Casimir lay upon to transport him to the cave, Woja stopped him, saying, "road too rough, he must be carried." Paul understood. But with so few uninjured troops and most of those with their hands full helping the others, where would he find men to lift the pallet and carry it between them?

Then Bazarek, stepped forward and said, "I carry little general across my shoulder, he not heavy."

What a godsend this man is, Paul thought, as he quickly agreed.

So, the wet, weary, and wounded troops began yet another march. At least this time there was warmth, food, and rest, rather than another fierce battle waiting for them. The falling snow was a blessing, it covered their tracks, leaving no trail for the Russians to follow.

As Paul led them into the caves, they were greeted with the warmth and the smells of hot cooked food. Spit roasted goat, boiled beets, and bread smeared with goat cheese were a welcome repast. After eating, they drank grog, a warm spiced wine which induced a deep sleep. They were safe, at least for the moment.

Woja turned her attention to Casimir, who was dreaming peaceful dreams now — dreams about his father and Frank teaching him how to take a lady's hand and brush his lips across it; dreams of Franciszka's beautiful hands playing the harp, and dreams of Paul riding with him across the Pulaski lands.

Bazarek hovered close, watching her every move. She ordered their leader's arm straightened while Casimir slept, and used a piece of sharpened bone to dig in the wound. She found two pellets and dug both out, then took a piece of cloth which was had been soaking in a bucket of foul smelling liquid and wrapped it around the wound. Her eyes met Bazarek's and he nodded in approval.

"She wise," Bazarek told Paul. "These gypsies from my land; some good, some bad. This one good. She is medicine lady. Very good.

"She said she could see our wounded back at the river before we left the cave. What did that mean? And what's that powder she uses to stop pain?" Paul asked.

"Medicine women will never say, but in my country beautiful red and purple flowers grow everywhere. Gypsy women pick the flowers in summer, seed pods in fall, and dig roots in winter. They dry and cut seed pods, scrape pulp from inside, mix with herbs and potions from Far East, and ferment part and dry other part to make powder. Some leaves are mixed with powder and kept to smoke in pipe. Tea is made from boiling roots. All forms make men feel good, whether wounded or not. When our men start asking for more liquid, we know they getting better and need to stop all medicine before they just want to sleep all time."

"And the other liquid she soaked the bandage in before wrapping it around Casimir's arm, what is that?" asked Paul, who had deduced that the powder and liquid medicine were opiates of some kind.

"Piss of pregnant mare." Barzak was obviously taking pride in his knowledge of gypsy medicines. "It full of many things to keep foal from sickness and make new growth while inside Mama, so very good to heal wounds."

"And how could she see our wounded before we went to them? Was she lying?"

"No, medicine lady never lie. She can see things others cannot both, now and later."

"You mean she can tell fortunes, see the future? That makes her a witch."

"No, no. She has a special gift. The owl is her eyes and her wisdom." Bazarek explained.

Casimir healed slowly from the many afflictions from which he suffered—a musket wound, hyperthermia, infection, fatigue, all crowned by fever. With the help of Woja and her potions, his progress was steady. He slept and dreamed while his body healed. He heard voices in his dreams, particularly Woja's, *'You will struggle through salt, snow, and sand. Death will always be near. One woman will save you, another will love you. Your heart will find a peaceful home. The confusion within you will be settled on the man side. You will lose your freedom but fight for the freedom of others. In a distant place, you will meet immortal men and become immortal yourself. A child will bear your name. Water will threaten you but land will claim you. Beware the Bishop.'*

Bazarek, ever-watchful and close by Casimir heard her whisperings. He talked with her often in their native tongue, and she told him more about what she foresaw for Casimir. She hesitated when he asked about his own future, instead she found an excuse to leave, to help the wounded.

With Woja's care, the warmth of the caves, and the food her clan provided, Casimir and his men recovered from their wounds. When Casimir saw the men showing interest in the young women and walking into the back shadows of the caves with them, he knew it was time to resume their effort to find the Russians and fight them.

When he heard Casimir say, "It's time we leave." Bazarek told the gypsies the men would go soon. The following day oxcarts laden with beets, cabbage, radishes, dried goat meat and grain for the horses began arriving. Casimir was grateful his men would have supplies and did not ask where the food came from, fearing the gypsies had lived up to their reputation as thieves and stolen it from nearby farmers. Only after they left was he able to confirm that the gypsies really had stolen the supplies. Some of the sacks and barrels were clearly marked with the Russian Army insignia. Casimir smiled at the thought that his men would be eating better than some of the Russians.

Casimir had no winter quarters, so he decided to cross the border into Turkey. He had recovered enough to be restless, and his hunger to resume his place in battle returned. He met with

Frank, Maurice, and Paul and said, "The Russians don't know where we are and probably think we are dead by now. They won't be on guard. Now is the time to hit them—hard."

His men were ready and anxious to avenge their fallen friends, but only a few were left, and provisions were again growing critically low. Casimir did not want to risk a shortage of supplies resulting in another surrender so he was forced to wait while Frank returned to Poland to raise more men, arms, and money.

When Frank returned, he brought not only limited supplies, but crushing news. Putting his hand on Casimir's shoulder he said, "Kas, have the men unload the supplies while you and I take a walk."

"But Frank, I want to see what you brought, how many guns were you able to bring?"

"Kas, we need to talk . . . alone"

"But Frank, Maurice and Paul need to know whatever you're going to tell me. Did you spot the Russians? How many? Where . . . Frank, what is it? You look awful."

"Casimir, what I have to tell you, you need to hear first. Paul and Maurice will learn later. Now, please come with me."

Casimir had an ominous feeling of dread as he followed Frank down a rocky path that led to the horse corral.

When they were beyond the hearing of the others, Frank turned and looked into Casimir's eyes, his face reflecting the pity he felt for his younger brother

"Kas, there is no easy way to say this. Father is dead, he died in the Turkish prison. The Turkish authorities said it was the plague, but our friends believe Bar Confederate War Council members offered the guards bribes to kill him. They wanted to make sure he did not regain his leadership role."

Casimir's knees bent and his world spun out of control.

"NO! NO! NO!" he cried, screaming like an injured animal as

pain shot through his chest. He instinctively rubbed the painful spot just over his breaking heart. He stumbled forward while Frank put a steadying hand on his arm.

"This cannot be, this cannot be. Oh, Frank please say it isn't true, that it's a ruse to trick the Russians and the Bar conspirators into believing he is dead. That's it. He's brilliant. He made it look like he's dead so he can raise more support and come to help us. That's it Frank. He is okay, and we'll hear from him soon."

He only prayed that he was right. But it was a prayer that went unanswered.

Frank, his hand still on Casimir's arm and spacing his words to make sure Casimir understood and accepted them, said, "Kas, I claimed the body. I was taking him home to have a burial service and place his body in the Warka Church cemetery, but a large Russian force was massed on the Polish side of the Dniester River, making it impossible for me to cross over to get to Warka. I had to bury him in an unmarked grave so his body would not be disturbed by the Russians."

"I can't bear it," Casimir cried. "To lose him and know that he is not in consecrated ground. It's too much. He was so devout, so faithful. He believed he could not go to Heaven unless he was buried on Church grounds. He should be at Jasna Gora or St. Nicholas, not in Turkish soil.

We must go get him now and take him home. We leave tonight."

"Casimir, you know he would never risk our lives for any cause," reasoned Frank. "There are too many Russians and he certainly would not want us to die trying to find his body. We must leave it where it is for now. Later, we can find it, have a proper service conducted, and return him to Warka."

Casimir knew Frank was right. He had always done what his father wanted, and he knew he wanted his sons safe, not risking their lives to retrieve his earthly remains after his soul had departed.

"I will wait, but as soon as we can, we must find him Frank. Promise to take me to his grave the minute the Russians are not a threat."

"I promise, my brother, we will find him and bury him the way he would want."

It was so unfair to lose his father so soon, without any warning, lingering sickness or injury that would have given them a chance to say good-bye. Just the words, 'Father is dead.' They hung in the air, like heavy fog over a forest.

Frank sensed Casimir needed to be alone and turned to go back to camp. Casimir walked to the horse corral and rubbed Wolny down as his Father had taught him. When night came he was still with his horse, crying softly into his mane.

After Paul and Maurice heard the news they were careful to give Casimir time to himself, time to remember his father and time to heal. He appreciated their thoughtfulness and noticed that Maurice seemed particularly sensitive to his loss.

A few days later they heard about a large Turkish Army at the Dnieper River which was getting ready to fight the Russians. Frank and Casimir rallied their men hoping to join them. With a large combined force, they might be able to break through the Russian lines and find their father's grave.

But before they reached the Turks they were overtaken by Colonel Suvorov, the most celebrated Russian fighter of the day. A fierce battle ensued. The severely outnumbered Pulaskis were pressed by Suvorov's troops on every side in a heavy rain, limiting their visibility. With their men, Casimir and Frank retreated into marshy terrain as the relentless downpour turned the bog slick and soft. Their horses' hooves plunged through, becoming stuck in the mire that made sucking sounds each time a horse freed a hoof, only to have it stuck again, each time it tried to move forward. They were trapped. The Russians had the advantage and their attack intensified as the battle dragged on for several hours.

Casimir led a desperate but futile attempt to find an escape route for his troops, while Frank struggled against a never-ending onslaught of Russians. He was running out of dry gun powder and his horse was shot from under him, exposing him to musket fire, but he kept fighting with saber and knife. Both he and Casimir fought frantically to evade capture while the Russians chased them, hoping to capture the brothers alive and collect the reward Empress Catherine offered.

"Urra, Purlashchuk popula" the Cossacks shouted as they surrounded Casimir. When Wolny stumbled in the muck and stranded him, Frank dashed to his side with a group of soldiers, enabling Casimir to jump onto another horse and continue the fight.

Colonel Castelli arrived to support Suvorov, and set up a formation in place to fire upon Casimir. Dazed and bleeding, Casimir didn't see him. Frank saw that Casimir was their target, raised his sword, and charged directly at Castelli who fired his pistol at point blank range knocking Frank to the ground. He died instantly. Frank's heroic charge succeeded in saving Casimir — it momentarily distracted Castelli until Casimir had moved out of range. Casimir, still fighting desperately, never saw Frank fall.

As more Russian soldiers charged, Casimir and his few remaining men slipped through a weak spot in the Russian line, aided by the cover of the heavy rain. Unaware that Frank was dead, Casimir led his men through a nearby forest to take refuge at one of the villages he and Frank inherited from their father. He assumed Frank would join him there because they had friends and relatives in the town who would help. Meanwhile, he needed rest to heal another wound in his right arm. He longed for

Woja's healing powers while waiting for Frank to arrive. But Frank would never come.

After several days, the rain ended. The Russians were on the move looking for him, forcing him to find safer ground where he could wait for his brother's arrival.

Maurice went on a scouting expedition and when he came back, looking grave, he found Casimir at the village church, kneeling in front of a candle burning for his father. Maurice knelt with him, silently praying for the soul of both Josef and Frank Pulaski.

They rose and walked toward the door of the church where Maurice stopped, turned to Casimir and quietly said: "Kaz, I am so sorry, but you may want to light another candle for Frank."

"What do you mean Maurice, why would I . . . No, Oh God no!"

"I found Frank's wounded men in the next village. They said he was shot by Colonel Castelli during that last battle, and died instantly. That he died without suffering is the only solace I can give you. I am so terribly sorry, Casimir."

Casimir gripped Maurice's arm with his good left hand, then asked, "What about his body? Did the Russians get it?"

"No, thank God. In the rain and confusion, his uniform was covered in mud and one of his men dragged him to the edge of the field at considerable risk to himself. Paulite monks came later to give last rites to the dying and to commit the dead to the hereafter. An injured man told them who Frank was and they took him to the Church at Wlodawa to be buried in the cemetery there."

Maurice had hoped that knowing Frank received a proper Catholic burial would ease Casimir's suffering. But when Casimir realized that the location of his father's grave died with his brother he could not be comforted. Turning to Maurice, he asked anxiously, "Was there anything in his belongings to indicate where he buried father's body?"

"I'm sorry, Kaz, there was nothing," Maurice said sadly. "I went through his saddle bags, and found a journal or two and the usual personal items. I asked that they be sent to your mother for safekeeping until you can return home."

"Thank you, Maurice," Casimir said, "I would like to light another candle and spend some time alone in the chapel." He could no longer deny or challenge the truth of words that told him another loved one was gone. Those barbed arrows that pierced his heart and left lasting scars came so frequently that he could only open his arms and embrace the pain, knowing full well that more arrows would come.

"I understand Kaz. I will be in camp near your tent to brief you on the Russian situation when you're ready," said Maurice as he turned sadly away from Casimir, wishing there was something he could do to comfort him, while knowing in his heart there is nothing that can ease the pain of losing a loved one.

This was the lowest and darkest of days for Casimir. His father and brother were dead. The location of his father's remains was probably lost forever, Antonin was in prison, and his own right arm was no longer able to hold a lance. He knew his men had been demoralized by the losses they had suffered. He felt totally alone.

Maurice came to him and reported that Russian General Drevitz was on his way to capture the fort at Jasna Gora Monastery, in Czestochowa. Casimir, now the only remaining seasoned commander in the Confederacy, asked the Bar leaders to let him defend the fort. They agreed and gave him 2,000 troops to hold the sacred site and prevent Drevitz from ransacking it.

It was a significant responsibility. Jasna Gora Monastery, the holiest shrine in Poland, was a special place for Poles. It was founded by Hungarian Paulite monks in 1382 and housed the painting of the Black Madonna with the child Jesus, which was said to have been painted by St. Luke on the very table where

Jesus sat at the last supper. The painting had been credited with performing many miracles for the sick and dying.

Casimir had a special affinity for the monastery. It was where his father made his pilgrimage and donated large sums of money in hopes of one day being buried in one of its chapels. The family often went there together to observe religious holidays and, like his father, Casimir wanted to be buried at Jasna Gora. It could not fall to the Russians. They had taken enough from him. He was determined they would not take his holy place.

Aside from the miracles accredited to the painting of the Black Madonna, also known as the Lady of Czestochowa, the fusion of glorious art and architecture within the church created a spiritual richness that made all who entered reverent.

In addition to its spiritual richness, Jasna Gora held other treasures. Gold and silver chalices, crucifixes, and the robes of popes and bishops, all encrusted with precious stones, were on display throughout the sanctuary. The church coffers were full of gold coins donated by worshippers like Josef, who were hopeful the money would help secure them a burial place on the sacred grounds. The Russians hungered for these riches.

Just off the courtyard and adjacent to the main chapel was a hall favored by Casimir. Centuries earlier, craftsmen carved wood panels and chiseled stone columns for the hall, which was dedicated to the knights who had defended Christianity against the Muslim invaders. At the end of the hall, a door opened into a large room. There on display were shields, with coats or arms engraved in gold, lances, swords with gold hilts, and sheaths encrusted with precious gems, which the knights had carried on their crusades. The Hall of the Knights and adjacent weapons room was a special place for Casmir because he felt a comradeship with those who fought valiantly for their faith.

In defending this spiritual capital, Casimir sought not only revenge against the Russians but solace for his aching soul. He vowed that Drevitz would not set foot inside the monastery's walls to despoil even an inch of its beauty and spirituality.

The Church sat on a low hill protected by a fort that encircled it with thick earthen walls rising fifty feet straight up. It had a moat, towers, and bastions, and like Fort Berdyczow, the only approach was across a drawbridge. Over the centuries, little maintenance had been performed on the fort but its massive walls had withstood the test of time. In addition to the gold, silver, precious stones, and religious icons it housed, there were other valuable items within its walls — large supplies of gun powder and cannons.

The Russians coveted the monastery's treasures and had always threatened to move in and take them unless large tributes of money were paid to them. In addition, the local Bar Confederates required large payments to defend it from the Russians. When the priests inside had finally had enough, they closed the gates to both factions and when Casimir and his troops arrived, the priests would not allow them to enter.

Casimir was a devout Catholic. He was indebted to the Paulite Monks for retrieving and burying Frank's body at Wlodawa. He would never go against the wishes of the church. But his soul cried out for relief from the pain of losing his father and brothers. He needed to light candles, pray, and receive communion and he desperately needed to confess his sins. He had killed scores of men and was responsible for the deaths of many he had led into battle. He needed absolution.

A priest who came to the main gate saw his anguish and admitted him for confession and the sacraments, but denied access to his men. Some of his men spoke with a priest at the monastery's back gate, and when the priest turned to close the gate and reenter the monastery, Bazarek Izman, stuck his oversized foot between the gate and post and pushed his way in, allowing the remaining troops to enter behind the giant Muslim.

The Paulite fathers were shocked by the forced entry. They worried about the possibility of Russian revenge and reprisals, so they found it easy to rationalize that Casimir had tricked them. This gave them the excuse they needed to placate the Russians should they overrun the fort and Casimir's forces.

The church was within the walls of the fort and the town of Czestochowa spread across the plain below. The faithful citizens of the town were integral to the defense of the monastery.

Each week, when they finished confessing their transgressions and had received absolution they would often also confess, "And father, please forgive me but I spied upon the Russians and saw that they have moved the main body of their troops to the outskirts of town and stockpiled their munitions near the old mill on the river."

"You are forgiven, my child. You must repent by also confessing to Friar Benedict." Of course, Friar Benedict then passed the information along to Casimir who immediately began making improvements to the walls, knowing an assault by the Russians was imminent.

It was late November when one of Casimir's men intercepted a courier with a dispatch for Russian Colonel Drevitz. It detailed how many men and weapons he would receive to lay siege to Czestochowa, and instructed him to overcome Casimir's resistance, occupy the monastery, and send all the Confederate defenders to Siberia.

The document detailed useful information about the size of the Russian force and its provisions, but Maurice's analysis of the mood, placement, and condition of the enemy troops was even more valuable. He described the leaders and their men as lazy, incompetent, careless, and self-indulgent. Casimir continued to marvel at the many talents of this man who seemed totally dedicated to him but the fact that he had the mannerisms and traits of someone Casimir knew still nagged at him. Who did this remarkable man remind him of?

Casimir began a strategy of continual harassment against Colonel Drevitz's larger force when they moved into the area. He and his men dogged the Russian troops constantly, taking small bands outside the fort to attack where and when the enemy least expected it. Remembering the lessons his father taught him about anger, he became the hornet that stung Colonel Drevitz until he was driven to madness and error.

Finally, on a bleak winter morning in December, the infuriated Drevitz ordered a full attack, and the Russians emerged from beneath a low slate sky to begin their assault. Casimir opened fire with his cannons preventing the Russians from getting close enough to dig in near the fortress walls. Drevitz's losses were heavy, but Casimir did not let up. He sent his men to burn the outskirts of the city occupied by the Russians, forcing Drevitz farther away from the fort.

Several days later, Drevitz's guns started a strong bombardment that lasted all day but resulted in little damage to the fort's walls and no Confederate casualties. The next day Drevitz sent his negotiators to call for Pulaski to surrender with a provision to allow safe passage home for all Confederate troops. Feeling self-assured and completely in control, Casimir's old arrogance returned and he answered, "Tell your Devil Drevitz if he wishes to survive he will put down his weapons. In exchange, we will give him an escort out of Poland."

Drevitz was so angry he bombarded the fort the next day, again with little effect.

Casimir asked Maurice, to give him an assessment of the enemy's situation that evening.

"They are tired, discouraged, and ready to go home," said Maurice. "They wanted you to give up and leave when Drevitz called for you to surrender. They have fought for weeks without even a tiny victory. Their commander gives them no praise or encouragement, only belittlement for his failure to overrun us."

"What about their guards?" Casimir asked. "Are they alert and ready to respond if I take a small band into their camp?"

"There are no guards, at least none who are awake. They're exhausted from the beating they have taken from you and from their own general."

Those words were an intoxicant to Casimir who was anxious to punish and embarrass the Russian general. That night he used the cover of darkness to lead a sneak attack on the enemy battery, hitting them on three sides. The Russian gunners, weary from constantly loading and firing their guns, were totally surprised and quickly scattered and ran away. Casimir, always resourceful, ordered his men to pick up the weapons they left behind and use them to wreck the abandoned cannons.

By the time Drevitz was able to react, three of his largest cannons were destroyed beyond repair and Casimir and his men had withdrawn with only minor injuries.

"These Poles are receiving supernatural or diabolic help from somewhere," some of the Russian soldiers muttered after this attack on the Russian Orthodox Christmas Eve. "We can't beat them. If we stay, we will perish here."

The next night, Casimir made another raid, surprising the Cossacks again. Drevitz was infuriated, and sent troops to circle behind Casimir to prevent him from returning to the fort. But Casimir had laid one of his traps. As they attacked, Casimir's second cavalry unit rode out from the fort and Drevitz' men were caught in the crossfire of the two Pulaski groups

Drevitz tried to excuse his failure as a leader by reporting that the nighttime attack was a well-planned maneuver by several hundred troops. But he realized the siege would continue for a long time unless he could take the fort by direct frontal assault.

He decided to try Casimir's nighttime tactics and at two a.m. on a frigid day in early January Drevitz began a full attack. Three Russian columns advanced from the village. They drove peasants in front of them loaded down with bundles of branches to throw into the moat for the soldiers to walk across. The villagers' voices praying to the Lady of Czestochowa to save them, rose as one to the top of the fort walls where Casimir ran along his positions to direct the defense. His heart went out to the peasants. They were innocents who would surely die this day through no fault of their own.

The moat quickly filled with attackers futilely trying to raise ladders to scale the vertical walls. Casimir ordered burning wreaths thrown into the moat along with rocks, logs, storm pots, and grenades. His troops opened fire with pistols, carbines, and cannon—stopping the attack. After an hour, the assault collapsed and the Russians withdrew. Many of the peasants were trampled underneath the fleeing Russians and their screams echoed through the fort all day.

The friars organized a prayer vigil, and several of the priests went outside to minister the Last Rites to the dying but there were too many dying and too few priests for everyone to receive a blessing.

Casimir, dressed as a priest, moved among the dying. Knowing he had caused the deaths of many of them, he needed to see them and try to comfort them. The agony of those burned by the wreaths he had ordered to be thrown was unbearable for them, and excruciating for him. He bent over a woman whose skin had been burned from her face. Yellow fluid oozed from her forehead, cheeks, and chin and she whimpered, holding back screams of pain, while working her hands up and down a rosary. He bent over her, assuming the role of a priest to grant her some comfort, saying, "My child, this day you have absolved yourself of all sin. Your sacrifice helped save our glorious church and the

Lady of Czestochowa. Heaven and the glory of God's kingdom wait for you."

Her whimpering stopped and she murmured "Thank you Father," while Casimir held her hand as her breathing became more shallow and then ceased.

He looked toward the sky and questioned, "Why, oh why do so many have to die? Is freedom worth it? Would a thousand years under Russian rule be worse than losing my father and Frank?"

Casimir, with no one to guide him, felt alone, not knowing if he could continue with the killing. What would father tell him to do? Who could help him now?

The only answer was Franciszka. He found a horse and raced to her still wearing priest's robes. She was shocked by his haggard look, his injured arm, and the absence of pride in his step.

Dismissing the servants, she asked, "Casimir, what is wrong?" and he began to talk. He felt desperate. He needing relief from his heartache. She pressed his head down into her lap and stroked his hair. They remained together until morning. Then she had a large breakfast prepared, and was relieved to see he was better after finishing the meal.

Talking of his pain had helped purge it from his heart, though he would always love, and be devoted to the memories of Frank and his father. His spirit and body now nourished, Casimir said goodbye to his beloved Franciszka and returned to Jasna Gora.

He was heralded as a hero and the savior of the monastery by the monks and priests but his usual arrogance was subdued. The prayers and screams of those trampled in the moat still rang in his ears. While he knew the Russians were at fault for their deaths, he relived his own orders to fill the moat with stones and burning wood that brought such horrible pain to many. He knew that success in turning back the Russians resulted in others being trampled. Casimir went to confession often, always asking forgiveness for the souls of the innocents who died.

The priests were moved by this man who was one minute a warrior, killing the enemy that crossed his path, and the next a devout Catholic, praying for forgiveness and for the souls of his brother and father.

But there was no question he had saved the monastery. They were grateful to him and empathized with him for the moral crisis he sometimes suffered. When Casimir asked that they retrieve Frank's remains and bury him within the monastery walls, they readily agreed.

After the fighting ceased, they contacted the priest of Wlodawa who oversaw the transport of Frank's remains to Jasna Gora, where a small service was conducted and he was buried. Only Casimir, the presiding priest, Paul and Maurice were in attendance since the grave had to be hidden from the Russians who were still hoping to collect Catherine's bounty for a Pulaski.

As Casimir thanked the presiding priest, Maurice heard him say, "Father, if I may ask one more favor?"

"Of course, my son, if I can grant it I will be happy to," the priest replied.

"When I am no longer of this world, could you make room for me near the Hall of Knights?"

"There will be room, my son, there will be room," promised the priest, putting Casimir's mind at ease. "I will make provisions in our records since you will probably outlive me."

The next day was quiet but activity among the Russian troops made it seem as if the attackers were preparing for another assault on Jasna Gora. Instead, they were starting to leave. Less wisely, Drevitz decided to take revenge for his defeat by taking the few prisoners he had and running them naked through the snow.

Casimir, who was always gracious to prisoners of war, usually letting them go free, could not tolerate this humiliation, and charged forth with his men. Furious, Drevitz was forced to abandon the prisoners, but he burned his wagons loaded with provisions to keep them out of Casimir's hands.

That night, as they celebrated the victory and the return of the prisoners, Maurice seemed pensive and Casimir considered again how much he reminded him of someone. But who? Maurice was without question more intelligent and observant than most. He had a great ability to assemble and use numbers to achieve results, but his greatest attribute seemed to be his ability to read men. Yet when the times called for physical strength in battle or treacherous river crossings he was as capable as any man in the Legion.

What a great lawyer he would be, thought Casimir, who called to Maurice across the courtyard fire. "Come join me in my quarters, my friend, for some of the good friar's cognac."

"That sounds wonderful, lead the way," Maurice responded, walking toward Casimir.

CHAPTER FOURTEEN

A STORM AND A NEW
BROTHER

The Atlantic Ocean
Jasna Gora & Warka, Poland
1772-1777

asimir's right arm, battered by gunshot, and the slashes of swords and lances had finally healed — as did his collarbone that had been broken by a ramming rod. So had the wound beneath his right eye and multiple fractures to his ankles and legs caused by falls from horses and horses falling on him, but pain, usually in the form of a dull ache, was ever present.

He was a young adult when he sustained most of his injuries and he could always push through the pain to continue training, leading troops, and fighting. Now in his early thirties, the pain was harder to ignore.

After spending an evening telling stories to Sultan he awoke with a persistent throbbing in his right arm. This normally meant a change in the weather.

Walking onto the deck, he was greeted by a magnificent scarlet sky adorned with purple clouds floating from west to east across orange and red hues that stretched from horizon to horizon. *Red sky at night, sailor's delight; red sky in the morning, sailor take warning.*

That sailor's rhyme came back to him; but the sea was so peaceful, and the sky such a palette of colors surely it would be a calm day. Still, there was the pain in his arm. Looking around, he saw the crew scurrying about the ship tying all loose objects down, and taking great pains to batten the sails and make sure they were taut and tightly tethered.

At noon, the sea changed from dark blue to a churning, froth-capped green. Waves grew to thirteen-foot high swells and crashed against the boat. Charcoal clouds, heavy with rain hung low, and moved over the last patch of blue sky and light on the Eastern horizon.

Casimir watched as westerly winds whipped waves into undulating mountains that tossed the Massachusetts about like a child's toy sailboat in a waterspout. Water began to wash over the deck, knocking men off their feet, threatening to take them to a watery grave. At one o'clock in the afternoon it was as dark as midnight. It brought back the vivid image of the painting of a storm at sea. He thought it might be a bad omen after all, and that he would be consumed by sea monsters when the ship went down. But he also recalled Woja's whispered words in his dreams in the cave, *"Water will threaten you, but land will claim you."*

He didn't believe in witchcraft, fortune telling, or dreams — but the words did give him comfort that he would not drown.

He wanted to spring into action and help the crew, but he knew an untrained man would be more hindrance than help while the seamen reefed the sails to keep them from ripping. To get out of the crew's way he went below deck where the clamor of crazed and howling land-rooted farmers and merchants was deafening. Then, just as in battle, his mind moved to the most critical need, *I must take care of Visner! I need him and cannot lose him to this storm.*

Casimir went to his horse, began patting him, and said softly, "Easy boy, easy, it's just a squall. I'll feed you some hay when it passes."

He continued to try to calm the frightened horse and remain calm himself while thinking it was a miracle that the pitching ship had not knocked the stallion off his feet, causing him to break a leg or sustain other injuries. Visner's eyes were wide, wild, and terror-filled.

"Steady Visner, steady boy, he whispered. Then taking his red sash from around his waist, he put it under the horse's nostrils and said, "Visner, here smell this. I'm going to put it over your eyes so you won't see things falling and tilting."

The horse calmed enough to allow him to use the sash as a blindfold. Casimir then wrapped his arms around the stallion's neck and mounted him bareback. His scent on the sash comforted the horse and having a rider on his back calmed him, but the tossing of the ship caused Visner to stagger, and he whinnied wildly.

Casimir gently prodded him forward until his front legs were on one side of the sling lying on the floor and his back legs were on the other. As he sat astride Visner, Casimir reached for the ropes to the block and tackle that lifted each side of the heavy canvas sling, and talked reassuringly to Visner while he pulled and tightened the ropes.

The ship rocked the two of them from side to side, then heaved them into the air and back down again. Casimir's calm in the midst of so much chaos was the reassurance Visner needed. The horse's feet gradually left the ship's deck as both horse and rider became airborne, swinging harmlessly back and forth. Casimir secured the ropes to two posts to prevent Visner from banging into the beams and walls of the ship, then began retching repeatedly from seasickness. He thought of the distress the horse was suffering and was thankful that horses don't vomit.

The storm passed almost as quickly as it came, and all were thankful they hadn't been near a shore with rocks or land upon which to crash. Visner and Casimir had literally ridden out the storm together strengthening their bond. Visner's trust in his master was now total and it seemed he instinctively knew that Casimir had saved him.

"Some storm, hey Count?" Sultan asked.

Casimir had corrected Sultan many times, telling him that although he was born into a noble family he was not a count, but he eventually gave up. The fact that he was of Polish nobility deserved some recognition and count was as good a title as any. He decided he might adopt it when he arrived in America.

Casimir laughed and shook his head. "Well neither Visner nor the farmers liked it very much and I have to admit riding a horse suspended in midair was a new experience."

"From what I have heard from you and from others it seems you have had more than your share of exciting experiences. Not everyone's head is worth as much as yours," Sultan joked. "Let's have some brandy to celebrate surviving the storm and you can tell me more about your adventures."

"It's true, I do like talking about myself Sultan, but this time the entertainment will cost you, and you must pay before you hear more," Casimir teased.

"What is the price, Count? Anything that is mine is yours . . . except my new pearl-handled pistols of course."

"I want to know about you before I tell you more of my life story so the price is your answer to some questions," Casimir challenged.

"Okay, Count what do you want to know? But beware, my life is boring next to yours," said Sultan.

Casimir started with the questions that had been on his mind since first meeting Sultan. Within a half hour he learned Sultan had married a beautiful Tunisian woman who died in childbirth; that his infant son died shortly thereafter, and that Sultan was on his way to America to secure the release of his wife's only living relative, a man named Elijah George who was a slave on a Virginia plantation. He already knew Sultan had travelled the world serving as everything from a Silk Road trader to a mercenary soldier. Sensing that the loss of his wife and child were painful, he ended his questions.

"I am sorry for your losses," said Casimir, "but I am glad we met and can spend time together. Now what would you like to hear from me? I can promise to bore you the rest of the night if you can stand more of my bragging."

"Tell me more about your father and two brothers."

"Ah Sultan, I haven't been totally truthful with you. I needed to know you better before I told you I have a third brother, Maurice Beniowski. Now that is an interesting story.

"You see Maurice joined my troops early on and was an invaluable asset. His ability to analyze any situation and recommend the best action nagged at me because he reminded me of someone, but I couldn't decide who it was. Finally, on the evening after our great victory at the Jasna Gora Monastery, I decided to ask him."

"Let me hear," Sultan pleaded. "This sounds intriguing."

"Well, after inviting him for a drink, I led Maurice down the three stone steps to a small wooden door opening into a grain storage room which I had selected for my quarters. I knew that if the pompous General Drevitz ever gained entrance to the fort, he would never suspect another general of living in such a modest room. I lit a large candle, poured cognac into two brandy sniffers and warmed them over the flame of the candle. Handing one to Maurice, I said, 'you remind me so much of someone I know. You always have. It teases my brain but I am unable to remember who. Did you have family near my home in Warka?'"

"Maurice hesitated, looked away a moment, then drew a deep breath and said in a serious, almost pleading voice, 'Kas, I hope you will believe my words, and not be angered or disappointed by them. To answer your question, yes, I did. My father was the mayor of Warka.'

"But MY father was the mayor of Warka," I protested, before realizing what Maurice was saying. Of course, that is why he has the lawyer's instinct, I thought, as I tried to deal with the shock of what he was telling me. How could this be true, how did it happen? I wondered. Mother and father were so much in love and mother was so beautiful.

"I was confused and frightened by what Maurice might tell me, but I had to know. I idolized my father and found it hard to believe he had betrayed his wedding vows, but it was clear that he had. The affair must have been the great wrong he wrote about in his diary shortly after I was born.

"I am shocked beyond words, since he was a devoted husband and father who took all his promises seriously," I told Maurice, "but I do believe you. Please tell me how it happened, because I knew nothing of it."

'I know, my dear friend,' he responded. 'That's why I said nothing. Our father asked me to join you, Frank, and Antonin and to stay close to you and protect you when you needed help. You see, my mother, Jane Wolsky, was married to a nobleman who was killed by Count Joachim Potocki before I was born. He had been your father's client.

'When I was old enough, she told me the full story and I will try to tell it exactly as she did, if you want me to. This may be difficult for you,' he told me.

"I was overcome by shock, disbelief, and sorrow but I knew the words Maurice spoke were true. There was no other explanation for the physical and intellectual resemblance he bore to my father. Frank and my father told me so much about our family and my early childhood because they thought it was important for me to know the family loved me and saw, a . . . a . . . special problem I had at birth as an opportunity for me to develop into an exceptional person. But I knew nothing about this part of my family's history and I feel certain neither Frank, Antonin, nor my poor mother did either.

"I remember Dr. Borloff's notes describing father's agony when I was born with an abnormality, thinking he had done something wrong that caused my . . . birth defect. Now I think the affair with Maurice's mother was the wrong he committed that tormented him so.

"But I had to know more, so I asked Maurice to tell me everything he knew.

"He continued, 'first I must let you know your . . . our father spent as much time with me as he could and that I also called him father. I know it's hurtful to you but I must refer to him as father . . . our father. To call him anything else would feel strange and be a disservice to him since he always treated me as a son.

'What I tell you now are the exact words he and my mother used to describe how they met and I was conceived.

'Mother's first words to our father were, 'Please sir, help me. I am sorry to come into your office unaccompanied and without an appointment, but I need your help . . . please sir.'

'She said he leaped to his feet and rushed from behind the desk where he had been reading a history of Jan Sobieski's winged Hussars.'

"Sultan, a pang cut deep into my heart as I remembered how often father told me about the Polish Hussars, which left no doubt that Maurice spoke the truth."

Sultan nodded with an intense look on his face and said, "Amazing Casimir, please go on."

"Maurice continued telling me about that first meeting. 'Madam, please sit, let me get you water and a doctor,' father responded.

'No, I do not need a doctor, I need justice.'

'Father studied her face, and could see that her swollen and split lip, the bruises around her dark eyes, and the streaks of blue on her neck where fingers had choked and constrained her were proof that she had suffered a great ordeal. His heart immediately went out to her.

'Why? he wondered. In God's name, why would anyone do this to such a beautiful woman?'

'As he helped my mother into a large upholstered chair usually reserved for the wives of his clients, he asked, 'Are you sure about the doctor? Those bruises and cuts look serious and you could have broken bones.'

'No thank you. I'll be alright without a doctor.'

'He got her a glass of water from the pewter pitcher on his desk and offered her a sip of brandy to calm and warm her, then he asked, 'How did this happen? Did you fall? Were you thrown from a horse or did someone do this to you?'

'She nodded to the latter and he asked quietly, 'Who did this terrible thing?'

'She thanked him for the water and brandy before blurting out, 'Joch Potocki killed my husband and raped me.'

'What? I can't believe it. He is a client of mine,' came our father's stunned reply.

'Then mother calmed some and continued. He pursued me while I was married. He often came to our home when my husband, John, was away. My servants knew to stay close by when he was on the premises. Their presence protected me from his physical advances but not his vile whispers of his desire for me and what . . . what he wanted to see and do to me.

'I saw him riding up one day and hid in an upstairs room. My maid told him I was away with my husband on a buying trip but he knew it was a lie and walked to the staircase and shouted, 'Well one day she won't have her precious John, and things will be very different for her.'

'At that point, my mother collapsed into a small, sobbing figure and father said he was tortured by the pain and anguish she displayed. He thought she looked like a snared rabbit struggling to get out of a metal trap with no escape anywhere from its torture, just as poor mother had no escape from the hell she was going through.

'Our father had always been contemptuous of Potocki because of his lack of morals and cowardice. Now his flames of anger leaped higher with each word mother spoke.

'Father asked himself why Potocki had done these terrible things. He knew Potocki had bragged about having three mistresses at a time and that he neglected his wife. Just as some men needed liquor or gambling he seemed to need multiple women and to betray each of them. But why commit murder and sexual assault to get another woman when he could simply buy one with cash or extravagant gifts? It infuriated father so much he said he could have killed the bastard.

'After drinking the water, then taking a sip of the brandy, mother became more composed. She straightened in the chair, folded her hands over a tear soaked handkerchief, and looked directly at father. Her voice and demeanor made it seem she had shut herself off in a distant place, far away from the tragic abuse she had suffered. But father said her next words fanned the flames of his anger into a firestorm.

'Mother described in detail what happened. It was too embarrassing for her to tell me, but when I was old enough to understand our father repeated her words to me.

'My husband was ambushed on his way home from a horse sale,' she said. 'He was shot in the head and chest and his throat was slit. The horses vanished and Potocki put out a story about gypsy bandits in the area who were robbing travelers. But, no one else was murdered and if robbery was the motive, why kill him? It wasn't necessary.

'Before I could bury my John, Potocki came to the house. He leered at me and said maybe now I would be friendlier. I picked up John's musket from the table and ordered him to leave and he did, but not for long.

'John's funeral was last week. Two days ago, my maid went to market for produce and the servant who takes care of the stables and grounds was busy mending a fence several kilometers from the house. Potocki came in without knocking. When I saw him, I tried to get to John's gun again but he was too quick for me. There was liquor on his foul breath and he was on me before I could run away. He knocked me to the floor, grabbed my hair, dragged me to the bedroom, and used his dagger to cut my clothes off before pressing it to my throat. He forced me to get to my knees and said he would slit my throat the same as he did John's if I didn't service him. When I spat on him instead of doing what he wanted, he started beating and strangling me.'

'The scoundrel!' cried father, jumping to his feet and clinching his fists. 'He actually told you he killed your husband?'

'Yes Sir, he did,' she replied in a voice that remained flat, cold, and distant.

'He was too strong for me. I couldn't stop him. He raped me, and said if I told anyone he would come back and kill me.'

'Mr. Pulaski, I have heard of your success in court. Will you please help me? I want that devil to suffer for what he did to John and to me.'

She still had a blank stare and seemed to be in a daze, more composed on the surface than our father, who raged at the thought of such blatant cruelty to an innocent yelling, 'The shameless monster, preying on the defenseless. He deserves the gallows if any man ever did and you deserve justice.'

'Father paced rapidly across the wooden floor in deep thought and anger. He wanted to help her and he wanted to punish Potocki, but there was a problem. He was Potocki's legal representative. As detestable as the man was, our father had served as his legal advisor in a variety of business dealings and minor legal skirmishes for years. It was unethical in his legal world for a lawyer to prosecute his own client and, as you know, Casimir, he was foremost a man of integrity who honored his commitments. But wasn't it more dishonorable to let a helpless woman go unrepresented and let this despicable man go unpunished? Now he felt like the rabbit in the trap with no clear way out.

'He looked at the suffering widow, my mother, and said, 'Mrs. Wolsky, I must take some time to consider your request. There are complications that make this a difficult decision for me. Please come back tomorrow morning and I will let you know if I can help you.'

'There was an embarrassed hesitancy on mother's part as her head dropped down and she averted her eyes from his.

'What is it Madam?' father asked.

'I . . . I cannot stay overnight here in town, and I can't go home,' she sighed. 'Potocki might return. After he finished beating me, he stole all the money from the house. I have no funds for a room or anything else until I can sell some of my assets. But I give you my word I will raise the money to pay your fee. I have livestock and a beautiful horse which is worth a great deal. Please, if you will just take my case.'

'Our father, who as you know, Kas, was always devoted to doing the right thing, no longer needed to think about his decision.

'I will get you a room,' he said. 'The Penskis' run the coffee shop in town and they have an extra room above the café. You can stay there. I know them, they are trustworthy.'

'But, I can't pay for it.'

'I will take care of the room as well as your dinner tonight and breakfast in the morning. You need rest and food and I will ask Doctor Borloff to look in on you. Those bruises are bad and you may have other injuries. Besides, his testimony could help us in court.

'And yes, I will take your case. I want you to come by to-morrow morning, so that we can discuss how we will proceed against Mr. Potocki. It is the right thing to do and I will enjoy watching him pay for what he has done. His confession to you that he killed your husband should be enough to ensure he nev-er does such a thing again.'

'Oh, Mr. Pulaski, you are a good man. You will not regret helping me. I will pay your fee and forever be grateful to you."

'Of course, she could not pay the fee and he did have reserva-tions about his decision. Yet he held fast to his belief that it was right to bring such a murdering thief and rapist to justice.

'Mother said they met almost daily to gather evidence. Father was confident they would easily win the case. He thought Poto-cki's admission that he killed her husband, the doctor's report of her injuries, testimony from the servants, the coroner's report on her husband's wounds, and an extensive list of witnesses willing to testify about Potocki's reputation as an immoral man would convince the jury of his guilt.

'As anticipated, our father was criticized by some for turning against a client, and a good-paying one at that. Several others abandoned him, fearing that they would suffer the same fate if serious charges were brought against them. Rumors suggesting that you had to live by Pulaski's standards to be represented by him spread.

'Mother was unable to raise the necessary funds to pay him when other landowners in the area refused to buy any of her livestock, even the champion Arabian stallion with bloodlines dating back to the days of the Teutonic Knights. She and father suspected Potocki had threatened them with physical harm and financial ruin if they helped her in any way. Later she learned Potocki held a mortgage on her entire estate, including the livestock, and on several of the surrounding estates as well. Without income to pay off the note, Potocki would get it all, including her beautiful white Arabian stallion, which he would use to race and make even more money when put to stud.

'Even though Father had recorded most of those mortgages for Potocki, he had no interest at the time in which lands they covered. He had no way of knowing they would play such an important role in his most memorable case.

'It was this discovery that answered his question as to why Potocki would murder and rape. It wasn't just about the conquest of a beautiful woman. As was the usual case with criminals, it was greed that drove him, greed to have what he could never buy.

'Father kept it from you and the rest of the family but his income dropped drastically. He jeopardized your family's future well-being for one case. His land holdings produced enough income for the family to maintain its lifestyle and he never disclosed anything to your mother about the case or the impact on his law practice. He said he usually shared everything with her, but he didn't want to worry her unnecessarily. At least that is what he told himself when he rationalized that he took the case because it was the right thing to do. Still, he confided to me that in a secret corner of his mind he wondered if his desire to right the wrongs mother had suffered was his only motive.

'When her bruises healed and the weight of her grief gradually lifted, mother's beauty blossomed again. That she had both physical beauty and a sensual appeal was undeniable. Father said she had a childlike softness that made him want to protect her. He began looking forward to their business meetings and became reluctant to end them. Mother seemed to enjoy them as well, and depended on the focus of their work to help her through all that she had suffered.

'Then, as time went on, the inevitable happened. They worked late one evening as Father poured over legal books while she waited to be of help if she could. But being weary and warmed by the fire, she leaned back in the big upholstered chair and fell asleep. The fire cast a glow on her face and after father closed the last reference book he stood and studied her beauty. He told me that she looked fragile and alone, yet somehow sensual. He felt a great urge to defend and protect her but a much greater one to hold her.

'He said that when he walked over to the chair to awaken her, he could have spoken or called her name but instead he touched her softly on the shoulder. She shifted and her head dropped forward causing her face to brush his hand sending thrilling excitement up his arm and through his chest.

'Father told me that your mother and he had been married for more than ten years at the time and he had never desired any other woman. She was the perfect wife, mother, and life partner. But this was different. My mother had lost all the love in her life and had been savagely brutalized. She needed to feel loved again and accepted him eagerly. Maybe he felt that desire within her or was simply responding to his own attraction for such a beautiful, fragile, and lonely woman. Whatever the reason, it was a forbidden union and one repeated over the next few weeks in spite of the wracking guilt they both felt. They were stumbling on the dark path of desire and betrayal, and their moral light was now flickering too dimly to guide them.

'Although he was brilliant in the courtroom, our father failed to have Potocki convicted because Potocki paid bribes to the jury, threatened them and then, as a second insurance policy, did the same to the judge. After the trial, there were always hard feelings between father and him, and Potocki opposed everything our father supported, including raising an army to defend Poland.

'But father's kindness to mother didn't end with the court case, partly because he was unable to bring justice to Potocki and partly because of his attraction for her. He felt a responsibility toward mother and gave her a house near the square in town, making sure she maintained the same lifestyle she had with her husband. She was grateful and often cooked meals for him when he worked late or had time for lunch.

'He said in spite of his love for your mother the relationship continued awhile because their anguish over losing the case brought them even closer. I was the product of their brief union but I'm sure your father never stopped loving your mother and loved all his children, including me, equally with a single exception.

"At this suggestion of discrimination on the part of my departed and revered father my head jerked up and Maurice saw the anger on my face. Before I could challenge his words, he said, 'Surely you must know he favored you above all his children.'

"I had to admit it was true, and my anger was replaced by fond memories of my father lifting me in the air and carrying me into breakfast each morning. I almost choked on the emotion.

'I hope I have not offended you by telling you this or by calling him father. It is what I always called him.' said Maurice in conclusion.

"In truth Sultan, each time he uttered the word 'father' a pain went through me unlike any I ever felt in battle, but, struggling to keep my voice from cracking, I answered, 'I cannot think of a man I would rather call brother. Thank you for telling me, especially now that I've lost Frank. One man can never replace another, but it does ease the sorrow to know I still have a brother like you with me.'

'Thank you, Casimir, and there is one more bit of information I think you will want to hear.' said Maurice, while flashing the first smile either of us had shown all evening.

"What is it?" I asked, desperately needing a bit of good news.

'Pushka, your favorite horse and your seventh birthday present . . . '

'Yes, what about Pushka?' I interjected.

'He was the horse stolen from my mother by Potocki when he foreclosed on her estate. Potocki beat Pushka with a post wrapped in wire for losing a race just before your birthday. When our father heard about it, he bought Pushka for you. That's why he had an injured flank when you got him.'

"I was breathless. This was yet more proof of father's love for me. He gave me the greatest horse that ever lived.

'Oh Maurice, it is wonderful to learn about Pushka's origins," I said. "He has been my best friend since I was seven years old and I thank you for sharing that with me, but what happened to your mother? Is she still in Warka?'

'She and your mother and sisters knew each other from passing in the market place since Warka is small. Father arranged for her to leave Warka for my birth. She was gone for two years and when she returned she was wearing a new wedding ring. Our father had a notarized marriage certificate waiting for her, and everyone believed that while she was away she was married briefly to John Beniowski, a land owner, who died when he was trampled by a bull on their estate.

'Thus, I became legitimate. Of course, John Beniowski was a fictitious person, but Beniowski was actually my maternal grandmother's maiden name.

'Father sent me to private Catholic schools and made sure I had everything I needed, including time with him while I was growing up. Mother moved to Krakow to be near the school I attended. She is still there.'

"When I heard his explanation, Sultan, I was emotionally torn. You must have gathered how much I admired my father. I didn't have the sexual desires most men feel at a young age but I wondered if Franciszka had given me more encouragement, would I have crossed that line with a married woman? Wasn't that what father did? Ultimately, I concluded that I could forgive father and was thankful for having another brother. I went into the chapel at Jasna Gora and gave thanks for my new blessing named Maurice Beniowski."

"Wow," Sultan exclaimed, letting out a low whistle. "That was special. Thank you, Count, for sharing this very personal story."

"Yes, Sultan, now you know more about me and my life than anyone other than Paul and Maurice. I dare say you would have found some of the battles I fought more interesting but I tried to answer your question about my brothers honestly. I fear the brandy may have loosened my tongue a bit too much."

"Don't worry, I enjoy all your stories and, as you know, anything you tell me is not repeated," Sultan assured him. "However, you have not told me one important thing."

"And what is that Sultan," Casimir asked apprehensively, fearing Sultan wanted to know about the birth defect he spoke of earlier in the evening.

Sultan rubbed his thumb across the cutlass he had drawn from his belt, testing it for sharpness, then pursed his lips and kept his eyes on the blade as he asked,

"Why is there so much gold offered for that ugly head of yours?"

Never fearing that Sultan would harm him even when he tried to look menacing, Casimir answered truthfully.

"When Catherine of Russia and Ambassador Repnin could not capture or control us Pulaskis militarily, she spread rumors about us claiming we kidnapped King Poniatowski and planned to ransom and kill him. Monarchs across Europe were frightened that regicide could occur in their country if I escaped unpunished, so I was forced into exile from Poland.

Catherine offered the reward for me, dead or alive, but I will never be taken to Russia alive, so if I go, I will be dead. That's why gold is offered for me and one of the reasons I seized the chance to go to America to fight."

"But my count, kidnapping a king is serious business. I must ask, did you do it?"

"Of course not," laughed Casimir. "The plot failed. The fool of a king was able to escape. Two of the kidnappers were killed by his guard and he bribed the third into releasing him. That proves it was not me. I do not fail. He would not have gotten away from me."

"I agree Count. That seems to be indisputable proof that you were not guilty. But who did do it?"

"I am certain Catherine was behind it and was trying to discredit me," replied Casimir.

Shaking his head, Sultan observed, "My dear Count, you have indeed lived many lives. I regret that we land soon and our nightly tales of adventure must end."

"I will also miss our conversations Sultan. But perhaps they do not have to end. You have been a mercenary and have fought on foreign soil before. Why not join me in America? It would be wonderful to have someone who can speak so many languages with me and I promise you will not be bored."

"I have no fear of ever being bored around you, Count," answered Sultan with a hearty laugh. "But for now, I must decline your kind offer. I have an obligation to see that Elijah George is released from bondage and I have the money to buy his freedom. That must be taken care of first, and, first things first, you know. But perhaps I will find you after that and we can share some brandy and maybe fight a war together."

"I would like that, but we would be winning a war, not merely fighting one," corrected Casimir.

"Yes, I know, the man who wouldn't fail in a plot to kidnap a king would certainly not lose a war," laughed Sultan. "Now good night my dear friend and perhaps good-bye if we reach land tomorrow. Your company has made a tedious voyage enjoyable. Take care of yourself and your horse."

"I will Sultan. But remember, I plan to see you and Elijah George in America. Now, good night."

CHAPTER FIFTEEN

TROUBLED TIMES

Lesser Poland
1772

Again, sleep evaded Casimir. Sultan's question about the bounty on his head brought memories of the harsh times he and his men endured after Catherine spread her slanderous lies.

His exile began when he departed Jasna Gora, a place he had returned to so often. Before he left, he lit candles for his father and Frank, then dropped to his knees in front of the Black Madonna and silently prayed, *Oh Blessed Mother, thank you for allowing me to defend this holy place. I ask a special blessing. Please intercede on behalf of the souls of my father and my brother. Both were true to you and the faith. Please comfort my brother, Antonin, who is imprisoned in Russia, and please watch over my mother and sisters. They have not taken part in this war and should not suffer because of the charges against me.*

He crossed himself and felt at peace. Like the Latin chants he had heard so often here, his spirit floated upward, along the gold-inlaid walls that met the peaked ceilings covered by biblical scenes more beautiful and meaningful than the artwork in any royal's collection. Nodding reverently, he rose and stepped out into the courtyard to walk down the cobblestone path toward the Hall of Knights for a final visit.

I know how the knights felt when they sat at this great oak table with their chair backs against the raised wooden panels of the walls, he thought as he entered the great hall. *They were defenders of the faith, like me. I can see them giving thanks for their safe return and for the honor of defending Christianity. This is my special place within the monastery. I will always come back here. My heart is here and God willing, I will be laid to rest here.*

Casimir knew that during the years he defended this spiritual place, his faith had deepened. It was his faith and the friendship of the priests and monks that helped him through the loss of his father and Frank, and he believed they would once again be together in a better place one day. The clean purity and grace of the cathedral convinced him that he must continue to fight to protect it and his Catholic faith.

The monastery is a symbol of the Poland father dreamed of, he mused. *It is strong and beautiful, righteous and enduring, proud and most of all, free. I don't want to leave. I am at peace here within the monastery walls where I can meditate for hours in the Hall of Knights, but I have no choice. I must go.*

His sense of peace slipped away as he stepped back into the courtyard and walked toward the main gate of Jasna Gora.

For now, I have to leave this place and my Poland behind, he reasoned with a heavy heart. *Too many good Polish people believe Empress Catherine's lies that I tried to kill their king. And my mother does not need to lose another son. It is hard, but I, Casimir Pulaski, always a champion, must sneak off and hide like a dog with its tail tucked between its legs all because of Catherine's insatiable hunger for our lands. Some call her Catherine the Great but I never will. I vow I will return when the Pulaski name is again respected.*

When he approached the gate, Maurice was nearby with Wolny, still the wild war horse only Casimir could ride, and who, with him had become the subject of legends and even poems and songs. Like Casimir, the horse never seemed to tire. He lived for constant action. Casimir stood for a moment, looking at Wolny with pride. He and his horse understood each other.

With a leap that belied aches from the wounds he had suffered over the past five years, he mounted Wolny, and in somber tones, said to his half-brother, "I must leave Poland. As the last uncaptured Pulaski male, I am sought by almost everyone because they believe we tried to kill the king. Even the Polish people have turned against me. The Russians are offering five kilos of gold to anyone who delivers me or my head to the whore Catherine's court."

"No, No, my brother," Maurice protested. "I am also a Pulaski. We must both stay and fight the lies Catherine spread about our father and you. Think of the fame and praise you have received for saving Jasna Gora and for your bravery in the battles you won. The French, English, Germans and Dutch have written of your feats. Songs ridiculing the Russian invaders, especially General Drevitz, are sung in pubs all over Europe. You set an example of patriotism and confidence in the ability of Poles to win battles, much like King Sobieski did. You awakened a sleeping country and its gentry and led them in the fight to drive the Russians out. We must stay. Other countries will surely come to our aid. You are needed here."

"Maurice, you must know that my great popularity came before Catherine decided Poniatowski should be removed from power for standing up to her. She had him kidnapped and made it look like my family and I did it. I suspect she had Ambassador Repnin hire the bunglers who botched the job, but most of Europe chooses to believe a Russian whore rather than a Polish nobleman.

"Poniatowski is a popular King, so even in this country I have few friends and certainly none among the monarchs of other countries who fear the overthrow of any ruler could lead to a challenge to their throne. My fall has been steep and swift. Many would turn me over to the Russians for the gold they are offering. I am not sure where I will go to rebuild my life, but I know I will find the place and clear the Pulaski name. Then I will send for you, I promise my brother."

"I fear you are right but where you go, I go," Maurice responded, trying to show confidence and boost Casimir's spirits. "We will fight side by side just as we have in Poland."

"Thank you, my dear brother and comrade. But you cannot go with me now. You are not known as a Pulaski and you have not been accused of regicide like the rest of us," Casimir continued, "I need you here to try to secure Antonin's release from the horrors of that miserable Russian prison. I don't want to think what my poor brother is going through. For now, it's best that you take care of my interests here. Help my mother and sisters as much as you can without divulging your true identity since it would wound them deeply.

"Recruit more men dedicated to our cause and train them. When the time is right, you can join me and bring fresh troops with you.

"But Kas . . . "

"Please don't argue with me. You have proven your loyalty time and again, and I will miss your friendship and counsel, but you must stay. I will take with me the officers who also had their reputations destroyed because they fought with me. Sad, how being a Pulaski officer changed from an honor to a curse so quickly. I cannot abandon them now. They can help me rebuild an army—somewhere, and then we can return and fight."

"I will do as you ask Kas, as long as you promise to let me know you are well and send for me as soon as you can," Maurice reluctantly agreed.

"Thank you for understanding, Maurice. My trust in you is unwavering. Now I must leave before the Russians realize I am here."

Maurice begged him to tell him where he was going, but Casimir said, "It is best you don't know. What you do not know cannot be extracted from you by torture or by threats against those you love."

They embraced, shook hands, and with a nudge of a knee Casimir signaled Wolny to trot away.

Maurice watched them exit the grand arched gateway of the monastery. The first snow of the season began decorating the red blossoms of the still-blooming geraniums lining the driveway with white lace. The melting flakes on Maurice's cheeks concealed the wetness that was already there. *God protect my brother and friend*, he prayed.

As the snow clouds darkened and the flurry of white flakes turned to sleet, a forlorn Casimir was wet, homeless, and abandoned. In truth, he could not tell Maurice where he was going because he didn't know. He didn't know where to go or what to do since he was not accustomed to hiding and running away. It was as if in addition to his father and Frank he had also lost himself. The proud, confident, brave Casimir Pulaski no longer existed. He shivered in his wet clothes and dreaded facing the six officers who, because of their association with him, were also banished from Poland.

They were waiting for him in Krakow near Lanckorona, site of one of their earlier battles, and would be looking to him to lead them. But where could he take them and how would they avoid capture?

In his misery he wondered how things went so wrong—from glorious victories to total rejection and exile?

He thought to himself, *How can Father and Frank be dead? How can I support my officers who are outcasts because of me and my family? Where will we find the comfort of battle, where adrenalin fires the veins and danger is a drug stronger than opium that drives us to more action? We are all addicted to fighting, and I am addicted to leading. Where will I find a place to lead again?"*

By the time he reached Krakow on the third day, he was cold, tired, despondent and sick. He had come to the sad realization that words, either written or whispered, even if false, can be more powerful than the sword when spoken by a greedy and malicious empress.

His officers were in no better condition than he when they met at the clock tower of the grand Wawel Castle, a fortress built four hundred years earlier by Casimir the Great.

Casimir had visited the castle as a young man, many times attending galas in its grand hall off the central courtyard. He was impressed by its sheer size and commanding position. Built on a giant bend of the Vistula River, the largest in Poland, the stream barred access to the fort on two sides and offered water for the town and the moats that surrounded it. The fortress was so large it took a man on a fast horse fifteen minutes to ride around its perimeter. Its brick walls soared forty feet from the top of a twenty -foot embankment that rose from the river and moat. Invaders carrying weapons and munitions could not climb fast enough to scale the walls before pots of boiling oil were dumped on their heads; their ladders were thrown backwards to the ground, or stones were hurled down on them from the walls above.

Attackers could get inside the fort only by tunneling a great distance deep under the massive brick walls and moat. That had not worked for Turks, Swedes, Russians, or countless others who tried. Casimir considered this ancient structure, that could not be breached, a great military strategy in its own right.

He greeted his officers as cordially as he could, "My officers and friends, thank you for your service and your dedication to our country and to me and my family. I am saddened by our current situation which is not due to any fault of yours. We fought bravely and valiantly though there were some in high places who resented us for the glory we earned at a high price in our fight for freedom.

"We are all leaving our homes and loved ones and being exiled to some distant land. I bear the responsibility for this trouble but I swear to the Blessed Mother that I will never abandon you. I will protect you with all my strength and one day, God willing, we will return victorious."

Bazarek Izman, the Turk, was in better spirits than the others, most of whom avoided their leader's eyes and simply nodded. He was not leaving his home and family behind in Poland. A former mercenary who went wherever he could make money fighting, he considered Casimir and his troops his family. Big, robust, and bawdy at times, he was a self-appointed protector of Casimir, having saved him at the battle of Grab and tended to his wounds as gently as any mother or sister. He was the sturdy oak that sheltered and strengthened the others.

Casimir was grateful Bazarek was there. He had insisted that Paul Dobrachek, who was shielded from Catherine's reach by his family's ties to royal courts in France and Austria, remain in Poland for the same reasons he ordered Maurice to stay. He needed them there, ready to rejoin him when the time came. Bazarek would help fill the void their absence created.

The Turk phrased his words so it seemed he spoke for all the men, when he said, "We ride with you Little General, we are the Pulaski men and we will fight to the death. Where you lead, we will follow."

Casimir was saddened to note that his officers did not add their voices to Bazarek's. Though young, they had old faces. When they joined the Bar Confederation to fight the invading Russians they were drunk on the wine of youthful optimism. Now they were seasoned and sobered by the realities of war, including death, wounds, starvation, frigid weather, and finally exile from their homeland. War had aged them beyond their years. They slumped in their saddles and their eyes that once glittered in anticipation of adventure and fame were dull and tired. Casimir looked away and silently rode to the front of them. He started to unsheathe his sword, but decided not to raise it and simply moved forward as they followed.

They were once so proud to be part of the Pulaski Legion, Casimir recollected. *If they had not followed me, they would be raising families in their homes now, rather than running and hiding like thieves across the land they once defended. They know that three of the Pulaski men are either dead or in prison and that I am disgraced. Now they doubt that I can protect them. Yet, following me is the only option they have.*

His misery weighed him down more than the soggy clothes he wore as they trudged on, day after day in the wet and cold. Even Bazarek's big baritone voice was song-less and silent. Hunger, despair, and cold numbed them, closing out the warmth of hope.

Casimir rode ahead and found a modest church in a small village tucked away in a deep valley along the Skawina River. Mountains, too steep for an army to cross, especially in deep snow, rose from the river. There was only one way into the valley, a road barely wide enough for a team of horses to pull a wagon that hugged the river bank. After surveying the terrain, Casimir determined that it was a defensible position for even a few men.

He dismounted and walked to the door of the church. It was a narrow building, which was built of reddish brown cedar boards running vertically up to a steep roof making it look even more narrow than if first appeared. A talented woodworker had carved lacy designs onto boards and attached them to the eaves on each side. It was the only decorative thing about the church, which wore its simplicity elegantly. The snow clinging to the roof and windows was like white icing on a cake.

"Enter my son, all are welcome here," said the old, bent priest who answered his knock.

"Father I have six men with me and we have ridden several days through freezing rain and snow without shelter or much food. They need a place to rest and warm themselves. May we take refuge in the Church for a few days?"

The priest observed the Confederate uniform with its general's insignia and the famous black stallion, Wolny, he was riding. "My son, how could I refuse the savior of Jasna Gora? I was there when your brother's remains were buried at the monastery and when you made the request for your own earthly remains to be placed in the Hall of Knights.

"Yes, You and your men are welcome here. But, there are Russian patrols looking everywhere for you. They visit the valley every few days asking about you and nailing up reward posters for you which our grateful parishioners tear down."

The priest smiled and motioned with a palsied hand for Casimir to come inside the church.

"Thank you, father. Your words of welcome mean so much to us," said Casimir, waving the small band of men who had just caught up with him forward. Then in a whisper, "We will stay the night and be on our way. I will not endanger you, your church, or the villagers by staying longer."

Before dawn broke, Casimir ordered his men to pack up, mount and be prepared to leave at sunrise.

"But sir, we just arrived and we need to rest and shelter from the weather," argued his young sergeant from Radom. "It looks like another storm is approaching, and we may be trapped in the mountains. It would be easy to hold out against the Russians here, where we can pick them off as they come up the road."

Casimir knew what he said made sense but was quick to point out what the sergeant had not considered.

"All good points Sergeant but what of the retributions against the priest and his church once we leave? And how many towns-people would be wounded or killed by stray bullets, cannon shot, and the fires that would spread from one of these wooden buildings to the next and the next?"

Casimir, who was still haunted by the screams of the burned and dying townspeople at Jasna Gora, knew his men were de-moralized, cold, and weary but he would not risk the lives of in-nocent people who were loyal supporters. How odd, he thought, that someone else was arguing to stay and fight and he was de-termined to withdraw.

After the priest blessed them and gave them cheese, some hard bread, and a bottle of wine, they thanked him and rode back out into the cold. Casimir was distressed by their danger-ous and desolate situation. He had sworn to protect his men but was finding it difficult. He knew they needed warm and safe shelter away from anyone who might recognize them and turn them over to the Russians. But where to go? Anywhere close to home or the Russian border was far too dangerous. The warmth of Italy was tempting, especially since he spoke Italian, but there was no fight to join, and he and his officers needed to lead an army into the heat of battle again.

But for now, finding shelter, preferably warm shelter was most urgent. One night inside the church had been a mere tease, show-ing them what they needed to survive. He thought of the salt mines at Wieliczka. It would mean turning southeast and riding two days, but the labyrinth of tunnels would hide them. The mines were so far below ground that the temperature never varied from a tolerable fifteen degrees Celsius. There were hundreds of tunnels and only a few were worked at a time. He thought they could stay in dormant ones unnoticed during the day while the miners were working. Then they could make foraging expeditions at night to gather food and intelligence after the workmen left for the day.

The town of Wieliczka spread over the valley below the mine entrance. They reached it on the afternoon of the second day, then crossed a frozen river and rode down a vacant lane, stiff and numb from the cold. They hid until the workers left the mines, then Casimir led them up the steep hill to the mine entrance. They walked their horses down the tracks used for carts to haul salt. They couldn't risk a light until they were several meters below the entrance and out of view of anyone passing by. Even then, a light in the darkness could be spotted by any worker or supervisor who had stayed late and would sound an alarm.

Bazarek, the tallest of the group, walked in front carrying a torch to lead them through the twists and turns of the underground maze. The remains of miners who died from cave-ins, exhaustion, or disease, were piled in one small chamber causing Casimir to wonder why they weren't removed for a proper burial.

Suddenly they heard the snort of a horse from one of the side tunnels and Casimir went to investigate. He found a dreadful scene.

Horses were used to pull the carts up the track as well as to walk endlessly, mile after mile, in a small circle turning a giant wheel which lifted other carts through an opening in the roof of the mine. The horses were coated with white salt that filled the raw wounds that the rubbing of their harnesses made and sores lined their backs and flanks.

To a horseman like Casimir it was a scene from hell. He could tell the poor creatures were blind from the constant darkness and their pitiful whinnies and attempts to lick the salt from their wounds told him they were in horrible pain while their protruding ribs showed they were underfed. Carcasses and skeletons of horses ringed what served as the stable area. The horses of his men, hearing the distress of the other animals, whinnied nervously, the odors and darkness of the place pressing upon them just as it did the men. It seemed they were entering a dark underworld, even colder in spirit than the world they left outside.

"You will struggle through snow, salt, and sand," came back to him. How could Woja have seen that he would end up in a salt mine? He had to push the thought from his mind, her words were too much of a riddle.

They found a small circular chamber that had served as a storage area. It had only one entrance, making it easy to defend. Although they were finally warm, they spent a restless night as did their horses. The mines became an iron maiden that encased them, puncturing their spirits with doubt, hopelessness, and fear.

Their lives deteriorated during the ensuing days into a depressing cycle of determining night from day by the sounds of the miners coming and going; trying to keep their nervous horses quiet during the day, and counting the hours until they could go out at night to find food and water.

They couldn't store water in the mine since the floors, walls and ceiling were salt, which turned any water they put in the shallow pits they dug to an undrinkable brine. They broke the ice in the river to fill their goat skin water bags and give the horses a spot to drink. Water for bathing or shaving was out of the question.

It pained Casimir to steal grain and hay from the starving work horses in the mine, but he had no choice. Their lives depended on their mounts and they had to be fed.

The darkness, along with the growing stench of horse and human waste and inactivity weighed heavy on his men, and Casimir knew they couldn't stay in the mines long. The men were demoralized and fearful. They might rebel against him and leave the mine during the day which would expose their position. He had to find a better place for them.

Meanwhile, he started disguising himself as a miner by using clothes he stripped from a miner's body that he concealed under other corpses. Then, while his men gathered food from unlocked store rooms and cellars each night, he slipped into town to learn as much as he could about the hunt for him and what was happening in other parts of the world.

"I am new to the mines here," he told one of the shopkeepers. "I came from the coal mines up north. This is the first time I have worked in salt mines."

"Ah, that's why I have not seen you before," the shopkeeper responded.

"We had explosions and cave-ins in the coal mines but we always dug our friends out and buried those who died," observed Casimir, still troubled by the corpses left in the mine. "Why is this not done here in the salt mines?"

"Superstition my friend," explained the shopkeeper. "Because the salt preserves their bodies, the townspeople believe their souls are also preserved and stay in the body. If the body is removed, their spirits will wander aimlessly in the dark underworld for all eternity. Relatives build shrines and leave flowers for the departed and other miners pray for their own safety at the shrines of friends."

"Ah, that explains it, thank you for telling me."

Casimir thought the tobacco shop was well situated. It was on the main highway at the edge of an arched stone bridge that all travelers, whether on foot, horse, or carriage had to cross to go through town or get to the salt mines. A fine hotel occupied the opposite end of the bridge where glittering chandeliers cast dancing lights on the windows well into the evening. The Grand Hotel was the place where the mine owners met visiting merchants seeking to buy stockpiles of salt to be shipped all over the world. Salt was a precious commodity. Meat could be preserved for months at a time with it and vegetables could be pickled to provide a steady supply of food even when weather or seasonal factors prevented hunting or farming. It also contained minerals people and livestock needed to survive. Whoever controlled the production or distribution of salt could make a fortune overnight. The mayor was often included in the negotiations between seller and hopeful buyer because the fortune of the town depended on the success of the mines.

After dinner, these gentlemen stopped by the shop for fine cigars or flavored pipe tobacco to enjoy back in their rooms or in the spacious, hotel parlor carpeted with thick Turkish rugs. They saw no reason to interrupt their conversations as they pointed to the tobacco they selected and paid for. As a result, the shopkeeper was better informed of the news of the world than either the mayor or the mine's owners.

At the beginning and end of their shifts, miners came to exchange gossip while enjoying a cup of tea in front of the big wood burning stove. Casimir timed his visits just after the shift ended and stayed late until after the hotel guests had made their purchases. He noticed that some of the visitors left correspondence with the shopkeeper and guessed the envelopes they gave him contained contracts and other business matters as well as letters to family and friends.

He took the risk of staying in a stable for several nights even though he knew he might be discovered and that his absence from the mine could cause his men to become rebellious. He trusted Bazarek to keep them focused on the brighter days ahead when they would leave. But first he had to decide which direction to lead them. From the stable loft, he watched the shop during the day to see what the shop owner did with the posts. He saw that couriers picked up pouches around noon and rode off to the north on Mondays, to the south on Tuesdays, to the west on Thursdays, and the east on Fridays. He also noted that they delivered packets of mail to the shopkeeper.

He thought back to when he was facing exile and Franciszka raised funds for him and his men. The money was meant to pay for food and ammunition and to recruit and equip new men. Oh, but where would he find recruits now and where would they fight?

He regretted not following her advice and forging diplomatic relations with the reigning monarchs and aristocracy of European courts. If he had done as she said, perhaps a few doors would be open to him and his men despite Catherine's cunning.

He had promised to let her know when he found a position in another country, but he doubted that would happen anytime soon. He decided to write to her now, while he had a means of contacting her. He knew she would be anxious to hear from him.

He wrote to her that evening.

Dear Franciszka,

Thank you for the monies you raised to sustain us in our exile. I am embarrassed to tell you that I am again in need of funds.

What you so kindly sent is needed for food, shelter, and ammunition for the few men who are with me. It is not nearly enough to outfit a contingent large enough for me to gain a commission in another country. I fear I must prevail upon you again and ask you to use your influence with the French diplomat, Claude-Charles de Peyssonnel, and Prince Karol Radziwill. I plan to write both asking for loans and your recommendation would be of immeasurable help.

As always you have my undying affection and gratitude.

Your devoted protector,
Casimir

He couldn't say more as she was a married woman. But they both knew their hearts were bound together.

He wrote to de Peyssonnel, and to Prince Radziwill requesting loans. He asked them to send their replies to Darius Pruneski, in care of the tobacco shop.

It would be unusual for a miner to read and write so he told the shopkeeper, "I have noticed that people leave letters with you to post. I have an uncle who married well and has business dealings in France as well as Poland. He entrusted me with correspondence to deliver. Perhaps because he had tired of my presence. He gave me money for my travelling expenses but I was enticed into a card game and lost it. He doesn't know of this and I thought if I could get the letters delivered he would never have to. Could you help me? It is important that I stay in his good graces as my mother hopes he will include me in his will."

"Not without payment, my friend. I have to pay the couriers and feed their horses. Doesn't sound like you have much money. It may not be possible."

"Well, I didn't lose all he gave me and I have my wages from the mine. I can pay."

"In that case, I can help you. Give me the letters and I will see they get delivered."

"Thank you, Monsieur. I realize I have not introduced myself. I am Darius Pruneski."

"You may call me Andrew," the shopkeeper replied.

Casimir knew the letters to France would go to the Thursday courier and the one to Franciszka to the northbound courier on Monday.

There was nothing more to do but wait for a reply to his loan requests.

He continued to visit the shop for two weeks. The dark miners' clothes and his small build allowed him to fade into the shadows in a corner and observe and listen without being noticed. Several times he heard local men talking about the reward for the Pulaski who tried to kill good King Poniatowski.

One said, "The Russians think he is in this area and they patrol the streets daily. We finally get a Polish king and another Pole tries to kill him. I don't understand it, but I do understand gold coins. If I see him I'll turn him in and collect the reward, you can be sure of that."

Bazarek came to him one evening to report that things were getting more desperate in the mines.

"When do we go Little General? It's not important where, but the others need something to look forward to, a purpose. Hiding is no good for them. They are like you, proud and brave, craving action. They are all good soldiers, but now very sad."

Casimir knew better than Bazarek how this miserable and unfair exile had broken the spirit of his men. His mood was melancholy. Hope had deserted him, but hope was what his men needed.

"Tell them we will go where it is warm. We'll go to Italy where I speak the language. We will stay in the sun and regain our strength while we wait for reinforcements from home. Tell them we will leave in a few days and they will be glorious again."

Casimir didn't like to lie to his men, especially Bazarek, but it was important that the Turk believed the story so the men would believe him and have something to look forward to. They needed that. And it might not be a lie. He might indeed take them to Italy if a better opportunity did not arise soon.

"I will do it General," Bazarek promised, then disappeared back into the night.

The next day Casimir heard hotel guests talk about the danger of traveling while the Russians and Turks were still fighting. His heart jumped at the news. He would love to fight the Russians again. He and the men must go to Turkey and help the Ottoman Empire defeat Russia. They were anxious to leave the oppressive salt mines, and heading for battle against the Russians would boost their spirits even more than the warm weather of Italy.

The next day the shopkeeper handed him a letter from de Peyssonnel, the French diplomat, and asked, "Would you like me to read it to you?"

"No, thank you," Casimir replied. Then, to conceal his real plans, he said "I have decided to return to my home near Gdansk and will deliver the letter to my uncle myself. It will show him I did the job he gave me. I do not understand business matters, so the contents are unimportant to me."

After leaving the shop, he slipped into an empty stall in the back of the stable where he could read the letter. Good news. Surely his fortune had turned again. First, the Russians were at war with the Turks and he could join the fight. Now, de Peyssonnel was promising to lend him money. But he had to get word to him to send the money to Istanbul where he planned to help the Turks fight the Russians. *But how can I explain another letter to the shopkeeper*, he wondered.

After returning to his men in the salt mines that night, his voice rose in excitement as he told them they would go to Turkey to fight the Russians.

"My brave soldiers," he said, "My head has nearly burst from the pressure of this salt hole full of evil while my heart struggled to escape and fight. I know you suffered even worse than I. We must exit or die. That has always been clear, but where we could go was the unanswerable question I struggled with. Now, finally, we have our destination. Turkey! We will fight against the Russians in Turkey and regain our glory. With only the seven of us remaining, we should be able to slip past the Russian patrols and regroup with more of our men in the mountains. The horses are in bad shape from being in the dark without any exercise. Spend tomorrow brushing them, rubbing them down and checking their feet for cracks from the drying salt. Then get the saddle bags ready. Pack at least three of them with salt, it is valuable and we may use it to barter. Tomorrow night we will leave this place. We will have the cold weather and the Black Madonna on our side, but we must be careful because many enemies are waiting for a chance to collect the gold on our heads."

"But what about Italy?" the argumentative sergeant asked.

"Sergeant there is no war in Italy. The Pulaski Legion fights Russians. We go where we can fight them. We will never give up the cause."

Some of his old bravado had returned and it was infectious. There were no more questions from his men, just a flurry of activity to get ready to leave their salty hell.

In the early morning hours, under the cover of darkness, Casimir rode Wolny out into the crisp white snow-crusted landscape and down to the empty stable stall. He had drafted a reply to de Peyssonnel during the night. It instructed him to send the money to another tobacco shop in Istanbul, where his father bought his fine Turkish cigars and pipe tobacco in better times. He told de Peyssonnel to again use the name Darius Pruneski.

As luck would have it, the next day was Thursday, the day couriers rode west. Casimir stepped from a side street and waved down the westbound courier who had just left the tobacco shop. "The mayor asked me to make sure you got this," Casimir said, extending his hand with the letter up to the horseman.

"All letters are to be left with the shopkeeper," yelled the courier as he prepared to kick his horse into a trot. "I can't take it. I have to follow orders."

"Perhaps you did not hear me my friend, the mayor asked me to give you this," snarled Casimir. Then, having gotten the courier's full attention, he started to pocket the letter while whispering, "I think it is a matter involving a young woman he wishes to be discreet about, if you know what I mean. He's addressed the letter to her brother, who is sympathetic to their situation. He will give you money. But I'll be happy to tell the mayor you refused both the letter and the gold piece that will be waiting for you when he receives a reply from her. I should think there will be more messages and more gold in the future if things go his way."

"Maybe I can take it after all. The mayor is an important man and my employer wouldn't be pleased if I angered him. Let me have the letter and I will see that it is delivered to the right person."

"And how do I know you will keep your word to personally deliver it, the mayor would be very embarrassed if the letter fell into the wrong hands?"

"It is in my interest to wait for a reply, don't you think," was the courier's canny reply.

Casimir handed him the letter, chuckling softly at how easy a greedy man can be tricked. He knew there would be no gold coin waiting and de Peyssonnel would not reply. Instead, he would have members of his trusted personal guard deliver the money. But by the time the courier figured things out, he and his men would be headed for Turkey. And the courier could not complain to the shopkeeper as he had disobeyed his instructions.

Still smiling Casimir headed back for the stables to get Wolny and return to the mine to make sure his men were prepared for an early departure.

CHAPTER SIXTEEN

HUNTED

Lesser Poland
1773-1774

After exiting the mine in the pre-dawn before the first workers arrived, Casimir's little army plodded along snow-covered roads and onto rocky mountain trails. A freezing rain had coated everything in ice. Tree limbs snapped under the heavy burden, and became slippery stumbling blocks for the horses that punched and pitched through the crusted snow. Their hooves became packed with ice as they plowed on, adding weight that pulled on tendons already weakened by the lack of exercise. Still, being in the frigid outdoors was better than the depressing darkness of the mine.

Leaving the poor working horses to their fate in the salt and gloom troubled Casimir. He had wanted to end their suffering before they left, but they could not risk killing the horses giving evidence that someone had been there.

Now as they moved forward, he knew activity was the right medicine for him. Even being exiled and riding to an unknown future was preferable to idleness. A good battle was what he and his men needed to regain their spirit, stamina, and self-esteem but until they reached Turkey and joined other forces, they had to avoid engaging any enemy. There were now only seven of them, and adversaries who wanted to collect the reward on their heads were everywhere. They could not afford to lose even one of their group.

Casimir, still wearing a miner's clothes, dismounted and walked into villages they passed to gather food and news while the others, still in uniform, stayed out of sight. He saw the reward posters now offering eight kilos of Russian gold for him, dead or alive, and suspected that Ambassador Repnin, disgraced and driven from Catherine's court because he could neither control, contain, nor capture the Pulaskis, had distributed the posters and inflated the reward from the original five kilos.

If so, Catherine would have a choice. She could either pay the full amount on the posters and restore Repnin to a prestigious position at court as a reward for bringing about Casimir's demise, or refuse to pay more than the five kilos she had authorized and continue to banish Repnin. Either way, Casimir would be dead.

He would not allow himself to be captured and taken to Russia to be tortured. If cornered or wounded, he would force them to kill him, possibly by trying to escape, since he feared torture and ridicule far more than death, and suicide was a sin that he must avoid. Those searching for him would not want to risk losing such a prize so if he tried to escape they would kill him and his men would fare no better.

That evening Casimir entered a village and stopped in a tavern for hot stew, cheese, and bread he could take back to his men. The barmaid was on crutches, and had a cut lip and bruises on her face and arms.

Casimir was shocked by her appearance, and asked her what had happened.

Observing his miner's clothes, she searched his face with cautious eyes and asked, "You are not a Russian soldier sent to spy on us, are you?"

Casimir almost laughed at the thought but assured her, "No, I am but a poor miner headed home to my village. But what happened? Did you fall or did someone beat you?"

"We tried to tell them, it was just a silly song my brother heard at another roadhouse many months ago," she responded, reassured by his apparent concern. "We were singing it because it had a catchy tune and the patrons liked it and started singing along with us.

A Russian colonel, Drevitz, his men called him, heard the song and went crazy. He shot my brother, beat me, and threatened to burn this place and my father's shop. We knew the song praised our Polish General Pulaski for saving Jasna Gora but we didn't know he was the stupid Drevitz talked of in the song who Pulaski had outsmarted so many times.

"He said he heard rumors that our Polish men were rushing to join Pulaski to continue the fight against the Russians and vowed to kill anyone who joined the general or helped him in any way. Then he showed us the reward posters for General Pulaski, and said he would guarantee that anyone who offered information about where he was hiding would get the money. Now, of course, no one will help him. He is a pig, a Russian pig.

Casimir felt a surge of gratitude toward the woman. A moment earlier he doubted there was anyone left who did not believe the lies about him or didn't want to collect the bounty on his head. He needed the boost her words provided, and he wanted more of it.

"I am sorry for your suffering that I may have helped cause, and I'm definitely not a Russian spy," Casimir said, holding her gaze as he removed the blackened miner's hat, sat it on the table and replaced it with the fur fez he kept in his shirt. When he adjusted it at a rakish angle on his head, the barmaid's eyes grew wide. It was the one he was wearing in the sketch on the reward poster. She gasped and Casimir raised his two fingers to his lips, cautioning her not to speak, then removed the fez and put it back in his shirt.

She leaned close to him, whispering, "If you need anything, there are people here who will help. Get word to me, I am Roksana."

Smiling and nodding to confirm her words, she clutched his hand in a warm friendly gesture and her kindness touched him so deeply that he pressed her hand in return. After putting the miner's hat back on, Casimir left quickly, fearing he might attract attention and endanger her.

He did not share the news she gave him with his men when he returned to camp. While it was uplifting to know he had some support in the area, her words told him that Drevitz was near and remained determined to find them.

For a while they were energized by the mission to join the Turks fighting against the Russians, but now the isolation in the mountains and the cold were taking a toll and he didn't want to burden them with more bad news.

They were only two days from the salt mines when a farmer gathering firewood in the forest saw them. Slipping back to his house, he saddled his horse and rode out to find one of the Russian patrols and collect the reward money. He found a Russian squad, and was taken to the main battalion of Drevitz's troops where Colonel Blukerchev was the commander in charge. The farmer said he saw a band of soldiers wearing Confederate uniforms in the forest with a small man wearing dirty civilian clothes in the lead.

Blukerchev couldn't believe his luck. From what the farmer, said there were only six or seven of them. He gave orders for his best infantrymen to move forward at a double pace and for the cannon to be pulled up front. Not wanting to take any chances of losing them, he would hit them with everything he had and take the pieces of their bodies back to Russia to claim the reward for himself, the farmer be damned.

Meanwhile, Casimir and his men rode in silence so the Russian patrols couldn't hear them. He nodded for Bazarek to ride next to him.

"It is too dangerous now, but when we stop for the night the men will be weary and heavy hearted. We can't risk a fire to warm our bodies but will you teach them one of your bawdy barroom songs to give them some cheer?"

"Yes, my general. I will also tell them the great story of Roxalena who rose from a slave girl to become the sultan's number one wife. She helped rule his entire empire. It is a true story that shows there is always hope."

"Thank you Bazarek, but you must stop referring to me as general. We can't let the Russians know who I am, and as soon as we can find other clothes the men need to get out of their Confederate uniforms. The Russians will never stop looking for us as long as there is gold offered for our heads."

"I understand, my gen . . ." he trailed off, "I mean sir," Bazarek said. He fell back to join the other men who were slowly riding along in soggy clothes and sagging spirits with bodies slouched and heads lowered. Each man was lost in his thoughts of home, family, past glories, and what the future held for fugitives.

With snow muffling the sound of the approaching horses, they did not hear the advancing Russians. Suddenly, Wolny tensed, snorted, and whinnied. It was already too late.

Casimir and the men saw they were surrounded. With only six men, Casimir had not risked sending one out to reconnoiter, a decision he now bitterly regretted.

Russian whistles alerted the entire battalion that the fugitives were found. Casimir estimated there must be at least 300 of them and his mind raced, wishing Maurice was here to analyze the situation and tell him where the enemy's weakness was. All he could do was look for cover since he would never surrender. They were on a steep wooded mountainside making it impossible to outrun the Russians on horseback with all the boulders and limbs blocking their way.

"Dismount. Set the horses free," he said, as he motioned with his pistol for them to follow him between a large rock and a gigantic boulder within a dense thicket of trees. The two rocks formed a protective pocket to shield them from the first round of enemy fire, but after that he could think of no way to repel hundreds of armed men who would overrun their position.

"There he is behind that boulder," yelled Colonel Blukerchev, "He has no horse. He can't run. Move in and take the cocky little Polish bastard. He doesn't look so cocky now, does he? Looks more like a trapped rat to me. Get him. I want that eight kilos of gold for him dead or alive, but I prefer dead. Go in and get him. I'm going to take his head back to St. Petersburg myself. To hell with Drevitz and that stupid farmer. I'll collect the money and share it with the one who brings him to me. But first I'll have some fun torturing him. Over there is that demon horse of his. Go get it. I want it crippled and then gutted alive. I'll make it pay for the men it trampled and for helping Pulaski escape so many times."

Casimir heard it all and believed that this time there was no escape. Surely, they would all perish. He turned to the men crouching next to him holding their pistols and swords and said quietly "I don't have time to properly thank you for your faithfulness and dedication to me, but I'll leave you with this, you must each decide your own fate here today for we are sure to meet God soon. As for me, I will not be captured, tortured, and killed. I will fight as long as I can and kill as many as I can, but when they close in on us, I'll throw myself into their fire and swords rather than be taken."

Casimir reasoned that this would not be suicide and he was not recommending it to his men. He hoped the Blessed Mother would agree.

"Me too, Little General, we go out together," Bazarek declared with a strong nod of his head. The other five men were silent, struggling to decide between the two terrible choices. They had believed Casimir would protect them from anything, but now they knew his luck had changed from good to bad, and each tried in his own way to prepare for the end of the Pulaski unit and his own life.

Their leader's words of hopelessness swept away their will to fight. Some pulled rosaries from their pockets and clutched them in trembling hands while others kept a watchful eye on the Russians. They were all brave, but facing death in the heat of battle was far different from crouching like cowards behind a rock, waiting to be shot or killed at the end of a bayonet in the snow.

When Colonel Blukerchev's Cossacks started firing, the bullets ricocheted off the rock in rapid succession . . . ping, ping, ping . . . and Casimir prayed aloud to the Lady of Czestochowa, "Blessed Mother grant us a quick death and a peaceful eternity," before he jumped up and shot the man standing next to Blukerschev, then ducked back behind the boulder. While he was reloading, Bazarek did the same thing, shooting Blukerschev's horse from under him causing the colonel to fall face first in the snow. Next the troublesome sergeant popped up and shot a Russian, before taking cover. Adrenalin now surged through the little group. They might be in a death struggle but they were once again the Pulaski Legion and even outnumbered a hundred to one, they would not be easy to take as the Russians soon realized when the men continued to take turns shooting, hiding, reloading, and shooting again.

They heard the colonel's order to move a cannon into place and winced, knowing it would destroy the boulder protecting them. But just as the cannon was being loaded and directed at the boulder, the snow clouds parted, allowing the sun to shine from behind Casimir directly into the eyes of the cannoneers. They were temporarily blinded and the cannon ball missed the rock by several feet, hitting a huge tree and toppling it. The large trunk of the tree fell across the stones near Casimir and his men just as a deep rumble began far up the mountain and a Russian shouted, "Avalanche, avalanche, Run! Run!"

The vibrations from the cannon started the snow moving downhill, and as it moved it picked up speed carrying everything in its path with it. It was moving too quickly to outrun and it appeared that both the Russians and Poles were doomed.

They all saw it coming, the Russians, Casimir, Bazarek, and the men. The snow crashed down the mountain uprooting trees, sweeping up rocks and scraping the earth clean as it carried it all toward them. Just before it hit them Casimir's voice yelled over the roar, "Get on the ground, flat on the ground, under the tree," and in a final act of desperation they followed his order as trees, men, horses and cannons were swallowed by the swells of snow undulating like giant ocean waves down the side of the mountain

It was unstoppable, but the thick woods surrounding the boulders served as a partial buffer and while the smaller boulder was tossed down the steep slope, the larger one held fast and the tree offered some support. When it finally stopped, Casimir and his men were buried in three feet of hard packed snow, but they were alive.

The Russians fared worse. Most of them were killed or injured. Their cries were pitiful as their comrades tried to dig them out and, mercifully, Casimir and his men were forgotten in the panic.

Casimir dug at the snow with his dagger, occasionally thrusting it straight up, hoping to feel it pierce through to open air.

Soon, he felt movement above him, heard a stomping noise, and thought the Russians were digging him out. He wondered if he had survived an avalanche only to be tortured and killed.

Then he heard a snort, felt something pawing at the snow above him and rejoiced. It was Wolny! Wolny was trying to get them out. Casimir stabbed at the snow faster and kicked at it frantically with his feet while Wolny pushed it aside with his head, his warm breath softening the snow, making it easier for Casimir to dig through it. When Casimir dug free he saw a huge Turkish hand break through the surface nearby and he and Bazarek quickly shook off their coating of snow and rushed to help dig the rest of the men out of their icy prison.

Wolny and the other horses had scattered when the cannon fire toppled the tree and were far enough away to avoid the avalanche. But they were nearby and the men gathered them up and rode off while the Russians were still frantically trying to dig out their comrades.

To Casimir's jubilant men he was invincible once more. Like most Poles, they grew up hearing about the miracles performed by the Lady of Czestochowa and now they had experienced one first hand. Riding with Casimir, they believed they rode under her protection and their hopes ran high for great victories when they joined the Turks to fight the Russians.

The surviving Russians also believed Casimir had supernatural powers and a satanic horse and all they wanted to do was to get off the mountain and away from him and Wolny. Drevitz received and passed on an exaggerated report that Casimir somehow set off an avalanche and channeled it toward the Russians while his demon horse reared up and diverted it away from the Poles. Both Drevitz and Blukerschev now believed Casimir and Wolny were the most demonic and detestable creatures on earth, and they vowed to destroy them both.

For the first time in weeks, Casimir raised the Sobieski sword over his head and trotted down the steep slopes to the valley below to head east toward Turkey. He knew the valley road was risky but he took the gamble that Russians would not spot them because his men needed to see him as their courageous leader again and he desperately needed them to view him that way.

As they approached the valley, Casimir heard a familiar voice singing with other voices quickly joining in. Bazarek was not waiting until nightfall. He was teaching the men another one of his bawdy songs and buoyed by their renewed confidence in Casimir, the men sang robustly as they picked up the refrain about the lascivious carpet merchant and the lusty wife and seven daughters of a miller. Casimir smiled. It felt good to be enjoying life again.

They risked a small campfire that night and talked of joining the Turks to fight the Russians. They would be part of a large army and certain to drive the Muscovites from Poland.

The next day the sun remained with them and Casimir took that as a good omen until fate quickly reminded him of his weakness.

Another Russian patrol had spotted them the day before but decided to wait until they were farther down the valley, away from the dangers of another avalanche, to capture them. They planned to keep their discovery secret from the Colonel in order to split the reward money between themselves rather than turn it over. But to a couple of the troops the secret was just too good to keep. To counter the story of the shameful defeat of Colonel Blukerchev's 300 men by six Poles, two of them went into the village and bragged that they had Pulaski in a trap they would spring the next day.

As Casimir and his men neared the mouth of the valley, the patrol rode down upon them from high up on the mountainside. They were suddenly surrounded by thirty armed Russians who dragged them off their horses. Struggling against the fourteen men who were holding them, Casimir and his men managed to push against them in the slick, thawing snow and slide themselves and their captors away from their mounts. Then Wolny led the charge of horses into the other sixteen Russians, trampling, kicking and even biting the terrified Cossacks until a Russian captain started firing his pistol at the other horses while calling to his men to catch Wolny. "Get him, get him, get that damn horse now!" he yelled.

The blood of slaughtered horses flowed across the white snow and into the creek, as the captain methodically killed each one. Then just as the captain turned toward the men, gun raised, Casimir gave a mighty heave, twisted free of the Cossacks holding him, drew his sword and lunged forward killing one of the soldiers with a well-aimed thrust. He had his pistol in his left hand, aiming at the captain when he heard one of his own officer's shout, "No, stop, leave him alone," and turned to see that one of the Russians was holding a knife against Bazarek's throat and a small trickle of blood was running down the Turk's neck.

"No," shouted Casimir, "no, take me. There is no money on his head. You can have gold for mine."

"No, no, Little General," interrupted Bazarek. "Let them kill me. I am worthless. You are a mighty warrior who will lead great armies one day and have glory beyond any you have known. The old gypsy in the cave saw it and told me. You must live."

When Casimir protested again, the captain looked at the soldier with the knife and raked his hand across his neck. The soldier understood and slit Bazarek's throat, but the big Turk never flinched. He flashed one last smile at Casimir as life gushed from his body.

Casimir knew he and the others would meet a similar fate except that his head would be severed and taken to Russia for the reward. Enraged, he raced toward the man with the bloody knife in his hand. The man jumped toward Casimir pointing the knife at his throat, but suddenly fell to the ground at Casimir's feet with a long bow arrow sticking through his neck.

Wheeling around, Casimir grabbed the nearest Russian and rammed his dagger between two ribs, piercing his heart as more arrows flew dropping Russians like leaves in the fall. Still mounted, the Cossack captain took deliberate aim at Wolny's kneecap and fired his pistol. The big stallion was still screaming in pain, when the captain hurled a lance into his neck before turning to escape down the road with the few remaining men in his troop who had survived.

He had made sure Casimir would have to kill his beloved horse. Casimir loaded his pistol in the hushed silence that followed. No one spoke or moved out of respect for the horse who had proven himself the best soldier among them.

Wolny was thrashing on the ground in excruciating pain but he still gazed at Casimir with a look of loyalty, love, and understanding. Casimir gave him a final rub on the forehead before backing up and firing through the brain of his devoted comrade in arms, ending his friend's pain forever.

Miraculously, everyone except Wolny and Bazarek had survived. Casimir looked up the mountainside to find the place from which the arrows were fired and spotted Roksana, the barmaid, astride a white mare with a sheaf of arrows across her back.

A woman will save you. More words from the cave dreams rang in his head.

Roksana was accompanied by six mounted men, who were also armed with arrows. Casimir recognized one of the men as the tobacco shop owner and wondered how he got there and if he had always known his true identity. Then he remembered Roksana told him her father owned the tavern and a shop and realized Roksana must have sent for him when she heard the Russians had spotted them. He gave thanks that she and the men came to their rescue but, gazing at the bodies of Bazarek and Wolny, earnestly wished they had arrived a little earlier.

When Roksana, her father, and the other men rode down, Casimir attempted to thank them but was choking back sobs over the loss of Wolny and Bazarek. Roksana broke the silence saying "My church is nearby and the priest is with us. Your friend can be buried there." Then, seeing Casimir's mournful look at Wolny, added, "I think I can talk our priest into placing your mount in a nearby grave."

After regaining his composure, Casimir replied, "You are being very kind, but no thank you. My father was buried in foreign soil and it has grieved our family. We're taking Bazarek home while the weather is still cold enough to transport his body. It is the least I can do for one who saved me so many times and was of such invaluable service to me and our cause."

"As for Wolny," he went on, "it would be good if his grave is made to look like that of a human so the Russians will not mutilate his body. He was too fine a horse and friend for that indignity. I want to bury him myself, but taking the time to do so will endanger the lives of my men. Is there a gravedigger I can hire?"

Roksana's father, the shopkeeper, stepped forward saying, "That is not necessary, General Pulaski. It will be an honor for these men and for me to take care of everything. The Muscovites will never find him, but when you come back we will show you the grave if you like. I think, perhaps we will put a grave marker that reads, 'Darius Pruneski.'

"You knew then?" Casimir asked.

"I knew you were not a miner all along. You didn't have the pale skin, red eyes, and hardened look of a miner, but I did not know, until my daughter told me of your visit to the tavern, that you were the hero of Jasna Gora. We have civilian clothes, extra food, and blankets in our saddlebags and we'll help your men roundup some of the horses the Russians left behind. But, for you, we offer my daughter's mare. She is not a warrior horse like yours, but she is fast, sure-footed, very loyal and she doesn't tire easily. Now, God Bless and God Speed. I believe patrons of a certain tavern will be talking tonight about seeing you and your men heading west rather than east."

Casimir was overwhelmed with gratitude for the kindness of this barmaid and her father and thanked them again. He directed the men to use the largest and best looking Russian horse to carry Bazarek's body back to Turkey with them. Fearing Russians would soon be after them again, they quickly departed without bothering to switch gear and saddles from their dead mounts to the Russian horses.

It was hard for Casimir to leave Wolny behind, but the new mare lived up to the shopkeeper's description. She was dependable and loyal and, in some strange way, Casimir thought of her as a blend of Bertha and Pushka.

CHAPTER SEVENTEEN

PRISON AND A NEW WAR

Turkey And France
1774-1777

Now he had only five men with him. Each felt the loss of Bazarek and Wolny, but none as much as Casimir. These, added to the deaths of his father and Frank, and the imprisonment of Antonin, made the weight of the grief he carried almost unbearable. But he shouldered it in silence, pressing on toward the Turkish border believing they would be welcomed there to assist in their fight against the Russians. He knew his men needed a purpose, and he believed fighting Russians once more was the perfect objective for them.

Suddenly his mind was jerked back to the present when an arrow flew by his ear and landed in a tall pine tree in front of him. Instinctively he pulled his musket from his holster and turned in his saddle to see where if came from. Silhouetted against the blinding sun he saw the outline of Roksana and her father. They had a large group with them.

He rode back to them. "I welcome the sight of you, but why have you followed us?"

Roksana pointed to the back of their horses where the Russian captain, who shot Wolny and ordered Bazarek killed, was being forced to march in the snow with the remnant of his patrol.

Casimir had always treated prisoners kindly, but this was a different matter. Roksana and her men moved their horses aside as Casimir rode back to where the captain stood. He looked at him, raised his pistol and fired, shooing the captain between the eyes. Showing no remorse, he then rode back to Roksana.

"Thank you. Leave his men to find their way on foot in the snow. Do not risk your life for me again. Your death is more burden than I could bear."

"May the Blessed Virgin Mother protect you General. You have given our people cause to hope again. Some of them will be joining you," she said, as she and her men turned and rode back into the sun. Casimir and his officers heard the Russian patrol troops begging not to be left behind as they rode toward Turkey, but he paid them no mind. It was the cruelest thing he ever did to prisoners.

Exaggerated tales spread about the Lady of Czestochowa miracle that saved the Pulaski band and Casimir's mystical horse Wolny who pulled them from the snow. Soon it was told that Casimir had called forth an avalanche that saved him from more than a thousand of Blukerschev's Russians and that his little group killed more than a hundred Muscovites who ambushed them on the road shortly afterwards. Both stories were gross exaggerations, but the villagers needed and wanted a hero who would stand up to the hated Russians. Roksana rejoiced and was tempted to write a song for the patrons to celebrate Casimir's victory over the Russians, but, remembering the rest of her family, she composed it in her heart, and kept it there.

Men started appearing from behind trees along their route asking to join the great Pulaski troops and each addition boosted everyone's spirits. The new troops were trained by Casimir's seasoned officers as they travelled, and by the time they approached the Turkish border their ranks had grown to a troop of forty-five competent men.

Casimir and his five officers rode ahead, taking the horse carrying Bazarek's body with them. Casimir hoped he would meet a Turkish officer or dignitary who could help him locate his father's grave on the Turkish side of the border. He and his men were still wearing the clothes Roksana gave them. They were out of uniform and riding horses with saddles showing a Russian army insignia. A Turkish patrol, thinking they were Russian spies, stopped them.

"Halt," yelled the Turkish Captain. "Why do Russian spies try to cross our border?"

"We are not Russians. We came to fight them. I am Casimir Pulaski, a Polish General, and these are my officers. We came to join your fight against the Russians," Casimir indignantly shouted back.

"Yeah, and I am the grand Sultan Abul Hamid," laughed the captain and his men. It was absurd to think that the legendary Casimir Pulaski would be riding a Russian horse and be with a few scraggly looking men in civilian clothes.

"My father died in one of your prisons because he defended our homeland against the Russian invasion, just as you are doing now. Please take me to someone who can help find his grave, and then let us help you defeat our mutual enemy, the Russians."

"If your father was in a Turkish prison, he must have been a spy also. Now go. Before I order my men to shoot all of you and keep those horses that look better than you do." At that the Turkish soldiers cocked the rifles aimed at him.

"Take your dead friend with you. And, go now."

"He was one of your countrymen. He was a hero fighting against the Russians with us. We brought him so he could be buried in his country. Let us do that for a brave man."

"No, go."

"Then please take his body and bury him," Casimir pleaded.

The captain motioned for one of his men to look at the body slung over the large Russian horse and confirm it was that of a Turk. When the soldier nodded yes, the captain said. "Why did you kill him and bring him here?"

"We didn't kill him," Casimir shouted in exasperation. "We can pay to have him properly buried. Sergeant, get some of the salt from the saddle bags."

He handed the salt to the captain and said, "this is worth a lot of money as you know. Will you take it to see that he has a proper burial?"

The captain, moistened his finger, stuck it to the white grains and raised it to his lips to make sure it was salt. "We will see that our brother, who you murdered, has a Turkish funeral and burial. Now go."

And with that, the Turkish troops grabbed the reins of their horses and escorted them several kilometers back into Poland.

There was nothing to do but submit. Casimir thought they were fortunate to be released since they could have been shot as spies.

He couldn't believe all his hopes for the future had been undone by some Russian saddles. He pondered the problem and his next move, while he and his men camped along a river that night.

The next morning, he had the answer. He ordered the sergeant to take the new recruits into Istanbul, infiltrate the city, learn details about the fight between the Russians and Turks and send the information in dispatches to Roksana's tavern. He thought she would be willing to have her father's couriers forward them to him.

Continuing his instructions, he said, "I have received a promise of money from Claude-Charles de Peyssonnel, a French diplomat who is to send it to a Darius Pruneski. It will be delivered to the Aromatic Tobacco Shop located along the wall leading to the Galata Tower. Go there and wait for the money. If you need to use some of it to raise men and arms, do so, and then rejoin us. I'll send a courier to let you know where we are. Prince Karol Radziwill may also send funds. If that money arrives do not spend it. I need it to pay debts. I will take only the other four officers with me since we must travel as fast and inconspicuously as possible. Understood sergeant?"

This time the sergeant didn't argue, saying only "Yes, general, I understand." Staying inside a warm tobacco shop was plainly preferable to the harshness they had endured since leaving Krakow.

They rode off in opposite directions, with Casimir heading to France figuring that if he could meet de Peyssonnel and Radziwill personally they might further support him by recommending a commission for him in the French army. *The French are always at war with the English, Austrians, or some other country and they need an officer with my superior experience and leadership abilities,* he reasoned. Still disappointed that he was unable to join the Turks to fight the Russians or to find his father's grave, he was comforted by knowing Bazarek would be buried at home.

Longing for friendly faces and familiar surroundings, he risked a side trip to Krakow to meet his sister, Joanna. The sight of the Wawel Castle thrilled him as it always had and he gazed longingly at the entrance gate. . . *If only I could stay here and ride out with troops to confront the Russians.* The pull of his homeland and the need to lead troops into battle was strong.

Most of Joanna's news was good.

"The Russians are still offering a reward for you but they are not sending as many patrols to find you in Poland," she said. "For some reason, patrons in a tavern near where you escaped the avalanche said they saw you headed west and someone else said they overhead one of your men say you were going to

Spain," causing Casimir to chuckle who again gave thanks for Roksana and her friends.

Joanna brought his uniforms and some money with her but warned, "Casimir you must be careful. It's risky to put on a Bar Confederation uniform, especially a general's. Even though the Russians aren't patrolling as heavily as they were, there are plenty of people who will turn you in or kill you for the reward money."

"I need to show the men I am still their leader," he replied, while in reality, he needed to boost his own morale by wearing a splendidly decorated uniform that made him appear dashing. He felt better as soon as he put it on. *It's so much better to be a general — the great General Pulaski — than to be travelling incognito in the dirty clothes of a dead miner or a townsman,* he thought, *it's worth the risk.*

"How is Mother and what news have you heard of Antonin?"

"Mother is in good health and misses you, father, and Frank terribly, but her faith consoles her and Antonin's letters help."

Perplexed by her response, Casimir asked, "But Joanna how can Antonin's letters from a horrid Russian prison be of solace to her?"

"I don't understand it either Kas," she answered, shaking her head, "but he insists he is well treated and is friends with his captors. He sends little stories about them and the freedoms they grant him. He is actually invited to the homes of the nobility and is apparently somewhat of a celebrity. And, Casimir . . . " she hesitated before going on, "in his last letter he even wrote that he was considering joining the Russian Army."

Casimir was astounded. While he was thankful that Antonin was not being tortured in prison, he felt his brother's friendship with the Russians was a betrayal to the cause their father and Frank had died for and thought there must be some explanation for his behavior.

He wondered if it was all lies the guards forced him to write and, if not, what else could convince him to socialize and possibly join Frank's murderers. He hoped Antonin had a plan that he couldn't share with the family.

"He wouldn't do such things without good reason," Casimir muttered, a twinge of bitterness in his voice. He tried to put the puzzle of Antonin's behavior aside by asking, "And, Joanna, what of you? What are your plans? Will you marry? Is there someone you are betrothed to?"

"I join the Sisters of Charity at Jasna Gora in April," she said, smiling at her brother.

Casimir was delighted to hear the news. While he would love to have nieces and nephews, the family was devoted to their faith. It was appropriate that one member join the Mother Church and there was no better place than Jasna Gora to serve.

"You make me proud my dear sister," he said wrapping her in a warm embrace before saying, "Now I must be on my way. Please give my love to Paul and Maurice and let them know that I am going to France. I will send for them as soon as I start forming a new cavalry there." Then reluctantly he mounted the white mare and rode away, they both knew it might be the last time they saw each other.

His reception in France was barely better than the one he received in Turkey but at least he wasn't accused of being a Russian spy. He soon learned that de Peyssonnel and Radziwill did not want their names linked with someone accused of attempting to assassinate a king.

"Monsieur Pulaski, I regret that I cannot be of further service to you," was de Peyssonnel's greeting to him.

"I appreciate your using a fictitious name to receive the money I sent to Turkey and I hope you will keep my support a secret between us. Our king grows more unpopular each day and fears losing his throne. He could easily suspect anyone assisting you of sympathizing with one who tried to overthrow his own king. I hope you do understand."

"But I did not . . . ," Casimir started to proclaim his innocence of the charges against him, but was stopped by de Peyssonnel's raised, lace-ruffled hand.

"Of course, Monsieur, I do understand. But had not the Duchess of Courland's letter been so persuasive I would not have sent you the money, I did. But now I must think of my family's position and safety."

"I would never want to endanger anyone who acted on my behalf," Casimir said softly with a downcast look just as a doorman arrived to escort him out by a side door. "I understand and thank you for your past generosity to our cause."

At least de Peysonnel saw him and explained the situation. Prince Radziwill either ignored or declined all requests Casimir made to see him.

He approached several French officers about joining the army to lead a cavalry legion. Rather than receiving the admiration he expected from fellow military leaders, he was received coldly, and later ridiculed behind his back. They resented the fame he had achieved having heard the songs and stories about his feats and feared he would compete with them for the top commissions.

It did not help that Casimir boasted of his many successes against the Russians, his superiority over much larger forces, and his military genius. The French accused him of arrogance, haughtiness, and a desire to start at the top without first proving himself. Most of the charges were true. What they ignored was his brilliance on the battlefield and mastery of military strategy.

"Monsieur Pulaski, we might have something for you in my infantry division. You would be walking with the rest of the troops and would have no need of a horse. If you survive a couple of years you might rise to corporal," Taunted a snobbish colonel.

255

After a few weeks of such rejections, Casimir decided it might be better to be called a Russian spy. He knew he was in a battle against jealousy and fear that he could not win. He gave up the attempt to secure a commission and took his men farther south. They had been subjected to enough cold, both from the weather and humans.

Again, Casimir and his men were unwanted and were left with little to occupy them physically or mentally, but the men stayed with him. He was touched by their loyalty and provided for them as best he could while trying to survive in a foreign land with no employable skills other than leading troops into battle, skills he was barred from using because of jealousy and mistrust. To fight the loneliness and depression he turned to drinking and playing cards. His losses soon exceeded his wins at the card table since he was too despondent to do his normal, almost automatic, card counting. In desperation, he borrowed from unscrupulous money lenders to support himself and his officers, to whom he felt a deep obligation.

He had no means to repay what he borrowed, since the money from de Peysonnel never made it out of Turkey and he assumed the assertive sergeant either spent it trying to raise troops or partying. Whatever the reason, the sergeant wasn't rushing to join them.

Days turned into months, and two years passed without any substantial support or sponsorship materializing for his army. Still mourning the loss of his father and brother, his country and his wealth, along with his family's prestigious name, his dream of leading a great army began fading.

He was growing older and less famous as the months dragged by with no change in his situation. His losses from gambling and other debts grew and, for the first time, Casimir realized that total defeat was possible.

When his creditors weren't paid, he and his men were seized and thrown into a dark hole in the French debtors' prison.

Although the debts were his, his men were jailed so they could not help him escape. It was a dark, dang, and dangerous place full of heartless thugs.

The French army officers, remembering his haughtiness, mocked his fall from the aristocracy and encouraged the guards to torment him. They gave him one of the filthiest cells where thieves, rapists, and murderers fought him for the meager food and water rations while mocking him as "the great general who was going to command all our French forces."

But his worst fears were realized when the guards shouted, "Pull that fancy uniform off him and let's see what he has to be so proud of," taunting him as they stripped him of his finely tailored uniform and exposed the secret of his anatomy.

The guffaws of the guards and ruffians were far more painful to the proud Pulaski than all the physical abuse they inflicted on him. To add to his misery, they forced him to wear a ragged burlap tunic, further humiliating the man who was always so proud of his appearance and hygiene, even on the battlefield.

He was always able to ignore pain and adversity and rise above it to win another battle but his degradation and depression reached even his limit when he was forced to endure such humiliation, and then to watch helplessly as his own captain was brutally beaten by six cutthroat thieves. It took eight other ruffians to beat Casimir into submission as he fought to defend Captain Monski who had been stripped and forced spread-eagled on the floor. They assaulted the defenseless officer repeatedly from their pure hatred of anyone who showed superior intellect, courage, and civility.

One in particular, a Moroccan called Boshka, smirked at Casimir, as he pointed between Casimir's legs, then laughed while cupping his gigantic balls in his hands and thrusting them at him. Boshka then repeated the action before exposing his oversized penis and shoving it between Monski's legs.

Suffocating, all-consuming depression drove Casimir to thoughts of suicide since it seemed the only way to end this torment and ridicule. Even if he managed to leave this quagmire of filth and abuse, nothing good waited for him outside the dungeon's walls. Not only had he failed to bring glory to his family, he had further tarnished the Pulaski name. Now he felt useless since he was unable to either help or console his captain or to protect his family from more heartache. The press of hopelessness and despair were overwhelming for the proud man who had accomplished so much in his short life. But his faith remained strong and, believing suicide was an unforgiveable sin that brought everlasting torment and damnation, he pushed thoughts of ending his life aside and vowed to endure this test of his faith with as much dignity as the situation would allow.

Just as he had so often eluded death on the battlefield, Casimir miraculously escaped this miserable fate when Paul Dobrachek raised enough funds to secure his release. After washing the prison filth and stench from his body, he donned the fine new clothes Paul brought him and hurried out the prison gates to meet him. Paul was shocked at his friend's appearance, even in the colorful uniform. There was no trace of the old, carefree, boasting Casimir in the haggard man who grasped his hand saying, in a subdued and serious voice, "My friend you have saved me from a fate far, far worse than any we faced on the battlefield. The words, "Thank you" cannot convey my gratitude, but please know I will be forever grateful and indebted to you."

Paul, equally serious, replied, "I know you would have done more for me." Then, quickly flashing the old smile that so often passed between them, said, "To set me free, you would have stormed the prison, climbed to the roof, poured buckets of oil on the heads of the guards and then ordered wagons of burning hay pushed through the doors. Of course, with all that oil and fire I would not have survived but you would have tried." Their old camaraderie returned as if their years apart were but a day and they walked in step to a local café for lunch.

Casimir was surprised and thrilled to see the Duchess of Courland, Franciszka Kransinki, escorted by a Courland Guard, rushing to him from across the room. His heart raced with excitement as they greeted each other, clasping outstretched hands and brushing lips against turned cheeks. For a moment, he thought he must still be in prison wrapped in some cruel dream and waited to be awakened by a kick in the ribs from one of the brutish guards. But the affection and concern shining in her emerald eyes were real, and she had a new warmth and wisdom that came with maturity, adding a new layer to her already breath-taking beauty.

He noted that, as always, she was dressed elegantly, but in a more mature style. She wore heavy gold brocade and maroon velvet rather than the feathery light pink and blue silks that in former years had made her seem to float across floors. The gold coin still hung around her neck and pearl hairpins matched the earrings she wore.

"Oh Kas," she cried, "I have suffered such nightmares, imagining the treatment you were enduring in that terrible place. When we found out you were arrested, Paul and I never stopped working to secure your release."

"My duchess, my sweet duchess," he sighed. "It is so good to see you again. Better friends do not exist. Despite my troubles, I am more fortunate than most men."

With great restrain, he resisted raking the food of the first decent meal he had had in months directly into his mouth. His sense of etiquette was strong, especially in the presence of Franciszka, and he forced enough time between each bite of the delicious roast beef to tell them of his disappointments in Turkey and France.

"I don't understand it. Don't they want to be strong? Don't the Turks want to win against the Russians? And the French. They're always fighting with someone. They need a leader like me. Their weak, stupid, petty and jealous officers will cause them to lose wars.

Leaning closer to Casimir and Franciszka, Paul excitedly proclaimed, "There is a bigger fight, underway, Kas. It is in America. The rebelling colonists are welcoming foreign troops to help them fight for freedom against the British. They are untrained and untested volunteers fighting against the strongest military nation in the world, yet there is a chance they could win. The British have to transport their men, armaments and supplies across the ocean, they are weakened by debt from wars they have fought over the last century, and they are fighting on unfamiliar foreign soil. Some of the American natives have joined the colonists to fight against them and it looks like the French may join them as well.

"Still, the trained British soldiers outnumber the inexperienced troops of the colonists. They are in desperate need of foreign support and strong military leaders with new ideas. This sounds like your kind of fight, Kas."

Casimir lost interest in the roast beef as the words flew from his mouth so fast, Paul could barely keep up with his questions.

"How would I get there? Who is in command? Where will I get the money for passage? I have no troops, or horses, or uniforms but I must get there before the French take all the leadership roles."

At the word uniform, both Franciszka and Paul joined in a laugh.

"Oh Kas, I see you still know what is important," Paul teased. "Of course, you and your men must have flashy uniforms with matching capes and hats. It's a good thing you're in France, where silks and brocades are so abundant."

Now laughing at himself, Casimir responded, "Oh Paul, you know what I mean. It's just the kind of cause I love. It's a fight for freedom. Of course, I want to go, but how can I do it?"

"Well," Paul replied, "we have started to work on that, since we thought you would be interested. Franciszka used her considerable influence, or perhaps I should say pressure, to convince some of our wealthy relatives and members of other prestigious families throughout Europe to support you. In fact, that's also how much of the money for your release was secured."

"Support?" asked Casimir. "What kind of support?"

"With their help, Paul was able to arrange a meeting for you with Monsieur Benjamin Franklin, the American Minister to France." Franciszka interjected, becoming as excited as the two men. "Franklin is legendary here in France for his inventions and humor as well as his eye for pretty ladies. But he is also practical, wise, and patriotic when it comes to gaining freedom for America. He is anxious to find men willing to fight in their revolution against the British. Kas, if you can distinguish yourself there, your place in history will be assured in the New World and you can return home a hero."

"When and where is this meeting to take place?" shouted Casimir across the table.

"Next month in Versailles," answered Paul. "That means you have four weeks to have a new uniform made and to polish your sword, which, by the way, I was able to bribe one of the guards into selling me."

"So, what do you think, blue jacket with white pants, or blue pants with white jacket?" joked Casimir.

"I don't know, Kas, you decide, but make sure you're not too big for those pants when you see Franklin," Paul countered, as all three laughed.

It had been a day that began in the nadir of his life and by evening he could see the zenith. He couldn't remember a more pleasant afternoon, spent with friends, free again, and now with a renewed hope for a glorious future.

Casimir found it hard to say goodbye to Franciszka but was grateful for the few precious hours he spent with her. After she left, he became serious as he turned to Paul to ask for a favor.

"My friend, some bad things happened in the prison to me and to my men. A big brute named Boshka was especially mean and with others got information that could be damaging to me and my family. Is there anything you can do through your connections here to keep them quiet?"

"Don't worry Kas," said Paul. "I'll handle it. I may not have wanted to carry horse manure to a rooftop for you, but this kind of filth I'm happy to remove, in spite of the risk and smell."

He didn't know how, but Casimir was confident Paul would take care of his problems at the prison since he had never failed him. Casimir thought once again about how blessed he was to have Paul as a friend.

It was a glorious morning splashed with sunlight that made the spray from the hundreds of fountains on the lawns of Versailles sparkle. The palace was grander than anything Casimir had ever seen and he wondered how anyone could afford such opulence. A footman dressed in finer livery than his own uniform ushered him into a dazzling room of baroque furniture upholstered in gold and pink brocade. The walls were covered with the same cloth. Floor-to-ceiling windows looked out on landscaped lawns with gardens that stretched as far as the eye could see. Water danced in the fountains, cascading into pools where brightly colored, imported koi fish swam. It was a dramatic change from his putrid prison cell of a few short weeks earlier.

Five French women with powdered wigs stacked high on their heads and red rouge flushing their cheeks surrounded the elderly Franklin when Casimir arrived. The women wore elaborate dresses made of silk, with lace and ribbons that formed borders on their sleeves, necklines and bodices. Their tight fitting under corsets pressed their breasts so high that they threatened to spill over the tops of their plunging necklines. He was sure the American Minister was hoping for just such an event as he luxuriated in their company with a perpetual twinkle in his eyes while the giggling ladies placed chocolates on his tongue. After each bite, he smacked his lips and then puckered them to receive a light kiss.

Casimir saw another, younger man, sitting in a large French provincial chair watching the scene with amusement. He was well dressed and wore a finely styled wig, but had a seasoned, suntanned face that suggested days spent outdoors in physical activity. At the same time, he seemed comfortable in the midst of the palace's opulent furnishings.

Franklin greeted Casimir warmly and invited him, in English, to join him in a cognac. Casimir, who spoke no English, declined with a shake of his head, as Franklin switched to French, a language both he and Casimir understood. When possible, Franklin preferred to speak in English since most of the ladies couldn't understand what he was saying and he could conduct business and enjoy their company simultaneously. Now, he reluctantly asked them to leave the room, promising to rejoin them in a few minutes, then began conversing with Casimir in French.

The ladies lingered to look admiringly at Casimir, who was resplendent in his new uniform consisting of white pants, blue jacket and a blue and white striped vest, with the highly- polished Sobieski sword hanging at his side. He knew Paul would have laughed outrageously at his vanity, but it felt good to look striking again. If there was any doubt about how he looked, the ladies removed it when they asked Franklin, "And the new man, will we see him as well?"

"No," replied the ambassador. "I want all your attention for myself and he may distract you. I don't want you distracting him either because he has important work to do. Now off with you ladies. I have work to do also, but I'll find you later, my pretties."

Then Franklin turned to Casimir to say "Monsieur Pulaski, allow me to introduce you to one of my countrymen, a member of the Continental Congress, Mr. Silas Deane. Mr. Deane, this is the famous Casimir Pulaski who I hope to convince to join our cause."

"I am very pleased to meet you General Pulaski," Deane said in French. "I have heard much of you, and if time permits I would like to talk to you about your defense of Jasna Gora and your many other accomplishments. Now I must take my leave of you both. I have a meeting with Jefferson in a few minutes." Then, turning to Franklin he said, "Ben, as always, it has been most entertaining. Thank you for the uh . . . tea."

Casimir realized this man was a close friend of Franklin's and could be influential so he held out a hand to him and said, "Thank you Monsieur Deane, I would enjoy meeting with you when circumstances bring us together." Silas Deane departed, leaving Franklin and Casimir to talk.

"Monsieur Pulaski, my country is young, but rich in natural resources and brave men," began Franklin. "We are facing a powerful adversary with professional soldiers, the strongest naval fleet in the world, the newest made cannons and the latest muskets, plus a monarch's wealth behind them. We have volunteer militiamen who only a year ago were farmers, merchants and tradesmen. They bring their own horses and equipment, some of it antiquated, and they commit only for a year of fighting. That's all they can sacrifice away from their farms and shops. Our finances are limited, so much so, that I used my personal funds to secure wagons and horses for use in the war effort.

But we are resolved to fight to the death for our independence from the tyrannical Mother Country. She has become too mettlesome and too greedy for men who sacrificed everything to carve out a living in what was a wild and dangerous place to tolerate. We received little help from our sovereign to succeed and now that we have succeeded we feel no obligation to contribute our wealth to his unearned lavish lifestyle. We need natural leaders like you with fresh ideas and the drive to overcome what will seem insurmountable challenges, along with the experience to train, discipline, and lead disparate groups of men. I hear that you have witnessed tyranny from a distant monarch and were victorious over superior numbers on the battlefield so surely you can identify with our cause. If I help you get to America will you help General Washington with your tactics fighting on horseback?"

Casimir was incredulous. Benjamin Franklin, a man revered on both sides of the Atlantic, was offering him the chance to redeem his life despite knowing he was a disgraced man in most of Europe where the royal families thought he was guilty of an attempt on their king's life. What Franklin was offering was a chance for him to restore honor to his family's name and at the same time, prove the value of his cavalry tactics in battle. His mind was exploding with the possibilities. This was a chance for him to once more ride triumphantly at the head of his Pulaski Legion, the most glorious and effective legion in the world.

"Monsieur Franklin, I am honored by your trust and confidence," responded Casimir. "You have no doubt heard the slanderous lies that were spread by Empress Catherine about my family and me. The British Ambassador to Russia brought Augustus Poniatowski to Catherine's court in hopes that a romance would develop. It did, and she later placed him on the throne of Poland. The Russian invasions that followed cost me my father, two brothers, many dear friends and my family's good name. I welcome the chance to fight any monarch who tries to subjugate people. I have little regard for the British and their interfering in the governments of other countries. I will gladly leave for America as soon as passage can be arranged."

"General Pulaski, I was loyal to the English monarchy longer than many of my contemporaries, but now I have little use for kings. The charges against you are minor in comparison to the feats you accomplished fighting against much larger forces in Poland. To me, and to General Washington I hope, that is the important thing. You can win battles. And that is what the Continentals sorely need.

"Ah to be young and spirited, and to have an adventuresome soul with a strong body to support it." Franklin smiled, then added, "Sir, I will prepare letters of introduction for you to present upon your arrival to the General. My secretary will have them ready for you tomorrow. A privateer, the Massachusetts, sails in five days from Le Croisic, near Nantes. You will have full passage on it."

Then, with a mischievous grin, he said, "By the way, I do enjoy that little jingle about you and the Russian General Drevitz. I hope they'll be singing new ones about you in America. Godspeed my friend."

"Merci, Monsieur Franklin, I will begin preparing for the trip immediately."

Casimir bowed to Franklin and walked across the room. He turned around at the doorway, planning to offer the senior Franklin a salute but continued on when he saw the octogenarian playfully tiptoeing across the carpet to the door through which the ladies disappeared earlier.

CHAPTER EIGHTEEN

LANDING IN AMERICA

JULY 1777

The monotony of sailing weighed heavily upon Casimir. While he enjoyed the evening story swapping with Sultan, the days dragged by slower than the spring thaw in the Pelicia River at Winiary. He spent the days bonding with Visner, rubbing, brushing, feeding and telling him grand stories of his father, Pushka, and how Franciszka sent Pearlina, his mother, to the Pulaski Family Estate. Even though the horse didn't understand, he sensed he was meant to be with Casimir and they would always be bound to one another.

To relieve his boredom, Casimir picked up the leather pouch holding the stack of letters Paul gave him to be delivered in America and untied the straps that held them in place. There was the letter from the Marquis de Lafayette's wife, Adrienne, which Paul had told him about, along with several merchants' letters regarding business transactions. As he thumbed through the stack he noticed a familiar scent. The aroma of Christmas spices, spring roses and fresh cut grass entered his nose and he breathed it in as deeply as he did the first day Franciszka went riding with him. Hurriedly digging through the rest of the documents, he spotted it near the bottom and held his breath. It was a letter from Franciszka.

The memory of their first meeting, their first ride together, her perfume and her astounding intellect and beauty tore at his heart. He missed her so. His hands trembled as he gently removed the Courland wax seal and opened the folded paper. He read:

> My dearest warrior and protector,
>
> You cannot imagine the sadness in my heart when I think about the great distance between us. My fondness for you has never, will never, diminish. I pray for your safety each night and your triumphant return to Poland. Remember our conversations about strategy over strength and the lessons of the great generals—Xerxes, Attila, Genghis Khan, Caesar, Alexander, Philip and the 300 Spartans. Just like you, they were creative, unpredictable, fearless and never gave up. They always went into battle knowing they would win, even when outnumbered. You will also win and return to the ones who love and miss you.
> Franciszka

He loved her the moment he saw her when he was fourteen. Being with her at the Courland Estate after her marriage to Duke Karl was bittersweet. He enjoyed her company but it was torture not to openly declare his love for her and hold her. He wondered at the time why his father had subjected him to such agony by sending him to spend time with her and her husband.

When he asked his father why he sent him to Courland, Joseph responded, "Ah, you were older then and I thought you had outgrown your infatuation with her. I wanted you to learn about diplomacy and politics from Duke Karl as well as some of the finer points of etiquette, music, literature and, much to your chagrin, dancing while at his court."

"Your mother feared reigniting the romance between you and Franciszka. She's a wise woman, your mother, but I assured her you would be too busy watching the Russian Cossacks and working in the Court as a page to be distracted by any woman. She reluctantly agreed to let you go."

"I still think it was beneficial for you. You returned to Winiary with a greater knowledge of Russian army tactics, some expertise in dancing and a pretty good knowledge of history, at least the parts that dealt with great generals."

Casimir was struck by how he missed his father's humor and wisdom, and how much he missed Franciszka. They were bound by an unbreakable bond. She was his mentor, counselor, adviser and solace. Franciszka was the one who interceded on his behalf when his arrogance and stubbornness alienated other officers and leaders of the Bar Confederation. She always gave sound advice, and that advice reinforced his father's counsel.

When he picked up her letter to read it again, a medallion fell to the floor. It was gold with imprints of Jasna Gora on one side and the Black Madonna on the other. The medallion was meant to provide its wearer with the Blessed Virgin Mother's protection. It was the coin he had seen hanging near Franciszka's heart so many times.

When his father left for Turkey, he gave his watch and gold chain to Casimir saying, "Keep this for me until I return." Casimir thought little of it at the time. In retrospect, it seemed his father had a premonition that he would not be returning to Poland. Casimir had little need for watches, so he gave it to Antonin, but he kept the chain and fashioned it into a necklace that he always wore. Now he unfastened it, threaded it through the loop on the medallion and put it back around his neck.

Franciszka's letter meant more to him than she could have imagined. It reinforced his pledge to deliver all the letters to the husbands and sons who might be as uplifted as he to receive news from home and loved ones.

He spent considerable time thinking about his arrival in America and how to approach General Washington. It was critical that he quickly secure funding to outfit and train his new American cavalry. He remembered what Paul said about Lafayette possibly helping him. Unlike Franklin, Washington was not fluent in French and would not have spoken it even if he could. He was a patriot who believed the local language should be spoken. Casimir wondered how he could convince the general of the advantage his cavalry would have over the British if the two had no common language.

He knew the British mode of warfare was to walk stiffly across battlefields in straight lines. They would be no match for charging horses whose riders were firing pistols, swinging swords and pushing long lances. He thought Lafayette could be persuaded to interpret for him, and decided to deliver his letter first.

At the breaking of dawn on the forty-eighth day at sea, land was sighted off the coast of Massachusetts, although "land" might not be the best description. The first sightings were of giant rocks marching out into the ocean from shore, but even rocks were a welcome sight to the weary crew and passengers. Visner, catching the scent of land, whinnied his desire to be free. Casimir was filled with gratitude for the safe passage but also had a good deal of trepidation about whether hostility or hospitality awaited him on shore. It could be either.

By early afternoon, Captain John Fisk had expertly maneuvered past the boulders and entered Marblehead Bay where Tucker's Wharf jutted out from shore. Townspeople lined the wharf watching the landing of their own American privateer, a big event for their small fishing village.

Captain Fisk could not risk running aground on the stone sentinels in the shallow harbor and anchored beyond them and waited for workmen on the dock to row out to the ship to take passengers, crew, and cargo ashore. But Casimir had an unusual problem. The long boat was not built to hold a horse. The animal's weight and unpredictable movements might sink the boat, drowning all aboard. The ship couldn't sail to another deep-water port where the horse could disembark because the British fleet was patrolling the coast. Everyone on board had witnessed the bond between Casimir and his horse. No one suggested it, but Visner may have to be abandoned.

With a French crewman acting as interpreter, Casimir asked Captain Fisk, who was anxious to be on shore himself, to "Let everyone go ahead of me. I'll get my horse ashore. I promise it won't take long. One attempt is all I ask."

Fisk, still smarting from his quick chess defeat by Casimir, carefully considered the request. He admired Casimir's bravery in Poland and his interest in the ship and navigation. He had a great intellect, after all he had beaten the captain soundly at chess, and his dedication to his military profession was impressive. Knowing Casimir was an extraordinary horseman, he agreed to give him one chance to get the horse ashore.

Casimir went below and returned leading Visner from his dark quarters in the hold onto the main deck. After so many days in semi-darkness, Visner was skittish. The bright daylight and the urgency he sensed in his master were frightening.

Casimir slung the pouch of letters over his shoulder, jumped onto Visner and prodded him toward the steep cargo ramp. The horse, now emaciated and weakened by the long voyage, balked and reared up with a high-pitched squeal. He tossed his head furiously from side to side as his hooves landed and skidded from slit to slit on the steep board ramp. Casimir kept a firm grip on the rein and gave him a strong nudge with his knee while leaning backward giving weight to his rear for traction. "Go Visner, go. We can do this." They inched forward.

As they entered the water, Visner's eyes widened and he whinnied wildly. Casimir knew he had never experienced salt water or ocean waves before. With no other option, the horse started swimming. Casimir slipped into the water beside him, directing him toward land as he clung to his tail, letting Visner pull him through the water. Casimir could see that the distance to shore was too far for a horse in Visner's condition to swim. He knew a longboat could pick him up, but he would lose Visner.

Then he spotted a small spit of sand behind one of the giant boulders and eased Visner toward it. Casimir crawled onto the lifesaving land and scrambled on top of the rock. Visner tried to follow, but worn out, with salt water blinding his eyes and burning his nostrils, he couldn't find firm footing in the sand. The gallant stallion struggled and struggled again and again only to fall back into the water. Casimir knew Visner would not survive another attempt. Almost as frightened as the horse, he jumped from the rock onto Visner's back, shouting "forward Visner, forward!" The horse leapt forward, found footing, and pulled wearily out of the water.

A huge roar went up from those on shore. "Hurrah, hurrah, hurrah," rang across the water and up the hillside of the town.

But Visner was now too weak to reach the distant shore. Casimir wasn't about to leave him and was saying, "Good boy, good boy, I'll get you ashore."

Fortunately, the tide was not rising onto their little island and the sea was calm, but that began to change as the hours went by and the sun started disappearing behind the buildings of the wharf. Night was fast approaching. Casimir looked westward toward shore and saw one of the flat boats used to haul cargo moving in his direction. Two teenagers, Samuel Abbot and his cousin, Abe Hawkins, boys of an age where the thrill of adventure outweighed caution, were rowing the big boat toward them.

They reached the isolated pair as the fading red glow in the western sky hung over Tucker's Wharf. There was just enough light left to guide them home.

John Bishop, the aide General Washington sent to meet Pulaski, was fuming on shore. He thought, "What an idiot! Who would bring a horse all the way from France when there are plenty of good horses in America? It is just my bad luck to be sent to babysit this foolish foreigner while General Washington plans his next battle." He cursed his fate for being left out because of this stupid man and his horse of all things.

When the boys reached the sandbar, they saw Casimir's uniform and were immediately in awe, the white horse and its decorative saddle only deepened their admiration. Abe snapped to attention and saluted Casimir and Samuel bravely stepped forward and stuck out his trembling hand. "Abe Hawkins and Samuel Abbot at your service sir," shouted Abe.

Casimir didn't understand a word they said, but he understood bravery and respect when he saw it. He straightened his back and shoulders and saluted each and then motioned for them to drag the flat boat up on the sand for him to climb in while pulling Visner's reins forward. The horse hesitated for a second, then followed, again trusting Casimir. With constant encouragement, the horse stood stone-still and forty minutes later they stepped ashore to roaring cheers from the townspeople. Everyone on the flatboat was a hero that evening.

But Major John Bishop did not cheer. He just wanted to get back to General Washington to butter him up to get a promotion to Brigadier General. He wanted that position and he wasn't going to let this little Polish moron delay him.

Neither Casimir nor Visner were surefooted ashore after being at sea so long. The land rolled and pitched like the ship for both man and horse. Visner stumbled on the cobblestones and looked more like an underfed plow horse than a fine cross-bred

Arabian stallion. Casimir knew he had not made a good first impression on Washington's aide.

Bishop smugly stepped up to Casimir proudly saying, "I am General Washington's aide, Major John Bishop. I am to take you to the general tomorrow morning, post haste."

"Casimir Pulaski at your service," Casimir replied in French.

"Yes, yes, you nutter," said Bishop. "I know who you are."

Obviously exasperated, Bishop motioned Casimir to follow him. The major walked with a decided limp making it possible for Casimir and Visner to keep up with him though they didn't yet have their land legs. They entered King Street, which ran up a hill from the wharf. Flickering candles in lanterns lit the way as they struggled upward. Smiling citizens waved when they passed but Casimir sensed this did not please John Bishop. He certainly didn't greet them with the warmth and charm most Poles extend and Casimir wondered if bad upbringing or something else was the cause of Bishop's agitation.

As in Europe, flowers of every color blossomed in window boxes and in the small front yards but, unlike the aristocratic brownstone and brick homes with which he was familiar, these houses were square, wooden, two or three-story structures, painted dark blue, yellow, or deep red. He thought, *Maybe the forests have not been depleted here and it is easier to build with wood.*

While he was processing and pondering his first glimpses of America, they passed a bright yellow, three-story wood building that housed the town hall. The well-travelled Sultan had told him that citizens of America assembled in such places to make decisions about the rules they would abide by. He found this strange and thought it odd that the town hall was made of wood, rather than stone or brick, and was modest in size. He wondered why it wasn't larger and more castle-like given the important work that was done there.

Visner was an unexpected complication for Bishop, who now had to find facilities for a horse. The townspeople were so taken with this man and his blasted horse, that Bishop had no choice but to appear concerned.

He had less affection for the horse than he had for Casimir because of a bad experience he had as a young man. After being beaten with a riding crop, a horse had reared up, throwing Bishop off its back, and then fell on him, crushing his leg.

Even killing the horse had not given him the satisfaction he thought it would. In fact, life gave him little satisfaction. In addition to the limp, he bore the scars of small pox on his face and body. Women shied away from him, even when he forced a smile and tried to be charming. That didn't matter to him since he didn't like women, but he did need acceptance and adulation, and he firmly believed that wearing a general's uniform would give him both.

He thought of the pretty seamstress back in Philadelphia sewing the general's stars on his uniform. His last encounter with her hadn't gone well.

She yelled, "I'll cut your liver out, if you ever touch me again, you pock-marked, cripple," after he tried to kiss her and get a squeeze of her breast. She lunged at him with a pair of sharp scissors in her hand and he then decided to make a fast exit, while thinking, *she'll act differently when I return as a general with guards who will look the other way while I have her.* His lewd acts toward women were driven by hate. He felt no sexual attraction. He simply wanted to punish, control and subjugate them, especially the pretty, bright ones. They were the ones that stole the attentions of young, handsome men. What better way to demean them than through sexual assault?

He needed the general's rank. He could hear his father's condemning voice, "John, your youngest brother, Martin, just made

Colonel and is well on his way to being a general. It seems all my sons, save you, are successful in the military. The eldest son of the Bishop family has always been the most decorated — until now. Perhaps one of your sisters would be better suited to becoming a full general?"

He emigrated to America from England to escape his father's wrath, but it reached across the Atlantic and crushed the breath out of him. He had to have relief. He had to become a general.

This damn Pole and his horse wouldn't ruin his chances. By getting back to General Washington quickly, he would prove that he should be promoted over the stupid, untrained colonists.

Bishop was trying to think of some way to get rid of Visner permanently, when Samuel Abbot rushed up to them. He had tarried down on the dock basking in praises from the townspeople for his and Abe's bravery and daring. It was just too good for a fourteen-year-old boy to pass up.

"Excuse me sir," he said, addressing Casimir. "If you need a place to sleep and board your horse for the night, my mother and father have a home just up the street, and I know they will be honored to have you."

The offer caused Bishop to grow more irritated. The last thing he needed was to have this Polish imbecile housed in one of the finest homes in Marblehead. Knowing Casimir couldn't understand a word the boy spoke, he thought about refusing the boy and walking on leaving Casimir wondering what he had said.

But Casimir, grateful for this young man's courage that reminded him so much of his own at that age, raised his hand, grasping Samuel's in a warm handshake. Samuel smiled with delight and motioned for Casimir to follow him. Casimir looked at Visner, then back at Samuel who nodded enthusiastically and for good measure took Visner's reins from Casimir's hand, escorting them both to his parents' home, a three-story, slate-blue clapboard house.

Samuel had never been far from Marblehead Bay, so world travelers fascinated him. He was completely overwhelmed by Casimir. He had studied history enough to know an officer's uniform when he saw one, regardless of the country. He could tell this man was special and he wanted to spend time with him. Besides, he, Abe, Casimir, and Visner were famous in the town. Samuel suspected his parents would not be happy, with the risk he took but he reasoned that if he brought Casimir and Visner home they wouldn't reprimand him in front of the officer he had saved, or at least partially saved. Abe did help a little. He escorted them past the house to the stable in back where a servant accepted Visner as if this were an everyday occurrence.

After a brief introduction consisting of a nod and bow from Casimir and a shocked look on her face in response, Samuel's mother recovered her sense of hospitality enough to show Casimir to a third-floor bedroom with a wide view of the harbor. Samuel knew he should leave Casimir alone to get some rest, but he was excited about having this interesting and daring man in his house, he couldn't stay away long. When Casimir answered his knock on the door, he motioned for his guest to follow him down the hall to a small room containing a claw-foot bathtub filled with steaming water. Casimir tried to express his gratitude by again clasping Samuel's hand and then pointed to the door's keyhole twisting his hand as if he were turning a key. The boy understood, but thought male modesty must be some strange European custom not practiced in America.

In spite of his urge to plunge into the inviting bath, Casimir waited until Samuel returned with the key, then he locked the door, undressed, and slipped into the warm water. He couldn't afford to have any prying eyes see him naked. After the long days at sea with nothing but a wooden pail for bathing, the warmth of a full tub of water and the homemade, rosemary scented soap, felt like great luxuries. He lingered until the water grew cool before reluctantly climbing out to dry himself with a large towel decorated with a border of blue and white gingham. He realized how much he had missed such feminine touches so reminiscent of his mother's household.

When he returned to his room, Samuel brought him a supper of cabbage, potatoes, and ham and placed it on a small wooden table in the center of the room. Thoughtfully, Samuel also brought writing paper, ink and pen and placed them on the night stand.

Meanwhile, John Bishop was left on his own to find lodging. After Samuel and Casimir left, he straightened his back and marched stiffly up the hill to the public boarding house.

In spite of his fatigue and the comfort of a warm bath and meal, Casimir found sleep impossible. He tried with little success to adjust to the strange food, customs, and scenery as well as all the voices around him speaking a foreign language. Thoughts of how best to win Washington's support kept circling through his mind, but he still had no clear answer on how to proceed. Surely the value of the cavalry that he would form and lead would be obvious to a battle seasoned general...wouldn't it?

Bishop arrived at the Abbot house early the next morning ready to depart with the troublesome Pole. General Washington wanted to get the meeting with Casimir over as soon as possible and so did Bishop. The sooner the general dismissed this Pulaski for the idiot he was, the sooner he, Bishop, could get back to being the general's trusted aide. It was his job to get Casimir to Neshaminy Creek where Washington had his headquarters, and he intended to get him there fast. He hoped the little Pole and his skinny horse could keep up with him.

He found Casimir in the parlor with correspondence spread out in front of him and Samuel eagerly pointing to each merchant's letters indicating with a nod of his head and a finger directed at himself that he knew the recipient and would deliver the letter. Bishop winced when he spotted the last envelope on the table. It was from Adrienne Lafayette to her husband, the Marquis de Lafayette, one of Washington's most trusted friends and advisers. Would this Polish menace never stop tormenting him? Now it seemed he knew Lafayette.

"Boston, he is in Boston," Bishop said gruffly, pointing to the Lafayette letter, to feign support of Casimir.

Casimir had studied maps of the colonies while on board the ship and knew Boston was not far from Marblehead. He looked from Samuel to the major and made a motion as if he were holding the reins of a horse and riding.

"One day," Bishop said between clinched teeth. "You can make it in one day on horseback—assuming you know how to ride."

Samuel reinforced Bishop's remark by holding up one finger and nodding. Casimir pointed to a drawing of the harbor on the wall. Samuel understood that he needed a map and quickly drew one for him. Bishop fumed, knowing he was still responsible for getting Casimir to Neshaminy Creek north of Philadelphia.

Mrs. Abbot entered the room to tell Samuel his father wanted to have a talk with him, and since she spoke a little French, she offered her assistance to Bishop and Casimir.

"Try to get him to understand that I will meet him at the wharf in Boston in three days and we will go to meet General Washington by boat from there, and," he paused for an emphasis he hoped Mrs. Abbot would convey to Casimir, raising his voice, "no horse this time."

Once she interpreted Bishop's message, Casimir stood, nodded, and saluted him with a click of his heels. The aggravated aide stormed out the door and a downcast Samuel headed to the library where his father waited.

After telling Mrs. Abbot how grateful he was to her, and her son in French, hoping she understood his words and the sincerity behind them, Casimir took Visner from the stable and headed toward Boston to meet Lafayette. Since neither he nor Visner had fully recovered from the voyage, they were fortunate it was an easy ride to Boston. It felt good to be riding again, and Visner seemed to be calmed by the normalcy of having his master on his back and a good footing. The salt air was much better when breathed on land rather than on a tossing sea, thought Casimir. Flowers seemed to thrive in it. Their bright colors spilled down over the rock walls separating stately homes from the wagon road he rode along on a hill above the beach. The sun was bright and hot, hotter than in Europe. His wool uniform soon became uncomfortable but he refused to unbutton the shirt or take off the coat. Appearances were important.

When he reached the outskirts of Boston he showed the Lafayette letter to customers in a local pub. Since Lafayette was already famous, it was easy to get directions to the home where he was the honored guest of the James family.

Once he expressed his desire to deliver a letter to the Marquis, Mrs. James who spoke French, offered him a seat in the parlor. Casimir asked if he could sit on the veranda instead where he could feel the cool ocean breeze and see the green ferns in their wicker baskets swaying back and forth. She understood, and served him a glass of water on the veranda where he relaxed in a large swing.

Bumble bees and hummingbirds buzzed around the flowers in pots lining the porch railing. Their drone and the warmth of the summer sun made him drowsy and a young man burst out onto the porch just as Casimir was about to drift off. Recovering quickly, he stood and bowed to the nineteen-year-old Marquis, who returned the gesture before they clasped hands.

"Bonjour, welcome to America Monsieur Pulaski," said Lafayette, greeting Casimir in French. "I have heard of your courage and am honored to meet you."

"And I have heard the same of you Marquis de Lafayette," responded Casimir. "It is a privilege to meet you. Your wife entrusted a letter to my friend, Paul Dobrachek, when she heard I was making the journey to America. I pray it brings you good news from home and lifts your spirits as much as such correspondence does mine."

"Merci, I am sure it will and if you will please forgive me Monsieur Pulaski, I have not heard from my family for many months and I would like to read it now," he said, obviously excited by the letter and grateful to Casimir for delivering it. "Will you be kind enough to excuse me for a few minutes? I very much want to talk with you if you have the time and are willing to wait. I promise I won't be long."

Casimir would gladly take all the time needed to talk with someone who was from Europe, spoke French, and could tell him about this country and its customs. He was especially interested in learning more about General Washington and Lafayette knew him well, so he quickly replied, "Oui, take all the time you need. I have all day and all night."

Shortly after Lafayette returned, Mrs. James announced an early dinner and led them into the formal dining room. Casimir knew he and Lafayette were being honored when he saw place settings of fine blue and white Wedgewood plates, Baccarat crystal stemware, and heavy silverware.

Mrs. James was impressed with her European guests and was delighted that their presence gave her an excuse to do some formal entertaining. Their refined manners made it fitting for her to bring out her rarely used, but treasured, dinnerware.

After being seated, they were treated to an elaborate meal of red meats and seafood, fresh garden vegetables, yeast rolls and a special claret wine. When Casimir commented on the quantity of fresh and in some cases, unfamiliar vegetables, Mrs. James replied, "Thank you. It took years to get enough land cleared of the heavy forests here to raise crops like cabbage and, farther south, tobacco and a variety of vegetables."

Hearing this, Casimir understood and was impressed by these industrious people who had cleared the trees to farm and used the timber to build their houses. No wonder there were so many wooden structures in a land full of stone.

After dinner, Mrs. James sent the gentlemen off to the parlor with coffee, brandy and cigars. They chatted in French well into the night as Lafayette gave Casimir details about the war.

"It is not going well for the Americans. Our brave General Washington suffered a defeat at Long Island and now Britain's General Howe is poised to strike at Albany or elsewhere. Our intelligence is contradictory. Washington is camped off a road between Philadelphia and New York with several thousand troops. It is rich farmland and, since its summer, the troops are living well off the land to the detriment of the farmers. But I'm worried if we have another harsh winter our men may die of exposure and starvation unless Congress finds the funds for food, uniforms, and most especially boots. If they don't get supplies they will abandon their posts and return home. Who could blame them?"

"His army seems ill-equipped and lacking discipline." Casimir observed. "What of the cavalry? Is it disciplined and trained? Will the troops stay and fight for me?"

"I am sorry to say that neither the general nor Congress have much confidence in fighting from horseback. It is very different here. Heavy undergrowth with vegetation and vines can entangle a man on a mount and the rough and rocky terrain and deep river mud can trip or mire a horse. Washington prefers work animals that can pull wagons and cannons, not cavalry horses."

The two aristocratic warriors liked and respected one another. Lafayette advised Casimir how to present his request for a commission of a cavalry legion to General Washington. Although thirteen years younger than Casimir, he had acquired knowledge about American diplomacy that Casimir lacked. They shared cavalry experience, Casimir in Poland and Lafayette in France and each had distinguished himself on the battlefields of Europe. But physically they were quite different. Lafayette had the advantage of being quite tall, with his height and posture giving him an authoritative, regal bearing beyond his years, while Casimir was diminutive and slight.

"I admire fine horses and can see that when your Visner recovers from the voyage, he will be magnificent." Lafayette commented. "The bond between you and the horse is obvious. I can imagine what a striking pair the two of you will make riding into battle."

"Thank you, Marquis, he is a splendid horse. But, I am to meet Washington's aide, Major Bishop, in two days and we are to travel together by boat to New York. From there we will ride inland to meet General Washington at his Neshaminy Creek headquarters. The major said Visner cannot go aboard the ship and I'm torn about what to do. I need my horse, but after the ordeal he went through during the crossing and at Marblehead, it would be selfish of me to try and take him."

The Marquis interjected, "I have an idea, leave Visner with me. I'll bring him when I come. I have field business to take care of along the way and won't be traveling by boat. It will be a long journey for him, but I suspect he will be ready for it after a few days of rest and good grain. Also, I'll prepare a letter of recommendation for you to give to General Washington. It will be ready for you tomorrow morning. I think you should leave when the next ship sails."

"Oh, and don't wait for Bishop. He is an ambitious troublemaker and will not be of help to you. General Washington is a good judge of character and he doesn't think much of the major trying to get promoted by flattering the general, rather than proving himself. You must reach General Washington as soon as possible to argue your case. We need you now."

"Thank you, Marquis. I am overwhelmed by your generosity. I am sure Visner will enjoy his stay with you." He then clasped Lafayette's forearm warmly before heading to the bedroom that Mrs. James insisted he use.

Lafayette gave Casimir the promised letter of introduction the next morning along with the news that a ship would sail for New York at four o'clock that afternoon. He had already sent a servant to book passage for Casimir. During breakfast, Lafayette told Casimir where he could find a horse once he arrived in New York for the trip to Washington's camp. He gave him a map of the route to take, asking him to memorize the directions and destroy it before traveling.

"Merci, Marquis. It is my good fortune to make such an important and gracious friend. I hope to return your kindness one day and to support you in your endeavors here in America."

"It is my pleasure, Monsieur, to help someone with such an impressive military record and who took such care in personally delivering Adrienne's letter to me."

While Lafayette was walking Casimir to the ship he said, "Don't worry about Major Bishop. I doubt he will reach Washington's camp for several weeks. You can always say you didn't understand what he meant when he told you to wait for him here."

Though he didn't know how Bishop would be delayed, Casimir smiled and appreciated Lafayette even more.

CHAPTER NINETEEN

THE
AMERICAN REVOLUTION

Pennyslvania
July 1777- July 1778

he sailing to New York was uneventful despite having spotted the British war ships, the Charlotte and the Maria, far off shore. In spite of the threat, it was certainly less dangerous than the crossing from France. Casimir kept to himself and tried to think of a plan to persuade Washington to grant him a commission and fund a cavalry legion for him to lead. Until he met the man and knew more about his military strategy it was difficult to prepare an effective argument. Still, he was excited about the meeting and hoped they could form both a friendship and a joint strategy to win the war.

In New York, Casimir lost no time in finding the stables Lafayette directed him to. Securing an acceptable horse and starting on the road to Philadelphia, his spirits were high. Life was good again. He was out of prison, no longer hunted and neither praised nor damned for his past. The only thing he needed to make it perfect was a command where he could fight and lead.

He soon learned firsthand of the thick vegetation Lafayette described. On a rise in the rutted, muddy road he saw a small detachment of British troops headed his way. He ducked in the brush. This was his first chance to engage the enemy in

America. He visualized riding into Washington's camp with Redcoat prisoners in tow who would report how he had single handedly captured them and killed several of their comrades; but he was alone on an untrained horse and this might be an advance scouting party with a much larger force down the road. No matter how disappointing it was to pass up the opportunity to fight, he knew it was wiser to turn off the road rather than risk losing his first skirmish in this unfamiliar land.

While riding cross-country to avoid an encounter with the British, the underbrush and thorny bamboo vines ripped through his clothing and tore at his flesh. He developed a rash made even more uncomfortable by enduring the sweltering heat in his wool uniform. The still air was heavy with humidity and leaves hung limp on the trees. Horseflies and other stinging and biting insects attacked him and his mount. Soon his beautiful blue and white colors were smeared with dirt, soaked with perspiration, and streaked with blood.

And the swamps were worse. Slithering water snakes, river rats, and beavers with teeth sharp enough to fell large trees swam among the moss-covered stumps. While seemingly non-threatening, these creatures were new to him and he kept his stirrups and feet well above the water.

As he rode through the woods early one morning, he heard a great crashing noise nearby. He knew soldiers wouldn't make such a racket and the native American Indians were supposed to be stealthy. His horse reared, jerked to the right and would have run headlong through a thicket if Casimir hadn't yanked back on the reins. The thrashing noise lessoned as the sound of short grunts, squeals and snorts reached him. That's when he spotted the hogs. But these weren't the domesticated farm animals raised in Poland. These were long-snouted creatures with huge sharp tusks, and were apparently ravenous since they ran around in circles rooting out grubs, tree roots and acorns. He cautiously nudged his horse away from the fierce looking beasts while thinking that animals must survive on their own here, much as the settlers do.

The tangling vines, murky swamps and the strange creatures they contained were all unfamiliar, and he began to understand Washington's skepticism about using horses in such woods. It was a constant torment for men and their mounts. But the British wouldn't expect such a tactic and surprise was a very effective weapon he had used many times.

After three days, he returned to the main road where he saw stone, rather than wood houses and they looked more familiar to him. Even barns, sheds and walls were made of stone, and some of the fields he passed were strewn with rocks. He admired the resourceful colonists who used stones to build their homes that they had cleared from the land to plant crops.

The following day he rode down a gently sloping bank into a creek, crossed its shallow water, and urged his horse up the steeper bank on the opposite side into a grove of woods where he saw Washington's encampment. He was surprised that he wasn't challenged by a sentry. Unknown to him, Washington's spies and Indian scouts had followed his movements for the past two days. They saw that he was travelling alone, and his blue and white uniform meant he was not a redcoat. His fatigued state and torn clothes meant he had either suffered some mishap or didn't know the terrain. Although hardly recognizable as a military uniform, he appeared to be European, so they mistook him as Lafayette's messenger and allowed him to pass.

The ride to Neshaminy Creek had taken a toll. He suffered from heat exhaustion, insect bites, and a rash from poison oak. His neck and wrists were rubbed raw by the scratchy woolen collar and cuffs of his jacket. He looked bedraggled which was not the norm for him, nor would it make a good first impression.

Washington's guards approached him to ask his business. Knowing what a poor appearance he presented, he decided using the title Sultan gave him might deflect the bad opinion they must have of him. He could not answer their inquiry in English other than saying "Washington" and then "Count Pulaski" while pointing to himself, and handing them the letter from Lafayette. He planned to give Franklin's letter to Washington personally. The guards seemed satisfied and motioned him to wait while they informed the general.

Casimir used the time to kneel in the creek as best he could, while leaving his uniform on and buttoned all the way to the top, befitting an officer. He splashed the cool, refreshing water on the insect bites and rash on his hands and face. He was still in the creek trying to use his damp handkerchief to wash the mud, dirt and blood from his uniform and boots without becoming soaking wet when the tallest man he had ever seen walked up to the edge of the creek bank above him. With the bank adding to his height, Casimir wondered if this was a human giant.

When he heard "Good Afternoon, Count Pulaski," he realized he was finally meeting General George Washington.

"General," was all Casimir could manage in English.

Since Washington knew he couldn't speak English, he motioned for Casimir to climb out of the creek and follow him. They crossed a grove of grass and trees where low tents were staked to the ground and campfires were lit despite the heat of the day. Casimir later learned that smoke from the fires helped keep the flies and mosquitos away. The troops watched the pair as they walked by. Washington, who stood six-feet four inches tall dwarfed the five-foot, three-inch Casimir. His small size diminished his importance in their eyes, as they wondered how he could be of much use to them.

They entered a stone house with a large reception room in front and a smaller room in the back. Two women sat in the front room in straight backed chairs with cane bottom seats. A pot of stew bubbled in a huge iron pot hanging over the fire in the fireplace. A blackberry pie with black juice streaming down its sides was in the warming oven beside it, reminding him of the raspberry sauce Sarah drizzled over his birthday cakes. It smelled delicious and Casimir thought, *they must have some kind of black fruit here. It is remarkable how they live off the land.*

One of the women, dressed in black, sat at a spinning wheel, while the other stitched edging around what appeared to be a banner or flag with alternating red and white stripes and white stars on a blue square. Both women seemed oblivious to the room's stifling heat.

"Mrs. Moland, Mrs. Young, this is Count Pulaski," said the general, introducing him. The ladies nodded and Casimir gave each a deep bow from the waist. When the one at the spinning wheel looked surprised, he wondered if he had done something wrong and whether men bowed to ladies here.

It was all a mystery to him, like all the different colonies with arbitrary boundary lines. He knew there were thirteen, each with different governing bodies, yet they were all part of the same America. How strange. There was so much he didn't understand about this land, and it was doubly frustrating that he couldn't ask questions because most people neither understood his attempts at English nor spoke any of the languages he knew.

Washington led him to his office in the back room and offered him a seat. He was curious as to why Casimir hadn't stayed on the main road and why John Bishop was not with him, but there was no one who spoke French or German, or even a smattering of Latin to help them communicate. For his part, Casimir wondered how people could function without speaking a second language. These frontiersmen and revolutionaries obviously thought the world should learn English and he wished now that he had learned the confusing language rather than Italian as a child.

Finally, he drew a map of the road and pointed to the spot where he saw the British troops. Then while touching the red sash around his waist and making a fist, Washington understood he had encountered British redcoats. But when Washington furrowed his brow and seemed to want more information, Casimir was unable to give him the usual military report of what were they doing on the road, how many were there, and how were they armed. He knew his failure to supply such information was just as frustrating to the general as it was to him.

Since Washington was a courteous man, he tried to conceal his irritation but Casimir knew the meeting was a disaster. He regretted that he had not charged the British on the road and made a grand entrance with prisoners in tow. That was a language any military man would understand.

General Washington was in command of his country's entire army — and made sure this Pole was aware of that fact. But Casimir knew from his conversations with Franklin and Lafayette that Washington needed him, and he was not going to let the general overlook that fact. The stage was set for a contest of wills and Casimir seemed to be out maneuvered.

Fatigued and confused by almost everything he encountered, and desperate to make Washington understand, he decided to act out his military hit and run tactics so the general could see the advantages. Unsheathing his sword, he started to swing it over his head as if leading a charge, but four of Washington's personal guards raced to Washington's side. Washington shook his head disbelievingly and motioned the guards back to their station. Casimir took that as approval to continue.

He sheathed the sword but used one hand to wave in the air as if he were swinging a sword in it while clasping imaginary horse reins in the other. He charged forward, thrusting the invisible sword into empty air, fighting an unseen enemy, then turning to run back behind a tall wardrobe, waving his arm in a circular motion to direct his hidden troops to come out of hiding and encircle the enemy pursuing him.

It was one of his worst ideas. Washington could hardly conceal a smile since the small man's arrogance and comical riding gestures made him appear silly. He looked like a young boy playing soldier rather than a great horseman and certainly not a general in command of a large force.

A major problem was that Franklin and Silas Deane had peppered Washington with letters of recommendation and sent, in Washington's words, "a swarm" of young men, mostly French, to capture high-ranking positions in the Continental army. Some claimed, falsely, to be connected to the French royal court which the Americans were trying to convince to support the Revolution. And others had actually been promised money and rank when they arrived in America. The shallowness of these self-serving foreigners infuriated Washington. Why had Franklin now sent him another pompous, glory seeker?

In his defense, the popular Franklin was approached by many young Europeans from well-to-do families who dreamed of adventure, status, and officer titles in America. Their wealth could help the Colonists finance the war and Franklin needed to woo their rich families. He knew Washington was working with untrained men who gave only short-term commitments to the Continental Army and when planting or harvesting season came they would likely leave to tend to their farms. So, Franklin recommended almost all the wealthy young men who approached him since they had no crops to tend and would stay with Washington for the duration of the war. This meant Casimir's endorsement from Franklin was commonplace and an irritant, not nearly as special as he believed.

General Washington wanted Franklin to stop wasting his time. He thought the foreigners were self-interested mercenaries, and while they might not leave during the growing season, they would return to their homelands once the war was over. In his mind, the brave men who had tamed the frontier and were willing to sacrifice all to achieve freedom for their children and grandchildren deserved the officer positions. After the war, they would stay and help build a new country that would endure for centuries, free of the tyranny of monarchs.

On this day, the general had another, more painful problem. His teeth were killing him. He had learned to live with the dull ache in his lower jaw, but a sharp new pain had moved into the upper jaw, a pain so severe that he had little patience for anyone.

Internally, he raged, *Damn that Franklin. He solved his own eye problems with those blasted spectacles. Rather than sending another arrogant, chattering foreigner, why not send something to fix my teeth. That would be a real help.*

But Washington needed fresh ideas and leaders. The war was not going well. He barely escaped disaster when Commander John Glover, of Marblehead, Massachusetts saved the Continental Army from annihilation the previous year by evacuating him and his men from Long Island on flat boats. He was acutely aware that he was vastly outnumbered by the British who were far better equipped and trained than his own Continental Army.

So, despite his pain, he tried to follow what Casimir was saying. He was swayed not by the fact he had a letter from Franklin, but by how different the ambassador's words were from his normal prattle of, "This young man comes from a fine and influential family with means to help our cause . . . " Instead, it read:

My dear General Washington,
General Casimir Pulaski and his mounted troops
distinguished themselves on European battlefields

against overwhelming forces. I believe his military
genius can be put to good use on American soil
against similar odds.

"Against similar odds" struck a chord with Washington. He
needed some quick victories against the larger British force to
encourage his troops to reenlist when their one-year terms were
up in December. And the letter from his friend and trusted adviser, the young Lafayette, carried even more weight in support
of Casimir by confirming what Franklin had said about his victories in Poland.

Finally, Washington motioned for Casimir to stop his tortured presentation and indicated by pointing to his own sword
and an almanac that Casimir could accompany him on a future
expedition.

"Merci, Generale," Casimir said trying to convey a positive
forcefulness in his voice as he had no option but to agree. He saluted General Washington and attempted a gracious exit, bowing as he left.

Disheartened, he worried he could not conquer this English
language quickly and he wouldn't be allowed to do anything
worthwhile to convince Washington of the value of his cavalry
tactics. All might be lost in the next major battle.

Casimir received encouragement when a letter from the
Marquis de Lafayette arrived assuring him that Visner was
gaining weight and strength. The marquis said he was exercising him daily and the two would soon start their journey to
Neshaminy Creek.

"I may be able to assist with the language problem when I
arrive," he wrote. Casimir was ecstatic.

When Lafayette, splendidly dressed in a blue and white Continental Army uniform rode into camp several days later on
Visner, Casimir felt a pang of envy. He should have arrived in

such style, and on Visner. That would have made a far better impression than slinking into camp in a torn and dirty uniform mounted on a plain looking horse.

But his envy was short-lived. The Marquis was a friend, and he was overjoyed to see that he had taken good care of Visner. After greeting each other warmly, Lafayette handed Visner's reins to Casimir and, displaying a wry smile, said, "It is good to see you my friend. I hear you are a count now. So, Count Pulaski here is your splendid mount."

Casimir blushed red, then realizing the Marquis was joking, replied, "Yes, it's a title I acquired on board ship from a fellow called Sultan. When I first used it here, I was sorely in need of some quick prestige and I thought the title might do it for me."

Lafayette smiled and nodded, saying, "I'm sure once people here get to know you, the prestige will come." Then he excused himself to report to General Washington about his progress in securing supplies for the Army. Once alone, Visner whinnied and nuzzled Casimir. They were together again, to protect and care for each other.

The Marquis brought quite an entourage with him. There were several mounted horsemen acting as guards and scouts. Behind them a wagon laden with cooking gear and supplies. A separate wagon carried Lafayette's tent and furnishings. Then came the oxen trudging behind, pulling carts filled with cages of chickens, turkeys and geese. Another team, this one composed of odd looking work horses with none of the noble Visner's sleek features, pulled a wagon loaded with muskets and gunpowder. Cows ambled along behind. Lafayette had bought the animals with his own money from farmers along the way to supply troops with milk, cheese, eggs and meat. The gunpowder and muskets were sent to him by a French brigantine arriving at Tucker's Wharf just prior to his departure.

Drawn together by their European heritage and military backgrounds, Lafayette and Casimir quickly renewed their friendship.

One day Casimir asked, "Marquis, what are those ugly horses that pulled some of your wagons into camp?"

"They are called mules," the Marquis answered. "They're stronger and more sure-footed than horses and make excellent beasts of burden, since they can pull heavier artillery and wagons than horses, and are faster than oxen.

"And, here's something else you might find interesting. Our General Washington was the first person in America to produce them at his Mount Vernon farm. They are what is called a hybrid, a cross between a Jack donkey and a mare horse. The Jacks originally came from Spain where it was unlawful to export them. Spain valued its control of the market so much that death was the penalty for trading in either mules or the rare Spanish Jacks outside the country. But, a grateful baron secretly shipped a magnificent Andalusian Jack to Washington as a special gift for saving his son's life during the French and Indian wars. It took a couple of years to get the Jack, 'Royal Gift' as he was called, to breed, but the general eventually got a line of mules and those you saw are part of that line.

"When this war is over, I plan to visit Spain and arrange for more Spanish Jacks to be sent to Washington so the line can be diversified and strengthened."

"How I would love to be able to converse with General Washington," Casimir said, sighing. "What an amazing man he is, and what a surprise."

"Well you may be in for more surprises," Lafayette responded. "One of the wagons I brought carried more than cooking gear and food items. It concealed an ex-slave. A black man freed by his owner in Boston. He is educated and served as his master's personal valet for twenty years. He goes by the name of Elijah, Elijah George. When his master became ill, he worried that after his death Elijah might be sold and shipped to a Southern plantation to be worked in the fields. That was an unbearable thought for him, so he signed the papers setting Elijah free."

Casimir gasped and, almost shouting, asked, "How is that possible? I met a man, Sultan, the one I told you about on the ship. He was on his way to America to buy the freedom of his dead wife's only living relative, a slave named Elijah George. I must go to him and let him know Sultan is looking for him. Where can I find him?"

"Now I'm the one who's surprised," the marquis replied. "What a coincidence. This is astounding. Elijah decided the general needed a personal valet and prevailed upon me to bring him to Washington's camp. Washington isn't accustomed to valets and declined his offer but he needed undercover agents to report British movements and thought a black man could blend into the crowds in cities like New York, Baltimore, and Philadelphia.

"People would assume he was someone's slave, running errands, and wouldn't question him. But I'm afraid you're too late to meet him here. He left several days ago, and I hear he's already relayed some valuable information to our great general.

"Now I regret that he didn't stay here because he is Tunisian and speaks Turkish and some French. I had hoped he could help interpret English for you."

Casimir was disappointed that he would not meet the ex-slave, especially as he could have helped him with his language problems, but he was still stunned by such a coincidence and asked if Lafayette had any more surprises for him.

"Only that I hear the general is receiving conflicting intelligence reports about Howe's movements," he said. "That's why he needs more spies like our Mr. George."

Casimir surmised, "The man must carry a huge weight on his shoulders with so many problems facing him. I wish I could be by his side to take some of the responsibility." Then he thought to himself, *one day, perhaps one day soon, I will get my chance.*

Casimir spent the next several weeks moving between Washington's encampment and Philadelphia pleading for funding for a cavalry from reluctant members of the Continental Congress who had little understanding of either the use of cavalry, or the mix of French and broken English this little foreigner used in his attempt to explain it.

They too, were tired of the seemingly endless parade of foreigners asking for the same things Casimir wanted, title and money. General Washington's vacillation didn't help. At times, he was supportive and at other times reluctant to spend his limited funds, so sorely needed for supplies, on a military strategy that was not yet proven in the forested terrain of America.

Casimir was becoming increasingly frustrated. His French, broken English, heavy accent and small stature made it easy for Congressional members to dismiss him as just another foreigner trying to make a name and a fortune for himself in America. He made a point of dressing well for his presentations to Congress since, for him, this was a show of respect.

He thought his high heeled boots and the cape that swished about him added to his stature as he walked briskly in to the chambers but, the impression he gave was not the one he desired. The colonists thought he displayed 'princely airs' which smacked of monarchy, the very thing they were fighting against. What a quandary. In Europe, he was denied commissions when accused of being an enemy of kings while he suffered here because his appearance suggested he supported kings.

Returning to Washington's camp he was even more frustrated by the inactivity he found. The troops didn't train regularly.

Instead, they lounged around talking about crops, 'huntin' dogs, and women. He wondered why they weren't practicing formations, shooting, and hand-to-hand fighting and why they didn't want to be as tough and smart as possible when they met the enemy. Did they think the well-trained British would be easy to defeat?

Casimir complained to Washington through anyone he could find to translate.

"General, I must have funds for my legion. The war is not going in our favor and we must act quickly. Your men lack discipline. All day long they loaf, telling tall tales. They should train ten to twelve hours each day to be ready for the British."

Washington had little time or patience for such complaints, especially when they were voiced in broken English, and let Casimir know it.

"Count Pulaski, these men have crops rotting in the field, and their children may starve if they are not harvested. Their families are unprotected and may suffer at the hands of the British or Indians because they are serving with us. We are doing well to keep them in camp. Discipline? These aren't the kind of men you reprimand for lounging. They will need all the rest they can get before engaging the British. Where will General Howe strike? That is where we should be focused, not on how the men gossip. When the time comes, they will prove that they have all the training they need. Now, leave me alone if you have nothing better to contribute. And on your other issue, I cannot give you funds that I don't have."

Disheartened but determined, Casimir busied himself training and practicing military tactics alone, riding Visner, who had completely recovered from the ordeal of the ocean voyage. Lafayette occasionally joined him and the two sparred on horseback or held races up and down York Road along the camp's border.

The troops, particularly Washington's elite guard, enjoyed watching the daily exercises. They were among the few troops who rode, and appreciated good horsemanship. It appeared Casimir was a friend of Lafayette, whom they knew was a close friend of Washington.

Aware of the attention he was getting, Casimir began showing off and performed ever more challenging feats. He dressed a straw dummy in a British uniform then leaped on Visner's back and charged toward the dummy with his gleaming sword raised high overhead shouting, bezplatnie (charge), and do przodu (forward), while drawing his pistol with his left hand and throwing it to the ground, thirty feet in front of him. As Visner raced toward it, Casimir leaned over to scoop the pistol off the ground and fired it with his left hand while still leaning over Visner's side. The troops saw the smoke from the gun and a wad of straw fly from the dummy's chest. Then they saw the red-coated dummy lose his head as Casimir galloped by, swinging the sword with his right hand to sever its neck. Wheeling Visner around he then charged at the guards sliding Visner to a stop right in front of them just as they were about to scatter. When he dismounted, the guards no longer saw him as a trivial little man.

Casimir wanted to get to know the guards, but his poor English placed a wall between them. His inability to communicate was a blessing in one regard, however. It allowed him to keep to himself. Unable to converse, most people left him alone. He found a little grassy island just big enough for his one-man tent in the middle of the creek and kept Visner hobbled on the bank to graze on the grass. When no one was walking by, he slipped into the water to bathe. He could always tell if someone was approaching by watching Visner's ear and head movements.

One day Lafayette informed Casimir, "Major Bishop should be arriving any day and was outraged when he arrived in Boston and learned you hadn't waited for him."

Casimir responded, "Did he come to your home looking for me after I didn't meet him on the wharf?"

"No, I sent him a dispatch, saying that you had left to offer your immediate assistance to General Washington and that the general wanted him to ride overland and gather as much intelligence as he could about Howe's movements as he returned. That is why he has been delayed," Lafayette replied.

"Marquis, is that true? Did the general want him to ride overland?"

"No, of course not. I just wanted to give you a head start and some uninterrupted time with the general. I believe the cavalry could be a valuable complement to the French and Continental troops and I didn't want Bishop trying to discredit it. I doubt that he will be in a good mood when he arrives, so watch out for him."

Casimir was stunned, amused, and unsure of how to deal with the situation, but decided not to be overly concerned about the grumpy major.

Lafayette had gotten a full account from his courier of Bishop's reaction when he received his dispatch.

"How dare that stupid little foreigner disobey me. I told him to wait in Boston. Washington expected me to escort him to Neshaminy Creek. The idiot probably got lost on the way or, better yet, captured and if he didn't, there's no telling what trouble he'll cause in camp. While he's working close to Washington, I'm ordered to take the time to gather intelligence. I'm the one who should be close to the general. I am his aide. How else can I impress him and advance my career? All I need is to make a good impression in one battle and I'll be promoted to brigadier general. Blast that little Polish upstart.

"He keeps strutting about in that fancy Polish general's uniform. What if Washington is naïve enough to be taken in by it and decides to give him a generalship? My generalship. That is a nightmare I cannot shake."

When Bishop finally arrived at Neshaminy Creek he rode toward Washington's quarters repeatedly kicking his horse, shouting at soldiers to get out of his way, and cursing so hard that spit flew from his thin lips. He saw Casimir and Visner practicing their maneuvers and cursed anew when he realized that not only was the little Polish thorn there ahead of him, but so was his dammed horse. He knew Casimir took a ship to New York, and wondered how the horse got here after he expressly forbade him to bring it.

Concealing his anger, Bishop told Washington the agents he talked with had said Howe would attack in Albany, New York. Washington listened to Bishop's report and praised him for taking the initiative to contact agents along the way on his return to Neshaminy Creek. He didn't ask why the major had tarried to interview spies, since his network of agents sent coded messages by carrier pigeons to his headquarters almost daily. Bishop never knew the general didn't give the order for him to interview them.

Meanwhile, Washington's new spy whom he had grown to trust, Elijah George, had performed admirably. George reported that he had overheard British officers talking about an attack on the Continental capitol of Philadelphia. That seemed to affirm the information Casimir had given earlier.

Pulaski had pointed to the map of the area and traced his finger south, indicating that the redcoats he saw on the road were headed toward Philadelphia. Now, when he was asked, Casimir, with Lafayette interpreting, said it was a small party, perhaps just scouting the area, certainly not Howe's entire force.

But Washington thought they could have been travelling south to meet the main force. One thing was certain, he couldn't leave Philadelphia unprotected. Losing the capitol would be a devastating blow to the morale of the troops and the colonists. He decided to stay close to Philadelphia, until he could be sure of Howe's intentions.

Then, on a crisp, clean morning with dew sparkling on the grass in a nearby shady area, General Washington ordered his officers to assemble near a flagpole in front of the Moland house. The men gathered before the general. Curious, Casimir and Lafayette moved to the edge of the group. When the front door of the house opened, a woman walked toward them carrying the flag she was working on the day Casimir arrived.

Addressing the group, Washington said, "Gentlemen, this is the flag of these united colonies. The militia flags of each colony may still be carried on the battlefield, but this is the one the entire army will follow. The stars represent our thirteen colonies. They form an unbroken circle, just as our commitment to each other and to our new country will never be broken. The red stripes are to remind us and our children of the blood that must be sacrificed for freedom. The white stripes give us hope for peace and the blue reaffirms our unity.

"Your being here shows that you are ready to die for our country and to lead others who are willing to do the same. You have earned the right to be the first to raise this flag, America's flag. Please step forward two at a time, hoist the flag a few feet, and allow the next pair to do the same. Messieurs Lafayette and Pulaski, you are also willing to die for our freedom even though you call another country home. You may join us in raising this flag of freedom for the first time."

Then, looking solemnly at the assembled faces, he cautioned, "Gentlemen this flag must never fall to the ground."

Sergeant William Jasper, the South Carolinian who saved South Carolina's flag from such a fate at the battle of Sullivan's Island, heard Washington's words, *"This flag must never fall to the ground."*

The sergeant understood the significance of Washington's words. Flags were the symbol men followed into battle and that led them out of danger when retreat was required. They had to be held high to be visible to the troops as a constant reminder of why they were fighting and Jasper vowed to always protect this new symbol of America's unity in the fight for independence.

Lafayette whispered to Casimir, "We are being honored. We are to have a turn at helping raise the flag."

Casimir was touched by Washington's gesture and, swallowing hard, he stepped forward with Lafayette as the general slowly unfurled the flag showing the details he had just described. Because of the general's unusual height, he was able to attach the flag to the pole so high it didn't touch the ground.

After each man had taken a turn pulling the flag to the top of the pole, a breeze caught it and the stripes began to ripple in the air. Casimir instinctively took off his hat and saluted the flag. All present did the same. It was the first unfurling of 'Ol Glory' and its very first military salute.

It was early September and the coded messages became more consistent. Howe was headed to Philadelphia and Washington had to stop him. Calling a meeting with Generals Anthony Wayne and Nathaniel Greene and his other officers, he stated bluntly, "Gentlemen, Howe is headed to Philadelphia. We have to block him. If the capitol falls, we may lose the war. Our seat of government would be in enemy hands, our own citizens would lose faith in us, and the French could see our cause as hopeless and refuse to support us. We must use our entire force to stop Howe. Get the men ready. We march tomorrow."

There was no debate. Everyone understood the gravity of the situation. According to reports provided by Elijah George and other agents they would be outnumbered again. They had 11,000 militia and Continentals while Howe had 15,000 trained redcoats.

Lafayette attended the meeting and reported back to Casimir that General Washington wanted him to come along as a volunteer observer.

Casimir was both angered and excited. "An observer," he moaned while thinking, *I have been the leader, the hero, the one who was 'observed' but never a bystander. This is a slap in the face, although I believe unintentional on Washington's part. Still, it is a chance to be near a battle, a huge battle that could determine the fate of America and England in this sphere of the world. This is exciting, very exciting.*

By sunrise, 11,000 troops were on the move with everything from cannons to cook wagons following. General Washington invited Casimir to ride with his officers, near him. Their march took them across rolling hills that were often capped with a farmer's house and barn. They rode through fields where resourceful Pennsylvania Dutch farmers had planted pumpkins, squash, and pole beans between the corn stalks. The orange pumpkins stood in contrast to the khaki corn stalks bearing large ears of corn and yellowing pods of beans, ready for picking and shelling. Green striped crook neck squash nestled on the ground while pack saddles, bees with a vicious sting, swarmed around tassels at the top of the corn.

The crops were meant to provide food for the farmers, their families and their livestock throughout the coming winter but it was being trampled into the ground by Washington's troops. Eleven thousand soldiers with cannons, horses, wagons, and other provisions of war scraped the countryside clean. It pained the farmers among them to know their march would result in a stark winter for the families in the area, but the worst was yet to come.

September was dry and less humid than July and August but the sun was still hot, especially for those in heavy homespun woolen uniforms carrying weapons, bedrolls, and canteens. The regulars slapped at horseflies, wiped sweat from their faces with the backs of their sleeves, swigged at their canteens and complained bitterly that they joined the army to fight, not to be walked to death.

Casimir, wearing a clean, colorful uniform while sitting astride Visner, looked like the general and leader he had been in Poland. He ignored the heat, biting flies, and dust, exemplifying professionalism and a total dedication to military strategy and fighting.

Washington, called to Lafayette to move closer and said, "Please tell Count Pulaski that I agree with him that appearances make a leader as much as action. He is truly a man who loves to fight. He lives for nothing else. My men tell me he and his horse train every day, day after day, regardless of weather. He deserves a chance to see how we fight here so he can adapt his tactics to our terrain. I will try to give him that chance on this campaign. While I don't anticipate encountering the full British force for several days, there might be a skirmish or two that Count Pulaski can watch."

Lafayette repeated Washington's words to Casimir who was obviously moved. That the general would take time on such a day to think of him and give him assurance was more evidence of what a fine leader the general was. And it gave Casimir confidence. He had received so little praise in America, that now, to receive it from one as revered as Washington, was meaningful. He would do his best to distinguish himself in the battle ahead.

On the evening of September 10, 1777, they entered a long, narrow valley with a creek running the length of it. This was Brandywine, a bucolic valley covered with verdant fields of grass sloping gently down to the west side of the creek. The land was steeper and covered with rocks on the east side. Two streams farther up the valley merged to form the larger Brandywine Creek which flowed wide and deep at the mouth. Washington headed north to Chadd's Ford, where a stone bridge built more than one hundred years earlier made crossing easier.

A large church with a cemetery clung to the hill above the bridge on the Eastern side. There were three stone mounting steps for parishioners to mount and dismount their horses near the front door. It reminded Casimir of the old churches that dotted the streets in Polish villages and towns and along roads in the countryside.

He saw three plainly dressed women in white bonnets and aprons hurrying inside a faded wooden house. It appeared to be a mother, daughter, and granddaughter. "Marquis, why are they dressed so plainly?" Casimir asked Lafayette.

"They are Quakers, referred to as Friends, because they are a peaceable people who do not believe in fighting. What a horrible ordeal this battle will be for them."

Casimir nodded his understanding and agreement.

Washington, still heading north, rode to the top of one of the highest hills from where he had a good view of the entire area. The view was truly frightening. Howe's army of more than 15,000 troops was moving through the valley.

Washington summoned Major John Bishop, who rushed up the hill to Washington's side, while casting a haughty look toward Casimir, displaying his arrogance. It was obvious that a huge battle was about to start and his expression showed that he assumed he was being recognized for a special assignment.

Lafayette and Casimir watched as Washington spoke to the Major and saw his look go from smugness to surprise to anger. "Major Bishop, I need your assistance in a matter of utmost importance. Moylan stayed behind in case Howe changed course and headed to New York. Go tell him to join us here, now. And find Doctor Rush. Tell him to bring every surgeon and nurse he can find. We're going to need them all. Leave now. Much depends on your success in getting to Moylan and Rush in time."

With those few words from Washington, Bishop was both entrusted to a critical mission and barred from being a hero on the battlefield, a battlefield where generals would be made. He had no choice but to obey orders and leave immediately.

At five the next morning Washington and his troops were on a promontory overlooking Chadd's Ford which was the logical place for Howe to attack. Daybreak was still an hour away and, as always, Casimir's mind was racing. He remembered his second battle at Lanckorona Castle, high above the Skawina River Valley, and his defense of the Jasna Gora Monastery which sat on a plateau above the city of Czestochowa.

Casimir's pulse quickened as he began to visualize alternative moves General Washington could make to surprise and defeat the British. He thought, *Commanding the high ground is a key advantage. General Washington should do well against the superior numbers of the British just as I did against much larger Russian forces.*

If he will only give me a chance to fight, this is the type of terrain I know. It is like that of Lesser Poland, where my guerilla tactics with only a small force of mounted Polish Cossacks worked so well.

He recalled how they had ambushed the Russians who marched in strict formation, as do the British, then retreated into the rocky ravines to hide behind large boulders. It drove the Russians mad and made him famous.

At what should have been sunbreak, fog moved in, concealing everything. Sounds were distorted by the heavy, damp air. The clang of a cook's coffee pot bumping against stone in a fire ring carried across the valley as loud as cannon cart wheels scraping over rocks. Neither army could see the other.

This is a perfect opportunity to sneak around them and create havoc from behind the lines, Casimir thought. But Washington failed to seize the opportunity and waited. Casimir was an observer, not an officer, and couldn't intervene in the general's plans.

When the sun sliced the fog into misty channels of light, it offered fleeting glimpses of shadowy figures moving toward them. A series of small skirmishes began.

As the sun slowly rose higher and the fog moved into smaller and smaller patches, the battle intensified and Casimir became disgusted at the carnage he witnessed. Both the American and British troops marched blindly to within musket range of each other, fired, and in turn were fired upon. Soldiers fell like wheat before a scythe. It went on for most of the day as the sun burned hotter, removing the last threads of the protective fog.

The weather befriended the British that day. Howe's General von Knyphausen attacked the Continental Army with 5,000 troops while Lord Cornwallis, under orders from Howe, moved the rest of the army far to the north. Fog masked their early morning movement enabling Cornwallis to move 10,000 troops across Brandywine Creek at Trembles Ford, undetected. Washington had dispersed a sizeable number of his troops to defend various fording spots along the creek, but none as far north as Trembles Ford.

Without resistance, the British came down the east side of the creek and encircled Washington's entire army. Too late, General Washington realized he was in a trap, a trap very similar to the one he had escaped from on Long Island. But now such a water evacuation and retreat were impossible.

Generals Anthony Wayne and Nathaniel Greene, two heroes noted for fighting valiantly and inspiring their troops, were trapped with him and he feared the core of the Continental Army would be destroyed on this very day. Would the war, American independence, and his own life end here?

Lafayette, who had been on a reconnoitering mission saw the peril and led his troops far to the left of the advancing British to meet Washington in the middle of a shrinking circle. Casimir sat on Visner near Washington with his sword and lance in hand, ready to move. He understood the danger they were in and started looking for a way to escape, but time was running out. Surrender or death could be the alternative and neither were acceptable to him.

Washington greeted Lafayette with courteous realism saying, "Monsieur Lafayette, I fear our position is tenuous. I can see no escape. I fear the battle is lost and we may all perish on these very rocks, or, worse yet, on a British prison ship."

"My great and heroic General, there is always the victor and the vanquished. Like you, I see no way to avoid defeat. Today we will not win but there will be other battles. The cause of independence is just and we shall prevail," replied Lafayette.

Casimir watched, gathering from their gentlemanly gestures that they were trading niceties to each other in the face of death. He was angered by such foolishness and he, for one, was not going to sit idly by while the enemy overran them.

Overcome by rage, he shoved his sense of protocol aside and spurred Visner forward to approach Washington and Lafayette. In French, with agitated arm waving and hand gesturing, he turned to Lafayette to interpret.

"General give me your personal thirty-man horse guard. With this small force, I can break through the British line and open a retreat route. This is exactly what I have done in the mountainous regions of Poland against stronger, fiercer and braver forces than these redcoats."

Fervently, he hoped Washington would agree, thinking, *it will be easy. I can slice through the British lines and show what can be done with a few men on horseback but, with no men of my own, I have to have the general's approval.*

Washington thought Casimir's proposal was suicidal but he saw no alternative.

It would also be suicide to stand where they were. With Howe's noose tightening, they must surrender or retreat, and there was no path to retreat through. It was another battle lost and this time the loss of the capitol. It was catastrophic. *The war could end right here on this rocky Pennsylvania hillside,* thought Washington. *The lives lost at Saratoga, Trenton and Long Island and in countless smaller skirmishes would mean nothing. The colonies would still be under British rule. If there is any chance for survival, I must take it and Count Pulaski is the only one offering any hope.* He turned to Lafayette and sighed, "I agree, but the men of my guard must decide if they are willing to follow Pulaski.

"Gentlemen," he said, turning to his guard, "Count Pulaski has requested permission to lead you to attack the British front in hopes of opening a retreat route. It is a highly dangerous mission, and it is up to you whether to follow him."

Having watched Casimir's amazing feats on the training field, Washington's elite guard moved forward as one, signifying their unanimous agreement.

Washington looked at Casimir and nodded his approval as the heroic Pole glanced at each member of the guard, raised the Sobieski sabre over his head, yelling "bezplatnie, do przodu," as he began the charge.

They had heard those words before and knew they meant 'charge forward'. Realizing he was the only one doing anything to get them out of this deathtrap, they didn't hesitate. They rushed forward as he rode headlong into the advancing British.

Urging Visner forward at a full gallop, he drew his pistol with his left hand and fired at the British troops. Then, as he rode closer to their return fire, he fell back in his saddle as if shot, while clutching his hooked lance. The British broke the line to allow the charging horse through, thinking the rider was mortally wounded, then closed ranks behind him, cutting Casimir off from the thirty men in the guard.

Once through the line, Casimir straightened in the saddle and, drawing his sword, spun Visner around and started attacking the British backs, hacking and cutting redcoats with his sword and piercing them with his lance. Screams of men being trampled by his horse's hooves, slashed by his sword and impaled with his lance filled the air.

Casimir was deadly accurate. He knew where the aorta artery met the collarbone, and his trained swordsmanship meant he rarely missed his mark.

Blood spurted and slickened the ground as his adrenalin flowed equally as fast, erasing all caution. He rammed his Pulaski lance through the chest of a British officer on horseback and used the hook to pull him to the ground.

While it was Casimir alone who kept attacking their rear, the British thought they were being outflanked and surrounded. They began breaking and running which created an opening for Casimir to race through to rejoin Washington's guard, now aggressively engaged at the front of the line. Then he led the guards from the British line, pretending to retreat. The British thought they had won the skirmish, but then, when he was just out of musket range, Casimir whirled Visner around and led another charge—directly at them. This time, he and the entire guard broke through the line.

When Lafayette saw what was happening, he charged in to assist, bringing more troops, eager to join the fight. Chaos ensued. Redcoats encircled Casimir at one point but Visner stomped three men in front of him, then used his mighty back hoofs to kick those behind him sending them sailing through the air like stones in a giant catapult, while Casimir severed a head from its body. Clearing everything in their way, Casimir never thought of risk or danger, but only how he could create more mayhem.

Lafayette and his men were mowing their way through the red-coats and the British scattered in all directions.

Casimir and the guard then rode back through the line toward General Washington but again, just outside of musket range, he turned Visner and headed back toward the British. When he approached the British muskets and bayonets, he slid down Visner's side and continued riding until he was on top of the red-coats. The man they thought had fallen from the horse rose and shot at close range as he moved back up in the saddle. Muskets were notoriously unreliable but Casimir had trained himself to judge just where the spinning musket ball would land, and adjust his aim accordingly.

He had gotten through the line a third time, bringing with him both the personal guard and Lafayette's contingent of men. Swinging around, he hacked, cut and slashed more British as he drove at their backs. The terrified British ran from Visner's deadly hoofs and the madman who rode him.

When General Nathaniel Greene saw the British line break under the relentless assault from Casimir and Lafayette, he led Washington and his other officers through the opening, saving their lives.

Casimir saw that the British were moving in position to block the Chadd's Ford bridge, which would prevent Washington's cannons and supply wagons from crossing. Casimir led troops, now anxious to follow the masterful little Pole, on a frantic dash to Chadd's Ford, where he used the same tactic yet again.

He charged at full speed, breaking through the line, and then attacked from the rear. It worked again enabling the supply wagons to make it across the river and rendezvous with Washington's main force.

Casimir had saved Washington and countless officers and men. But, he was horrified by what the day had cost. The bodies of horses and men from both armies littered the fields, the churchyard, and the creek. The moaning of men and their pleas for water and help filled the air but there was little that could be done. Doctor Rush had finally arrived with eight assistants, but amputation was the only treatment for almost all wounds to the arms and legs. Body wounds were usually fatal due to loss of blood, and infection with gangrene being the biggest killer.

The stone church cemetery was soon filled with fresh mounds of dirt, although only those men who lived in the area were buried there. Most of the British and American bodies lay next to and on top of one another across the hillside. The water in Brandywine Creek was no longer a gurgling, cool, and clear stream. Now it crawled along like oozing blood, coloring the stones in its path dark-red. Buzzards gathered in the tall elm trees gazing down at fallen bodies that rats were already working on. It would be a winter filled with starvation and the stench of rotting bodies for the people in the valley.

Casimir saw Quaker women dressed in aprons and bonnets moving among the men with water and prayer books. They gave what comfort they could to the dying in spite of their beliefs on fighting and war.

Other women moved across the battlefield, holding handkerchiefs to their noses as the smells of urine, blood, gunpowder, and the deathly odor of gangrene filled the heavy night air. They carried kerosene lanterns and shined them into the faces of the dead and dying soldiers, crying out, "Tom, are you alive? Call to me. Willie, my boy, please answer your Mama, please answer your Mama. Oh God, let him answer." Few were rewarded with an answer.

Musket shots continued all night as wounded horses were shot, and wounded men committed suicide to gain relief from their pain or avoid capture. Casimir understood and thought how he would prefer death to capture.

The sound of those muskets penetrated George Washington's bones. Each shot reminded him of the price paid for another lost battle, one for which he felt responsible. It was a demoralizing defeat, since troops were more likely to accept the loss of comrades if their lives were sacrificed for a victory. He wondered how long he could hold the army together.

Now he was being forced to retreat to Lancaster, Pennsylvania and he had to admit that Philadelphia, the capitol, might soon fall. That loss would dishearten not only his army and members of Congress but all those brave citizens who supported 'the rebellion', as the British liked to call their fight for independence. How many would decide it wiser to convert to Loyalists? Another defeat might also convince the French to withdraw their support which would be a devastating blow to the cause.

General Washington looked back at the soldiers following him. After making sure the supply wagons were safe, he saw that Casimir was riding back toward the main army. In spite of a deep gash in his left thigh, Lafayette rode up to join his heroic Polish friend. Riding proudly together toward the front, they were cheered by a chorus of "hip, hip, hurrah, hip, hip, hooray, boys you showed 'em. Those redcoats couldn't run fast enough," shouted the troops as they passed.

When General Washington heard the cheering, he motioned for Casimir and Lafayette to join him. He was more thankful to these two for boosting the morale of his troops on this dark evening than he was for his own life being saved.

Fighting men need a hero. The Continental Army troops thought of Washington as a god, far above fighting hand to hand, and they saw Lafayette as daring and dashing, but still royalty, hence a bit removed from the common man.

What they really loved was "seeing the redcoats run from that mad little Polish guy." Casimir had rallied them when all seemed lost and they would follow him again, given the chance.

Major Bishop, arrived at Brandywine in time to see Casimir save Washington. The troops heard him rage, "What possessed this little man to think he had a right to risk the general's personal guard? And now the idiot looks like a hero.

"And, you ignorant, illiterate troops are cheering him. What is it about him that makes people overlook his arrogance and rashness? Can't you see he's a self-centered foreigner doing as he damn well pleases? No, instead you applaud him. What if the rest of the troops acted like him? There would be no organization. Surely Washington can see through him. One little successful skirmish does not make officer material. Officers must be disciplined, cautious, serious, and obedient, not spur of the moment glory seekers. Oh, his day will come and I ask only that I get to see his fall when it happens."

But Washington saw Casimir's charge against the British as more than a skirmish. He was impressed with Pulaski the man, his military assault tactics, and the inspiring impact he had on the men with his cavalry charges.

After Brandywine, much to Major Bishop's chagrin, Washington petitioned Congress for funding for an American Cavalry and the rank of brigadier general for Pulaski. The rank, along with approval for Pulaski to lead the cavalry, were awarded, but little funding followed, partially due to lack of follow through by General Washington himself.

Vacillating, Washington sometimes wondered how he could, in good conscience, pull money away from food, ammunition, and equipment for his men who had endured frostbite, starvation, musket wounds, and separation from their families to fund a military strategy led by a foreigner that was unproven in America's forests. It was a high risk and costly venture. Still, the British were afraid of him, he inspired the troops, and his new way of fighting might succeed where the old ways failed.

"Damnation," Washington lamented to himself, *"I wish I had more money so I could fund the needs of the army and the cavalry this heroic Pole is so fired up about.*

CHAPTER TWENTY

FRIENDS AND FOES

Pennsylvania
1777-1778

asimir was grateful for the promotion, but frustrated beyond words. He had been given the rank of Brigadier General with no funding for his cavalry. To Congress he was like a burr dipped in honey and tangled in long hair. The more the members tried to dismiss him and be rid of him, the stickier and deeper the snag became. He kept demanding money for the cavalry that they authorized him to lead, and was at the chamber doors daily to persuade anyone who spoke both French and English to help him explain the value of a cavalry and the urgency of the present situation.

It was September. A cold October was in the wind. There had been no great victories to encourage the men to reenlist. Casimir was convinced that if he had enough money to get the cavalry battle-ready, victories would come. He wished that the pessimistic sloths in the Continental Congress knew how effective his tactics were in Poland against overwhelming odds. But they were using his lack of English as an excuse to close their ears to reason.

It was not his nature to quit. He continued to show up at the chamber doors daily, but what he considered the injustice of the situation was now wearing his patience and spirits sorely thin.

It was at this crucial moment that Silas Deane of Connecticut, who had been authorized by Washington to secretly negotiate with France for aid, returned to America. He saw Casimir at the chamber doors constantly beseeching everyone from clerks to John Hancock, the president of the Continental Congress, to help him obtain funding.

Deane recalled his conversation with Benjamin Franklin a few weeks prior to Casimir's visit at Versailles. "The bravest, brashest, and most determined man I have ever heard of," Franklin said. "He successfully stopped the Russians from driving deeper into Poland again and again with a force a fraction the size of theirs. He inspired men to join his cavalry and follow him into what looked like certain death, time and again. I hope to convince him to join Washington and do the same against the British."

From what Deane had heard since arriving back in the colonies, Casimir had already proven himself having saved Generals Washington, Wayne, and Greene at the Battle of Brandywine. Why on earth was such a man having a problem getting money to equip a cavalry that could be of such great help in the fight against the British?

He didn't approach Casimir directly to find an answer, but when Congress took a brief break he cornered several members and asked, "I see General Pulaski here requesting funding for the cavalry that was approved. Why is he having so much trouble getting it?"

"Have you seen him? He doesn't speak English and he acts like some sort of sissy royal prince strutting up and down the aisle in high heeled boots with a cape swirling around his gaudy brigadier general's uniform, one that he had modified to suit his tastes," replied a member. The others quickly added, "here, here."

"But what does any of that have to do with winning battles, which he has proven he can do?" Deane asked.

There was no credible answer. Just the lame excuse that he was a foreigner and while his tactics worked in Europe, they were untested in America. According to some, Brandywine didn't count, because most of it was cleared land, not forested.

Deane dropped the issue as it was obvious Casimir's style was not to the liking of the congressional delegates. But he admired Casimir's persistence and fortitude, arguing day after day to seek funding to fight for an American cause, so far from his homeland. It seemed this little foreigner was more patriotic and dedicated to winning independence for the colonies than some self-serving members of Congress who spent most of their time bickering. Deane was not sure he himself could endure this daily dose of bureaucracy and drama. His admiration for Pulaski grew.

As he expected, he found Casimir at the congressional chamber doors the next morning, ready for another battle with the stubborn members. "Monsieur Pulaski, I'm Silas Deane, I'm not sure you remember but we met briefly at Benjamin Franklin's quarters in Versailles. I trust your journey to America was not too arduous as you look very fit, albeit a bit frustrated," Deane said in French, as he bowed to Casimir. Casimir responded "Oui, Of course I remember you, I thought at the time that I would like to meet you again and it seems fate has allowed that to happen. It is good to see you also made a safe crossing," as he returned the bow.

"I heard of your success at Brandywine saving Washington's life. I also heard of your difficulties in receiving funds for the cavalry congress authorized."

"Oui, Oui. You have read my frustration accurately Monsieur Deane. I need to train and equip my cavalry to win battles against the British before the enlistments are up. The men will surely leave Washington if he cannot provide them with more hope that the war can be won."

"Count Pulaski, I believe you and your cavalry can help turn the tide for Washington. Unfortunately, I am embroiled in disagreements with some of the delegates myself. There's a little matter of my endorsing the wrong Frenchman and some issue with money that has helped my detractors discredit me. I am no longer a Delegate. But I do have a little influence remaining and will do what I can for you. I cannot authorize congressional monies but I believe our current situation grows more desperate each day. I will personally provide what funds I can, hoping they may help carry you through until Congress wakes up."

Unbelieving, Casimir grasped Deane's hand. "Merci, I am most grateful for your financial support and even more so for your confidence in me. I won't disappoint you and I hope others in Congress will follow your example. It can make a great difference in the outcome of this war."

Deane's support, although not nearly enough, lifted Casimir's hopes of receiving additional monies and he soon had another source.

After that, Casimir received a letter from his sister, Joanna.

My dearest brother,

Your last letter disturbed me. It seems unfair that after traveling so far to be of aide to the Americans, that they have not accepted you, and that you are hindered from proving yourself by a lack of funds. I have no use for money myself as all my needs here at the convent are provided for by the Church. I asked Mamma to sell my jewelry, another luxury I have no need of here, and have arranged to forward the proceeds to you. It is not much, but I hope that the love that comes with it will replace the frustration you have experienced and in some small way make life brighter for you.

Mother is well and sends her love with mine. We hear from Antonin regularly now and he is also well. God protect you and return you to us one day soon. With love, your sister, Joanna

Casimir was overcome with emotion. The combined funds of Deane and Joanna would give him a start but were not enough to properly recruit and equip a cavalry to his liking Yet, their gestures gave him renewed enthusiasm.

He began immediately to build a cavalry with the meager funds he had, but the men were untrained, belligerent, and some who were defectors from Washington's Army, expected less discipline in this foreigner's horse legion. The latter group could not have been more mistaken.

Casimir knew complaining to General Washington would only anger the general, so he began his own strict training program to upgrade the troops who would serve with him. After the press glorified his saving of Washington at Brandywine and ran articles about his new cavalry and his need for men who were good riders, a steady stream of woodsmen, farmers, apprentices, blacksmiths and clerks began pouring into camp seeking the adventure of riding with a hero.

With a renewed energy in his dream of creating an elite force, he set up a rough-hewn recruiting table, strategically located in the very center of camp where others were sure to see how many men wanted to be part of his legion. He wanted the best to apply and he meant to choose the very best.

Henrik von Hessen, a German soldier with a thick neck and drooping moustache, approached him one day with an unusual offer. Von Hessen spoke both English and German and could converse with Casimir who spoke German, and the English-speaking recruits. "I can help you General Pulaski," he said. "I'm not a horseman, but I am good at keeping track of things. I kept records for my father, who was a butcher, recording all the inventory, sales, spoilage losses, prices, and daily tallies of net receipts. Father said I have a plain, easy-to-read hand, and Father rarely gave praise. I think you need to keep track of men who wish to ride with you, and those you want to ride with you. Am I right?"

Casimir, never one for record keeping, needed precisely this kind of help and responded immediately, "Yes, I would be most grateful for someone to help me interview the men in English and record the information about them, especially the ones I plan to recruit and train."

Von Hessen proved to be up to the task and quickly established a process of communicating with the applicants. In a ledger, he entered their names, ages, locations of their homes, and family names — for notification purposes in case of death — and presented it to Casimir in legible, straightforward handwriting. Whether by coincidence or because von Hessen was assisting them and Casimir also spoke and read German, a large number of his new troops came from Germany. There were also many from France, for Casimir to converse with.

All day, the line of hopefuls wound through the camp. The man at the front of the line would step forward to the recruitment table announcing his name and hometown, which von Hessen dutifully repeated for Casimir. On the afternoon of the third day, Casimir was delighted to hear two voices he recognized, "Samuel Abbot, Marblehead, Massachusetts reporting for duty, Sir. Abe Hawkins, Marblehead, Massachusetts reporting for duty, Sir," came their strong and loud young voices. Casimir looked up from his long list of potential recruits and smiled, moved toward them grasping their extended hands signaling enthusiastically toward von Hessen to record their names in the smaller ledger with those being accepted into the Pulaski Legion.

When the newspapers had reported Casimir's rescue of Washington at Brandywine and on the other skirmishes he and his men won, the boys dreamed of joining him.

Sketches in the papers showed Casimir astride Visner, in a tailored uniform, with sword raised overhead — he was the most interesting and romantic figure they had ever encountered. Not even the knights of old, whom they had read about, had his flamboyant flair, and there was a mystery about him that drew the boys to him like the tide is drawn to shore. They had told Samuel's mother they wanted to learn French in case they needed to trade with France after the war and she had been pleased to teach them. She wanted Samuel to have some of the graces so common in Europe where most people spoke several languages. Of course, they had already been planning to join Casimir and wanted to be able to speak with him, perhaps even act as personal assistants, translating for him. Their parents could no longer restrain them when they read that he was looking for recruits.

Although Casimir had met these young men only once, they were like old friends. He knew they were in awe of and genuinely devoted to him and he vowed to protect them.

The pace picked up as the afternoon progressed, with more qualified candidates stepping forward. Casimir's interest having been heightened by the arrival of the two Marblehead boys. He listened more closely to the applicants, studying their facial expressions when he couldn't understand their words. Although he did not comprehend what they said, he did discern a dialect that was becoming prevalent in the new men applying. It was firm, short and almost curt in its delivery, somewhat similar to von Hessen's direct way of speaking. It was clear that Abe and Samuel had convinced many of their New England friends to join them, and all of them spoke in the no-nonsense, flat cadence of the New England Yankee.

In late afternoon, as shadows turned the canvas tents gray and cooled the air, Casimir heard a different accent. It was softer and stretched words out longer, leaving them drifting on the air. It was a pleasant dialect, like a romance language — perhaps French or Italian — but still in unfathomable English that he couldn't understand. It came from a young man who approached the table and said,

"Lee McElveen—no home, only some Indian relatives —but I can ride and shoot and I can talk with the Indians . . . speak some French too, if that will help."

Casimir glanced up at the recruit in front of him expecting to see a mix of curiosity and hopefulness from a youngster hoping to be accepted into the Pulaski Legion. Now, at thirty-four, Casimir was nearing old age for a soldier, but he was young and eager, like these boys when he had begun fighting, and he still liked having the vibrancy of youth around him.

Looking closer at the applicant, he didn't find what he expected from Lee McElveen, his eyes weren't eager —they were serious, sad and defiant; his young face was mud-streaked, his jaw rigid. His body was slight and seemed almost frail, but Casimir thought the man's size, like his own, was unimportant as long as he had other attributes to overcome his small stature.

Von Hessen turned to Casimir, "He says he can talk with the Indians, and you said you want an interpreter who can convince the natives to help us—this could be your man. With no family and no home, he may be willing to take more risks—oh, and General, he can speak some French."

Casimir thought, *divine providence must have sent this young man to me, there is no other explanation.*

Not wishing to display his enthusiasm to the new recruit, he said to von Hessen, "He seems different. Ask him where he is from and how he knows the Indian language."

"The general wants to know where you grew up and how you can talk with the Indians," said von Hessen, looking directly at Lee, who responded,

"South Carolina, sir, near Charles Town, my mother was half Cherokee and I lived with her tribe several months a year. They taught me their Cherokee language and ways, I can ride a horse, track animals or men, and live off the land as well as any Indian."

After von Hessen had interpreted, Casimir asked,

"Why does he want to fight, and why for me—the name 'McElveen' sounds familiar—does he have a relative here?"

When von Hessen passed the question on, he got a hard, cold answer. "The British were brutal to me, my family and my cousin, Jimmy McElveen, who served with General Pulaski—he died at the Battle of White Horse Tavern fighting the British at Warren. I was told that he fought and died next to the general."

When von Hessen repeated what Lee said, Casimir remembered the name and the fight. One of his patrols had spotted a small detachment of British soldiers. It was pouring rain and the Redcoats were not expecting an encounter—exactly the type of situation Casimir liked, since it gave him the advantage of surprise, and he could hit them hard and then run. He had jumped onto Visner's back and spurred the stallion forward. It was easy for his men and their mounts to see and follow the white horse in the rain, but they had to ride hard to keep up with their sword-swinging general who repeatedly turned in his saddle to urge them on.

The heavy rain soaked the gunpowder, making it useless, and the skirmish was inconclusive. The British were ready to leave the field, but Casimir seized the opportunity to storm into them with his men at full charge, using his Pulaski lance and sword to full advantage. The British were stunned by the attack and fought savagely to save themselves. During the melee, Casimir was knocked from Visner's back, his boot spur became tangled in the stirrup, and his frightened horse, being beaten with lances, tried to run, dragging Casimir with him. Seeing his general's plight, young Jimmy McElveen had raced over, grabbed Visner's reins, and helped free the general's foot.

Just as Casimir started to stand, a raging Redcoat ran toward them with a raised lance aimed directly at Casimir's chest.

"No," cried the young cavalryman, knocking Casimir back to the ground and falling on top of him. The Redcoat drove the lance through Jimmy's back, killing him instantly. Casimir squirmed from under Jimmy's body, slashed the Redcoat's knee with his Sobieski saber, and when the British soldier clutched his leg and fell, Casimir finished him off by bringing the sword down on his head.

He knew his life had been saved by the sacrifice of young Jimmy McElveen. Now, he remembered that Sergeant Wilkes had told him one of the recruits had a cousin who could talk with the Indians. This must be the man. Of course, he would accept the cousin into his elite cavalry. Casimir needed an interpreter to communicate with the Indians and if Lee was as brave as his cousin, he would be a fine recruit.

Casimir understood the wisdom of working with the Indians and that it would be good to have someone who could talk to the natives and report the conversations directly to him. He nodded his approval to von Hessen and reached out to shake Lee's hand. Then, not wishing to continue the masquerade of being unable to talk with the young man he said, 'bien venue.'

It was a good day, many fine young men joined his force, and he was confident at least three of them, Samuel, Abe and Lee, would distinguish themselves like he had at their age.

Still, Congress dragged on, giving no additional funding, as General Washington moved cautiously. He assigned Casimir and his cavalry to trivial escort services for generals and dignitaries and a few minor battles, exasperating the Polish warrior to the point of madness.

He had ridden across Poland leading thousands of men when he was only twenty-two. He had been shot, stabbed, beaten and imprisoned while fighting the Russians and had survived to fight again, not to wait for tight fisted bureaucrats to debate endlessly about whether to give him the money he needed. He was vibrant and invincible on horseback charging the enemy. He was as addicted to fighting as some men are to drinking, gambling or women — and he could not give it up. Fighting for freedom from overbearing monarchs was right and he needed to fight. Why couldn't General Washington and the Continental Congress see that and turn him loose on the British?

Joanna and the rest of his family continued to raise money and forward it to him, but it was never enough despite the fact that he used it wisely. He and one of his sergeants knew horses better than many who raised and sold them and he got the best horses at bargain prices. He also designed marvelous uniforms for the troops and had them made by the Moravian Sisters at a nearby monastery who would accept only a small donation for their work. He improved the old equipment and the Pulaski lances, which now included a hook to pull men from their mounts. He bought all the best saddles, blankets and munitions wherever he could find them at reasonable prices.

Von Hessen kept meticulous records of the men as Pulaski's troop numbers grew, but he didn't keep records of Casimir's expenditures to outfit his cavalry, nor did Casimir ask for such information.

In spite of Casimir's consistent victories in the small skirmishes assigned to him, congressmen remained cool to his monetary requests. They dribbled funds to him, with the excuse they could not provide more until they had the records they needed documenting where the last paltry sum they gave him was used and how the requested new funds would be spent. Since the money they approved was so much less than what he needed, Casimir didn't think it was worth his time to try to answer their request for details. Especially since he had more than matched the Congressional funds with personal money from his family. He simply saw no need to give an accounting since his family was not asking for one.

Some members were cautious and concerned about committing scarce resources to untested military tactics while others were simply jealous of Casimir's popularity with the press and the way women reacted to his European flourish. Casimir peppered them with petitions to reimburse him for the personal funds he had spent as well as additional funding for his unit to no avail. They still turned a blind eye, demanding details of past expenditures, which infuriated Casimir. Due to his inability to state his case in English, the dialogues were short and Congress was dismissive. He was never allowed the time or the skilled interpreters to explain why he needed the funds and how successful he could be with a fully equipped legion.

Major John Bishop, still seething about Casimir getting the Brigadier General's rank, was becoming a pressing problem. As Casimir's legion of well-dressed, finely mounted, and well-trained soldiers, came together as an elite group, Major Bishop was often seen stomping through camp, fists clenched, while muttering to himself or watching Casimir from a distance with a sinister smile stretched tight across his thin twisted lips.

"This cocky little man struts around in his general's uniform like he deserves to wear it," Bishop muttered to himself. "I'll bet that pretty seamstress in Philadelphia made it for him. Oh, yes, he'll get what he deserves, and it won't be more unearned glory. I will see to that."

Bishop was not the only one who envied Casimir. Several other officers resented his quick promotion after Brandywine. It was his first fight and most of them had fought several battles with Washington and suffered severe privations, only to be passed over for the brigadier general rank by a foreigner who couldn't speak English.

Foremost among the disgruntled officers was Colonel Stephen Moylan. He had served as Washington's aide before Bishop and then assumed command of the dragoons. He envied Casimir's cavalry which made his dragoons appear shabby compared to the Pulaski troops. His men were more seasoned and just as brave as these fancy-pants soldiers and Pulaski's promotion was an insult to them as much as to him.

As former aides to Washington, it was natural for Moylan and Bishop, both bitter men, to form a vengeful alliance to discredit Casimir in the eyes of Congress. They began spreading rumors about his use of the small sums awarded him.

Casimir felt the biting jaws of jealousy. It hurt more than he would show to be brushed aside by Congress and to be denied a leadership role in the planning of military tactics. His general's title that others coveted was an affront to him. Without the funds to properly train and equip his legion and prove the effectiveness of his military strategy, it was a joke. He had no power beyond the notoriety he gained from winning each small skirmish assigned to him. In his homeland, he had been in command and led his troops to stunning victories. From childhood, he was a champion in everything he attempted and the lack of recognition from General Washington and the Continental Congress cut deeply.

Bishop's incessant rantings about Casimir stealing his promotion and his growing display of disloyalty to the Revolution concerned Moylan, causing him to be increasingly uneasy about his pact with Bishop.

"I earned the right to that uniform," Bishop raved to Moylan. "I played a far more important role at Brandywine than Pulaski. I brought you back to the battle where you fought as hard as anyone. And it was Greene who saved the general, not Pulaski. But did I get credit for you and the doctor being there? No, this arrogant little wart stole the glory that was mine. Now the fancy peacock is a general, promoted over me."

As Bishop raged on, spittle now flying from his mouth, Moylan became more uncomfortable and asked him to slow down and be quiet lest he be heard.

But instead of heeding the warning, Bishop rattled on, saying, "My family produced military leaders in England for centuries. I should have joined the British Army instead of this ragtag bunch of illiterate backwoodsmen who could care less about gaining promotions or honoring those who deserve them. They just want to fight for what they call freedom. Well, they'll have their freedom—freedom to freeze and starve—and eventually the freedom of a prison ship or death.

"I signed up with the Americans because there were so few men qualified to be generals. The British Army is full of career men. I chose this army where I would stand out. I don't give a tinker's damn about either the British or American causes. I just wanted the general's rank to shut my father up. I chose the side where I thought I could get it the fastest. I do everything Washington asks and more, and anything I think he will notice and appreciate. I even studied farming so I could talk with him about his precious Mount Vernon and those stupid asses called mules. And this little nitwit of a banty rooster, who can't even speak the General's language, got the title that was reserved for me. My promotion!"

Since Moylan believed in the American Revolution, it disturbed him that Bishop wasn't devoted to it. But he also harbored a seething animosity towards Casimir. Against his better judgment he continued to support Bishop in his attempts to destroy the new general.

When not arguing for funds from Congress, Casimir spent his days and nights devising battle strategies and training his men. He and his troops proved themselves again and again when they were permitted to engage the enemy and his reputation for bravery, leadership, and evading capture grew even more.

After a triumphant battle at Haddonfield, New Jersey, newspapers praised his cavalry's exploits and Casimir's notoriety soared.

The battle occurred after General Washington ordered General Anthony Wayne to forage for food and supplies to feed and clothe his freezing and starving men at Valley Forge. When Wayne received intelligence that a large British force was in the area he sent for Casimir and his cavalry to come to his aid. The Pulaski dragoons were in poor shape themselves, with many suffering from wounds inflicted in other battles. Casimir was able to assemble only forty-four men and five officers who were fit for service.

Colonel Stirling, the British commander, wanted to stop Wayne's foraging and confiscate the few supplies he had gathered supplies, so needed by the troops at Valley Forge who were in desperate straits. But, Casimir arrived just in time to thwart Stirling's move by launching a stunning night-time raid.

He and his forty-four men charged on the two thousand British troops. The brashness of the move startled the British into believing they were being attacked by a much larger force than their own. Casimir ordered his troops to attack in all directions furthering the certainty on the part of the British that they were besieged by a major segment of Washington's army.

Visner charged forward with Casimir astride him thrusting his sword and lance into any Redcoat within range, while the horse kicked those on the ground with his mighty hooves.

As they turned to chase the enemy soldiers fleeing their deadly assault, Casimir saw Abe Hawkins tumble from his horse after being rammed in the chest by the pike of a mounted Redcoat. The boy was in danger of being trampled by the horses of his own troop or speared with an enemy lance. Casimir rode to the fallen boy, dismounted, and lightly touched the back of each of Visner's front knees instructing him to gently step one leg at a time over Abe's body shielding him from the other horses and Redcoats. Abe was still gasping for breath and Casimir was exposed to attack on the ground. Casimir Pulaski, the ferocious warrior who had just killed several men, cradled the young Hawkins in his arm as tenderly as one would a newborn until Samuel Abbot rushed to them and Casimir ordered him to take Abe away from the battle.

He remounted Visner and stormed into the British again, leaving them in confusion and disarray in the dark. Now with total certainty that they were being overrun by a much larger force, the Redcoats retreated to nearby Coopers Ferry, where Casimir quickly struck again, causing the British to flee. In their haste to retreat, the British abandoned their supplies which were then diverted to Valley Forge. General Wayne was once more free to forage for food.

Newspapers jumped on the story of his heroic encounter and praised Casimir, with a New Jersey Gazette article printed on March 11, 1778 reporting,

> Though they (the British) knew our inferiority of number, our attacking them with a few light horses at Haddonfield, under the command of Brigadier General Count Pulaski, made their fears get the better of their knowledge, as well as their courage, and happiest was the Briton who had the longest legs, and the nimblest head. Leaving bag and baggage, they retreated precipitately to Cooper's Ferry.

Like Wolny before him, Visner also gained fame. One newspaper wrote,

> Count Pulaski becomes one with his white stallion and in their swirling and twirling they are indistinguishable. One is shooting, slashing and spearing while the other kicks, stomps, and tramples. A formidable pair that the English fear and the Continentals cheer.

Despite his battle successes and recognition in the press, congressional members failed to budge. When he requested money, they only asked how he spent the pittance they gave him rather than listening to why he needed more. Casimir's frustration turned to anger. What difference did it make? The little they had allotted him wasn't nearly enough, certainly not enough to warrant all this detailed and time-consuming recordkeeping they wanted of him. It wasn't nearly as much as Deane, Joanna and his family had contributed. Besides, he thought, *I have a war to win. I have no time for clerking.*

Bishop and Moylan tried to discredit him by secretly meeting with members of Congress. They lied that Casimir couldn't give them an accounting of funds spent because he had used the money on unneeded equipment and fancy uniforms for himself. In truth, Casimir was frugal with the personal funds he raised as well as Congressional funds. He didn't have money for sorely needed provisions and he certainly didn't spend his own or Congressional funds for anything useless. But like the lies Catherine spread about him in Europe, the slander was effective, especially when he had no records to disprove the charges against him and, prodded by Bishop and Moylan, congressional delegates became mistrustful.

Von Hessen could have kept the proper records but Casimir thought it was a waste of time for such minor amounts and the big German was too valuable helping him train troops than to be sidetracked by bookkeeping. Having been raised in an affluent household where there was always money for things needed or wanted, keeping an account of small expenditures was as foreign to him as English. Even the Bar Confederation leaders didn't make such senseless demands. They allowed him to focus on fighting.

And fight he would. He would lead a daring charge, but this time it would be a political one. Never one for courting those in power, he decided to take his cause to the people. The newspapers had made him famous and that gave him ammunition to use against the nit pickers in Congress.

He assembled his Pulaski Legion dressed in their most resplendent blue and white uniforms. For himself he chose his flashiest parade uniform. Gold braids hanging across his chest connected two rows of gleaming gold buttons lining both sides of his indigo blue vest. The gold hilt of his Sobieski sword hanging at his side was mirror-polished. His cobalt blue cape had a gold lining and his red waist band matched his red fez that sat at the usual rakish tilt atop his coal black hair. White pants met black thigh-high boots with golden spurs that rested in brown leather stirrups decorated with small silver ravens.

He sat regally atop Visner whose white mane was braided with black and gold silk ribbons intertwined in it. A black leather saddle with a silver horn and amber gems imbedded in the hand-tooled borders sat atop a lapis blue blanket with borders of red and gold. The horse's tail was braided and had long free-flowing satin ribbons of blue, gold, and black. Visner pranced with a high step as if knowing he had a special role to play.

Casimir could see that his troops' chests bulged with pride to be part of the Pulaski Legion and to look so grand. He knew their morale ran high and was in sharp contrast to that of the other Continental troops. They were elite. He had them ready and prepared for this great political battle, one of the most important they would engage in.

Casimir paraded them through villages and towns in New Jersey, Delaware, and Pennsylvania. His campaign was a complete success. People rushed out of homes and shops to see such striking examples of courageous and dynamic young men and beautiful horses. It was uplifting after seeing the ragged and demoralized Continental troops trudging through mud and snow to challenge the well-dressed British. And only men as disciplined as the Pulaski troops could have resisted the young women rushing out to them with cakes, pies, and hot biscuits with the fresh baked smells filling the air. Like Tower of London guards, they took no notice of what the women were offering, which was surely more than pastries.

Casimir's charisma was infectious. As word spread of his route, reviewing stands were set up for mayors, town council members, and even a governor or two to watch as his legion passed through town. He accepted several offers to meet with dignitaries and told them about his need for funds to expand his cavalry and better equip it. Soon the congressional delegates were receiving letters from the areas they represented demanding that they fund the Pulaski Legion.

General Washington remained silent, but those around him noticed that when General Pulaski was mentioned, he simply nodded with the smallest of smiles parting his lips. He had always admired Casimir's bravery and military genius and now he marveled at his cleverness. He wished he had more men with his resourcefulness.

His aide, John Bishop stormed and stomped, cursed and fumed each time he overhead General Washington receiving a new report of Casimir's popularity.

"We will never be able to discredit him now," he shouted at Moylan. "We will have to do something else. The only solution I can think of is to kill the bloody cockamamie idiot. I would take great joy in shooting him, but now he is so popular the general would never promote me if I were found out.

"No, he must have a flaw, a weakness, that we can discover and use to our benefit. We need to stay close to him and watch everything he does."

"I think you should focus on something else for a while, John," Moylan advised.

"How can I? My mind will not give me peace as long as he is tormenting me with his antics that everyone sees as heroic, or grand, or pleasing?"

"Major, try to avoid destroying your own happiness over this. I don't like being passed over either. But we do still have a war to fight," Moylan counseled as he walked away.

Samuel Abbot's parents came to Delaware to see him and the rest of the troops. "Look what a fine uniform our son is wearing, Dad. If they move south, like the papers say, he will need a lighter one."

"He'll need something bigger too, Mother, whether they move south or not, he's about to pop the buttons off that one, his chest is puffed out so far."

"Well, I'm going to make him a new one," she continued. "I'm scared all the time that he's going to get hurt or killed, but just look at what a fine young man he has turned out to be and what a great general is leading him."

The Pulaski Legion swung inland and ended their grand march in Lancaster at the steps of Congress. Having been bombarded by letters from their constituents and now facing the cause of all the commotion, the delegates had no choice but to give Casimir money for his Legion. It was still not enough, but the recognition he received combined with the token financial support gave him hope that there might be more in the future. He had won a great political contest and it guaranteed his place in history on the eastern seaboard of America.

A few weeks later, Lafayette brought two letters to Casimir at his training grounds, that had just arrived by ship from France. Casimir's heart jumped when he saw a folded paper, sealed with the Pulaski Black Raven insignia and he wondered if it was good news, or bad. Was Antonin alive or had he been killed in prison like their father? The other was addressed in Paul's handwriting.

"Monsieur Lafayette, I am grateful, but I am concerned about the contents of one of the letters," he said to his friend. "If you will excuse me, I prefer to read it in private."

"Of course, Casimir," responded the Marquis. "Please let me know if I may be of help."

Casimir found a quiet spot away from the troops beside the horse corral. Visner snorted a welcome when he saw him walk up, and sit on a nearby grassy spot. Frightened of what he might learn, Casimir's hand trembled slightly as he broke the familiar seal and unfolded the letter. It was from Antonin.

> My beloved brother,
>
> I know you agonized over my fate while I was a prisoner in Russia, I am sorry for any distress I caused you. The truth is, I developed a rapport with my guards and received good treatment in return. Even the Russian court honors me. There is much to relate and explain.

Casimir was overjoyed that Antonin was not only alive but seemingly well and that he spoke of being in the Russian prison as something in the past. But he was quickly disillusioned when he read on.

> I know you will be shocked, my dear brother, but please read all I have to say. First, I have joined the Russian Army.

Casimir read and re-read those words but he still couldn't comprehend them. How could a Pulaski serve in that hated military? But Antonin's reasons became clear as he continued reading.

> Through my service with the Muscovites and the connections I developed, I have been successful in clearing our Pulaski name of treason in the King Poniatowski charade that Catherine orchestrated.

Casimir's heart raced wildly as he went through the complicated emotional contradictions. On the positive side, his brother was safe and he was no longer charged with a crime he hadn't committed. It was possible for him to finally return to Europe as a victor. He could kneel at the feet of the Lady of Czestochowa to give thanks for his safe and triumphant return just as so many conquering knights of long ago had done. Surely, he and Washington would defeat the British soon, and he could go home as a hero and be with his mother and sisters. And he could see Franciszka again.

But what a price. A Pulaski had served in the detestable Russian Army. It hurt him to the core, regardless of the reasons. Then Antonin's letter offered more insight,

> I am on my way to Warka to see Mother and our sisters and there's a good possibility my new Russian acquaintances will restore some of the Pulaski lands to our estate. I hope we can meet there soon under happier circumstances than we've known in a long, long time. However, I must warn you that in even though the regicide charges against you have been dropped, Ambassador Repnin, probably at the urging of Empress Catherine, is still offering a reward of five kilograms of gold for you dead or alive. That bounty is good in any country, so be careful wherever you travel.

Antonin's letter ended with,

> Because of your former friendship with her, I thought you would like to know that the Duchess of Courland is well and has a daughter.
> God Bless you, my brother. May the Blessed Mother protect you and bring you safely home.

Casimir shook his head as he reread the letter and thought, *Antonin, the youngest may be the strongest of us all. He put saving the family name and lands above all else.*

One thing was certain, Antonin's imprisonment in Russia was far different from his in France. The letter boosted Casimir's spirits. His brother was safe and one day he too could return home with his reputation restored. Then, considering Antonin's warning, he realized he was no safer in America than in Poland as long as the Russians wanted him. He wondered what they would do to him if he were captured by the British and turned over to them. One thing he was sure of, he could never allow himself to be captured again.

While pleased to hear that Franciszka was well and happy, the mention of her name failed to bring the thrill it once did. They lived in distant and different worlds now with dissimilar lives that no longer overlapped in any way. He knew he would always be fond of her and was sure she felt the same but he no longer dreamed of how life might have been if they had married.

He opened Paul's letter next.

> My dear Kas,
>
> I heard that you have become a Count in a country that does not have royal families. Somehow, I am not surprised. News of your saving General Washington's life as well as your theatrical tour through many of the colonies has also reached us. I am glad to hear you have not changed.
>
> I will soon settle my business here and be ready to join you. Sadly, Maurice buried his mother months ago and is haranguing me daily to prepare to sail to America. I think he fears you will win the war without him. I, on the other hand, know how much you need our help to win.
>
> Please let us know where you will be in the coming weeks so when we land we can arrange transportation to your camp.
>
> Always your devoted friend, Paul

"Monsieur thank you again for delivering the letters," Casimir said, as he returned to where Lafayette waited. "My apprehensions were not warranted. All is well at home."

"Good Casimir, I am glad to hear it, but I do detect a bit of sadness in your face and voice. Did the letters make you wish to be with those you left behind?"

"You read me well, Marquis. I do miss my Polish homeland, especially when it is so difficult here to get the things I need for my cavalry. My brother, Antonin, sent word that the charges against me have been dropped and I can return home without fear of arrest, although the bounty remains on my head wherever I go. But I committed myself to help Washington win this war and I feel an obligation to remain."

"Well, Casimir, perhaps I can help. The same ship that brought your letter brought me news from my homeland as well. It appears that France is ready to recognize the colonies as an official country and will be giving more support to the effort here. Benedict Arnold's daring defeat of Burgoyne at Saratoga a couple of months ago gave Benjamin Franklin the ammunition he needed to convince our leaders that we may win this war if the French join the fight."

"That is wonderful news, Marquis, wonderful news indeed, but what does it have to do with my returning to Poland or remaining here," Casimir asked.

"Everything, my Count, everything. You can help Washington from France," came the Marquis' answer as he spread his arms wide in a grand gesture. "Don't you see, you are credited with saving the life of General George Washington, the commander of France's newest ally. Your military prowess will not be questioned by those jealous and small-minded officers who rejected you before.

"You can go to France, my friend and choose your position. If you want to lead a cavalry you can lead a French cavalry here in America, or you can train troops in France, or you can be a valued consultant to the French. You have fought on American soil with George Washington, and trained an elite force, you know the terrain, the generals, and of course, the recalcitrant congressmen. You will be invaluable to France's efforts and while it is not Poland, it certainly is much closer to your homeland. Once you have distinguished yourself there it will be easy to go back to Poland, as a conquering hero."

Casimir's mind raced with possibilities as he absorbed Lafayette's words. "You have certainly given me much to think about, Marquis. And I will consider all you have suggested very seriously. I know you have my best interests at heart. I appreciate your friendship more each day. The other letter was from my dear friend, Paul Dobrachek, he and my half-brother, Maurice, want to join me here. It would be unfair to allow them to come if I'm not staying."

"I understand, Casimir. Take all the time you need. There is no one with qualifications better than yours to help the French."

"Thank you. Now I must return to training my men, while I still have a bit of money to outfit them," Casimir said, as he left Lafayette.

Although he wanted to respond immediately, he decided not to answer either letter until he had determined whether he would stay in America or go to France.

With the additional congressional funds, Casimir's real work began. It was his mission to build his small core of Pulaski Legionnaires into a much larger force, the American Cavalry. He would have to train, equip and build it into an effective fighting force. There was no precedent for such a military unit in America, and the new path he was clearing was littered with the stones of doubt, jealousy and envy from fellow officers. His foreign status and language barrier continued to plague him and funding was still meager, certainly not enough to build a new Legion with the proper equipment and decent mounts for an army struggling for birth and recognition. But he was as determined as the brave settlers to remove those rocks to build something strong, sturdy, and enduring: his Pulaski Cavalry.

The venom of John Bishop and Colonel Moylan flew through the air as they falsely accused Casimir of sleeping before an important battle, laziness and failure to follow orders. They worked tirelessly to destroy him. Knowing Casimir would likely fail without money to outfit his additional troops, their campaign against him escalated. Bishop and Moylan cornered congressmen at pubs, meeting houses and outside the chamber doors to spread lies about Casimir squandering the latest funds gambling and drinking. They had no proof, but the seeds they sowed began to sprout and Casimir's disdain for details and recordkeeping fertilized and watered the weeds of mistrust.

Lafayette's tantalizing description of the glory awaiting him in France were never far from his mind, but for now he would give his best effort to help Washington and to build the first American cavalry.

Too soon, however the congressional funds, his personal money, and that provided by Deane and Joanna were exhausted while his men were still not properly equipped to his rigid standards. Many had no mounts until horses began mysteriously showing up in his camp, usually at night. He recognized some as ones he had pointed out to Abe Hawkins as being good stock when they were riding past some local farms near Washington's camp.

Casimir and George Washington were similar in their adherence to a higher set of moral standards than most men. The difference between the two was that the stoic Washington strictly adhered to the literal dictates of his faith and never saw a sufficient reason to lie, cheat, or steal.

I believe in and practice the tenets of the Catholic faith every day. But some are deeper, more important, than others. Casimir thought.

If I can save lives, maybe hundreds of lives by 'borrowing' horses from farmers, or even soldiers who do not know how to properly care for or ride them, and end this war early, how I got them is irrelevant. God will credit me for saving lives rather than condemning me for taking horses that are not being put to good use.

Such rationalizing led to trouble when a Pulaski Legionnaire refused to pay the inflated price a butcher asked for a smoked ham shank. He laid down the money he thought was a fair price and walked out with the ham over his shoulder. The store owner called for the constable and the soldier was arrested and thrown into jail.

Outraged, Casimir stormed into the prison demanding the release of his soldier. "This patriotic man should be given the best food available free of charge," he shouted. Of course, the jailor did not understand anything he said, but knew the little foreigner in a general's uniform wanted him to release a thief and he refused.

Spinning around on his high heeled boots, Casimir headed straight for General Washington's headquarters where he learned that the butcher, Bartholomew Dandridge, was the general's brother-in-law. When Casimir demanded that the military, not the local authorities, decide if his man had committed a crime, Washington had already heard about the incident from Martha, his wife, and was in the unenviable position of being caught between his fiery Polish general and his spouse.

Letting wisdom rule, he said "This will set a precedent; hence congress must decide what to do in this case, and future ones like it." For once, the delegates sided with Casimir, ruling storekeepers could not inflate prices during wartime.

However, that victory was hollow. The glory of the publicity parade that forced Congress to give him funds had been sweet, but now that money had run out, and he was back in the same frustrating position as before.

Never a quitter, Casimir had to face reality, especially with the news from Antonin that he could return home and Lafayette's encouragement that he would be welcomed in France. The thought of commanding some of the French officers who had first rejected and taunted him and later encouraged his harsh treatment in prison was tempting. The lack of money, jealous enemies, mistrustful congressmen, and saboteurs like Bishop and Moylan, plus the language barrier, and the constant fear of having his physical anatomy used against him, were becoming too much to bear.

He could think of no reason to stay in this inhospitable country where someone could collect the bounty offered for him. He wondered why he shouldn't go back home.

The pull of home where family and friends would embrace him and he wouldn't struggle to be understood was becoming stronger each day. He missed his friends and the places where he had grown up, played, and fought. He knew and loved his Polish hills, mountains, rivers and rolling farmland. He sorely missed the Church. Most people in America were Protestants and Catholic churches were almost non-existent. The souls of the many men he had killed in battle weighed heavily upon his conscience and he desperately needed the absolution of confession. Then, there was still the matter of locating his father's grave. It all tugged at him and each rejection by Congress and jealous officers made staying his course harder.

He carefully considered what he should do. *My treatment here has been little better than in France, or Turkey. I do not see the opportunity for the glory Woja spoke of in America. Poland is home where I can have peace.* He reasoned.

He thoughtfully and artistically wrote his resignation to General Washington in French, using a fine quill and ink that allowed him to write in flourishing letters befitting his sense of style. He felt the proper presentation of his resignation would show his deep respect for the general.

Expressing his gratitude and admiration for a man he considered a great leader, he wrote:

General:

You have my highest regard for the leadership you have shown under the harshest circumstances and I am grateful for the privilege of riding with you and your troops. It is my strongest wish that you and the colonists are successful in gaining freedom from a distant and demeaning monarch interested only in the riches your country can pay in tribute to him.

My troops are well trained and they will continue to serve you well. To my great disappointment, I am unable to personally deliver the service I wished, because of the many obstacles I face here. Therefore, I am resigning the Brigadier General rank awarded me and returning to Europe.

I hope that through contacts of the Marquis de Lafayette, I may still serve the American cause in France, after a short visit with my family in Poland.

God speed in all you do,
Count Casimir Pulaski

Casimir asked Lafayette to arrange a meeting with General Washington, accompany him to personally deliver the resignation, and read it in English to the general.

Washington's modest white headquarters tent seemed dull in comparison to Lafayette's grand blue and white pavilion that covered more than an acre of land. The furnishings were also in stark contrast, with Washington having only the necessary tables, chairs, and desks to perform his work versus Lafayette's plush French furnishings. But despite their differences, the bond between the two was undeniable. Washington welcomed

Lafayette warmly, as if he were greeting a favored son, clasping his hand and wrapping an arm around his shoulder. Lafayette's glowing face showed the adulation he felt for the man who had become an iconic father figure for him.

"Gentlemen, please have a seat," he invited, then turned to Casimir expectantly.

"How can I be of assistance? Monsieur Lafayette, has Count Pulaski enlisted your assistance in requesting more funds for his cavalry?"

When the Marquis did not answer, Casimir stepped forward, saluted the general and handed the letter of resignation to Lafayette who began reading it aloud to Washington in English.

General Washington nodded slowly, with a sympathetic look in his eyes. "Please interpret for me Monsieur Lafayette," he requested as he continued to look at Casimir.

"I know you as a brave and decisive man and I completely understand your impatience with the lethargic and ungrateful Congress. I've been forced to deal with them myself. I appreciate that for a man of action, inactivity and uncertainty are stifling. But I believe it will be a loss for both of us and this country if you return to Poland.

"Your bravery, I will never forget. I wish I could do more to properly thank you. No man I know has such a combination of ability, leadership, and courage. It is with a heavy and grateful heart that I accept your resignation if you are steadfast in your determination to leave us."

Casimir nodded solemnly and said, "Oui Monsieur, Oui," affirming his desire to return to Europe.

General Washington extended his hand and smiled before slightly squatting and bending his legs into a semi-circle, stretching his arms out, and bouncing up and down as if riding a horse just as Casimir had done at their first meeting. They both laughed heartily.

While the gesture was lost on Lafayette, it was a joke the two of them shared in a special bond. It reminded them of all they had gone through since the first meeting at Neshaminy Creek.

Nothing could have surprised Casimir more than finding Paul and Maurice waiting for him at his headquarters tent when he and Lafayette returned. He rushed to them where all three embraced in a brotherly hug. Maurice was openly weeping with joy and Paul slapped Casimir on the back with a hearty laugh, "Well, Casimir I see you found some nice uniforms here."

Casimir was speechless, and deliriously happy to see them but dread soon set in. They had left their homes and everything familiar behind and travelled almost five thousand miles to help him fight against the British. He knew better than anyone how hard that was. But when he left Europe he had little choice. They, on the other hand, were willing to risk their lives for a cause that was not theirs just to be with him. How could he tell them he was leaving on the next ship to France? What a terrible turn of fate. It wasn't fair, to him or to them.

Lafayette, sensing this meeting was not going to be easy for Casimir quietly left the threesome alone.

"Why didn't you let me know you were coming?" he demanded.

Paul and Maurice were shocked at the tone of his voice. What had happened to their friend that he would greet them in anger?

"Kas, what is it? Why are you upset to see us? Soon after I sent the letter to you, another ship set sail for America. Maurice was chomping at the bit to join you, and we decided to surprise you. We thought you would welcome your friends, not be angry with us. What is it Casimir that makes you resent our being here? It was not easy crossing that damn ocean as you very well know."

"Oh Paul, please come inside my tent with Maurice where I will explain."

They followed him inside his small tent and waited for the promised explanation. But what he offered seemed trite and petty in comparison to their display of loyalty.

He tried as best he could to convey his frustration at the back-stabbing jealousy he had encountered, his inability to raise the funds he needed and at not being assigned major battles. He went on to tell them that he could return home now that the regicide charges had been dropped against him and that there could be a suitable position for him in France as well.

They listened but could not give him the acceptance he sought. Maurice's words were sharp, "Casimir, our father would never have given up over such trivial matters and he would not have expected you to. I am sure I speak for Paul when I say we hope you will reconsider."

They stayed a few moments longer, but the three felt awkward in each other's presence which was something they'd never experienced before. Saying they were worn out from their travels, another barb that pained Casimir, they excused themselves. He called his aide de camp, Captain Bentalou, and ordered him to show them to a good tent. It was not a time of excitement or anticipation for him. He regretted he had to disappoint close friends and comrades. Plus, he still had to tell his troops he was leaving and that was a task he dreaded.

He hoped that on the long voyage back to France, he could make Paul and Maurice better understand his reasons for leaving. He had no doubt that they would go with him and join him in winning more glory.

After seeing that his friends had what they needed, Captain Bentalou mustered the troops who were expecting a training session. Casimir came outside and addressed them curtly, avoiding the eyes of some of the most dedicated.

They were surprised and saddened by his announcement. What would happen to the Legion? They joined to ride with him and took great pride following him. They would never desert him, so why was he deserting them? Again, his answers did not carry the weight he had hoped. He could see in their eyes that they couldn't fathom how one who defied death on the battlefield could be beaten by what he vaguely described to them as "barriers, obstacles and restrictions" and "better opportunities in Europe."

As word spread through Washington's camp, other generals could be seen huddling in small groups, soldiers were sitting around campfires in serious conversations, and the Pulaski troops wandered aimlessly around the training field. Only one person was smiling, Major John Bishop was ecstatic. "I don't know what the silly little bastard did, but I don't believe for one minute that he resigned. He got caught doing something cowardly or dishonest and Washington kicked him out. Well good riddance, now it will be my turn," he gleefully told Moylan.

That evening, Lafayette's tent was overrun with Casimir supporters petitioning him to intervene. Paul and Maurice assumed Lafayette had encouraged Casimir to go to France, and if so, he must help them keep him here. They hadn't travelled seven weeks on a ship only to board another one.

Lafayette had no idea that what he considered a helpful suggestion to a friend would result in such an upheaval. He was amazed and chagrined to find his elegant tent now being mobbed and muddied by soldiers.

When Maurice urged him to summon Casimir to his overcrowded personal quarters under the pretext of having a farewell dinner and drink, the Marquis reluctantly agreed, knowing the crowd would not disperse otherwise. He sent a note to Casimir's tent that read, "My friend, I will miss our evenings together and regret that I will not hear more of your past experiences. Please join me for a small dinner and a brandy so we may bid each other a fond farewell."

When the group heard Visner approaching, they rushed outside surprising Casimir who thought he and Lafayette would have a quiet dinner together. He thought the Marquis must have arranged a farewell gathering for him and that was why the others were here. But why were Paul and Maurice included if they were all leaving together the next day?

In fact, desperate to keep him, Abe and Samuel had pleaded with Paul, Maurice, and Lafayette to do something, anything, to convince Casimir to change his mind. Others felt the same way and had congregated at the tent of the marquis. Lafayette would miss Casimir and the common heritage they shared, even though he was partially responsible for his decision to resign.

Now Casimir tried again to explain why he must leave saying to Maurice and Paul, "I feel terrible that you made the long journey to join me only to find that I am departing for France, but you must understand how it is here. There is no support, no equipment, no respect and most of all, no battle plan. You . . . you . . . will leave with me, won't you?"

Again, Maurice spoke first. "Brother, we will not return with you. We have come too far to be turned back by what sounds like petty politics. You must go alone to find this better situation in France. We appreciate that we were able to stay in our homeland during the years you were in exile and you have been away far longer than we have, but now we are together, ready to fight again as we did in the homeland. We will not follow you to yet another dream of glory."

It was a crushing blow to Casimir to think that having just gotten them back in his life today he would lose them again. Paul, who gave him no quarter, simply said, "What of Visner? You know he cannot make the voyage again."

There were so many things that he, the great strategist had not considered. Realization that his decision may have been premature began to gnaw at him.

He looked around to see that at least thirty people had gathered. In addition to Maurice and Paul there were many officers and troops he had trained. Noticeable for their absence were Bishop and Moylan.

One of Washington's personal guards seemed to speak for all of the officers when he said, "General Pulaski, we are deeply saddened by your decision to leave us. But for your quick actions at Brandywine and Haddonfield many of us would not be here tonight. We know you have not been properly recognized by Congress and others, but your contributions are appreciated by many. We hope you will reconsider."

Samuel and Abe looked inconsolable. They could not conceal their distress.

They looked at him with pleading eyes, and calling up the French he had learned, Abe said, "Monsieur, if there is anything we can do to persuade you to stay, please let us know what it is. We will follow you wherever you lead. If there are not enough horses for everyone, we'll steal more or walk, just as long as we can be part of your troop."

Samuel added, "General Pulaski, my life will be forever changed because I have known you. Again, if there is anything Abe and I can do to convince you how important it is for you to stay we'll do it. Just tell us. He said we would walk if necessary to follow you, I say we will crawl. Please do not leave us. We all need you."

Casimir was defeated but it was a sweet defeat. He had to rescind his resignation, knowing now that he was valued and wanted in America. Now that he had Paul and Maurice with him, they would be unconquerable.

CHAPTER TWENTY-ONE

OF HOME AND HORSES

1777-1778

eneral Washington was relieved to welcome Casimir back. He knew about some of the difficulties jealous officers and congressional members had created for him, though he was unaware of Moylan and Bishop's treachery. He decided it was best if Casimir functioned outside the regular Army. The general gave Casimir the authority to lead his Pulaski Legion independently and report directly to him. Casimir was grateful that he would not be reporting to officers who were inferior to him and that was everyone except Washington himself.

General Washington placed Moylan, the dragoons' leader, in charge of the regular Army cavalry. Bishop was behaving less rationally each day, and his appointment both appeased Moylan and gave him an excuse to terminate his alliance with the major.

Casimir was euphoric until he realized that he still had very little money for his legion. Now that he knew he was recognized and valued, he applied himself to work with what he had and what he had were some damn fine fighting men. He might have to skimp on their mounts and equipment, but they would be the best trained troops in America.

Lafayette continued to lend a sympathetic ear to Casimir and they often spent evenings together. It was during one of their sessions of cards and chess that Lafayette told Casimir, "The French brigantine that brought the guns and ammunition I transported to Neshaminy Creek has undergone refurbishing and repairs in Marblehead and she's ready to sail back to France next week. I've asked General Washington for permission to carry some letters to the captain for my family and business associates. If you would like to send some as well, I'll be happy to include them. It's the least I can do considering the part I played in your brief resignation."

Casimir, who was disappointed not to be seeing his family after all, was delighted by Lafayette's offer. "Oui, Oui, Monsieur Lafayette. I have many at home I wish to communicate with. But most of the correspondence will be to people in Poland. Will it be possible for them to receive it if the ship goes to France?"

"Yes, Casimir, I'll have one of my former cavalrymen deliver them, and it won't take long to reach the recipients since my cavalrymen ride almost as fast as you do," Lafayette joked.

They played to a draw, and Casimir returned to his tent where he opened his leather letter pouch and withdrew the paper and pen used to keep a diary and draw battle plans. He wrote well into the night, using the light of his campfire to write letters to Antonin, his mother, Joanna, Father Joseph at Jasna Gora, Edward Kransinki and, of course, Franciszka.

To his mother, he wrote:

> I am well and have achieved the rank of Brigadier General reporting directly to General George Washington, the Commander of all American forces. The Pulaski name and insignia are emblazoned on a banner that the soldiers of my Pulaski Legion Cavalry proudly follow.
>
> I am happy to know that Antonin is well and headed home to visit you. It is a great relief to know he is no longer a prisoner in Russia.

Although my heart will always be with my family, I must finish what I have begun here. I now know that General Washington and many others rely on me and I cannot leave them until the British are defeated.

While all has not gone as Father wanted in Poland, I do look forward to leading a quieter life there by helping Antonin manage the estate. He tells me we may be able to recover most of our lands.

I send you, Antonin and my sisters my love and pray I will be with you again soon, perhaps to celebrate my thirty-fifth birthday with a piece of Sarah's delicious cake.

Tell her so and God Bless you all,
Casmir

Remembering Lafayette's counsel that many lives are shortened by war and it is prudent to give guidance on how matters are to be settled, Casimir asked Edward Kransinki, Franciszka's father and a long-time friend of his own father, to be executor of his estate. He couldn't think of a better person to take care of disbursing what remained of his possessions and he asked Mr. Kransinki to use any funds available upon his death to continue the search for his father's remains near the Turkish-Russian border. He asked if their location could be discovered, that they be retrieved, and interred at the family church in Warka.

In his letter to Father Joseph he said he prayed daily for the safety of the monks at Jasna Gora and for the preservation of the monastery. He feared the Russians would again try to sack the sacred site, especially now that he was not there to defend it. He also reminded the priest of his promise, "I am so grateful that my earthly remains will rest at Jasna Gora. Thank you for your kindness in reserving a place for me near the Hall of Knights."

To Franciszka he wrote:

Precious Duchess of Courland,

My poor pen cannot describe the delight given me by your presence at Nantes, the gift of passage for Visner and, most of all, your letter. Nothing could have raised my spirits more. Your gold coin hangs around my neck as it has since the moment I received it. The memory of our times together and the knowledge that you may cherish those memories as much as I do, sustain me.

I miss your encouraging words and counsel. Your diplomacy is sorely lacking in me and I fear I have made some enemies here. I am sure if you were by my side your charm would convert them to the staunchest of allies.

Paul and Maurice arrived a short time ago and it will be good to build a new legion with them. We will create the finest cavalry the world has ever known.

Antonin wrote me that you have a daughter. She must give you great happiness. I am sure she will grow up to be as smart and beautiful as her mother. I often think of your smile and it gives me great pleasure. So, smile often and please remain safe and happy.

With the greatest admiration and fondness,
Kas

While signing the letter, Casimir realized that was the way he felt about Franciszka now, with "fondness and admiration," not with the burning love he had once known.

After struggling with his reply to Antonin's letter, the honest words finally came to him,

My dear brother,

What a relief it is to know you are safe. I did agonize over what fate may have befallen you at the hands of the Russians. I trembled with uncertainty when your letter arrived, worried about what I might learn from it, but instead it brought such good news. Having our names cleared of the regicide charge is unbelievable. I can't imagine how you accomplished so much while in prison. You certainly outdid me as a prisoner. All I got was brutal beatings but then I was never a humble person as you know. For some strange reason my guards thought they should be in charge, not me.

I must admit I was shocked to learn you joined the Russian Army, but when I realized the reasons, I accepted it as a very clever move on your part to restore our family's status. Thank you for that. It took strength and brilliance to do what you did. Through astute diplomacy and manipulation, you did more than anything I did on the battlefield of Poland.

The bounty on my head is a darkness I must live with. I will be careful, as you cautioned, and I hope the war here is soon over so I can rejoin you and our family at Warka. Meanwhile, if your new, rich Russian friends have rubles to spare, perhaps they will donate them to the new cavalry I am building here. I would much rather have them used for that than to buy my head.

God willing, I will be with you soon.

As always, your devoted brother,

Kas

He hoped Antonin would see the humor in his suggestion that Russians would help fund his efforts in America, and chuckled to himself at the idea of Antonin funneling rubles to him from unsuspecting Muscovite aristocrats.

Casimir decided against writing to Antonin about Maurice. If he were careless with the letter, his mother or sisters might discover it and the knowledge that his father had been unfaithful would destroy his mother.

As he gathered the letters together Casimir reflected, *I do not fear death nor have time to think of it when I am in battle. Still, we all must die, even my father who I thought would always be with me, and Frank, and wonderful Dr. Borloff. I have cheated death many times. Musket balls broke my hand and fingers so I can no longer make a fist, while swords and lances have cut through my flesh to the very bone, making them ache in damp weather. Even my faithful horses have died. I know I will die someday. I just hope it is in a glorious charge rather than from disease or some lingering sickness, with the Blessed Mother leading the way.*

The next afternoon, Casimir delivered the letters to Lafayette. He found him writing in his journal while sitting on a rock near a deep, still pool of green water that broke into ripples when a frog, frightened by his footsteps, jumped in.

Casmir dismounted to hand the letters to Lafayette who rose to greet him saying, "I will see that these are delivered, Casimir. There are several letters I see. Do they all go to Poland?"

"Yes, they are to family and friends, all in Poland," smiled Casimir. "It means a great deal to be able to communicate with them — in Polish."

Lafayette laughed while opening the satchel he used for his journal to place the letters inside. Casimir could see that he still carried the letter from his wife, Adrienne, with him and realized that the Marquis too understood and appreciated the bond with home and loved ones.

"I'll see that your letters reach their destination," said Lafayette. "Now, how about joining me in my tent for dinner tonight?

Just watching your endless training makes me hungry and I have read every book and paper I brought with me. My evenings seem endless."

"Yes of course, Marquis, I'll be delighted to visit." He cheerfully replied, "Visner ran out of interesting things to tell me last week." Both men laughed as they agreed to meet at Lafayette's tent at seven that evening.

Lafayette's quarters were far more elaborate and comfortable than either Casimir's small sleeping bivouac or his headquarters tent. It had obviously been cleaned after its occupation by Casimir's supporters the evening of his resignation. Inside were all the comforts of home plus a dining table, writing desk, and a playing board for cribbage, cards, or chess.

Casimir, who always rode fast and hard and was ready for battle at all times, couldn't understand how a warrior could travel so encumbered, but he did enjoy the luxury accompanying Lafayette's hospitality. He smiled broadly as he entered the spacious headquarters and was greeted by the aroma of a stew. Now that he had run out of Polish sausage, the beans and cornmeal mush he normally ate had become even more tasteless and boring. He looked forward to a good, well-cooked meal.

"Marquis, you certainly know how to travel in style," Casimir said while accepting a glass of wine.

"Thank you for your offer to have my letters delivered in Poland. It means a great deal to me. They contain personal correspondence with family members and friends along with some business matters. I took your advice and prepared a will of sorts."

"Good, my friend, it's best to take care of such matters while we are healthy, Oui?" Lafayette replied.

"Yes, Marquis, now maybe I can return your favor by allowing you to finally win a game of chess?" Casimir joked.

After spending a long and enjoyable evening playing chess and talking of the war with his friend, Casimir arose early the next day to start readying his men for the battles to come. They were truly his men now, the Pulaski Cavalry Legion, separate from the regular army, and he wanted them to distinguish themselves at everything they did.

The Pulaski troops were trained to surprise and charge the enemy, a tactic that wasn't considered feasible in the forested mountains and valleys of Colonial America. To succeed, each man had to become like him, a centaur, indistinguishable from his horse.

They had to be good riders to be accepted into the Pulaski Legion, and to stay they had to become extraordinary. Casimir was determined to make them the best horsemen in Washington's army. He remembered his father's words about knowledge of the horse and how it helped Jan Sobieski's Polish Winged Hussars defeat the advancing Muslims. He made sure his men knew and understood their horses so well that they could anticipate their animal's every movement.

He held daily classes on the horse, explaining how it developed from a twelve-inch high mammal that was prey to lions, cheetahs, and other carnivores into the beautiful and strong creature they now rode.

"The horse's large eyes evolved to enable them to detect predators at a long distance, giving them time to run from danger," he explained, "they have good night vision but lack clarity up close. Anything moving quickly in front of your horse at close range can frighten him. Their muscular hind quarters have become large and strong for running away from danger or delivering deadly kicks to lions and tigers trying to spring onto their backs. Those bone-crushing kicks can also be deadly to our enemies. Never drag anything behind a horse, because that will frighten the most disciplined one to the point of stampeding.

"They must be trained to recognize that when a rider mounts them, that he is a friend and master and not a predator attacking. Their large rotating ears were developed for hearing distant movement but they're sensitive to loud, nearby noise and a rider's shout can cause them to bolt because the sound is magnified when close. If a soldier watches the direction the ears turn, he can determine where the enemy is hiding or moving in the brush. Flight is the horse's method of escape; their knees lock while they stand, even when they sleep, allowing them to make a quick start if a sudden sound alarms them."

He showed them how to care for their tack and equipment and he continued to refine the new lance he designed with a hook on the end for pulling enemy fighters from their horses. Casimir, who trained and led by example, took impeccable care of his own equipment and horses.

Samuel Abbot and Abe Hawkins never missed a session. They were like shadows trailing after him, training all day and continuing to practice after the others left the field. But the new man, Lee, became his most impressive student. Lee was never too tired from the many assignments Casimir gave him to miss a training session.

Odd, thought Casimir, *he seems to already know most of what I teach. So why does he come to the sessions? They are not mandatory.* He was intrigued when he saw Lee frequently talking with Indians at the tree line in the evening. Their bodies seemed to drift and float in and out of the dark pools of tree shade just after sunset and he noted that when Lee went out to meet them, his walk was not the same as it was in camp. It seemed to shift to an easy, natural gait with a shuffle of the feet, rather than his usual open stride with swinging arms. It reminded him of the way his sisters walked, and he wondered if it was some sort of tribal gait. After these clandestine meetings, Lee frequently brought him news of British movement that he said his Cherokee Indian friends had passed along. Lee excelled at everything and volunteered for additional work. Casimir thought: *much like me.*

CHAPTER TWENTY-TWO

LEE

1779

asimir's Pulaski Cavalry Legion became the center of attention in camp when they continued to win every skirmish they engaged in, and gained a reputation for being the most disciplined unit in the army.

General Washington remained grateful to Casimir. Had it not been for Pulaski, he might have perished at Brandywine, and the men at Valley Forge may have starved without the British supplies he and Wayne commandeered. Washington knew Casimir was a strong leader, and as his trust and confidence in him grew, he decided to give Casimir a major assignment. He ordered him to head south to Charles Town, South Carolina and hold it until reinforcements could arrive.

This was what Casimir had longed for. Excited, he sent his aide, Captain Bentalou ahead with a small squad to survey the situation around Charles Town. In his regular aide's absence, he thought of Lee. Surely the man's work and devotion, not to mention his cousin sacrificing his life for him, deserved recognition and making Lee his aide was the only reward within his means at the moment.

When Lee responded to his summons, his face was still smeared with the black mud that he explained was necessary "to be able to slip through the woods and meet with the Indians."

But under the mud, there was not a trace of a beard. *Strange, he's like the Indians, who do not have beards,* thought Casimir.

Ignoring his unkempt appearance for the moment, Casimir said, "Lee, I have sent Captain Bentalou ahead to do some scouting, and I need a new aide. You have distinguished yourself in the short time you've been with us, and I am assigning you to that position until he returns. That is, assuming you would like to serve in that capacity."

Lee looked directly at Casimir and responded, "Thank you, General, it will be an honor to personally serve you. Others would feel the same."

Casimir knew the others were Abe and Samuel—and he also knew he was becoming completely distracted because he had never seen eyes like Lee's.

They were deep, deep brown, almost black, that grew larger as the rays of the setting sun bronzed the young man's face, but he detected a great sadness in them. Casimir knew most Indians had dark eyes and he wondered if Lee's Indian and white heritage fought for dominance in his. When Lee's gaze dropped away from his own, Casimir sensed that the young man was hiding something. Having kept his own secret hidden away from people all his life, he felt a kindred spirit and thought he should get to know his new aide better.

"Good, you will start tonight," said Casimir. "Go find Sergeant Wilkes and have him show you around my headquarters area. Ask him to introduce you to my cook, wrangler and the others you'll work with. And Lee, wash your face and put on a fresh uniform. My aide can't look like a backwoodsman."

When Lee started to protest, Casimir raised his hand, saying "I know you need to be inconspicuous when you talk with the Indians and I need you to continue to do that. When you go to meet them, you can change out of the uniform and dirty your face."

"Yes sir," Lee responded, again avoiding direct eye contact with the general. While Casimir was convinced there was something secret about this young man, he had no time to dwell on it. He must prepare for the approaching battle at Charles Town.

Casimir was right about Lee. Lee was keeping a secret, a secret from everyone in camp and, like Casimir's own secret, it had to do with his anatomy. Unbeknownst to Casimir, Lee, in fact, was Leah, a woman dressed as a man, whose goal was to fight the British to avenge her husband's death.

Casimir was also right about her mixed heritage. The traits she inherited from her Irish, Scot, and Cherokee ancestors made her a multi-talented and very beautiful woman. She had the stoicism of the Scots, the quick wit of the Irish, and the spirituality of the Cherokee.

Leah's father, Drake, was a Scot while her mother Ellen was half Irish and half Cherokee. As soon as she could crawl, her mother's Indian friends began teaching her about the woods and all its creatures. She seemed to have a natural talent for languages. Her Grandpa O'Rourke who had worked with a Frenchman at a print shop in Dublin, and helped the Indians sell their furs to the French traders, had taught her French. She learned the Indian languages from her relatives and friends. As a child, she would often switch from Cherokee to Creek, to French, to English, while talking with her mother or her Indian friends. Leah grew up knowing she had nothing to fear from nature or the Indians.

While walking around camp looking for Sergeant Wilkes, her thoughts turned to her childhood, growing up in South Carolina, her Cherokee ties, and the stories her grandfather, Devon O'Rourke, told her about his arrival in the New World.

According to Grandpa O'Rourke, he was a typesetter at the Dublin Times in Ireland. He lasted there until losses from gambling on horses turned against him, and his creditors gave him two choices: he could become an indentured servant in the New World or go to a squalid debtor's prison with no means of paying the debts and little hope of surviving the filth and cold.

He agreed to be the servant of a candle-maker and shopkeeper, an Englishman named Adam Burke, and signed a seven-year indenture contract with him. Burke paid off his creditors in exchange for his new servant's contract, and within a week carefree Devon O'Rourke was working in Burke's shop in London. When Burke decided to move his business to Pennsylvania, Devon was shoved below decks on a ship bound for America to finish his servitude in the colonies.

He had gotten a taste of the candle making business in London. Bending over and stirring iron pots of boiling lye and animal fat then pouring the steaming, stinking stuff into molds, packing boxes of candles, then carrying them to the shop, sweeping floors, emptying the family's chamber pots, sleeping on a straw pallet, and all the other indignities the fat, pompous Burke demanded of him became too much for an Irish lad to endure, contract or no contract.

He risked jumping overboard when a storm drove the ship near an island off the coast of Carolina. He was barely able to swim to shallow water where he walked barefoot through mud and razor-sharp oyster shells to reach the sandy beach.

He was exhausted from the exertion and suffering from deep, jagged cuts on his feet. Living for weeks on starvation rations for which he had fought rats and starving men in the dark, damp ship's hold had weakened him, and the swim sapped his last reserve of strength. When he tried to stand on the beach, his legs buckled and he collapsed.

The next morning, he was awakened by movement and a sense of danger nearby. He couldn't tell what it was. His eyes were unaccustomed to the bright sunlight and he was blinded by the brilliant rays reflected from the bleached white sand. Slowly raising his hand to shield his eyes, he saw a figure wrapped in a halo of bright light. It gradually took the form of an angel, a female angel of mercy, bending down to press a leather bag filled with cool, sweet water to his lips.

Then he became aware of other figures standing near the angel. But these weren't angels. They were massive males with strips of bark, grass and seashells wrapped around their loins.

They were curious about the pale, red haired white man covered in clothes who had just risen from the sea. Thinking he might have supernatural powers, either good or bad, they hesitated before closing in on him. When they started plucking at his clothes and red beard, the angel said something in a foreign language, motioned for the goliaths to back away, and ordered them into the nearby woods. When they were alone, she rubbed her stomach and raised her hand to her mouth asking him if he were hungry. Devon shouted, "Yes, Oh, my God, Yes. I'm starved. I need food, please." Then he nodded his head up and down and patted his own stomach when he realized his words were unintelligible to this beautiful, angelic creature.

The Indian camp was near, and though walking was painful, his instinct told him he mustn't show weakness so he forced himself to keep up without limping. Curious about his red hair and strange clothing, the children and old ladies in the camp laughed and pointed at him. The angel maiden stopped them with a quick gesture of her hand and they hurriedly cleared a path for them.

She brought him fresh fish, corn, roasted oysters and more water. Devon was so ravenous he scooped the food up in his hands and gobbled it down until his shrunken stomach could handle no more and tossed most of it back up. Sick as he was, he took solace in the thought that he ate some of the bloody oysters that had cut his feet.

Completely spent, he passed out on the ground and the Indian maiden had him placed on deer hides to rest and recover over several days. Once mobile again, he observed the Indians' movements and habits. Unable to understand the language, he paid close attention to their rituals and daily activities. It was the women, rather than the men, who gathered firewood, built fires, cooked and took care of the animals. It seemed like a good life for the males who did very little while their women waited on them.

As the days passed Devon realized how lucky he was. *Only the luck of the Irish brought me to this place,* he thought. *I'm free and I have the most beautiful woman I've ever seen taking care of me.*

She was beautiful, with olive skin, long shapely legs and full breasts. Her eyes were a devilish brown, while her hair, hanging to her waist, was a shiny, deep indigo red tied in back with a thin leather strap laced through a hole in a white conch shell. Two long eagle feathers placed between the leather tie and the shell extended from the base of her neck to the crown of her head. It was a sign of royalty, he later learned, but it was already obvious by the way the others deferred to her that she was an authority figure to be obeyed. The moment he saw her in that circle of light, she cast a spell, mesmerizing him completely.

After some days, he pointed to himself saying, "Devon, Devon. I am Devon."

"DEV-on," she repeated. It was close enough for him and he smiled and nodded, then pointed to her.

"Choppa, Choppa," she said, pointing to herself. It meant strong, pretty one, but he didn't know it at the time, nor did he care what it meant. Shaking his head from side to side, frowning and wagging his index finger in a negative motion, he said "No, no," then pointing at her, "Angela. You are Angela, my Angela, my angel."

"Angela," she repeated softly, almost whispering the name.

"Yes," he said nodding, "From now on you are Angela." To him she could have no other name. She would always be his angel, his guardian angel.

While his wounds mended he regained his strength and he tried to return her kindness by offering to assist in the work of the tribe, but there wasn't much a typesetter could do in an Indian village. The other Indians avoided him and he wondered if it was because of his relationship with Angela. With her dancing eyes and soft smile and his quick laugh and love of life, they enjoyed walking along the beach together in the evenings, learning about each other through gestures, a few words they now understood and some sign language they developed between them. Communication became easier and easier as they fell in love.

One evening her hand found its way in his, and he knew they were meant to be together. Devon worked hard at gaining approval from the tribe. He learned how to spearfish, harvest oysters and crabs, hunt deer with bow and arrow, trap, and carve beautiful canoes from the giant oaks on the island.

The tribe eventually accepted him as Choppa's Redbeard and, still thinking he might have magical powers, no one objected when he married his angel maiden, who was the daughter of their revered Chief Attakullakulla.

They named their daughter Ellen, after his Irish mother. Then a second child was conceived but died in the womb during Choppa's sixth month of pregnancy. His beloved Angela, Princess Choppa, died from the subsequent infection.

Devon couldn't bear the constant reminders of Angela surrounding him in the Indian village and he moved inland with Ellen to a small town where he found a job in a print shop. Since Ellen's only relatives in America were Indian, he allowed her to live with them several months each year as a tribute to her mother. They could tell her things he could not about what her mother liked as a child and what her favorite Indian stories and legends were. They also told her about her grandmother and how her grandfather became the revered chief.

Like many bi-racial children, Ellen was confused about what her place in life should be. Was she Indian or White? She met and married a white farmer, a Scot, named Drake Barton, but she treasured her Cherokee heritage. And when their daughter Leah was born, she wanted her to have all the advantages and opportunities of a white girl while still honoring the Indian ways.

Devon visited his granddaughter, Leah, often during her early years, entertaining her with stories far more fascinating than any fairy tales. She especially liked the ones about her grandmother, Princess Choppa, grandpa's Angel, and she always carried herself with the regal bearing befitting the granddaughter of a princess.

After her Grandfather O'Rourke died, life was lonely for Leah. Like her mother before her, she was allowed to visit her Indian relatives and learned their ways. She cherished her times with the Indians and made many friends among them. One buck, Tathtowe, became her teacher and protector. He taught her how to sneak up on deer and ride bareback just using her knees to guide the horse, things her mother frowned upon but didn't deny her.

At home, she and her mother worked the fields of tobacco, corn and cotton beside her father and two brothers on their one hundred twenty-acre farm in South Carolina. Her father inherited eighty of those acres. Through hard work, some savvy horse trading, and rising cotton prices he was able to buy another forty, and was considered wealthy, almost to the point of reaching 'planter' status, in the South Carolina low country.

Truth be told, the farm did well mostly due to Tathtowe. He showed them the richest soil for planting and told them when the danger of frost had passed in the spring so planting could begin.

With Tathtowe as their mentor, Ellen and Leah also learned how to dry vegetable seeds to plant the following year, to use cow and chicken manure along with fish to fertilize their vegetable garden and to bury cabbage, sweet potatoes and sugar cane in a mound to preserve them well into the winter.

Leah liked Tathtowe, and spent as much time with him and her mother's other Indian relatives and friends as she could. She learned to hunt, track and slip quietly through woods and streams by stepping heel first, followed by toes.

The usual peace on the farm was sometimes disrupted at night by the bitter arguments Leah overheard between her parents about acquiring slaves to work the crops.

"And just how far above slavery is our working in the fields from sunup until sundown when a drought, flood, crop diseases, or swarms of insects can mean we starve in spite of all that work?" argued Ellen, urging Drake to buy slaves.

When he wasn't moved, she went on, "It ain't fittin' for women to work in the fields, callousin' up their hands and lettin' the sun wrinkle-up their skin like the back on a gator hide, 'specially now that we can afford some slaves."

"It ain't right to buy another human being," Drake countered. "My paw told me about watching slaves being sold at markets in Barbados before he came here. Says he saw young'uns pulled from the tits of their maw's and stuck two or three to another maw, same as cattle. Slaves bring money, so producing young'uns is big business. I ain't even talkin' about the men using them to satisfy their urges. It just ain't right and I ain't havin' nothin' to do with it.

"And it ain't just the black folks. Pa said white folks who couldn't pay their debts were sold as servants indentured for as long as seven 'n sometimes even fourteen years. A lot of the Irish were sold outright as slaves. He said they brought lower prices than the blacks 'cause they couldn't take the sun and they were called 'red legs' 'cause of it. When they got to the colonies, they were worked, starved and beaten nearly to death, white and black alike. The worst of it was they could be sold at any time at another market moving 'em away from their families. I ain't havin' no part of it Ellen."

"Well, Leah ain't workin' the fields no more and I mean it," Ellen vowed.

"She needs to take care of her looks and get some book learnin' where she can marry up with a man of means, not some poor dirt farmer tryin' to scratch a livin' from this sorry land. That's what she needs and that's what she's gonna git. She's gonna be a lady married to somebody rich one day."

While Leah was more comfortable in cotton and flannel than silk, she understood her mother's reasons for wanting her to become a lady. Grandpa O'Rourke had told her about her Irish great grandmother and great aunts. He described them as "fine ladies, sipping tea in the afternoon and making fancy cushion covers and wall hangings with their needlepoint threads the rest of the day while always appearing dainty and delicate to their menfolk."

"Grandpa, didn't they help the men make a livin' and didn't they cook and clean," asked Leah when she was seven.

"Well no, my Darlin'," he explained. "The servants did all the housework and the men took care of providin' for 'em."

"But what if there was no man," Leah asked, causing Devon O'Rourke to shake his head and think, *this one is too smart for her age,* before responding, "Well my little Princess, women were raised and trained to get a man to take care of them. They couldn't own land and they had to leave home when the eldest son inherited the farm, or preferably before. It was considered a disgrace for a girl not to be married by eighteen."

"But Grandpa, what if she couldn't get a man, or what if the man died?"

Devon didn't want to tell her the truth. Spinsters went into convents and widows became destitute, begging off relatives or trying to find work as a laundress or seamstress, so he answered,

"Why my little Leah, there were always gentlemen willing to care for them. Men know it's their job to take care of women because they're weaker than them," he answered, although he knew this was only true if the widow was young, pretty and could remarry fast, while most ended up in workhouses, or on the streets as prostitutes.

"Well it seems like a very dull life to me," sighed Leah. "I would rather have a garden to work in like mama, and lots of animals to care for. If I helped work the land, then at least part of it would be mine and I would know how to make a living from it."

Devon decided to change the subject. His granddaughter was smart, strong, and independent and he didn't have the heart to tell her she might have to hand over her independence to a man in exchange for a home.

Yet, in time, things could change and Leah's vision of how life should be might become reality. This new world was full of strong, ambitious men willing to risk their lives to defend their beliefs and build a fortune. But most of them couldn't do it alone, especially those who migrated to the rugged wilderness areas of Western Virginia, Carolina and remote backwater areas of Georgia. They needed a strong and determined woman by their side to load the muskets while they were under attack by Indians, French, or British and to bear and raise the sons they needed to help clear and farm the land. They depended on their women to plant, harvest, and prepare the vegetables that would feed them and to tend the tobacco or rice that would pay for the supplies they couldn't grow or make themselves. Gradually, men began thinking of their women as partners who might not be exactly equal, and couldn't own land, but were definitely necessary and valuable. The velvet shackles loosened as each successive generation of men and women became more American and less British, Irish, German or French.

Ellen, constantly trying to improve their status, was successful in getting some books into the house when a family traveling to Charles Town had to lighten their wagon. A cracked axle and a pregnant daughter made that necessary. She desperately wanted Leah to have a better life than hers, and hoped through reading she would educate herself and become the wife of a merchant, lawyer or doctor, but not a farmer. Leah had a quick mind, and just as easily as she picked up languages, she retained most of what she read in books.

Jimmy McElveen was not the man Ellen would have chosen for a son-in-law. His Irish heritage was a plus, but he was poor and, worse yet, he was an itinerant farm hand who didn't even own the land he farmed. He and Leah met at a church revival when the Reverend Whitfield, a famous circuit-riding preacher, came to South Carolina all the way from Virginia. People from miles around attended the revival and Jimmy arrived on its second day.

There was a mutual spark of interest when Jimmy made sure he could sit with Leah by placing the highest bid for the peach pie she brought to the revival. He bought homemade ice cream to go with the pie, and Leah couldn't remember having a better day.

When the crescent moon climbed high toward the Big Dipper, and the evening drew to a close, Jimmy said "Miz Leah, I can't ever remember eatin' a finer piece of peach pie, or talkin with somebody as nice as you. Would you be willin' to let me come callin' on you Saturday after I get off work at Mr. Huskeby's farm?"

Leah's sixteen-year-old heart nearly exploded as she clasped her hands together and exclaimed, "Why Jimmy I surely enjoyed sitting with you and hope you'll ask my maw if it'll be okay with her and paw. I could make you another peach pie."

Ellen reluctantly granted permission and he came calling, not only that Saturday but almost every Saturday thereafter, making the eight-mile hike to her house with such regularity that Ellen said, "Leah, if that boy keeps coming around, he's gonna get mighty wet when I throw out the dish water 'cause he's always hanging around the kitchen door."

Jimmy and Leah sat in the front porch rockers talking for hours about the farm they would one day own and how they would build it into one of the best plantations in Carolina. The sitting and rocking led to a marriage proposal, but Ellen was dead set against it.

Leah pleaded her case, begging, "Maw I am almost seventeen and Grandpa O'Rourke said it was a disgrace to the family for a girl not to be married by eighteen. Please, Maw, I'm not going to marry anyone else — ever."

Drake had no problem with Jimmy marrying Leah, because he seemed to be a hard worker and he didn't have grand ideas about her being a fine Charles Town lady as did Ellen. Ellen was outnumbered and there weren't any men of means on Leah's horizon. So, she finally relented. She wasn't happy about it, but at least Jimmy was Irish and he surely did love her Leah.

Jimmy and Leah moved into a small cabin on Mr. Huskeby's land that they farmed together with a love that knew no bounds. They raised enough vegetables, corn and cotton to pay Mr. Huskeby his share and still have some left to sell at the Saturday market in town.

By saving every spare penny, they had enough money after the third harvest to buy the cabin and a little plot of land next to it from Mr. Huskeby. He hadn't planned to sell either one, but he admired the young people who had worked so hard and were so excited about having their own place. He sold it to them for less than it was worth, knowing that with their drive and energy they would turn it into a showplace that would make the rest of his land worth more.

They wanted children right away, but as month after month passed with no signs of Leah being with child, they realized that even though they hungered for a family, being childless gave them time to grow closer and build a love-filled home together. They worked side by side, rarely separated by more than a few feet. Leah helped him in the fields and cattle pens and he helped her in the kitchen, garden, and hen house, places men generally shunned.

Their intimacy flourished as their love matured. Some days as they worked together in the garden, the sweat would soak her cotton dress, making it cling to her body, and the swell of her breasts against the fabric and tanned legs pressed against the wet skirt were too much for Jimmy.

He would take her hand and lead her into the cabin where he slowly unbuttoned her dress, one button at a time. As each breast broke free he kissed it, then gently washed it in cool well water. After bathing her body from head to toe, he'd carry her to the bed, caressing and kissing her until neither could hold back.

On other days, the ripple of his muscles under his homespun shirt as he harnessed Nellie, their plow horse, then followed behind her in the plowed furrow, or the way he confidently strode from one chore to another would have the same effect on her and she would go to him and lead him back to their bed.

Sometimes Leah became melancholy and asked, "Jimmy, Why no babies? I couldn't love you more, and having your children would make life perfect for me."

"It just wasn't meant to be—yet, but they'll come, maybe a dozen, six girls with your raven hair and beautiful brown eyes and six boys with my thick red hair and blue eyes," Jimmy would say as they lay in each other's arms.

The world was changing outside their little paradise, however. As word of the Revolution began to spread, Jimmy knew he would be a part of it but he wanted Leah to be able to hold on to what they worked so hard to build if he went. He was glad they had Scrap, the big, shaggy, cur dog who followed them everywhere. Scrap was part of their little family. They loved him like a child and he returned their love tenfold. Jimmy knew Scrap would defend either of them if they were threatened and he felt better knowing that if he went to war, Scrap would be with Leah.

They talked about the war, knowing it would be excruciating for them to be apart, but optimistic about the opportunity it gave them to get more land. If the Colonists won, their leaders promised to deed a parcel to each soldier who served. They hoped the war wouldn't last long and Jimmy would soon be back home with deed in hand, perhaps for land near the plot they already owned.

It was Leah who thought of a way they could be together if the war dragged on. One night she sat up in bed and proclaimed, "I can dress like a man and come to you, Jimmy. I read in one of the books maw got from those people going to Charles Town that lots of women go to war, always have. Some dress like men and fight. Some carry messages behind enemy lines, and some are . . . uh . . . some service the men, which you know I wouldn't do."

"No, I won't have it," he said. "It would be too dangerous. I won't allow it Leah, no matter how much I'd miss you and you better not even think about servicin' any man 'cept this one."

"But Jimmy, you know we can't live without each other," she pleaded. "Nothing could be worse than being apart."

She was right and he knew it. He finally compromised, saying, "If I'm gone more than a few months without comin' home I'll get word to you lettin' you know where I am. Then you could come pretendin' to be my cousin, Lee. They'll probably need someone who can talk with the Indians and who could do that better than you? And the Indians would help look after you. But that's enough war talk for now. I may not even go."

That was how they left things until disaster struck.

She was nineteen years old and beautiful by anyone's standard. Against her mother's wishes, she wore her hair like an Indian squaw. Grandpa O'Rourke gave her Angela's conch shell and eagle feathers and she often wore them in her long hair like her grandmother did. Remembering her royal blood line, she walked proud with her head held high.

The British soldiers stationed at the Mt. Joseph Fort watched her intently. They hated — what they called the savages — who had once joined the French to fight against them. The constant flow of Indians visiting Leah's home and her regal bearing inflamed them. She refused to lower her head when she walked by them in the nearby village, and ignored them completely when they passed on the road near the farm. What right did a squaw have to put on such airs? They couldn't wait for a chance to teach her some manners toward white men, especially His Majesty's soldiers.

One afternoon, after Jimmy left to carry some hogs to the Charles Town market, they made their move. Three British soldiers rode their horses up to the rail fence Jimmy had built in front of the cabin and dismounted. Leah was working in her vegetable garden behind the house when she heard Scrap's low guttural growl and saw the redcoats.

The biggest one yelled, "Hey squaw, we come to call on you. Where's your hospitality?" As all three started to walk around the fence toward her, Scrap leaped in front of Leah to lunge at the man who was talking. The big man screamed like a child as Scrap locked his strong jaws onto the man's leg. His attack gave Leah time to run to the cabin, grab Jimmy's rifle and race back outside to see that in spite of brutal kicks to the ribs by all three of the men Scrap still held fast to the man's leg, tearing his flesh down to the bone.

"Get this son of a bitch off me," screamed the soldier, rolling in the dirt, blood gushing from his leg, as a fellow redcoat drew his knife and thrust it deep into Scrap's heart, killing him instantly. The man's gaping wound and searing pain incited him and his companions to far greater brutality than they had planned. Their intent had been rape, something they felt entitled to with any colonial woman, but most especially with the low-grade Indians. But now they had more vicious things in mind.

Surrounding Leah as she repeatedly yelled, "What do you want?" one of the menacing soldiers snarled, "To teach you some respect for white men, you filthy squaw."

She aimed the rifle at the leader and pulled the trigger but it misfired. Now angered to madness by the dog's attack and Leah's effort to shoot them, the three crazed beasts fell on her before she could reload.

Leah's only crime was being part Indian and being proud of her royal heritage, but they were going to punish her for it. No longer thinking of rape, they were bent on raw revenge and were seized by an irresistible pack instinct to destroy a weaker pray.

They grabbed her hair and dragged her back into the cabin where two held her while the third one punched her in the face. Her screams only drove him to hit her again, while the blood pouring down her face and neck fueled their frenzy. The one Scrap bit yelled, "Give her something to remember us by boys. Kick her in the stomach. There might be another redskin in there."

Through a fog of pain, Leah forced herself to remember their faces and names as they called to each other to hit her harder. Bert, a huge man with a bulbous nose was the one Scrap bit. Charlie with cold gray eyes and a beak for a nose was the cruelest. He had bony hands that delivered sharp blows, and he was the one who killed Scrap. Tom was the older man with a tomahawk scar on his forehead who egged the other two on.

Falling across the kitchen table, she reached a trembling hand toward Charlie to plead for mercy but he grabbed her by the hair instead and dragged her off the edge. As she was falling to the floor she slid against his leg. "You bitch," he shouted, "You got blood on my white pants," and started kicking her again as she tried to crawl away.

"Oh Hell, Charlie, make the most of it," Tom laughed, then cheered him on. "We'll report back to headquarters that you got in a fight with a redskin who jumped us on the road. Me and Bert'll claim you saved us after he cut Bert's leg with a knife. It is mostly true, that damn dog that bit him was a redskin's dog."

After what seemed like hours, they were finally through. On the way out, Charlie snatched two oil lamps from the shelf by the door, lit them outside and threw one back through the cabin window. It exploded on the wooden floor and flames climbed the log walls fueled by the gingham curtains Leah had made the week before. Barely conscious, she crawled through the door as the room filled with smoke. She had almost made it to the barn, where, Nellie, was still tethered in her stall when the hay inside burst into flames. Helpless, Leah listened to Nellie's screams until she lost consciousness.

On their way out, they deliberately rode their horses back and forth through the vegetable garden she tended so lovingly, trampling the plants to take even that part of her home from her.

On his way back from market, Jimmy saw the smoke over the trees while still a mile away. He spurred his horse into a fast gallop, praying, "Please God, please let it be a forest fire. Let Leah be safe."

Seeing the charred barn and cabin, he searched frantically for Leah. He found her lying on the ground next to Scrap. Screaming in horror he cried, "What happened? Leah, who did this to you?" Cradling her head in his arms, he stroked her blood-soaked hair while asking, "Darling, who did this to you? I'll kill the bastards, right now, tonight. Who did this?"

Leah, now regaining consciousness, remained silent, pretending not to remember what happened. She knew what the British would do to Jimmy if he harmed the redcoats, they would hang him without the benefit of a trial. But she would never forget them.

Over the next several weeks, Jimmy watched Leah move to the other side of the street whenever British soldiers approached. He was convinced they were responsible when he saw a big one with bandages on his leg limping and another with a pale face and sharp nose avoiding his gaze.

After moving into their tool shed, the only building they had left, Jimmy held Leah night after night, weeping with her while begging her to tell him if those two were the ones. When he finally went to the British colonel for help, he was turned away after being told, "It could have been anyone, probably Indians wanting some fun with one of their own, or punishing her for turning white on them."

Furious, disheartened and determined to wreak vengeance, he kept asking himself, "Why are the British even here?" He knew the answer. Those in power in England wanted to steal their hard work by taxing everything they consumed or produced. It wasn't right. No nation could survive when work of its citizens held no reward. If he and Leah realized their dream of a farm of their own, he had no intention of giving his hard-earned money to some foreign king, especially one living a life of opulence without working, and who allowed his soldiers to act far worse than the 'savages' they despised and felt so superior to.

Something had to be done. He *HAD* to do something, to avenge the attack on Leah, and win freedom for the two of them and the children they might someday have.

Leah, didn't have to tell him. Watching her cringe in fear at the sight of soldiers, he knew who had attacked her and decided he could legally kill them if he joined the Revolutionary forces. The land he would receive in exchange for his service would be their chance to get a new start.

When he heard General Pulaski was making life miserable for the British and needed good horsemen, he decided to join the Polish leader's cavalry. Jimmy was an excellent horseman, having learned to ride as a young boy on his grandpa's horse farm, and was convinced the general would welcome him.

Before he left, he asked Mr. Huskeby to look out for Leah and let her stay with him and his wife. "Of course, son. We'll be glad to watch over her," Mr. Huskeby answered. "We feel terrible about what happened, especially here so close to us, and on the land we sold you. Just take care of yourself and come back to us soon. She'll be fine."

Leah was determined to rebuild their cabin by herself in defiance of those who tried to drive her out. That worried Jimmy, but he couldn't change her mind. All he could do for the moment was leave her his rifle and a pistol and tell her he would try to convince General Pulaski to take on his cousin, 'Lee', as an interpreter between the Indians and Americans. He wanted more than ever to have her close to him, where he could protect her. "If the war goes more than three months, I'll send for you," he promised.

When Jimmy arrived at camp, Casimir was impressed with his eagerness to fight the British, his knowledge of the local terrain, and his riding ability. He accepted him into the Pulaski Legion. Early on, Jimmy distinguished himself as an outstanding guide with excellent riding skills. He earned a reputation among the officers and men as a fearless fighter and someone easy to befriend.

But, sadly, death claimed him when he sacrificed his life to protect Casimir from a redcoat's lance. Jimmy hadn't given Leah's name as his survivor when he signed up with the Pulaski Legion since he wanted to keep his wife a secret in case she had to pose as his male cousin. So, Leah wasn't notified when he died or given any property that she might have claimed for his service.

Leah thought of the sad day when she had learned of his death.

It had been a warm day, with the air still holding the clean fresh smell of morning rain. Leah was working the garden that she had defiantly replanted after the redcoats trampled her spring plantings. She was picking large pole beans that dangled from strings tied to six foot stakes crossed at the top to form triangles. It was late summer and the mature beans would make a delicious dinner when cooked with pork fatback. Soon frost would come and she would harvest the remainder of the crop, shelling the larger beans and drying them for bean soup in the winter. The young smaller bean pods were for pickling and frying with corn pone that winter, when wind would whistle through the cracks in the small lean to she had built on the ashes of their old cabin.

Honey bees were working the pumpkin blossoms on the vines that climbed the corn stalks planted next to the beans. They reminded Leah that her Creek girlfriend had promised to help her find their hive in one of the nearby gum trees and rob the bees of enough honey to cook with, and drizzle over biscuits or corn bread on special occasions. They would be careful to leave enough for the bees to survive the winter. Leah knew and honored the Indian traditions and, like her native kin, she respected all creatures and shared the bounties of nature with them.

Jimmy had left four months earlier and there was no end of the war in sight. Leah anxiously waited for a message from him telling her where to join him as Lee, his male cousin. In the time since he left, she had found some relief from the anger that threatened to eat her heart out through completing her mission of defiance by rebuilding the cabin and replanting her garden. Admittedly, the cabin was at best a makeshift shed, built from scrap boards Mr. Huskeby gave her, but she slept in it every night hugging the rifle and keeping the pistol next to her. Deep down she hoped the British soldiers would return. She would be ready for them.

She and Jimmy were willing to work, and if he returned with a land grant and if their crops did well they could buy more land, and maybe raise horses as Jimmy wanted. They planned to raise corn to sell as feed to other farmers. Children would be a big help with the farm work and bring joy as they watched them and the crops grow.

It disturbed her that after four years they still didn't have a child. The desire for a baby to nurture and love gnawed at her like the vision of a fleshy rib bone would haunt a starving dog. She wondered if it was fair to Jimmy to stay with him if she couldn't give him children. But she couldn't bear the thought of living without him.

She continued working as the sun weakened in the sky and crawled toward the western horizon. She stood up from her bean-picking squat seeing movement at the edge of the woods. The glare of the setting sun blinded her for a moment and then her heart froze when the form of a man appeared in the tree line. Was he a friend or foe? A Redcoat?

She had worked her way down a long row of beans and the pistol was at the opposite end in the pocket of the apron she had taken off when the afternoon became too warm for that extra layer of clothing. A long-legged man could cross the small field to where she stood before she could retrieve it and aim.

Overcome by joy and relief, she gave silent thanks to God when she heard the whip-o-will call of Tathtowe, her childhood friend. After friendly gestures, they spoke in his native language.

"I bring news from the great battles between the settlers and the redcoats," said Tathtowe.

"From Jimmy," she squealed, words flowing from her mouth like a fast-moving creek. "Is he coming home? Is he alright? Does he want me to join him pretending to be another soldier?"

"My heart weeps that I can answer yes to only one of your questions," replied her tall Indian friend. "I have sad news and a request from the horse general. Jimmy is gone, he was killed by the British three months ago while saving the general's life. Before he died, he talked to a sergeant about a male cousin who speaks our language. The sergeant told the general and he said he wants this cousin to come to his camp to talk with the Indians and convince them to help him defeat the British. The horse general wants to convince them to become agents for him, to fight against the British."

It was clear that Jimmy had started planning for her to be with him before he was killed and she was heartsick, not only for her dead husband but for the child she longed for and would never have with him.

All of her hopes and plans for a life with Jimmy and their children disappeared with the news from Tathtowe. Her longing would never be satisfied.

There is no reason for me to go now, Leah thought, *I can't see him or be by his side to take care of him if he's wounded, or hold him at night. I'll never be able to do those things again because of the British. They've taken everything.*

But, then she knew in her heart that the brutal attack on her, the killing of Scrap, the burning of her home, and the killing of her dear Jimmy had to be avenged. She would go, and she would do everything in her power to make the British pay dearly for all they had taken from her. She could do that by getting her Indian friends to help the general to kill them all.

Leah buried her grief and added another layer of hatred in her heart for the redcoats. With balled fists and clenched teeth, she said, "I will go, Tathtowe, but first tell me what you know of Jimmy's death. I have to know."

Tathtowe's heart ached for this woman he had watched over, and protected as a child. But now he could not protect her from the hurt she was suffering. Quietly he told her what the messenger from the camp had said about Jimmy dying with a lance in his back that was intended for General Pulaski. When he finished, she swallowed hard, brushed away a tear and said, "I will need you to protect my secret. I'll be going as Jimmy's male cousin. Do you understand?"

"Yes, I will be silent," he replied. "You will be a young man trained in the ways of the Indian. That is what the horse general wants."

Her feminine body had to be disguised to look like a young man's. Her resolve to fight the British outweighed any concerns she might have for modesty or femininity. She used strong, rough burlap strips torn from feed sacks to flatten her breasts against her chest and wore Jimmy's pants and shirt that were big and baggy enough to conceal the curve of her hips and waist. She cut her long, raven hair to shoulder-length, tying it behind her ears as most men did, then covered it and most of her forehead with a hat. She welcomed the discomfort of the burlap bindings and clumsy brogan boots she wore as they strengthened her determination to get revenge.

The land she and Jimmy had worked so hard to buy would go to his oldest brother. The pistol, rifle, makeshift cabin and the garden she had calloused her hands building and tending, were her only worldly goods. She hoped that with service in the army she would be granted a piece of property even if it had to be in the name of a man. If she got it, she would build a proper cabin on it for herself and maybe a child, if only God would grant her an opportunity to somehow have a child. She needed someone to love more than ever with both Jimmy and Scrap gone. But for now, she was driven by hatred for the British.

"Tathtowe, we go now," she said to her friend, in a voice stronger than he had ever heard her use. "I won't wait. We must hurry to help defeat the British."

"Pack what you can carry," he replied. "We will cross the river and go through the swamp to leave as few footprints as possible. It's a long way and we must not speak since the British are near and may hear. But we should wait at least two days because the moon is full and the river is at flood stage. It's not a good time to cross."

"No, I go now, with or without you," she declared.

Tathtowe waited silently while she stuffed a bag with a change of threadbare clothes, food and the pistol, before tenderly adding the lock of Jimmy's hair he gave her when he left and another she cut from Scrap's fur before Jimmy buried him. She stopped briefly at the dog's grave overcome by the feeling she might never return. She silently thanked him for being such a brave and loyal companion and then prayed for Jimmy's soul and their eventual reunion in a better world.

When she slung the bag and the rifle over her shoulder, Tathtowe motioned for her to follow him.

The river was running high with a strong current. The crossing would be dangerous. They could be swept downstream toward a British camp and the bright moon would make them easy to spot. They would be helpless in the water, unable to swim and fire their weapons at the same time. But none of this deterred Leah. She wasn't going to turn back.

An eddy swirled at the river bank near where a hungry gator lay in wait, its eyes barely protruding above the muddy water, colored orange by the clay runoff from the hills farther north. Tathtowe spotted an otter ten yards upstream and threw his knife, burying it up to the hilt in the otter's side, killing it instantly. When the warm carcass floated near them, he grabbed it and tossed it on the far side of the gator which slid silently through the water after it. While the gator was distracted, they tied their bags to a log and pushed furiously, holding on for dear life while trying to guide it straight across. The current was so strong that they were carried downstream, and almost ended up in the redcoats' camp. They were so close they could hear the men talking and laughing and the clang of pots and pans being cleaned. The camp fire blended with the moonlight to illuminate the river's surface and they were forced to duck under the water as they drifted past the British.

Once clear of the camp, they climbed onto the river bank and slipped into the thick tree line, where swarms of mosquitoes and insects bit and sucked blood from any exposed skin. Smearing mud on their faces and arms slowed down the biting and buzzing and made them less visible to British sentries. They didn't dare slap at their flying tormentors or move through the brush too fast. The soldiers were everywhere. As they moved deeper inland, the camp sounds started to fade. Then, a frightened deer sprang up and charged away, breaking dried branches as it ran, and forcing them to pick up their pace for fear the British would come to investigate.

As they moved away from the river, thick brush gave way to open land sprinkled with large long leaf pines and live oak trees. Lengthy beards of gray Spanish moss swayed in the darkness like shrouded ghosts silently skipping from one giant oak to the next. The British, who were unaccustomed to anything hanging from trees in long, wide strands, found the place eerie and avoided the woods at night.

Yellow deer flies combined with the mosquitoes to make life doubly miserable for Leah and Tathtowe as they bent low, sometimes crawling, to avoid casting shadows, but when the British camp was finally behind them, the fear of being captured loosened its hold on Leah. She didn't fear dying as much as giving the British the satisfaction of hurting her again. She and Tathtowe spent the rest of the night on beds of deer moss and ferns in the woods, chilled but unable to risk building a fire to dry their clothes.

They walked all the next day without stopping. Tathtowe found witch hazel plants, and rubbed juice from the stems on their mosquito bites to relieve the itch. Although miserable in her soggy, dirty men's garb, and fearful of having leeches beneath her clothes, Leah felt every painful step was worth it if she could get to General Pulaski and help him rid the country of the English.

Casimir's camp was easy for Tathtowe to find, with his knowledge of the movements of both armies and help from his friends' coded bird calls along the way.

Even though the sun had lost the worst of its intensity as it surrendered the sky to the moon and stars, humidity still saturated the air, draining their strength. The air was full of mosquitoes and gnats when they arrived at the American camp. They saw the soldiers gathering moss and throwing it into the camp fires, creating an odorous smoke to keep most of the insects away until late evening breezes would offer some relief.

Tathtowe faded back into the woods, once they reached the outer edges of the bivouacked tents, leaving Leah alone to try her charade of being a man. She wasn't afraid. She had joined the war effort to wreak revenge on the British and now she was where she could do just that.

Jimmy had been her whole life, yet he sacrificed his life for someone else. She had asked herself a thousand times why he did it, wondering why their love hadn't been enough for him to live for.

But she knew the answer. Jimmy was a good person, the best she had ever known. He had been full of love for people, always thinking of others first. He couldn't hold back if someone was in danger, and she was sure his saving the General was pure instinct. He hadn't taken time to think of himself or her; he just did what he thought was right.

Now she had nothing, not him, not the home they worked so hard to build not even the child they dreamed of. Silently she swore, *I'll kill them Jimmy. I promise I will kill every last redcoat I come close to. You joined the war to avenge me and now I am joining to avenge you, Scrap, the child we never had, and the land we lost. I'll get them Jimmy. I swear my dead love, I will make them pay.*

Her thoughts were interrupted by the approach of a big bellied man asking her in a booming voice, "You a new recruit, laddie?"

"Yes sir," Leah said as low and loud as she could, trying to make her voice sound masculine.

"Well, Lordy me, you are a scrawny one," he observed. "The littlest one to show up today and they're coming in everyday like pigs to a slop trough. Everyone wants to ride with General Pulaski now that the newspapers have made him famous. Rightfully so though. He's the damnedest rider and shooter I've ever seen. Well come on, everybody has to line up at the recruitin' table to apply. He's about to close it down for the day so you best hurry. Call me Sergeant Wilkes and who might you be?"

"Lee McElveen, Sergeant," Leah shouted.

"Well follow me, the table's over here." For a large man, Wilkes moved fast. Leah had to practically run to keep up with him.

Her heart pounded while she wondered if she would be able to pull off the masquerade. Could someone smart enough to be a general be fooled by a woman dressed as a man? What would the penalty be if she were discovered?

Leah forced herself to focus on the moment, trying to match the sergeant's long strides as they entered the recruiting area.

She was the last volunteer allowed to enter the line that day and it moved quickly since von Hessen was in a hurry to get to supper. Moving closer to the recruiting table, she saw General Pulaski sitting next to a man with a big moustache and was taken aback by the general's appearance. She was expecting a much larger man but he was dwarfed by von Hessen and the towering Sergeant Wilkes. Leah had heard that General Washington was a giant of a man and she expected all generals to be big. Still, there was something about Pulaski that gave him a large presence, despite his small size.

"Next," shouted the mustachioed Von Hessen, as she realized it was her turn to step up to the table. Leah was looking directly at General Pulaski. He had piercing, highly intense and animated black eyes, wavy black hair and a slow, serious smile. In fact, he seemed to her to be a very intense, serious man.

His cleanliness and the neatness of his bright blue and white uniform was a sharp contrast to Sergeant Wilkes' appearance, but then she had already noticed that Wilkes was the exception in camp. Pulaski's troops exhibited pride in their appearance, standing out from the ragged troops of the Continental Army, and Leah wondered how someone as unkempt as the sergeant could be part of such a proud legion.

"Lee McElveen, no home, no family," she responded to von Hessen's brusque questions.

It was hard to understand Casimir's mixture of German and broken English. But while von Hessen interpreted, she answered the questions he asked in English, while looking directly at the general, he would be the one to decide if she could stay and fight, and he was the one Jimmy died for.

And now after just a few weeks since that fateful day, she was to be at the general's side as interpreter and personal aide. She prayed she could serve him well. The Continental Army was pinning its hopes on his ability to hold the south. Saving Charles Town was crucial as was re-taking Savannah from the British.

Her reverie ended when she saw Sergeant Wilkes walking toward her. Leah once more observed his bowed legs, the paunch hanging over his belt, his bushy graying moustache and eyebrows, enormous gnarly hands, and the caked dust and dirt on his face, boots and hat brim. *How can a meticulous general who is so demanding of cleanliness in his troops tolerate the sergeant's slovenly ways,* she again wondered.

"The general said you're a goin' be his new aide and I should show you around," Wilkes said, in a booming voice before spitting a stream of tobacco juice into the creek that ran through the camp.

"Yes sir," Leah yelled, trying to bellow back. "I need to see his headquarters, meet the cook, and get up to date on our next move."

"Alright then, come along," said Wilkes. "The cook is most important because he has to fix all kinds of God-awful stinking stuff to keep the General happy and we want the General happy, believe you me. So, you'll meet him first. Then I'll show you around."

Good to his word, Sergeant Wilkes introduced her to the big gray-haired cook who had his face turned away from the smells of pork sausages and sauerkraut frying in the skillet he was holding over the fire. The cook acknowledged them, coughed, and spat on a hot rock ringing the fire, sending up a hissing steam.

Wilkes moved out of range of the sausage smells and the cook's anger, and showed her the best spot in the river to get water upstream of the latrines, the aide's tent, and the horse corral. When they finished, the sergeant slapped his knee and said, "I nearly plum forgot. The general said you're to have supper with him. I'll take you back to his headquarters tent where he meets people.

Seems odd that he don't sleep in it, says he wants his privacy and crawls into a little tent next to the corral. His horse stays with him. Strange little fella, but a hell of a fighter. I'm afeared you just saw and smelled what you'll be havin' to eat."

Leah was nervous about being alone with the general. What if her voice or actions failed her and he discovered she was a woman? What would he do to her? Sending her home before she killed any British would be the worst he could do. She just couldn't let him find out.

She saw von Hessen talking with the General while pointing at a ledger with names in it. It was worse than she feared. Now she would have to carry on a conversation with both of them at the same time, while pretending to be a man.

Casimir knew his life and those of his men might depend on his aide's quick thinking and calm in battle and he was following up on his hunch that he needed to know his new aide better. He invited Lee to dinner to study him and included von Hessen because he seemed to be the only person in camp who shared his taste for Polish sausage.

His headquarters tent was sparsely furnished, with one cushioned and two cane-bottomed straight back chairs, and a narrow wooden bench providing seating next to a table with maps and papers strewn across the top.

"We're lucky to be invited today. He just received a package of good Polish sausages from a butcher he knows," von Hessen confided. "They're delicious."

Casimir laughed when he saw his thick-necked interpreter raise two fingers to his puckered mustachioed lips and make a smacking noise to illustrate his enjoyment of the Polish treat.

Casimir motioned to Leah to sit in one of the cane-bottom chairs, and studied her face with care. He could usually judge a man within the first moments of their meeting with an uncanny ability to sense a person's character, strength and loyalty. He thought this cousin of the man who gave his life to save him would also sacrifice his life if the situation called for it. He particularly noticed the fierce determination in Leah's eyes. They seemed full of hatred for the British but reflected something deeper, which he concluded was sorrow, and wondered if his own eyes held the same combination, given his resolve to win glory here after the losses he suffered in Poland and France. What had this man lost? Certainly, a cousin, but was that enough to create such sadness and hatred? He was puzzled by the man in front of him. Something was driving him, but what was it? He also noticed that some of the fellow's mannerisms were quite delicate and his voice was soft.

What an odd fellow, Casmir thought, *but if Lee can help me win the support of the Indians I'll gladly accept him and all his oddities.*

All the scrutiny was making Leah extremely nervous and she feared she might either start crying from the strain or bolt out of the tent if he continued to gaze so intently at her. The thought of running away was tempting.

Finally, he seemed to realize that his staring was making her uncomfortable and broke the silence by saying, "Allow me to offer you my condolences on the death of your cousin," he said in French. "I have not properly expressed my gratitude to you for his sacrifice. He was a fine soldier and a brave and courageous person and I owe my life to him. Having come from the same family stock, I'm sure you will be a valuable addition to our cause."

"Thank you, sir," replied Leah. "He was a very special person to me. And thank you as well for the opportunity to serve as your interpreter and aide. I will do everything I can to help you win the war and drive the British out."

"There's no need to thank me for the aide position," Casimir smiled, "It will mean hard work and long hours."

She nodded her head in acceptance, thrilled because she knew of Casimir's bravery, and as his aide de camp she would be close to the planning and fighting of battles. Soon, she would have an opportunity to kill the British face on.

"Good, we will start the real work tomorrow," he said. "Now tell me about your knowledge of the Indians. How did you come by it? And how did you learn their language as well as French? If you're proficient in both, I want you to stay close by for any emergency interpreting with the Indians and the troops. I don't understand why some of the natives have joined the British, but I hope to change their minds and use them as guides and spies."

The cook placed plates of sausage, sauerkraut, potatoes and pierogis on the long table, while Casimir decided that even though he needed his aide's help with the Indians, he would need to carefully test him until he was sure of his ability and loyalty.

There's still something strange about him that nags at me the way Maurice's familiarity did before I knew who he was, he mused. *My instincts are rarely wrong, and they tell me this young man is hiding something. I just need to make sure it isn't something that will cause trouble later*

Telling him as much truth as she dared while they ate, Leah said, "My grandmother was an Indian princess. My mother and father allowed me to spend time with her family where I learned the Cherokee language as well as a little Creek. My grandfather was from Ireland and learned French there; he taught me to speak it."

"Excellent!" Casimir exclaimed. "We need someone like you. Tomorrow I want you to talk with Sergeant Wilkes about our upcoming battle. It's an important one that could determine the outcome of the war."

After the meal, she said, "Goodnight, General, thank you for allowing me to work with you to get rid of the Redcoats."

She was headed to her small tent next to Casimir's headquarters, when a young soldier stepped out of the shadows, motioning for her to follow him. While apprehensive, she saw he was alone and displayed no weapon and she thought refusing him might cause more of a fuss than going with him, so she cautiously followed.

When they were far enough away from the campfires that they wouldn't be overheard, he smiled and said, "Hi, I'm Jack Turner and I know about you. Jimmy was my best friend. He told me about your plans for you to join him. He couldn't wait to see you. I'm terrible sorry for your loss. I was there the day he died and he sure is a hero, especially in the general's eyes. If you need anything here, you just let me know."

His disclosure caused a new fear that wrapped her tighter than the burlap bindings. She could hardly breathe. She had survived encounters with the troops, General Pulaski, von Hessen, and the sergeant, but here was someone who knew her secret. How many others knew?

"Thank you so much," she ventured cautiously. "I want to do all I can to make the British pay for what they did to him, and to me, and to our home before he joined the army. I can't do that if the general finds out I'm a woman."

"Your secret is safe with me," Jack reassured her. "I won't tell a soul. I knew Jimmy's plan so I volunteered to find you when Sergeant Wilkes said the general wanted Jimmy's cousin to help with the Indians. I told the sergeant I come from the same parts as Jimmy and could find you. Then I asked the Indian messengers to send word along the line to the Indians where you lived that you should come to camp and talk to the general. I knew you were friendly with the Cherokee and figured they could find you and let you know what happened to Jimmy."

"Thank you, Jack, I can tell you were a good friend to him," said Leah with a sigh of relief.

"I'm just sorry you didn't get here before he died. He didn't suffer none. There was no pain, he died so fast."

"Is it possible you could take me to where he is buried?" she asked hopefully.

"I can tell you where it is, I'm not supposed to leave camp without permission, but with you workin' with the Indians you can go and come as you please. I'll draw you a map you can follow," he offered, then hesitated, "But there are a lot of soldiers buried together, there always are at a battle site. It won't be like a churchyard cemetery."

"I'd appreciate it just the same, and I'm grateful for all you have done, and for your promise to keep my secret," she said.

"Sure thing," he replied. "It's the least I can do for Jimmy. If you're not too tired, how about sittin' a spell at my campfire? I'll try to fill you in."

Weary and emotionally drained from the intensity of being on her guard to keep her disguise convincing, the thought of talking with someone she didn't have to keep up the pretense of being a man with was appealing. She wanted to know more about the men she would be working with so she agreed, saying, "Sure, I'm not that tired. Do you have any coffee? I need to get the taste of those sausages out of my mouth with something."

"Yeah, we could smell the cook frying them all over camp," Jack laughed. "It's an honor to serve with the general, but eating with him is a whole other thing. Follow me and I'll get you some coffee."

After learning about the general's routines and preferences, she asked about something that had troubled her since her arrival, "Jack tell me about Sergeant Wilkes. Why does a general who's so picky about how clean his troops are, their gear, and even their horses, put up with someone so dirty and rough? He told me to wash my face and dress in a clean uniform but Wilkes walks around like he just climbed out of a pig pen."

"Well, I guess I can shed some light on that," Jack chuckled as he leaned toward her conspiratorially and lowered his voice. "I wasn't there but I've heard the story so many times I reckon it's the God's truth about how Ole Billy Wilkes and the general hooked up. It's a long story so you better have another cup of coffee to stay awake through it."

After stirring a stick in the fire that sent a shower of sparks into the night air, he tossed on another small log, reached for the coffee pot, poured her another cup, and began.

"The way they told it, the sergeant was a horse wrangler and trader in the Kentucky wilderness. He bought and rounded up good stock in Kentucky and brought them east for sale to big land owners and soldiers. It was a rough and lonely business and took a tough ol' boy to travel through backwoods thickets, fight off highwaymen and Indians, and survive rain, snow, bears and the likes. Some say he made friends with Daniel Boone himself, and that Boone helped him get through Indian territory along the Kentucky river.

"As the story goes, the general was on one of his favorite missions, buying horses. He had heard about a man who drove good stock from Kentucky to sell in the area and he was standing at one of his corrals when a group of loud and mean-looking ruffians swaggered up to him. It was the local troublemakers, the two Buchannan brothers and five other half-witted brutes. They surrounded General Pulaski who was on foot at Wilkes' corral, choosing the horses he wanted to buy for his troops. As usual, he was dressed meticulously in his blue and white general's uniform, red sash, and high leather riding boots. The hooligans began mimicking his accent and pointing at his small size. Then, they got whips out to teach this little 'cock of the walk foreigner,' as they called him, that real men don't take to such high falutin' airs. Just as Joe and Bobby Buchannan began closing in on him with whips cracking overhead, Big Billy Wilkes strode into the middle of them.

'Now boys, I don't take kindly to you'uns tryin' to chase my customers away,' "he said, real calm like." 'You best back off.'

"The Buchannan boys just sneered at him, with Bobby kind of snarlin' and saying, 'Well I reckon you should be more choosey about who you sell your horses to. This little dandy don't know one end of a horse from the other. You can tell that by lookin' at the way he's all trussed up in that outfit he's a wearin.'

"When he and Joe started moving toward General Pulaski cracking their whips up and down around him, the sergeant grabbed Joe's whip in midair, yanked it outa' his hand and stripes 'im right across his neck and face. Joe crumbled in pain while Bobby and the other four moved in to attack the general who just calmly pulled out his sword and slashed Bobby's arm and rib cage. Yes sir, they say he didn't bat an eye, acted like he was swatting a fly away.

"Then he and Wilkes turned toward the other four who were trying to get away. The general shot one in the leg causing him to whimper, 'No, no I don't want no more, mister, I've had enough,' while dragging his leg and limping as fast as he could toward his horse. Wilkes whipped another one until he was rolling on the ground also pleading for mercy. While that was happening, the Buchannan brothers slipped away. It was every man for himself as far as the gang was concerned, and each one painfully made it to his horse and rode off while the general and Wilkes watched. They never came near Wilkes' horse corral again.

"Then, the general walked over to Wilkes and shook his hand trying to thank him, and ask with sign language and broken English if he could ride and shoot as well as he could use a whip.

"When the rough horse trader figured out the question about whether he could ride and shoot he slapped his knees laughing, saying, 'Can I ri . . . can I ri . . . , can I ride a horse?

'Mister them horses were wild mustangs I caught, broke, and brought here. I'm the best damn horse rider you'll ever find. I know horses; know how they act in any situation, what they want, who they trust, and how to make 'em respect me.

'As to a pistol, no man survives out here without knowin' a pistol like his right hand. You bet your bottom I can ride 'n shoot. I've won more shootin' contests around here than any five men put together, no brag about it, just the way it is.'

"Well onlookers said the general seemed more surprised that Wilkes was talking to him in a mix of backwoods English and French than by his boasting. Seems he had learned French while dealing with fur traders and the Indians who fought with the French. General Pulaski, a good judge of character as proved by you and me being part of his legion, recognized that there was more to this tough, brave man than one would think by looking at his rough dress and talk.

"The general likes confidence in a man, has plenty of it hisself, and he needed good horsemen who could shoot and fight. He suspected Wilkes was such a man and decided to find out for sure.

"He challenged Wilkes by saying, 'Well perhaps we could do a little shooting and riding together, just for fun and maybe a small wager of say, that white mare of yours against my inlaid pistol?'

'You're on,' Wilkes hollered.

"It was obvious that although he didn't care about his appearance, he was proud of his riding and shooting. So off he went to the corral to get the white mare to ride. He told people later that he knew right away that the general had plenty of horse smarts because that Arabian mare was the prize of the lot he brought back from Kentucky. There weren't many Arabians in the wilderness, especially one as good looking as that one.

"The general called Visner over to him just as Wilkes swung up onto the mare's bare back with a look of pure one-upmanship. In response, General Pulaski jumped onto Visner and gave him the signal with his knee to raise his front legs high in the air, lifting him up to a commanding position. Wilkes leaned over, spit a stream of tobacco juice onto the ground and laughed. He slapped his leg, and said, 'Damn this is gonna' be fun.

'Tad, go git them two cattle skulls over by the corral.' He yelled at a boy about ten years old that was hanging round. 'Whack off the lower branches on those two young maple trees standing together over there and hang them skulls on each tree higher up than my head, but make em' even.'

"The boy, Tad, was just a little scrap of a kid. He ran over to a woodpile, grabbed a hatchet, collected the skulls and ran to the trees that were about a quarter mile away from where General Pulaski and Sergeant Wilkes were sitting on their horses, with the horse trader on the left side of the General. He shimmied up the first tree, hacked off the small, lower limbs up to ten feet above the ground and hung the first skull on a stub six-feet up, like Wilkes told him to. He then climbed the second tree and did the same thing.

"Tad ran back to the horse trader grinning from ear-to-ear. He had done this before and seen Wilkes win a lot of riding and shooting matches. The general could tell that the kid worshiped Wilkes, and thought he would easily win.

"The rules were simple. Race toward the tree, fire at the right eye socket in the skull, and get back to the starting point first. Whoever came closest to hitting the eye socket would get ten points and the one who got back first scored ten, so a tie was possible. In that case two more rounds would be played and the one with the highest score after three rounds would win the bet.

"Someone gave Tad a pistol and when he fired a shot signaling the start, both horses leaped forward, charging across the field toward the trees. Visner pulled slightly ahead and the crowd of onlookers saw the general perform one of his favorite tricks, he threw his gun to the ground, slid over Visner's side, scooped it up in his left hand, and fired from under Visner's neck while he was still climbing back into the saddle. Wilkes fired his pistol at almost the same time. The crowd, which was growing by the minute, roared at such riding and shooting.

"There was nothing said about what they did after they shot, just that they had to get back to the starting line. Well, Wilkes did what he had always done against other contestants. He turned his mare in a big circle in front of the tree on the left and headed back to the center of the track. But the general, stood up on Visner's back, ran between the two trees that were no more than three feet apart, and grabbed his skull from the right tree. He and Visner made a tight turn around the maple on the right and raced back toward the finish line. They gained a lot of ground on Wilkes while he was doing that wide circle and the mare seemed to lose momentum when Visner increased his sizeable lead.

"What a show. One man riding and shooting bareback and the other scooping a pistol from the ground and shooting from the side of his horse. The locals talked about it for months afterwards.

'Whew doggie, that was some ridin' you did. Tad, go get my skull, let's see if our friend can shoot as good as he can ride,' the horse trader crowed.

"When Tad handed up the skull to Wilkes, he pointed to the shattered corner of the right eye socket in his target and bragged, 'I hit mine.' Tad was grinning even bigger, showing a big gap between his two front teeth, and nodded in agreement.

"Then Wilkes looked over at the skull the general was holding and said, 'You did some fancy ridin' but I don't see a mark on that skull you're holding. Unless you're willin' to forfeit I guess we'll have to do it over since your horse edged mine out. After that I'll be collectin' that fancy pistol of yours.'

"He was still sitting there with a broad grin across his face waiting for an answer when the general said quietly, 'I beat you by more than a horse length, and I hit my mark as well. Take a look at the back of this skull directly behind the right eye.' "The crowd gasped when the general held the skull up and daylight shined through a hole in the back where his bullet exited the skull after going through the middle of the right eye socket.

"Wilkes shook his head and said, 'Well, dang it, I didn't know what I was up against. You shoot like that, you deserve this mare and I'll throw in a drink over at the saloon.'

"The general surprised everyone by saying, 'My new friend, I'll be honored to have a drink with you, and even more honored to have you join my cavalry. My men need a strong example to reinforce what I teach them about horses and good riding and shooting. Will you join me in driving the British out of this land?'

"Wilkes' face showed shock and admiration for the general and he said, 'Heck, I'm getting kinda tired of dodgin' Indians 'n outlaws just to bring a few horses east to sell. It's a lonely life and I could use some company, so yeah, why not? I'll join up with you. I don't like them redcoats no better than you do. Too stiff and starchy for me. One thing though, even if you did beat me and I might, might I say, learn a thing or two from ya', I ain't fancyin' up like you.'

"General Pulaski agreed, "Fine, and I'll buy all of your horses for my men. They look like good stock. And since I can't ride two horses back, bring the mare with you. When I'm not using her, she'll be yours to ride and she and Visner might become close friends and give us a colt one day. What a fine horse that would make. Oh, and it would be nice if you'd wear a uniform of some kind so our men don't shoot you by mistake, but you don't have to 'fancy up.' Agreed?'

'Partner, you got yourself a better deal than you know. I reckon that little sprout of a boy will be comin' with me. His Ma died havin' him and his Pa got hisself killed in a knife fight. Didn't leave the boy nothin' 'cept a juice harp. He's been taggin after me for months. He's scrawny but he can skinny up a tree and spot game a mile away, tote water, cut wood, build a fire, tend horses, or do just about anything else I tell him to do. Oh, yeah and you should hear him on that juice harp. He can even play some foot stompin', heel kickin' tunes on a washboard or a pair of spoons.'

Jack ended the tale with, "And that's how we got Tad, our drummer boy, and how Sergeant Wilkes and the General became friends. Even though they are as different as can be, I've noticed they always keep an eye out for each other, makin' sure when one needs the other he's there, especially in battle. That's why the general wanted the sergeant to show you around. He trusts him totally and will value his opinion of you."

As Jack finished the story, Leah began to feel the effects of the long day. "Thanks for the coffee and for filling me in on the Sergeant. I'll look at him different from now on. I'm pretty wore out, so I'll see you tomorrow. Goodnight."

"Goodnight Lee, and good luck," Jack called after her, stressing the name Lee as she made her way to her little tent. Once there, she relaxed and was comforted by the stillness in the camp. It was quiet, except for the movement of the horses on the picket line. She could sense their uneasiness. It was like they knew what carnage might be ahead for them and the men they would carry.

CHAPTER TWENTY-THREE

CHARLES TOWN

1779

asimir asked his aide to stay close and Leah did. She was by his side every day and her admiration for him continued to grow. At the same time, impressed by her dedication to eradicating the British, he found himself relying on her more and more. He began assigning her challenging and important tasks, and she finished every job beyond his expectations.

Sergeant Wilkes reported to Casimir that Lee "keeps to hisself and don't trade truck with nobody 'cept the Indians and every now and then Jack Turner, the soldier who found him."

Casimir still wanted to know more about the young man and invited Lee, along with Paul and Maurice, to eat supper with him several times. Each invitation pleased and frightened her. While she was honored to be included in his inner circle, she knew each encounter increased the odds that one of the men would figure out she was a woman.

At the first meeting Maurice, introduced himself and Paul, greeting her warmly, saying, "Welcome Mr. McElveen. I am Maurice Beniowski. The general asked me to introduce myself to you as his blood brother, and I'm to introduce this somewhat cocky young man as his lifelong friend; each of us would willingly die for the other. General Pulaski has high hopes that your influence with the Indians will convince them to help us against the British."

"I'm honored to meet both of you, and it's my dream to be of help to the general in ridding this land of the Redcoats," said Leah, speaking as forcefully as she could to sound masculine. When she shook their hands, she did so with the firm grip of a frontiersman, glad for the first time to have developed calluses from rebuilding the cabin and planting the garden.

Leah got to know all three men during these meetings and, while each was different, she liked them all. *How lucky I am,* she thought, *here I am an Indian farm girl, eating with European aristocrats. If only I could let ma know, she'd be mighty proud.*

Although it was hard to act like a rough, illiterate, uncouth man around such fine gentlemen, she had to. She remembered to take Jimmy's pipe from her pocket, strike a match on the heel of her boot to light it, and blow smoke rings toward the ceiling like he used to do.

She even forced a belch one evening, but could do it only once in front of such gentlemen even though the taste of those smelly sausages lingered long after she forced herself to swallow them. She never learned to like the general's sausages, but she was so happy to be near him and his friends, that she would have eaten rotten eggs if he had served them.

Casimir continued to find his aide, Lee, resourceful, smart and quick to respond to requests. He was constantly running messages, checking on roads, helping free wagons stuck in the mud, reporting anything that could slow the army down, and passing along intelligence about British movements he got from the Indians.

Casimir trusted and depended on Lee, and was somehow comforted by the aide's presence at his strategy meetings with Maurice and Paul.

Lee's friendship and ability to converse with the Indians helped secure local food for the troops, as well as directions on which routes to take. When the time came, they would have to cross rivers, larger ones than he had known in Poland, and they would be a challenge. He was counting on Lee to get valuable information about the best places to ford from the Indians. It was for those reasons, he told himself, that he kept Lee near.

With his unusually observant eye, it didn't take Maurice long to figure out the reason Casimir's new aide de camp didn't go to the latrine while other men were there, why he didn't bathe in the river with them, and why he slept in his aide's tent away from the campfires. Maurice guessed Lee was a woman. He knew women came to camp dressed as men for various reasons. He also knew they could be effective spies, posing as prostitutes or local women, and he wondered, *does she have such a mission?*

What Maurice couldn't figure out was why she was so driven to fight the British, but he suspected it had something to do with her cousin, Jimmy, who died saving Casimir. She did as much or more work than any man, never complained and was an excellent interpreter with the Indians who seemed deferential to her. He had heard Sergeant Wilkes and some of the wagon masters and frontiersmen describe such determination as 'grit' and was convinced she had an abundance of it. Casimir was wise to keep her close to him.

Casimir enjoyed keeping her near and although it took him a bit longer, he too learned Leah's secret. He would never disclose it since he identified with her, having a closely guarded secret of his own. She was a woman taking on the dress and traits of a man. He was a man with certain female characteristics. He had the ability to fight the fiercest battle, while at the same time analyzing the situation calmly like a woman. Another reason he would not disclose her secret was he needed her help. He had a mission to accomplish, and her work with the Indians had become crucial to his success.

Casimir knew women were drawn to him and he enjoyed the attention he received at balls and social gatherings. The newspapers had rightfully declared him a hero, and his Polish European flair was irresistible to many of the wives and daughters of the planters and army officers. But while he enjoyed their admiration, he couldn't waste his precious time courting them. His objective was to win a war and restore the family name. That was always foremost in his mind.

He had not enjoyed the company of a woman since leaving Europe. Franciszka was certainly different from Leah. While she could never be described as gentle, graceful, charming or eloquent, Leah had a down-to-earth, common sense astuteness he admired, and felt sure that with a similar upbringing she would have been Franciszka's equal in many subjects.

She was smart, no doubt of that. Her language abilities proved it. He admired her determination and knew she would willingly accept any assignment he gave her, regardless of the danger. Casimir identified with her lack of concern for her own safety, which reinforced his feeling that they shared a kindred spirit. Although he wasn't sure if her dedication was due to some sort of vendetta against the British or an attraction to him, he was thankful for her expertise with the Indians and for her company, regardless of the reason.

Casimir soon began inviting her to join him for dinner by herself, in the evenings, but he never gave her any sign that he knew about her gender. He was interested in the seemingly ease she could pick up languages since he was still baffled by English. Already she knew several Polish words and had actually taught him a few English words and phrases. They now communicated in a mixture of French, English, and Polish with some occasional humorous misunderstandings that they laughed about. It seemed they both enjoyed their evenings together.

Leah was not immune to Casimir's charisma and charm. She could see he was an extraordinary man destined for greatness. To be near him was to be caught up in the excitement of that destiny. She was drawn to him as only a sensual woman can be drawn to a man, but she had to hide her yearnings. If she didn't, she would surely disclose her real identity and be sent away.

None of this was lost on Major John Bishop, who stayed as close to Casimir as possible, waiting for the right time to destroy this prissy little foreign general he detested. He too, had seen through Leah's disguise, but kept her secret to himself, hoping she would inadvertently help him ensnare Casimir.

One evening, Casimir said, "Lee, have Sergeant Wilkes fill you in on our move to Charles Town. We leave the day after tomorrow and there's a lot to be done to prepare for the long march. The sergeant is in charge of logistics, and can use your help."

"Yes sir," replied Leah. "I'll talk with the sergeant right away and contact my tribal people tomorrow morning. If you don't need anything else, I'll say good night now, sir."

"That's all Lee," he smiled. "One day I'll have to find the time to make you an officer since you're already my aide. Remind me of that after we get through the battles of Charles Town and Savannah. Now, good-night and don't forget to find Wilkes."

Leah's heart pounded. If she were an officer, receiving a land grant after the war was almost assured. She would just have to pretend to be Lee when she filed the deed at the land office, or have a man do it for her.

She found Sergeant Wilkes in front of his tent cooking beans and fatback over his campfire.

"Hey Laddie, come eat with one of the common folks," the sergeant invited, smiling as he greeted her. "I just got beans, no fancy sausage, but your welcome to 'em." He liked Lee and it never occurred to him that he was anything other than what he said he was and looked like, just a skinny young boy, trying to help the general with the Indians because he hated the British.

"Don't mind if I do, Sarge," she said, as she lowered herself to the ground on the opposite side of the fire and crossed her legs. The tin plate he handed her had food from several previous meals clinging to it, which she quickly rubbed off with some sand before ladling beans from the bubbling pot on the fire. The plain food tasted good and she ate a second helping, then accepted the cup of burnt coffee he offered.

"And to what do I owe the privilege of your company tonight, Laddie," the sergeant asked as she leaned back, with her elbows bracing her in the sand.

"The general wants me to find out about our march to Charles Town, said you're in charge of gettin' us there," she drawled as she picked up a dry piece of straw and stuck it between her lips to chew on as she had seen men do.

"Well, I reckon we're a gonna' go on down to Charles Town and kick a little Redcoat ass," he replied. "Now, if I know the general he wants to get there fast, before they know we're a comin'. That'll depend on the weather, the route we take, and how the wagons hold up. The way we go is the most important part, the shortest, safest and easiest for horses and wagons is the one we want, but all those things usually don't come together on one trail.

"Your Indian friends know a whole lot more than any of us about this area and which way to go. That's what the general needs to know, but you don't have a lot of time to parlay with 'em. He wants to move in two days and once he starts movin' it's hard to keep up with him, even if you start out next to him. If he gets a head start, you'll never catch up."

Wilkes let out a loud fart as he rose from the campfire and said, "We've got a lot to do to get ready, so I'm gonna' git some shuteye. I figure you better do the same."

"Thanks for the beans Sarge, and for the information," said Leah, while vowing to herself that she would never again sit downwind of the sergeant. She remembered to belch, cough and spit as she rose, then turned toward her tent.

Leah felt better after eating familiar food, and decided to slip into the woods to contact Tathtowe rather than waiting for morning to find out about the best route. That way she could get the information back to General Pulaski as quickly as possible. She had watched him train enough to know Wilkes was right about keeping up with him, and didn't want to risk either the general's anger or being left behind.

Walking into the woods, Leah was wrapped in darkness but she was unafraid. She was more comfortable here than around the men at camp. Here she knew that no harm would come to her. Giving the low, plaintive call of an evening dove, she heard an answering 'whip-poor-will', 'whip-poor-will' call from deep in the darkness. Then she waited, dead still, until her eyes adjusted to the dark. A new moon gave enough light for her to watch a screech owl swoop low to snatch a chipmunk for supper. She made the dove sound again. This time the answering whip-poor-will call was much closer.

When Tathtowe appeared, he motioned for her to follow him upstream along the creek bank until they reached an oak tree where moonlight bounced off the silver moss hanging from its branches. There she told Tathtowe about Pulaski's plans to fight the Redcoats at Charles Town and his need to know the best trail to travel.

"It must be big enough for wagons and galloping horses, but hidden from the British," she told him.

His answer confirmed what she already knew. "Don't use the regular road. Those who want to travel fast and not be seen must use the small trail and swim across the river, while wagons must go by the bigger road and cross the river on rafts. If the troops, wagons and cannons go together, it will take longer and be too noisy. Either way the horse general must watch out for Cherokee and Creek who have joined the British."

"But why would they help the Redcoats?" Leah asked.

"They are promised horses, a rifle, and whiskey for each American rebel they kill or capture and much more for the general," he explained. "The British don't have many horses. Their promise is a lie, like all the other promises of white men, but some want to believe, so they do.

"Slaves help them also, believing they will be given their freedom and land if they help win the war. The Redcoats have no new troops to replace the ones killed until another ship comes from their land, so they lie to them as well."

Then he drew maps in the sand of two trails, one wide enough for wagons and cannons but more open and visible than the other, which was only wide enough for horses and men. Leah quickly committed both maps to memory and headed back to camp to report to the general, who would be rising from his usual few hours of sleep.

Tathtowe put a hand on her arm as she turned to go and quietly said, "along the trails I showed you only the bird with red feathers will talk in the day and at night only the dove." Leah nodded, knowing this was to prevent confusion with any other bird calls enemy Indians might make.

Casimir was sitting outside his headquarters tent when Leah returned to camp. His mind had not allowed him to sleep. He was anxious to get to Charles Town and save it from the British. They already held Savannah, and if they captured Charles Town they would dominate the Southern Colonies.

He motioned for her to join him and asked, "Did you learn which road we take to Charles Town?"

Leah picked up a charred stick from the campfire pit and redrew the maps Tathtowe made in the sand, pointing to the wider line to indicate it was the best way for the cavalry, foot soldiers, wagons and cannons to travel together.

Casimir pointed to the thin, straighter line, looking at her for more information. "Cavalry only," she responded. "It's too rough and narrow for cannons and carts and the river crossing is swift and deep."

"Maurice" he said, and, understanding instantly, she hurried away to rouse Maurice and bring him to the general.

It was three in the morning when she called through the opening in Maurice's tent and for once she was thankful she didn't understand much Polish. He started swearing at the top of his voice, every fourth or fifth word coming out "Casimir," followed by unintelligible one-word bursts.

When he finally emerged, fully dressed, he growled, "What does he want this time that couldn't wait 'til daylight?"

"I think it has to do with the move to Charles Town," she responded sheepishly.

"Oh, bloody hell, he'll want the whole damn army up and ready to move before daybreak," he moaned. "Let's go, might as well get it over with."

Casimir didn't waste time apologizing to Maurice for waking him, instead greeting him and Leah with, "Lee, get Visner's saddle bags packed. I'll need food for three days and the usual ammunition, but keep it light. We're going to move fast."

When a loud groan came from the direction of Maurice, he said, "Maurice, you and Sergeant Wilkes have to get the army moving right after sunup and take them down this road." He pointed at the maps in the dirt Leah had drawn, tracing the stick along the wider line, and continued, "We'll meet at Charles Town. I'm taking the cavalry with me. Lee, get a message to Paul telling him to join us there. He's scouting the situation around Savannah. You'll come with Maurice and Wilkes. They may need you to get information about the Redcoat movements from the Indians."

"Sir, I must go with you. There are Indians along the way who joined the British I'm the only one who can tell the difference between the bird calls of our friends and our enemies."

He nodded his approval. He'd been raised to respect women as very special, almost holy beings; and knowing she was a woman, and a valuable one who could talk with the Indians, he didn't like risking her life or having her make such a hard ride, but he realized she was right. He needed her beside him on the march.

As the aide de camp, Leah was responsible for getting all the cavalry officers ready to ride while Maurice and Wilkes were responsible for the rest of the army. When Casimir shouted, "Let's move," she was fast and efficient, ensuring that the Pulaski Legion troops were in their saddles and lined up behind Casimir before the sky started to pale in the East.

Casimir showed his complete trust in Leah and her Indians to guide them along the fastest route by directing his aide to lead the way.

Leah heard the low, mournful call of a dove off to the right, and motioned for the cavalry to move in that direction. The guiding dove calls continued until the sun was streaming through the forest. Then the chirps of cardinals replaced the cooing doves to lead them from the forest into marshland.

It was there that the fresh morning air surrendered to the heat and humidity of a coastal midday and sand gnats and mosquitoes tortured the riders who sweltered in their long-sleeved uniforms and leather gloves.

The heat was so oppressive, Casimir couldn't breathe. He felt like he was in a furnace and Lee's voice seemed farther and farther away, making it hard to focus on what his aide was saying.

The ground and marsh grass began spinning, and Visner seemed to sway while Casimir's sweat soaked jacket and pants began to stick to him. Then, without warning, he vomited and his wet clothes suddenly turned to ice, making him shake uncontrollably.

Malaria was common in the area and when Leah turned and saw him shivering, she knew he had it. The only treatment was to rest until the fever wore off, but she knew he wouldn't do that.

The trembling became so ferocious his teeth clattered and he couldn't control his speech. When it finally subsided enough for him to talk he called Leah to his side and whispered, "Lee, I cannot fall in front of the men. Tie my hands as tight as you can to my saddle horn and fasten my feet to the stirrups, then stay with me and guide Visner to where we must go."

"General, you have malaria, you must rest," she pleaded, but she knew it was useless even before he shouted, "No. Do as I say. Now!"

She had to follow his orders, but she wished Maurice and Wilkes, who had more influence on the general, were with her. But they weren't, so she had to lead on as best as she could.

Catching the eye of Samuel Abbott, who looked worried as he watched Casimir, she mouthed, "Halt the men," and though he didn't understand why, he turned in his saddle and shouted, "General says to stop here."

It was only through superhuman willpower, that he was able to stay in the saddle until she guided him under some trees where she tied his hands and feet as he had instructed. Then she led him and Visner farther down the road so the men would think he had lingered to reconnoiter the area.

Voices and visions filled Casimir's semi-consciousness as Visner plodded on. He heard Dr. Borloff encouraging him, *Don't give up, Casimir. You are special. You can do more than other boys.*

While the fever raged, he watched Bazarek Izman die and bodies being thrown overboard from the Massachusetts as it sailed to America. Leah heard his groans and an occasional muttering of "No, no, don't do that to him," and stayed close to make sure none of the men could hear.

Ten miles outside of Charles Town she heard the scream of a hawk and, sensing danger, she stopped Visner and her horse and waited until a fine black stallion carrying a man dressed in a Pulaski uniform galloped across the swampy marsh toward them. He went directly to Casimir, started a salute that ended in midair, then turned his bright blue eyes from Casimir's face to Leah's.

"I'm Captain Bentalou," he announced. "You must be the aide who took my place. General Pulaski wrote me about you. What's wrong with him and why isn't he getting medical care?"

"Yes sir, I'm Lee McElveen, the general's *acting* aide until you return," she responded, hoping he wasn't offended by her stepping into his role as aide de camp.

"General Pulaski has malaria. There's very little that can be done for it other than bed rest, and you probably know him well enough to know he won't stop to rest."

"Yes, I know how stubborn he is," the captain agreed. "The good news is that there is a plantation ahead where our officers are welcome. Perhaps we can get him out of the saddle at least for the night."

Casimir didn't know that Lee and Samuel carried him from his horse into the plantation house where Leah bathed his chest and arms in fresh well water, and kept cool towels pressed to his head day and night. Unable to resist, at one point she bent and kissed his forehead and ran her fingers through his hair then let them trail down his chest.

When he finally awakened, he found himself in a four-poster bed facing floor to ceiling windows. Light gauze drapes beside the windows billowed in a fresh river breeze. He was propped up on pillows, and beyond the windows he could see acres of emerald green rice shoots and the river that both watered them and provided the house with cooling breezes. For a moment, he imagined he was still delusional, but when he saw his aide watching him from a chair across the room, he knew the worst was over.

The fever and dehydration had weakened him and created vertigo, causing the room to spin when he struggled to an upright position. Knowing instinctively what he needed, he reached for the pitcher of water on a marble-topped nightstand next to the bed and after finishing two glasses, demanded to know, "How much time have we lost?"

"You have slept five days, Sir. It takes most people that many weeks to recover from malaria," she answered.

"Five days. Where are we? Has Charles Town fallen while I slept?"

"We are at a plantation outside Charles Town. Captain Bentalou said the owner welcomed the Pulaski officers to make quarters here. He has a full report for you but Charles Town has not been taken, yet.

"Bentalou?" he attempted to shout. "Bentalou is here? Bring him to me, now."

After she rushed from the room, Casmir hurried to dress. Unlike most generals, he never allowed his aide to dress him, and he wasn't sure how many of his clothes he still had on since his chest was bare. He sighed with relief when he found he was still wearing his trousers under the bed covers.

Not yet trusting his legs, Casimir put on his shirt, vest, and uniform jacket while sitting on the edge of the bed. Once fully dressed, he rose from the bed and steadied himself by leaning against the backs of chairs and other pieces of furniture. He struggled over to the wooden vanity where a pink-flowered washbasin and matching pitcher stood. He poured cold water into the basin, and washed his face and hands. Now revived, he sat rigidly straight in one of the room's silk covered chairs when Leah and Bentalou returned.

Leah started to leave while Bentalou was saluting but Casimir stopped her. "Lee stay. You will need to know what he has learned about this area to help get ready for the battle."

His words left her both confused and pleased. She had thought with Bentalou back she would be relieved of the aide's role and reassigned to the regular troops but, apparently, this was not the case.

Casimir turned to Bentalou asking in French, "What do you know of the situation here, and of the British plans?"

"Sir, there is a large British force commanded by General Provost moving toward Charles Town," responded the captain. "I'm not sure of the number but it must be in the thousands. The situation looks hopeless and the governor and town council are meeting right now to decide when and how to surrender."

Casimir couldn't believe his ears. Civilians were planning to surrender their own town to be burned and ransacked by the enemy? He wouldn't allow it. Only a commander of armed forces could surrender.

"Lee, get the men ready," he ordered. "We leave in thirty minutes."

"Yes sir, right away sir," she answered, knowing it was not her place to argue and it wouldn't make a difference if she did. She looked nervously at Captain Bentalou, wondering what role he would play and how he would feel about it.

As she was opening the door to leave, she heard Casimir say, "Captain, continue to secure information about the British Navy's movements and how many Loyalists may join the redcoats. I need to know whether some of the citizens of the town will turn against the patriots. Make friends and see what you can find out. It's vitally important work and I need someone I can trust doing it."

Leah thought the general was trying to soothe the captain's feelings with his last remark, but Bentalou showed no emotion responding in military fashion, "yes sir. I will see to it."

Infuriated by the town leaders' decision to surrender, Casimir quickly recovered and stormed into Charles Town at the head of a small cavalry unit. Fearing an attack on the Town Hall, the council were meeting in Mrs. Swallow's Tavern on Broad Street where, just as Bentalou reported, they were discussing how to surrender the town.

Casimir charged in shouting, "Surrender? Surrender? You dare speak of surrendering your homes and your town, you gutless, spineless cowards. You would give your children a future of being controlled by a foreign king? You don't have the authority or right to surrender. I am a general in the Continental Army and my men and I choose to fight, and fight we will, to the last man, if necessary, no matter what you decide."

Even though they didn't understand all the words, they understood the passion behind them and the message he delivered. They were stunned at such brashness, especially coming from a foreigner, but before they could protest, Casimir swung around, cape flying behind him, and stormed out.

He opted to sleep in a small tent near the river rather than impose on the mistress of the plantation for another night and, awoke before daylight the next morning. Stepping outside his tent to find a spot to relieve himself he was greeted by Leah, who held out a steaming cup of coffee to him.

"Uh, uh, good morning Lee. Excuse me for a moment and I'll be right back for that cup of coffee."

When he returned, she told him his light infantry had just arrived and asked, "Will we engage the British today? We seem so far outnumbered."

"Yes, Lee, we're outnumbered at least four to one so I must surprise and disorient them. I'll hide the infantrymen behind the sand dunes and palmetto palms lining the river below the road. Then, I'll lead the cavalry past the hidden men and charge directly into the British line. The redcoats are always surprised by courage and won't expect an attack from such a small group.

After the initial shock wears off and they get organized, I'll pretend to be withdrawing and the British will chase me. When we have all passed the hidden infantrymen, they'll run from their cover and fire on the British backs while I, and my cavalry, turn and charge their front. We'll have them in a trap, from which they can't escape."

Her heart pounded with concern. He would be in front, leading the men, and the British would be firing directly at him.

"Sir, it sounds dangerous for you and the men you lead," argued Leah. "Wouldn't it be better to wait for the rest of the army to arrive? They should be here by tomorrow."

"What and let these idiot town leaders have time to give their homes and families to the British," he raged. "No. We ride today. Stay behind me, but close. I may need you to ride back with information for Sergeant Wilkes and Maurice."

"Yes sir," she said, realizing that by staying close to him she would have her first chance to kill British soldiers.

Casimir showed his officers where to hide their infantrymen, then ordered the cavalry to prepare for a charge.

Like the Polish Winged Hussars, Casimir began slowly walking Visner toward the enemy down the sandy road past his hidden men, and then kept picking up the pace until he and his troops were at a full canter.

Leah was directly behind him in the middle of the first line of cavalrymen. Musket fire began flying all around them, but Casimir simply rode faster, directly into it. He seemed immune to the bullets. She rode just as hard as him and remained just as indifferent to her own safety.

Then, off to the right, she saw them — Charlie, Bert and Tom, the three redcoats who had beaten her and burned her home. Pulling on the reins of her horse, she broke from the line and rode toward them aiming her pistol at Bert, the one Scrap bit.

They didn't see her at first since, like their comrades, they were too surprised by the attack to be aware of details around them. She held her fire wanting to get close enough for them to see her, to know why they were dying. When she was within earshot she screamed a blood curdling Indian war cry and they turned in unison to see a crazed young man riding toward them. Too late, they tried to fire at her, but she had already pulled the trigger and Bert dropped to the ground. When the other two started to ride up on each side of her, she hooked Tom with her Pulaski lance, and drew him closer before pulling it back and plunging it into his heart. Then she stared at Charlie, growling like a dog, and the shock of recognition leapt across his face just before her lance found its mark again.

Riding back to the cavalry charge, she was numb and as cold as a rock in a barren field in February. She saw that the general's plan was working well. The British had fallen back in disbelief at his daring move, and were now beginning to organize into a line to fire. "Retreat, retreat," Casimir yelled in English so the British would hear and understand. His men knew the tactic and followed his orders.

But the second stage of the plan went awry. His infantry commanders saw the British line collapse and ordered their troops to rush forward to keep the British from escaping before Casimir had retreated past their hiding spot. The opportunity for them to move behind the redcoats as they pursued Casimir and his men was lost and the infantry troops were out in front of the advancing British along with the cavalry, leaving all of them open to attack by the much larger British force.

The losses to the infantry were catastrophic. Eighty per cent of his men fell but despite losing, and at such a terrible cost of lives, the battle was considered a success by the citizens of Charles Town. It showed the British they would not just sit back and be taken over, that colonists were capable of attacking and they would. There was no further discussion of surrendering.

Casimir, wracked with remorse and guilt over the loss of his men, lamented, "The fault is mine, I am the general, the leader. Somehow, I let the men down. I didn't explain the plan well enough, or I didn't leave the right men in charge, or I delayed the fake retreat too long, or miscalculated the enemy's strength, or . . . " The punishment he heaped upon himself went on and on throughout the night, and Woja's words, like bad dreams, haunted him, *you will struggle through snow, salt, and sand.* So now more of her omens had come true. *But she also told Bazarek my greatest glory is ahead. Surely the worst is over for my men and me.* He prayed that it was.

The next morning, when his aide greeted him with a cup of coffee, a memory of Lee riding away from the formation toward the British right flank drifted through his mind. He remembered seeing the bodies of three redcoats lying on the ground to the right of the battle as he feinted a retreat. Hadn't the battle been enough of a disaster without his own aide disobeying orders? Especially an aide he valued, and had more or less befriended. This Lee perplexed him more each day, and had now openly defied him. He wouldn't tolerate insubordination.

"Lee, why did you disobey my orders and ride away from our unit yesterday," he demanded.

"I'm sorry sir, I thought I could help break the right flank while you broke through the center," she said, avoiding his gaze.

Something was wrong. Lee didn't seem worried or nervous, even though this was a court-marshal offense. There was even a hint of satisfaction on the aide's face. He had to know why.

"Lee, you know how serious this is. I can have you court marshalled and hanged for insubordination and failure to follow orders in battle. If you have any explanation, give it to me now. Why did you break ranks and kill those three men?"

Leah looked directly at him and said, "I recognized them. They ganged up on me and beat me, killed my dog, and burned Jimmy's and my home . . . uh, I mean our grand pappy's home where we grew up."

Her eyes filled with the tears she had been holding back and Casimir looked away. He believed her words were mostly true, and he had already guessed she and Jimmy were more than cousins. Jimmy had saved his life, and so had Lee by getting him to Charles Town despite his fever.

"Do not ever question my orders again soldier," he said as gruffly as he could. "Do you understand me?"

When she nodded, he added, "Killing three redcoats is to your credit as is the work you have performed for me, so I'll let this pass — this time. But don't try my patience again, Lee."

"No sir, I won't, and you won't be sorry about giving me this chance to fight the British again," she answered, with a quick sigh of relief.

He was angry with her because he wanted to keep her safe and she had risked her life when she strayed from the main body of the troops. He lost enough men that day without losing his aide and interpreter.

Nothing more was said about the matter and Leah resumed her duties as his aide. The next day, she relayed to him information she had received from Tathtowe that British General Provost was leaving Charles Town with his troops, heading south, toward Savannah.

Casimir was astounded. Why would a superior British force withdraw? Even with the arrival of the rest of his troops later that day, the British would still have them substantially outnumbered.

Paul gave him the answer when they sat down to exchange information that evening. "Casimir, we found the body of one of our couriers just outside town. His mail pouch was empty. The British must have intercepted a message about General Benjamin Lincoln moving his troops south. We heard rumors from some of the new recruits that he is headed here with a Continental force of about 4,000 men to defend the town. I'll bet that's the message the courier was trying to deliver."

"The newspapers say that after distinguishing himself at the battle of Bemis Heights, Congress appointed Lincoln commander of the Southern Department. General Washington must have sent him south to retake Savannah. With Charles Town threatened, he is most likely diverting his army here to reinforce our troops and analyze the situation before moving on to Savannah. Provost is probably trying to get to Savannah before him."

"You must be right Paul," said Casimir. "Why else would they leave? Well, I'm not sure we should let them go, at least not without some trouble. Are you?"

"Of course not, Kas. I can't wait to see what kind of trouble you have in mind."

Casimir was happy to have his old friend to joke with, but he was deadly serious about harassing General Provost. He would worry him with delaying tactics and hopefully prevent him from arriving in Savannah ahead of the Continental forces.

He summoned Leah, and when she entered the room she nodded to Paul and turned to Casimir who said, "Lee, I want you to talk with the Indians and have them track the movements of General Provost's army. I need to know which roads they're taking to Savannah. I plan to delay them. Savannah will be our next big battle and I don't want them to have a lot of time to rest and dig in."

"Yes, sir, I'll leave now," Leah responded, then turned and headed outside toward the tree line.

Paul looked curious and said to Casimir, "I am surprised to hear you and Lee talking in French, English, and Polish. He must have picked up some Polish here and there and proven there is some hope of you learning English. And you seem nicer to him than to the rest of us, why is that?"

"He does his job well, without complaining, for one thing. And it is easier to understand and learn his slower Southern dialect than the English that the men from Samuel and Abe's region speak, or the immigrants with the heavy accents."

"Um hum, I still think it a bit strange. But I have a feeling I should go get some rest. I suspect whatever you are planning for General Provost will take place in the middle of the night."

Leah reported back to Casmir the following day. "Sir, the British are travelling down the Savannah Road near the river at Purryburg. An advance party is several hours ahead of the mounted troops and foot soldiers and they're a day ahead of the cannons, munitions wagons, and other supplies."

"Good," Casimir exclaimed. "We'll start at the rear and work our way forward, beginning tonight."

Late that night Casimir ordered Sergeant Wilkes, "Get me our thirty best riders and bring them here. Then tell Maurice to see me right away. We ride in fifteen minutes."

Shaking his head and muttering something about why couldn't anything in this dang army happen in the daytime, Wilkes wandered off to find Maurice and the select group of horsemen.

"What?" muttered Maurice. "He wants to see me at one a.m.? Why didn't he wait until three a.m. like he usually does? Don't even bother telling me what it's about Sergeant, I'm on my way."

Chuckling to himself at Maurice's sarcasm, the sergeant hurried on to wake those unfortunate enough to be considered the best horsemen in the troop.

"Maurice, we're about to go on some night raids, and I want you to ride ahead and scout out General Provost's supply and munition wagons," Casimir said. "I want to know where the horses are corralled, and if there are guards posted with the cannons. We won't be far behind, so ride and work fast. We have to surprise them in the dark."

The angry scowl left Maurice's face and was replaced with a look of admiration and then a mischievous smile when he guessed Casimir's plan. "Kas you are the best military man I have ever known, read about, or heard legends of. I am sure we are about to make life miserable for the British just as we did for the Russians in Poland.

"I'm on my way. I'll ride back to you as soon as I have what you need." He started to walk away but hesitated and added, "Take care of yourself," and then disappeared into darkness.

Leah rode up to take the aide's position on the general's right side while the other men were assembling, but he dismissed her saying, "Lee, I don't need you tonight. Go get some rest."

"Beggin' your pardon sir, but you may want to reconsider. I need to listen for the signals from the Indians who're helping the Redcoats. You don't want to risk having your men ambushed."

Perturbed because she was right again, especially after she had disobeyed him in the earlier battle, he snapped, "Then be quiet and keep up."

Casimir cautioned the men to be silent as he led them south along a road that hugged the river bank. It was a warm night and the smell of fresh mowed hay and harvested sorghum cane perfumed the air. Casimir smiled at the way Visner stepped high and pranced as he was prone to do when he was on a night ride. *Like me, he enjoys being in the lead,* Casimir thought. Stars twinkled in a black velvet sky and the horses moved smoothly and silently along the sandy road. Then the glow of dying embers from campfires twinkled back from the ground just ahead of them. They heard a soft, low whistle and Maurice appeared beneath a thick veil of Spanish moss draped across the limb of a 300-year old oak tree.

"Well?" Casimir asked.

"Fifty horses are hobbled along the river bank just south of the camp. It looks like a light garrison of soldiers. I counted thirty. The cannons aren't guarded, and the cook wagons and oxen were left between them. There's a lot of heavy snoring coming from the tents, drunk snoring is my guess. Boots and guns are jumbled together like a pile of straw outside some of the tents."

Pleased by the information, Casimir was now convinced that though he couldn't stop Provost's army he could slow it down. "Good Maurice, this will be easy. Take ten men and loosen the pin on the tongues of the cannon carts and cook wagons so they'll pull out and drop to the ground when the horses are attached to them.

"Lee, take five men with you and show them how to crawl Indian style so as not to frighten the horses. Cut their hobbles and lead the best ones back to me."

Leah nodded and started moving through the men. She selected, Sergeant Wilkes, who knew horses' instincts, Jack Turner, and three country boys who knew how to slip silently through woods and grass without being seen.

Casimir then turned in his saddle to address the remaining fifteen men saying, "You soldiers come with me. We'll relieve the British of their cannon rammers and sponges and then collect a few guns and boots."

The camp was like a busy anthill with Pulaski troops silently scurrying among horses, wagons, cannons, and tents, setting the stage for mayhem in the morning. They encountered only three sentries, one each on the north, south and east sides of the camp. The river acted as a natural barrier to the west. The sentries on the north and east sides were sound asleep while the one on the south was relieving himself in the river. None were aware of the Pulaski soldiers moving throughout the camp.

When the soldiers regrouped at the north end of the camp they had a string of twelve fine horses, twenty British rifles, ten cannon rammers, thirteen cannon sponges and fourteen boots, all for the left foot. Casimir thought it only fair to leave the owner the right boot and smiled when he thought about how much time the British soldiers would spend hobbling about in their right boot looking for the left one.

Wilkes was the last to join them, and had a wide grin on his face when he came sauntering in with a prize Arabian mare and foal. "She must've belonged to a high-ranking officer who had to leave her with the wagons to drop this foal. I reckon in a couple of years Visner will have his choice of mares to sire colts," he boasted.

Billy Wilkes never ceased to amaze Casimir, who was forever grateful to have the big rough horse trader in his Legion.

Everyone wanted to stay and watch the chaos the next morning, but they were far too outnumbered, and Casimir was not about to lose any more men on this campaign. A refreshing breeze started to cause ripples on the river and ruffle Visner's mane when Casimir noticed Leah looking up at the clouds that were rapidly moving across the stars above them.

"Lee, what is it?" he asked.

"Sir, the wind is coming from the northeast, the coast and the ocean," she replied. "It's blowing southwest and will keep blowing until at least noon."

"I understand, but what does that have to do with us?" he asked.

"It's dry and grass fires spread fast in a pine forest. Once the flames climb up the trunks they jump from tree top to tree top. A big hot fire travels a long distance real fast." She looked back at the British camp just south of them.

He quickly grasped what she was suggesting and smiled knowingly as he said, "Take two men and start the burn."

Leah dismounted. She motioned for Abe and Samuel to follow her, and was soon back with torches that she set to small mounds of pine straw, leaves, and sea oats. The wind whipped the flames high and swept the sparks southward, igniting tree tops, canvas tents, stored horse straw, and eventually the gun powder. The entire camp was ablaze and their earlier wish to witness pandemonium came true.

Redcoats raced out of burning tents, trying to find the mate to their right boot, chasing hobble-free horses, and looking for their rifles. On the ride back to camp, the legionnaires were filled with a conspiratorial camaraderie and bantered jokes back and forth about the British limping into Savannah on one boot. Casimir shared their jovial mood. His stay in Charles Town had been good to him and Savannah promised to be even more rewarding if he could take the city back from the British. And he had no doubt he would take it.

While the British were trying to recover from his first raid, he continued his night forays, moving farther down the road to harass the foot soldiers, many of whom awoke in the morning with one boot and no rifle.

The mounted British troops suffered the most. Cut belly straps and stirrups, stolen and runaway horses, pieces of thorny vines hidden in the folds of saddle blankets, causing the gentlest horse to buck when mounted, saddle bags emptied of provisions and filled with a mixture of sand and horse manure, missing swords and, of course, lost boots, made life miserable for them.

Tad O'Reilly, the drummer boy, took pleasure in putting snakes, lizards, salamanders and other crawling things in the remaining boots when he was allowed to go along on the night raids.

Casimir was having a fine time, as were his men, who laughed about the British all being foot soldiers now that they walked barefoot. When General Benjamin Lincoln arrived, he praised Casimir's conduct.

"General Pulaski, your valiant charge to save Charles Town and the initiative you showed in slowing General Provost's march on Savannah is admirable. I have sent a favorable report to General Washington," Lincoln said, and then with a wry smile continued, "Knowing that the general has a sense of humor, I included a note about the slithering creatures the Redcoats were finding in their one remaining boot."

"Merci, General Lincoln, I appreciate your praise and your thoughtfulness in sending General Washington a report on the activities here," Casimir said, then thought, *I do deserve the recognition.* Then he commented, "But I can't say I am pleased to see that an angry Major Bishop is with you. It is obvious from the scowl on his face that he still harbors a great deal of animosity for me."

General Lincoln explained the Major's presence to Casimir. "Apparently, General Washington became totally exasperated with Bishop's fawning and flattery plus the complaints he received from congressmen that the Major continuously assailed them with his accusations against you, General Pulaski. He ordered him here to serve under you, not to punish him, or you for that matter, but as he told me, he hoped the Major would come to respect you if he saw you in action. The general said he thought first-hand observation might show him how you earned the promotion he so covets."

"Well," Casimir laughed, "I see that winning the battle at Savannah is not the only challenge I have."

"I'm afraid you are correct General. Good luck — on both trials," Lincoln replied.

It soon became obvious from Bishop's red-faced demeanor and frequent tantrums that Washington's hope that he would come to respect Casimir was futile, especially after Casimir was hailed as the savior of Charles Town and British General Provost's tormentor.

He was again touted in the press and invitations to galas, balls, private dinner parties and to the inner circles of the local leaders started arriving daily. He was appointed by the governor as military advisor over all of the South Carolina forces, finally achieving the position of influence he had so desired since coming to the Colonies. Bishop was relegated to obscurity. Casimir didn't trust him enough to include him in decision-making or in any prominent roles, and he was certainly not invited to any of the balls.

Casimir relished the recognition, accepting invitation after invitation. The town celebrated him and he basked in the glory. He and his splendidly dressed Pulaski Legion promenaded down the streets of Charles Town in a parade given in their honor. Life was good.

His days were spent recovering from recurring bouts of malaria, thinking about the coming siege of Savannah, and training his troops. In the evenings, he attended lavish parties where he impressed the men with his talk of battles against Russian Cossacks and foreign generals, and dazzled the exquisitely dressed southern ladies.

Mrs. Samuel Bowen frequently attended the balls and became an ardent supporter. Her husband did not accompany her, and Casimir learned that he was a Loyalist while she leaned toward the Patriot cause. Casimir concluded they were hedging their bets, making sure at least one of them was on the winning side.

"Why Count Pulaski, you are the bravest and most refined man I've ever met," she cooed in French. "Our gentlemen aren't nearly as well-travelled as you and I don't know another person who has met a prince or has a royal title. We're honored to have you in our society. I do hope your stay here will be a long one."

"Thank you, *Madam* Bowen, you are most gracious," he responded, emphasizing the Madam, indicating her status as a married woman. "I will certainly continue to enjoy Charles Town's hospitality until duty calls me away."

After Jane Bowen curtsied and walked away, Governor John Rutledge joined him observing, "Count Pulaski I see you have captivated our South Carolina ladies, including Mrs. Bowen. I would advise selecting your words carefully with her. Perhaps you've heard of her husband's loyalty to the British?"

Casimir bowed to the governor before replying, "Indeed Sir, I have heard rumors that Mr. and Mrs. Bowen have different sympathies. One of them shall certainly be on the winning side."

The governor chuckled at Casimir's astute analysis of the Bowens, then said, "Damn shame that he's with the British. He's the best planter we have in this area. Sam Bowen has the creative genius of General Washington when it comes to farming. He imported a type of pea called soy bean from China and started growing them. Says they're the best food for cattle and humans. I don't know if that's true, but they're much less labor intensive than rice, and they don't need nearly as many slaves to work them or water to grow them. We'll need farmers who can think and plan ahead when this war is over. I wish he was with us."

"Well, Sir, perhaps he will change his mind. If not, I think you Americans are resourceful enough to develop a profitable farming industry. After all, you will have General Washington back at Mount Vernon cultivating new crops and breeding livestock after the war."

They smiled broadly. The future did look bright, and neither man doubted that with Casimir's help, the war would soon be won.

Mrs. Bowen was but one of a growing number of women who had fallen under Casimir's spell. He was a hero, leading his gallant men to victory and glory, yet there was a mystery about him that drew women. And, thanks to Franciszka's tutoring, he was a superb dancer. He twirled the southern ladies around and around the dance floors beneath the glittering chandeliers of the local plantation manors, making the layers of ruffles on their gowns bounce and their starched underskirts rustle. His brightly colored uniform in the midst of the pastel gowns was a magnet that no eye, especially a female eye, could turn from.

As time passed, he noticed the gowns became more elaborate with trims of pearls, gold threads, and an occasional diamond brooch. The bodices were cut lower and lower and the jewelry changed from onyx and pewter cameos to emeralds, rubies, and sapphires.

The Patriot populace had taken to wearing only homespun clothes in order to boycott anything imported from England, but how could a lady dance in homespun? So the women risked digging up jewelry they had buried to hide from the British to impress him and rationalized that abandoning their patriotic homespun garb boosted the morale of the troops by looking elegant for them. But, it was clear that it was Casimir's attention they were vying for.

He was flattered and enjoyed the adulation but never lost sight of his mission. *Ah, finally, finally, after all the accusations, jealousies and ridicule I have suffered, I am being recognized here for my genius and skill. But I won't let that or anything else deter me from finishing what I came to America to do. I will restore the prestige of the Pulaski name and defeat the British. No woman is worth turning me from my destiny,* he reminded himself.

Because he showed no more interest in one woman than another, and the men also enjoyed his company; enthralled by his tales of battles, the court at Courland and living in a foreign land, the local men were not jealous of him.

But, Major John Bishop was not swayed by Casimir's charm and charisma. The more accolades Casimir received, the more erratic Bishop's behavior became. He appeared to be obsessed with hate. He could be seen almost daily mimicking and mocking Casimir as he bowed to imaginary people, waved a sword over his head, and did his best to execute an exaggerated strut with his crippled leg.

He yelled at everyone within range of hearing, treated his horse so brutally that Casimir took it away from him, and refused to participate in any drills. The most troublesome scene for devoted Pulaski fans like Abe and Samuel was Bishop's clutching his chest and falling backwards as if a lance had pierced him when he was pretending to be the general.

Sergeant Wilkes couldn't take anymore and one day came to Casimir in a blustering rage, "General you need to lock that lunatic Major in the stockade before he does some real damage. He's as crazy as a bess beetle on a log in a fire. The man is mad with envy. He plays out his own war games, but you are the enemy he tries to kill. And I see him sneakin' around your tent at night when Lee, Paul and Maurice are with you. You can't just keep ignorin' him."

"And what would I tell General Washington? That I threw his aide in the stockade because he doesn't like me?"

"General, he'd understand if he could see the way the major stomps around the camp first ranting at nobody and then at everybody."

"Sergeant, I've had my share of being denied commissions and officer-ships, in more than one country. It can be pretty disheartening. I don't think he is doing any real harm to anyone other than himself."

"Well, I think Washington making him come down here and report to you, someone he already hated, accordin' to what I hear, drove him plum off his rocker. Most men consider it an honor to serve with you, but he said it is a 'great indignity for a real officer to report to a fancy pants foreigner."

"Okay, Sergeant Let me take care of it in my own way. Thank you. Now go on about your business of finding a way to get us to Savannah."

Casimir refused to be distracted by the pettiness of one man, and because Bishop had served with Washington, he wasn't harsh with him. Instead, he ignored the Major. He didn't include him in meetings or assign him duties. He didn't want to be bothered with childish behavior. And that was part of the problem. The more Bishop was ignored the more he seethed.

He was never far from Casimir, watching his every move. He fretted to anyone who would listen that his hopes of becoming a general, at least in the Continental Army, ended when he was assigned so far away from Washington. Thinking him mad, the men laughed behind his back at the idea of someone so childish leading seasoned troops, and his vow to discover some weakness he could use against Casimir was equally laughable.

It was now late in September. Maurice brought Casimir a dispatch in English and what appeared to be a letter from a family member written in Polish. Casimir put the letter aside and tore into the dispatch, then asked him to read it aloud.

Maurice read,

General Pulaski:

Retaking Savannah is critical if we are to maintain a strong position in the Southern Colonies. French Count Charles d'Estaing was in a position to win a decisive battle against the British, but made the mistake of granting the British commander, Colonel Campbell's request for a day's halt so he could consider the surrender terms he would offer the Commander. During that time, Colonel Campbell sent for, and received, reinforcements of eight hundred British troops from South Carolina. Now, several days of bombardment by Commander d'Estaing's fleet have not resulted in the promised British surrender. It is hurricane season and Commander d'Estaing must

move his fleet northward to safety soon. An attack must be planned and launched immediately. You are to join forces with Commander d'Estaing and begin the assault on Savannah as soon as possible.
Signed,
General George Washington, Continental Army

"Yes!"

"Finally, the siege of Savannah is about to begin and I'm ready for it. Maurice, it's what I've been waiting for, a win at Savannah following on the heels of my successful defense of Charles Town will make me second only to General Washington in recognition."

"That's all very good, Kas, but we do have to win the battle first, you know."

"Yes, yes. I know. Paul is already reconnoitering the area between here and Savannah. Go join him and report back to me everything you see — terrain, troop movements, fortifications, cannons, condition of the soldiers and all the things you're so good at analyzing. But first, translate my response to Washington."

He did know that taking Savannah back from the British wouldn't be easy. He immediately dictated a reply to General Washington:

General Washington:

I welcome this opportunity to help drive the British from your southern colonies. I will not delay longer than it is necessary to develop a strategy to defeat the Red coats, plan our cross-country march, and secure all the necessary provisions. My men and their horses are in excellent condition and eager to fight. We will be on the march to Savannah within two days, before the weather turns against us, or the

British receive more reinforcements. I will rendezvous
with Commander d'Estaing on the way.
> Count Casimir Pulaski,
> Brigadier General, Continental Army

He knew he was already outnumbered, and he couldn't afford for those numbers to grow worse. He must get to Savannah
before the British brought in more troops.

When he opened the other letter, he was delighted to find it
was from Sultan, who wrote,

> My dear Count,
> I hear that you no longer deny the title I gave
> you."

Casimir stopped reading for a moment. He could almost hear
Sultan chuckling. The letter went on,

> "I must for the moment decline your offer to
> fight in your Legion. As you may know, my quest
> to free my wife's relative is over. Elijah was freed by
> his master before our ship arrived. Since he does not
> need the funds I intended to use to buy his release, I
> have used a portion to book passage to my homeland
> and may use the remainder, along with certain funds
> I have acquired, to buy a small shop in the bazaar. I
> have travelled enough for one life time, and it is best
> that I leave this part of the world. Thank you for your
> friendship, good luck with your war. I hear a big
> battle is brewing. I am sure you will be victorious. If
> you find yourself in Morocco, please look for me at
> one of the carpet shops in the bazaar.
> Yours in Honor and Respect,
> Sultan

Casimir smiled. He was happy to hear from Sultan and to know he was well. Sultan was a special man, a kindred spirit and he missed their jovial storytelling. He wished he could let him know what a valuable asset Elijah George had become to Washington.

Then he picked up a sheet of paper that had been folded and tucked inside Sultan's letter. His smile widened. It was a wanted poster with a picture of Sultan in a white, wide-sleeved shirt, the white turban, and a black sash around his waist. It read, 'King Francoise Antoine, of the Dominican Republic. Wanted dead or alive for treason, piracy, and murder. Reward, 10 kilos of gold.'

The amount of the reward was circled and Sultan had written, "So my friend, my head is worth more than yours." Casimir laughed while thinking, *I still have no idea who he really is, but I am glad I knew him."*

The letter from Sultan was a brief diversion from the turmoil General Washington's message had triggered within Casimir. He must focus all his energy on the battle ahead. Thank goodness, he had Maurice and his quick analytical mind with him for this most important battle. He needed his half-brother's astute judgment of the enemy, but he needed even more, the old friendship and bravado he, Paul, and Maurice shared when they rode into battle.

He had accepted an invitation to a lavish ball at the governor's mansion that night and he decided he would still go, in order to keep his plans secret. There were many like Samuel Bowen who were loyal to the king. He didn't want to arouse their suspicion by cancelling his evening plans.

During the ball, a group of ladies excitedly encircled him far more easily than the British could have. He lingered to revel in their admiration until Governor Rutledge entered the room, at which time he escaped his pleasant imprisonment diplomatically saying, "Excuse me, ladies. It makes me sad to leave such lovely company, but I must consult with the governor on an upcoming military parade we're planning for some French dignitaries arriving soon."

It was a clever version of the truth since the parade would actually be his march to Savannah, and the French dignitaries were Commander d'Estaing and his four thousand troops.

"Bonjour Monsieur Pulaski, thank you for attending tonight," the Governor greeted him, as he held out his hand to Casimir. "News you would be here increased our attendance significantly, especially among the ladies."

"I am honored to be invited governor, but I do have some news for your ears only," responded Casimir in a low, secretive voice.

Arching his bushy gray eyebrows and twisting his voluminous moustache, Rutledge led him to an alcove at the side of the ballroom, where he leaned in close to ask, "What is it, General?"

"I must leave for Savannah within days," Pulaski whispered. "It's important that we retake the city soon as a hurricane could move in at any time. No one other than you must know this since our march will be far more dangerous if word of it reaches the British. I'm sure you understand."

"Oh sir, tell me it's not true," the Governor protested, suddenly becoming agitated and using his handkerchief to wipe sweat from his brow. "You can't leave us at the mercy of the British. Charles Town shall surely fall without you to protect us."

"We will leave enough men here to hold the British at bay," Casimir assured him.

"The British are now much more interested in Savannah than Charles Town, and most of their troops are being moved from this area to reinforce that city. They fear they might lose Savannah and I intend to make that fear a reality."

"I believe you will, sir, but please promise to return to us when you have won," pleaded the Governor. "We need your protection and your delightful presence."

"I will certainly try," Casimir replied. "My stay here has been most pleasant, but only God knows what lies ahead for me."

"Then Godspeed sir," said the Governor, and for the first time made a slight bow to Casimir, his protruding midriff not permitting a deeper one. "Our prayers for a speedy victory and your safe return go with you." Casimir returned his bow, straightened and gave the Governor a salute then returned to the ladies.

Maurice had met Paul near Savannah, the two of them returned the next day and went directly to a strategy meeting in Casimir's tent. Maurice reported, "The Redcoats are determined to stay the course and they have enough supplies, munitions, and food to last for several weeks. Many loyalists have joined them and they are firmly dug in. Their mood is serious and ugly. I guess some of them didn't like being harassed on their way to Savannah, and the others don't like getting their white pants dirty in the trenches in which they're hiding. They won't be as easy as the ones at Haddonfield, that's for sure.

Casimir, fell silent. *I lost too many at Charles Town to take this battle lightly, and, at thirty-four I'm getting too old to be charging at the enemy on horseback. I want to have a home with a family of my own, full of love and joy like the one I grew up in. Perhaps I could teach military strategy to my sons, the way father did to me. Doctor Borloff didn't find any record of a person with my anatomy producing children, but I've always been the exception to the rule. I may be the first to father children, or maybe there were other cases that were just not recorded.*

"Kas," Paul called, snapping his fingers to bring Casimir back to the present.

"Yes, yes, I'm sorry, I was thinking about the battle," he lied. He then turned to Leah, saying, "Lee, I need you to talk to the Indians. Have them tell you about the trails between here and Savannah. Getting there may be as big a challenge as the battle itself. It's not easy to move an army cross country especially over rivers with this sucking mud that can sink a horse to its belly. Take Sergeant Wilkes with you. He'll need to know everything in order to get supplies to Savannah."

Leah and Wilkes met Tathtowe and his friends that night, while Casimir made his final appearance at a social function in Charles Town. He still had much work to do: complete plans for the march, make contact with Count d'Estaing, and coordinate their tactics for the siege.

But it might have raised suspicions if he failed to attend, and anyway, he enjoyed such balls and the near idolization Charles Town bestowed on him. There would be little enough of that in the tough days ahead, so he strutted, bowed, and pirouetted around the dance floor, charming everyone around him until well past midnight.

When he returned to camp, he had already mentally planned the siege of Savannah, and he sat at the small table in his tent to write a dispatch to d'Estaing.

Commander d'Estaing:

I look forward to our joining forces to defeat the British. I know of your concerns about the weather and I am eager, like you, for our siege to begin. I can have my troops in place near the redoubt on the north side of the town in five days. My recommendation is that we meet there at midnight on Friday, October 8, with our regular troops plus the Haitians you brought with you. We can then advance in the darkness to a high point from where we can charge the British at daybreak, surprising and confusing them.

Perhaps you would like to meet prior to this date to finalize our plans. If so, I will make myself available to join you wherever you suggest for such a meeting. I look forward to our work ahead. May the Blessed Mother look over us and our men during this endeavor.

Yours,

Count Casimir Pulaski,

Brigadier General, Continental Army

Then he called for Leah, and handing her the dispatch, said, "Give this to one of the couriers. Make sure he leaves with it immediately. There is a landing on the Bull River they call Warsaw, I am not sure why, but he should find Commander d'Estaing there.

"Tell the messenger to wait for a reply. Everything depends on our joining forces at the right place and time. I have committed us to join his French force in five days. Somehow you and Wilkes will have to get us there."

"Yes sir," she responded, then adding before departing, "and sir, the Indians have always called that place Whispering Waters. White men didn't understand their language so they named it Warsaw, the same name as the place you were born, Maurice tells me."

He was astounded at how she could answer his every question, without being boastful. But he wasn't one to hand out compliments. Instead, he called after her, "And Lee, when you get back, find Sergeant Wilkes, Paul, and Maurice and have them meet me here."

No one was complaining about the early hour when she returned with the sleepy three, thirty minutes later. They knew how important the coming days were to the future of the American colonies.

If they took Savannah back from the British, the Americans would control two important ports, Charles Town and Savannah, making it difficult for British ships to bring fresh troops and supplies to the Southern Colonies. John Adam's navy was doing an effective job keeping them from docking in Massachusetts, so the war could end quickly if they were successful in taking Savannah.

Paul and Maurice had agreed earlier that another plus to winning the battle was that it would give Casimir enough fame to persuade him to return home to Poland. He was deserving of both the recognition and the chance to retire and enjoy peace without all the privations of war. He had fought for others all his life, now it should be his turn to surround himself with love and comfort, perhaps with a new family of his own after having lost so many loved ones. And they were also ready to return and start families. They had had enough war.

But first they had to take Savannah. Casimir ordered Wilkes to work with Lee to gather all the supplies and munitions they would need for the siege and plan the river crossing.

Pulling his wide-brimmed hat off, exposing the bald crown above his long hair, Wilkes wiped sweat from his forehead with a wrinkled handkerchief and said, "Yep, we'll have to cross the Savannah River and it's about to jump its banks right now. It shouldn't be floodin' this late, but it is. Heavy rains up in the Carolinas and Georgia are fillin' all the creeks and smaller rivers that feed into it. It's gonna be a ball buster to cross. It's probably full of snakes and alligators. That's gonna drive the horses crazy but there ain't no way around it. We've got to get everything across somewhere."

Casimir looked at Leah and asked if the Indians could help.

"Yes Sir, they go back and forth across the river to trade furs and cattle for cloth, corn meal, and other things they need and some they don't, like liquor, at the trading posts."

The timbre in her voice showed the pride she felt that her Indian relatives were being called on to provide such a valuable service when white men usually looked down on them. "They can tell us where the shallowest spots are and where it's most dangerous during flooding seasons."

"Good, go talk to them Lee and report back to us as soon as you can and take Sergeant Wilkes with you. He'll be responsible for getting everyone across," Casimir ordered. Then remembering that the Savannah river flowed to the ocean and had salt water, "Lee, one other thing, are there any . . . creatures that would be a danger to the horses and men in the river we will cross?"

She hesitated to tell him, but he had asked. "Well, Sir, like the sergeant said, there are alligators, you probably know about them. They can be ten or twelve feet long and have jaws that can rip a person's leg off or tear the side out of a horse. And they can outrun a man on land.

"Sharks sometimes swim upriver, but usually stick closer to the ocean. Sergeant Wilkes, and the men from this area like Jack Turner know what to look for and how to deal with all those creatures.

The Indians also know where they stay and can help steer us clear of them. But the main thing is not to show 'em you're afraid. Any animal can sense that, and will attack something scared, but will usually run from anything that stands its ground and fights back."

"Thank you, Lee," Casimir said, as a shudder crawled up his spine.

Anxious to reach Savannah and join forces with Count d'Estaing, he had his entire army on the move from Charles Town the following day. He was determined to win this battle — quickly and decisively.

The Indians advised crossing at a village called Purryburg. It would be easy to find because an early Irish settler had erected a Celtic cross beside the river, just outside a wrought iron fence on his property. A little family cemetery developed around the cross and the gravestones there told of the hardships of those early settlers who died in childbirth, drowning, snake bite, yellow fever and Indian attacks.

A road ran past the cemetery, then disappeared into the muddy waters where in drier times wagons were loaded onto a ferry to be taken across the river. But now the river was threatening to surge over the top of the riverbank.

Most of the locals in the area were Patriots and the British had punished them by destroying their means of getting goods back and forth across the river. The ferry and almost every other boat and raft in the area used to cross the river were demolished. One lone canoe was all Casimir found when he arrived with his army.

CHAPTER TWENTY-FOUR

THE PULL OF A BOOT

Savannah, Georgia
October 1779

Sergeant Wilkes pulled his horse up beside Casimir at the water's edge. "She's goin' be a bitch to cross, Countski," he bellowed, his face breaking into a wide grin revealing tobacco stained teeth. Wilkes knew he was the only one who could get away with referring to Casimir as 'Countski' and then only when they were alone.

"We got a double whammy on us, floodin' river and springin' tide. But now as I get a good look at 'er, I reckon the Savannah River ain't all that big even if she's swoll up from those heavy rains up north. It could be worse; the new moon is still a couple of days off, that's when the tide really pushes in. The British got their stuff across in five days with fifty barges, we should do just fine gettin' across in a day with the one canoe they left us."

"Good morning, Sergeant," Casimir responded, smiling back at the coarse, no-nonsense backwoodsman he liked more every day. "I doubt they left the canoe for us and I hope they aren't expecting us. But I do agree that it shouldn't be much of a problem for the Pulaski Legion to cross with one canoe assuming the Sergeant in Charge gets to it right away."

Casimir knew getting across wouldn't be easy, even at this narrow point. The Savannah was wider and deeper than the

Polish rivers he had crossed while fighting the Russians, and those had been challenging enough without creatures in them that could bite, sting, and eat men and horses.

"Lee," Casimir called, summoning his aide. When Leah rode up to him he said, "d'Estaing's reply came earlier this morning. I'm going to meet with him to refine the battle plan and to get to know him better. But I'll be back in the afternoon to see how things are going. I'm leaving Wilkes in charge, so make sure no one challenges him. If someone does, shoot them."

Leah involuntarily winced when she heard his words. She couldn't imagine shooting one of their own, but it was an order and she would if she had to.

Casimir went on, "Send men across in the canoe, three at a time. One will have to paddle it back to this side, so we'll only be able to move two per trip. I want Sam Abbot, Abe Hawkins, and the rest of the thirty men who rode with us the night you started that grassfire upwind from Provost's camp on the other side of the river as soon as possible.

When she turned her horse back, Leah spotted Sam and Abe standing near the bank watching the general, with their hero worship shining on their faces.

"You boys come with me," she called to them. "The general wants you in the first canoe across."

They grinned and strutted over to her full of pride at having been singled out by their Polish hero.

The place where wagons were normally loaded onto the ferry was under water and Casimir rode Visner out to it to get a better look at the other side. He called for Sergeant Wilkes, who had remained on the bank, to join him again.

"Dang it to pieces, I got to get my boots wet ridin' into the water 'cause he's in too much of a confound hurry to come back to dry land," Wilkes muttered. "Some days wranglin' horses back in Kaintuck don't look so bad."

But the way the Sergeant straightened in his saddle and hurried to Casimir showed his pride for being trusted to move the army across the river.

"Here I am Countski, what do you need?" asked Wilkes, splashing up to the general.

"I need you to get this Army to the other side by sundown," Casimir said. "I'll be back to help after I meet with d'Estaing. I told Lee you are in charge and he is to shoot anyone who disobeys you. Make sure that isn't necessary. Bully them into doing what you need. You're good at that."

"Alright, general, I'll bust some balls and we will splash this river dry with all our runnin' across it before we eat our beans tonight," responded the smiling sergeant.

Instinctively, Casimir reached out and shook the surprised Wilkes' hand. Wilkes, clearly moved, stiffened from his usual slouch to an upright position and executed a perfect salute to Casimir, before hurriedly turning his horse back toward shore.

To show he was in command, Sergeant Wilkes started barking out orders to the troops.

"Get the axes and saws. Go to them woods and start cuttin' me some logs. Use the horses to drag 'em back here 'n strap 'em together with ropes, we gotta make some barges. Blasted British. Move fellas, move now. We can't kill them Redcoats if we don't get across this mud hole."

They had seven makeshift barges built in short order. Then the loading began as the sergeant yelled more commands, "Thundering horse shit, you load the cannon in the center not on the end or you'll sink us before we get started. Stack the gunpowder on top of the cannon and balance the load with cannon balls and anything else that we'll need. Use sand if you have to, but make sure this hunk 'a floatin' wood is balanced. If it turns over, we'll be here all day and night divin' after supplies and I don't think you want to be swimmin' with the gators and no moon to see 'em by. Now move it."

The men, troops, cooks and blacksmiths, clear down to Tad the drummer boy, knew better than to talk back to the sergeant. He wasn't above planting a forceful kick to the butt of anyone he thought was 'dilly dallyin'.

Meanwhile, Leah assembled the thirty men, and made sure no time was lost when the canoe returned, getting two more men in it and headed to the other side.

After placing Wilkes in command of the crossing, Casimir slid off Visner into the waist deep water. He nudged the horse farther out into the river. Visner started swimming to the opposite side with Casimir holding onto his tail and kicking his feet to stay afloat and to propel himself forward, lessening the pull on the horse's tail. He was waiting on the opposite shore when Abe and Sam arrived in the first canoe with Jack Turner.

"Jack, you know the woods. Head north and scout out the area. Watch the British movements. Count the numbers, the direction they're headed and the equipment and supplies they have. Sam, go south and do the same thing. I'll need your report tonight. Abe, take the canoe back and bring von Hessen and another man across."

When von Hessen arrived, Casimir ordered him, "When the next two men get here send them east and west with instructions to watch for the British and any Indians who might be traveling with them. They need to slip through the woods quietly, I can't risk letting the British know we are already here and crossing. And when all four come back write down what they tell you. I'll need a report when I return.

"When they get here, set the rest of the men to work unloading the barges and setting up the wagons and cannons to start moving as soon as everyone is on this side of the river.

"Yes sir." Replied von Hessen getting his ledger and pencil out of his leather pouch.

As he rode off on Visner, Casimir was proud of his disciplined and well-trained troops and he relaxed somewhat knowing things would progress well without him during his meeting with Count d'Estaing. It was a glorious day. He was preparing for battle, perhaps the biggest of his life, and he had his elite Pulaski Legion to lead.

Casimir found the commander on the wharf in a small trading post midway between Purryburg and Warsaw. "Count Pulaski, it is an honor to meet you," d'Estaing greeted him graciously. "I have heard much of your bravery in Poland and here."

"The honor is mine Commander d'Estaing. You and your navy are serving a critical role in the fight for freedom here. I think together we can take Savannah and give the Colonials a good chance to throw the British out."

After the owner of the post provided them a private room, Casimir spread maps of the area on a table and they started formulating their battle plans by deciding the route each would take to Savannah.

Casimir's course, to the redoubt north of Savannah, where they were to meet on the night of October 8, was longer, and he couldn't even begin the overland trek until he got his army across the river. But he was confident that he could make the rendezvous on time. d'Estaing was anxious about the weather, insisting he had to move his fleet north within days, before a tropical storm or hurricane hit. Casimir agreed, anxious to take Savannah even though he wasn't sure General Lincoln's army would be able to march from Charles Town in time to join them.

The map showed a river flowing around a large island, then joining the Savannah River a few miles east of the city. The river curved around a bulge of land that Casimir thought would provide a commanding view of Savannah to the north and west, and the ocean to the south and east. It would be a good vantage point to watch British movements by land and sea. He decided to locate his headquarters there.

Their plan of attack was finalized within the hour but when Casimir prepared to return to his troops, d'Estaing protested, "Monsieur Pulaski, please allow me to show you some French hospitality. I have a wonderful Bordeaux wine and some fine cigars we can share over the cook's cassoulet."

"Merci, Count D'Estaing, but I must get back to my men, and I fear wine at this early hour would dull my senses," he responded. "I will gladly accept your offer when we have taken Savannah from the British. Then we can have a celebratory dinner."

"Very well, my new friend," agreed d'Estaing. "I'll see you Friday at midnight."

During his ride back, Casimir reflected on how well the meeting had gone. There was no doubt about the importance of the role the French would play in his plan to sneak close to the British during the night and feign an attack on their center the next morning. But he would bring the major force to bear on the redcoats' left flank. Then, he would have his troops fake a retreat to draw the British into the heart of the city where more Colonial soldiers would be waiting to crush them. *It's a good plan*, he assured himself. *May we be victorious and the Americans have the southern stronghold they need to quickly finish this miserable war. I want to go home and spend time with those I love in familiar surroundings.*

But, something was nagging at the corner of his consciousness as he hastened to rejoin his men to see how the river crossing was progressing. It was the image of d'Estaing's troops lazily lounging along the wharf, as though they had nothing to do and no one to direct them.

He wondered about their readiness, physically and mentally, to do a fast-paced night march through unfamiliar territory and

449

engage the enemy. As far as he knew, they had spent a great deal of time on ships rather than on land marching, training, and fighting. He hoped they were simply being given a day of rest before the battle and tried to drive the image from his mind.

He was glad to see everything was going well at the river. Von Hessen had men unloading the newly built barges that were hauling everything from cannons to cook wagons across the river.

Wilkes is right, Casimir thought, *it could be a worse. I moved thousands of men across flooded or frozen rivers in Poland, some filled with treacherous rapids and waterfalls, and often at night with Russians chasing us. I can cross a river in a hurry if I need to, and I need to today. Everything depends on our meeting the French troops at the agreed time and striking the British before foul weather threatens the commander's fleet. Thank goodness for these backwoods boys who learned how to build and load barges to float their timber and vegetables to market. That's an advantage we have over the British who are accustomed to being transported by ships to battle sites, rather than marching overland.*

They won't believe we can make the crossing in one day. When we do, we'll be able to surprise them by moving in close to their camp in the darkness. I like to surprise the enemy by doing what they think is impossible.

He was pleased to see that rank was temporarily forgotten while Sergeant Wilkes commanded everyone—Leah, Paul and Maurice toiled alongside the foot soldiers and cooks. He marveled at their teamwork while cutting trees, dragging them to the river and strapping them together, then loading the barges and poling them across as they clung to a rope stretching between giant oaks on each bank of the river. The British had removed the wire guideline that the ferry pilot had used to help maneuver across in storms and high water.

The men worked tirelessly loading the barges despite the mud, flies, and mosquitoes. Casimir watched closely as the horses were loaded, and was pleased to see Wilkes was doing it right.

To keep the horses from panicking and sinking the few barges they had, he had them placed in the center of the rafts with heavily loaded wagons counterbalancing each outer side and blocking them from jumping off. One frightened horse crashing through to the edge could dump the whole load. The loss of the equipment would be bad enough, but much worse would be the mutilation of the men and animals that would be attacked by alligators attracted to blood in the water. Plus, the horses carried saddle bags filled with precious gunpowder that would be lost if they fell in the water.

Casimir allowed Wilkes to make the crossing decisions but he watched closely to make sure all the wagons were loaded to capacity to conserve space on the barges and he and Visner swam across the river several times to watch the loading and unloading. Visner was now comfortable in the water and seemed to enjoy having his master hold onto his tail while he pulled him across the river. His troops watched as their general again led by example, asking no one to take a risk that he hadn't taken first.

Casimir was actually enjoying the day as much as Visner. He was in his glory training men how to get an army across a river. The water was cool and refreshing in the warm October sun, and the gnats were kept at bay by the river breeze. He knew that he and his white stallion created an impressive image, and were being admired by the troops and the large entourage traveling with them.

Casimir loved the attention and the beautiful fall weather and, while making his tenth trip across the river, he thought *how good it is to be alive.*

Everyone labored throughout the long and arduous day and as the sun started streaking the muddy water gold, the last barge landed and their job was done. They had transported an army across a flooding river in a single day that they began with only one canoe.

Everyone worked hard except Major Bishop. He was notice-able by his absence, finally showing up in a spotless, dry uniform with his usual smirking smile, just in time to be rowed across in the last canoe. Casimir was disgusted but not surprised by Bish-op's continuous attempts to provoke him, and he was confident that ignoring him was the punishment the major would feel the most deeply so he continued to do so.

Bishop thought, *Oh, these stupid idolaters. They think their gen-eral will win every battle and save them from harm. Well this battle will teach them differently. He'll neither win nor survive, and I'll get my promotion in the victor's army, not in this motley band of uncouth rebels. Too bad, the little foreigner will be dead before I get my general's uniform. I'd love to see the looks on his and Washington's faces when they realize that in future battles I'll be the one leading the forces that overrun them.*

I'll observe the battle in a British captain's uniform, for a start. It does flatter me, and my father will have nothing left to ridicule me about. Even he will have to show me some respect. I hope he doesn't give me a lecture on loyalty. I've tolerated enough of his talking about morality. All I need to do is get the battle plans to General Provost's aide and the generalship is mine. Provost said so today. He liked the idea of killing Pulaski after all the embarrassing, childish raids he led at night against his troops. That little showoff will learn his lesson not to mock real leaders.

Bishop smiled to himself. *Following Elijah George into the woods was a stroke of genius. He led me straight to Washington's agent who had infiltrated General Provost's camp, posing as a cook. After George left, I told the agent that Washington sent me, his personal aide, to meet privately with Provost. He bought it, even though Washington isn't anywhere close to this area, and took me right to Provost's head-quarters. I'll be able to use him again, telling him I'm carrying a re-sponse from Washington to Provost's most recent reply. I might even throw in that it looks as if they are negotiating surrender terms.*

Casimir dismissed Bishop and his arrogance to concentrate on the coming siege, thinking, *the battle begins in two days and everyone has to be ready. A quiet evening, going over the details and strategy one final time will be good after such a rigorous day. I'll have Paul and Maurice join me so we can strategize together and perhaps reminisce a little about other battles we've won.*

His mind continued to churn, *now that we are across the river, we have plenty of time to surprise the British after the French forces join us. We will win.*

He felt good about his selection for the site of his Savannah headquarters. It was far different from those he had in Poland, or anywhere else. Here, he had the taste of sea salt on his lips, a warm breeze tousled his dark hair and swayed the gold-green marsh grass to a slow harmony at the sparkling water's edge.

Statuesque white egrets stood on long, delicate legs at the shoreline, while blue and gray herons skimmed across the rippling river. A pelican plummeted from the sky and plunged deep into the water before surfacing again with a bulging pouch full of mullet. Land birds nestled in the arms of gigantic live oak trees talking to each other in calls Lee had taught Casimir to identify. He heard blue jays, cardinals, sparrows, wrens, woodpeckers and screech owls hiding behind veils of Spanish moss and saw squirrels playing up and down tree trunks. A curious raccoon peeked out from a hollow knothole in a tree. It was a serene, peaceful scene that soothed him.

Ah, if men could only learn to live as peacefully together, he thought, while tightening the ropes on his headquarters tent. When he saw Lee pitching a small bivouac near his, he thought, *it is customary to have the aide de camp close by. I'll continue the ruse that Lee is a man until after the battle. But then, I must deal with the fact that she is a woman, and decide what to do about her. She has served me well, but this hoax cannot continue. Regardless of the reason she is here, she will have to leave. War is no place for a woman.*

453

Casimir walked into his quarters and sank into a large wood frame chair, an unintended gift from one of General Provost's officers whose tent was raided by the Pulaski troops one night. It had carved wooden arms that rolled downward at the ends to provide a natural resting place for his hands and a curved mahogany back that was perfect to lean on after a long day. Lafayette had insisted that he bring it, and he had to admit it was more comfortable than his straight back cane bottom chairs. Still wearing wet pants and boots, he stretched out his legs in front of him, exhausted but satisfied. They had accomplished a small miracle today and soon they would accomplish a much larger one.

When Paul, Maurice and Leah arrived, and found him relaxed and pensive, they turned to leave and allow him time to rest. He stopped them.

"Please sit, all of you," he said. "I want to go over the battle plan. Commander d'Estaing and his troops are to meet us tomorrow night at the fortifications north of the city, so we must all know how to move the troops into the correct positions."

After pausing to make sure they were listening, he continued, "My strategy is to act as though the main attack will be a direct frontal assault to their center, while in fact the main force will hit their left flank. If the British are fooled into placing the bulk of their men in the center, our Pulaski Legion can charge and break through their line on the left then quickly circle around, and attack them from behind.

"Count d'Estaing will continue the assault on their front at the center. After we have destroyed the left flank and broken through the redoubt, we'll charge into the city, causing confusion and mayhem. When the main force turns to fight us, d'Estaing will be attacking their backs. Then we will turn and charge their front again, confusing and entrapping them with our rapid horse movements.

"Sergeant Wilkes will be hidden with the infantry, reserve troops, and cannons, moving them where needed after we start the charge. You three will ride behind me. Does everyone understand? Any questions? Lee, do you understand that you are to remain with us, even if you see the Devil himself off to the side?"

Leah nodded but was concerned about Casimir, who would be out in front, flamboyantly dressed, on his magnificent white stallion. The British would recognize him — he and his horse would be easy targets, but she kept her silence as did Paul and Maurice.

"Good," he said. "I plan to work late. Lee, go to the river and get some water for coffee. I'll meet with everyone tomorrow morning to go over any changes in the plan. Now all of you leave. I have work to do. I need to write letters to the families of the men we lost at Charles Town, and study the maps of the area before I go to bed."

Paul and Maurice headed to their tents to prepare for an early morning wake-up call fearing Casimir might not sleep at all and could call for them at any hour between sunset and sunrise.

When Leah left for the river, she saw Major Bishop standing close to Casimir's tent. She wondered if he was waiting to see the general but he didn't move. Instead, he flashed a menacing grin and crossed his arms as if he were standing sentry at Casimir's headquarters. She wondered how long he had been there, and decided it made no difference. He was one of Casimir's officers and could stand wherever he wanted even if no one liked him.

Casimir pulled the maps from his bags and began studying them. After a few minutes, he turned from his worktable and walked outside to gaze once again at nature's bountiful beauty. The evening sky began as a golden tan, the color of the underside of a gator, then gradually deepened to the orange of palmetto palm bark, and finally to a dark, beet red. A mirror image of the colorful sky lay across the water shimmering brightly. He wondered if it was foreshadowing the fight ahead. Were the scarlet sky and water an omen that so much blood would spill from men in the coming battle that it would turn the earth red? If so, whose men, his or the British? He tried to recall the sailor's omen. Was it red sky at night, sailor's delight, red sky in the morning, sailor take warning? And was that omen reversed on land?

That thought sent a chill up his neck and he decided to go inside to get out of his wet uniform and boots. When he saw Lee tending a pot of coffee on the campfire he called, "Lee, come over here. I need help getting these blasted boots off."

Leah rushed over eager to help and followed Casimir into his tent. When he dropped into the chair and tried to push his left boot off with the toe of his right, it wouldn't move and he looked at Leah, raising his left leg. She turned her back to him and straddled his leg to pull on the boot. He tried to assist her by flexing his foot to point the toe up in the air and then down toward the dirt floor, but the boot refused to budge and the movement threw her off balance. When she tightened the muscles in her calves and buttocks to steady herself, he unconsciously reached for her hips to help, then stared at her rounded bottom rocking forward, then backward as she pulled at the boot. He could no longer ignore her trim waist and the curve of her hip. She was undeniably a very sensual woman, and a sudden surge of sexual desire confused and frightened him. He had felt this strange and urgent throbbing between his thighs only once before, and that was with Franciszka, whom he could never have.

The military had been his only mistress, and a jealous, demanding one requiring all his time, focus, energy and attention. His 'maleness' came late, since he was not driven by lustful male hormones as a young man and instead of women, he focused on strategy, tactics, and training. Now at thirty-four, he was still a virgin.

When the boot suddenly flew off, Leah rocked forward and grabbed his leg to keep from falling. The pleasure of her hand on his flesh and the fiery passion it ignited were unexpected. It unleashed an alien, animalistic hunger that had to be satisfied.

Casimir's familiar world of control and discipline abandoned him. Nothing mattered but his desire to have this sensual and complex woman. He bent forward, caught her waist and pulled her onto his lap with such force that it took her breath away.

Pressing her body tightly against his, she turned her head to meet his waiting lips. They kissed hard and long while his hands caressed and explored. She had spent many troubled nights dreaming of him and longing for his touch while fearing he would sense her female desire and see through her male disguise. She was confused and distressed by such passion for another man after loving Jimmy so deeply. This was totally different. It was undeniable desire and yes, a new kind of love to which she eagerly responded.

He pulled her grandmother's leather tie from her hair, and it cascaded down to her shoulders and he buried his face in it. The aroma of her arousal filled his nostrils, fueling his own erotic inferno.

Reaching around her shoulders to feel the fullness of her breasts, under the straps of scratchy burlap that bound them, he asked as tenderly as he could between rapid breaths, "What is your real name? Please tell me."

"Leah," she gasped, while her chest rose and fell in sharp thrusts. He didn't understand the sexual frenzy that drove him to tear open her shirt, snatch down the straps and pull her to him, but it felt natural when he filled his mouth with her full young breasts. His tongue teased her distended nipples, and then he sucked them between his teeth and felt them harden even more. A throbbing sensation ran down through her abdomen and thighs. When his hands found her wet womanliness,

457

she tore open his trousers as her hips started thrusting against him and her kissing became love bites. There was no longer any sanity or control for either of them, only the pleasure of pent up desire being satisfied.

He heard her muffled cry and felt her body shudder as deep inside she felt something opening, unfolding, and accepting his surging warmth as it flowed into her. A vision of an exotic red flower opening one petal at a time filled her mind and she knew . . . knew with absolute certainty that this was unlike any experience she had ever had with Jimmy, and she knew why. This wonderful, brave and passionate man had just fulfilled her dream of creating a child. That had to be it. There was no other answer. She would finally be a mother.

Their hunger sated, they fell back, exhausted. Leah clung to him, eyes closed, face and lips pressed to his neck, her bare breasts nestled on his chest. He wondered how such a seductive, beautiful woman could have convinced him and his men that she was a man, even for a short time. It seemed impossible.

Casimir had never allowed himself to be softened by love of a woman, but Leah's complete surrender and the tender drape of her body across his engulfed him in her loving warmth. Her fingers curled through his hair and her hand drifted to his chest. It was disturbingly familiar as if he had felt her touch before. "I love you," she whispered, about to drift off to sleep.

Suddenly a terror beyond anything he had encountered on the battlefield, in prison, or on the stormy seas, gripped him like a giant claw. He had let his guard down. He had no time for women or personal indulgences. He was on a mission to restore his family name and to prove himself and his cavalry on the battlefield. He had to fight for freedom and he could allow nothing to deter him.

He jumped to his feet as he might if leaping for a sword to ward off an attack, hurtling Leah onto the hard-packed dirt floor.

She was stunned as much by his abrupt move as by the fall onto the ground. She looked up, shrank from his maddened gaze, scrambled to gather her clothes, and clutched them to her.

Mindful that others might hear, "Go, go," he shouted in a tortured, seething whisper with soul searing scorn for his own weakness.

Leah rushed away, seeing only the anger in his eyes, and hearing his suppressed shouts burning in her ears as she stumbled into her tent, thankful for the darkness that hid her naked body. Neither she nor Casimir saw the figure in a major's uniform slip into the darkness between the two tents.

Her shocked pathetic sobs carried through the night and wounded him more than a saber's thrusts could. The pain and confusion he felt heightened his resolve not to be weakened by romantic feelings, especially now, when he faced the greatest battle of his life.

Leah rose to retrieve the coffee pot, which left untended on the campfire overnight, had boiled the coffee down to a stinking, gooey mess. She grabbed it and went to the river to clean the pot and make the general's coffee as usual while waiting for him to decide if he would allow her to continue to play the role of his aide. Her eyes were swollen and her throat raw from having wept all night.

The shirt she had thrown on the night before revealed her prominent cleavage since she had not yet flattened her breasts with the uncomfortable binding. She could still feel Casimir's warm, demanding lips sucking on them and when her bare nipples brushed against the shirt, her passion and anguish surged.

Leah was tortured by unanswered questions. Why had he rejected her? What did she do wrong? Jimmy and she had always fallen asleep in each other's arms after lovemaking. Why did he push her away? Did he have no feeling for her? Did he hate her? She prayed that he would talk to her and be her friend even if they couldn't be together as lovers. Should she leave? Would it be better not to face him again? She could not bear to see hate in his eyes. But if she left, she would be a deserter and could be hanged. The thought of hanging did not bother her as much as not being near him if he needed her in the battle. No, she would not desert, she would stay by his side — if he would allow it.

She squatted at the water's edge splashing cold water on her face. She decided not to bathe today because she wanted to keep his scent with her. While relishing this thought, she heard a twig snap and thanks to her training with Tathtowe, she knew someone was near. Rays of sunlight breaking through the darkness revealed a distorted reflection in the water. Someone was standing close behind her. She froze, motionless, like an egret waiting for a fiddler crab to surface in the river mud.

As the reflection became clearer, she could see the person was not in a uniform. Good, she thought, it's not a Redcoat, it must be the cook coming to get water for breakfast.

Her legs were cramping from squatting so long and she struggled getting up, while pulling her shirt together and turning to face the cook, but it wasn't the cook. She recognized the man immediately, Major Bishop. He was wearing only his pants and a shirt without his uniform jacket. She knew he and Casimir didn't like each other, but he was an American officer, so she believed that he posed no threat.

She squinted into the rising sun behind Bishop and said in as masculine a voice as she could muster under the circumstances, "Mornin' major. I saw you outside headquarters last evening. Did you want to see the general? I reckon he'll be up soon, normally is up early."

His fist rammed into her stomach and she gasped for air, doubled forward and reached her hand out to steady herself and stop him. Didn't he recognize the general's aide de camp?

Bishop looked directly into her eyes before viciously kicking her left hip, knocking her to the ground, then snarling, "How dare you address an officer with such insolence, you little whore."

Leah tried to get up, but he was on top of her with his hand over her mouth and a knife at her throat and growled, "do you think you fooled me, or anyone else by dressing like a man so you could be with your puny little Polish bastard? You're a bitch in heat. We all knew you wanted to be with that Polish piece of shit.

"You didn't trick anyone. You might think you got what you wanted last night but now I'm going to give you a real treat. The feel of a full-sized man."

Leah spat in his face and shouted, "No you won't. I'll tell the general and you'll be sent to the stockades and hanged. Now, let me up."

Bishop laughed menacingly as he held her down. He liked boys better than girls. In fact, he despised women for their smug belief that they could get men to do whatever they wanted. Brutality aroused him, especially brutality against someone he hated, and he loathed Casimir. The pleasure he got from raping Leah would pale by comparison to the pleasure he would get from causing Casimir pain.

"Hanged for raping the general's aide de camp? What would his men think about their high and mighty General Pulaski hiding a woman he sleeps with? I'll have you and you can tell him. I want you to. See what good it does you.

"Resist and I'll kill you and report to your little general that I saw a Redcoat do it and chased him away. Then I'll slit his Polish throat."

Leah would rather have died than endure such degradation but she couldn't endanger Casimir. She knew he could be caught off guard if Bishop went to his tent and reported that she was killed by a British soldier. Bishop could get the jump on him and carry out his threat.

She lay rigid, forcing her mind to remove her from what was happening, while he tore open her trousers. She was totally dry and he forced himself into her with a savagery that was painful to both. Yet hatred drove him and he made the ordeal last as long as he could.

When he was satisfied, he cut a small gash on her right breast and said, "Just a reminder I was here and if you don't do exactly as I say, I'll kill both of you. Now listen very carefully.

"I want you to tell him exactly what just happened. Let him know that I took something of his just as he took my generalship from me. Do it soon. I want him distracted when he goes into battle. It will be his last. I'm seeing to that. He won't be around to hear it after the battle, and I want him to know I had his whore and enjoyed it. Now go. Go to your little prick foreigner. And remember what I said. I'll kill you both if you don't do as I say."

Then he let her up, but grabbed her by the arms and shook her while giving her a look of pure hatred and saying, "Remember, I will kill you and him."

When he released her, she stumbled back toward her tent, straightening her clothes as she went, still hearing Bishop's sickening laugh behind her. She was aware that someone was running down the hill but didn't dare to slow down to see who it was.

She couldn't tell Casimir. How could she? And no one else must find out about this. Bishop was right, it would distract him before the battle and cheapen her in his eyes. But she would watch the worm, Bishop, and when she got the chance, she would kill him.

The major recognized the figure charging toward him and smirked, "This is even better than I thought. I get to take care of another one of Pulaski's pets."

"You scoundrel. You horrible, dirty, disgusting coward. You don't deserve to be part of this Legion." Samuel Abbot screamed as he raced toward Bishop. He had seen Bishop holding Leah down with the knife, seen her run away clutching her jacket together, and seen Bishop's open trousers. The whole scene was baffling to him, and nothing seemed right. Lee was a girl? The major attacked her? Yet, he knew it had happened, he had seen it, and he lunged toward the major with the intent of choking him to the ground and then dragging him back to the stockade.

Bishop's only response was to stand still, wait until Samuel was close enough, and then thrust the knife he was still holding deep into his ribcage. Surprised, Samuel clutched at his chest, pitched forward, and fell face down on the rocks. Bishop grabbed the dazed, bleeding boy under the armpits and started pulling him toward the water. Samuel weakly tried to stop Bishop by digging his boots into the ground and twisting from side to side. But he was no match for the major, who dragged him into the water and held his head under until he stopped struggling. Then he shoved the body out into the current and as he watched it disappear a few hundred yards downstream, he called after it, "Pitiful, silly boy. Where is your great general now? Why didn't he ride in on his white horse and save you?"

By the time she reached her tent, Leah had barely composed herself. She bandaged her cut, dressed in her uniform and quickly emerged to resume her role as the aide de camp, getting a cup of coffee from the cook as the general's coffee pot was still at the river.

When she entered his tent, he didn't look up and simply pointed to where she was to put the coffee while busying himself with maps and battle plans, studiously avoiding eye contact.

She noticed a small stack of letters he had written on the table where he directed her to place the coffee. The one on top was addressed to the Duchess of Courland. Seeing it caused her still more heartache as she thought, *what a fool I've been. How could he have any interest in me? He knows royalty and is a noble himself. He is sought by wealthy plantation owners' daughters and wives. I have nothing to compete with such fine ladies.* Still she couldn't stop longing for him.

Leah was careful not to brush against him or allow her hand to touch his, despite the almost irresistible desire to do so. She trembled at the thought of how she wanted to climb in his lap, to be comforted by him, to kiss his neck and cheek, to tell him of the extraordinary pleasure he had given her. She would never tarnish the beauty of their brief union by telling him what Bishop had done, and especially why he had done it. She would block that memory from her mind and cling to the one of their beautiful moment together.

Casimir himself was so fearful of the flame she had ignited in him that he wasn't sure he could resist a touch from her. Her backwoods beauty and innate intellect attracted him far more than any of the well-dressed, refined women he had known. He was drawn to her strength and commitment to their common mission to kill the British. He identified with her being driven by a purpose. He surrounded himself with men like Paul, Maurice, and Sergeant Wilkes who had similar traits, and it was natural that such a woman would appeal to him.

Although he wasn't sure it was the right thing to do, he had written to Franciszka about Leah, telling her that he finally knew what it was like to consummate a love.

It was such a momentous event in his life that he needed to tell someone. He knew she would understand that it did not lessen his admiration for her. He believed Franciszka would be happy for him and would understand why he would avoid Leah until after the battle. She knew her gladiator's history better than he, and knew he couldn't be weakened by a woman before battle. But later, after the battle, after the war . . .

Casimir and Leah didn't speak of their prior evening together. Instead, they focused their disciplined minds on the battle ahead. The retaking of Savannah could be the turning point in the war and bring Pulaski's cavalry the acclaim and prestige he and many others had worked so hard to achieve. Everything depended on Savannah. Pulaski and Commander d'Estaing agreed their plan was a good one and Casimir was sure they would win the city back for the Colonists.

He turned to Leah and said, matter-of-factly, "Go get some rest. I don't need anything more and tonight's rendezvous with d'Estaing will come soon enough."

She gave a perfunctory salute and exited even though his cold voice and demeanor were breaking her heart.

CHAPTER TWENTY-FIVE

THE LAST BATTLE

Savannah, Georgia
October 9, 1779

eah . . . Lee! bring Visner, and make it quick. Then go get Abe and Samuel. They will be riding with you directly behind me," Casimir yelled.

He saw a puzzled look on Sergeant Wilkes' face when he snapped at Leah and was immediately sorry for his curtness with her.

He treasured Leah and the boys, and wanted to keep them close where he could protect them. Now, he was in a hurry to get to the designated meeting place with d'Estaing in case the commander arrived early.

Still, he was always courteous to his staff, even to prisoners of war. So how could he have been so abrupt with Leah? She had done nothing wrong. But she had created feelings that confused him and he did not know how to deal with them. One thing was certain, he could not let his guard down again, not as he was preparing for battle.

So, he pushed thoughts of Leah away as he felt a familiar surge of confidence return. He relished the burst of energy he got from fighting and leading. This battle could be a crucial turning point that would seal the fate of the British in America.

Leah found the horses pawing the ground and straining at their lead ropes. The excitement of the camp was contagious. Visner, the most seasoned, and normally the most disciplined, seemed more anxious than the others. What did he sense?

Most mounted soldiers had several horses shot from underneath them. Was that it? Had he seen too many horses killed in battle? She didn't think so. He was a war horse, accustomed to battle. Something else must have him spooked. But what, she wondered.

When Leah returned to his tent with Abe and Visner, Casimir ignored her. He took the reins, mounted and turned back to Abe asking, "Where is Samuel? There was a worried look on Abe's face and his jaw begin to quiver as he answered, "I don't know, General. I haven't seen him since he went down to the river to fetch water early this mornin'. I've looked and called for him but couldn't find him. I figured he was doing something for you and didn't think much about it at first, but now I'm scared something's happened to him."

Fear gripped Leah. She remembered seeing someone running down the river bank as she stumbled away from Bishop. It must have been Samuel and he must have confronted Bishop.

"Damn it to hell," Casimir exploded. "I can't go look for a man when I have to rendezvous with d'Estaing's troops. The outcome of this battle depends upon our meeting with them tonight, for a surprise attack tomorrow. Where could he be?"

"Sir, I'd like to go look for him, if you don't need me right now for anything else," Leah said.

"Yes, go find him, and the two of you catch up with us quickly."

"Yes sir," she said, and then silently prayed, *Oh, God please let me find him alive.*

Casimir rode off with Abe without looking her way or saying anything more to her.

He was soon near the redoubt where he was to meet with d'Estaing's men. Sitting straight in a brown hand-tooled saddle astride Visner, dressed in high leather boots, a flowing gold cape that matched the buttons and braided epaulets of his blue and white uniform, and a crowning red fez placed at its normal angle atop his flowing black hair, Casimir was ready and eager for the greatest battle of his life to begin.

He had no doubt of his success thinking, *I will win this day, and earn fame as a hero in both America and Poland. How can I not? My troops are well-trained and well-equipped and my strategy is flawless. Surprise is the sharp-edged sword that will slice through the redoubt and scatter the British and their sympathizers.*

His excitement began to ebb as time crawled by. *Where the hell, are the bloody French? We've been waiting for hours. It's almost sunrise and they were supposed to meet us at midnight,* his mind screamed.

His jaw was clenched until it became a tight, hard line, and he felt a pounding throb at his temples. His hands tightened into fists around Visner's reins. He was known, even criticized, for his impulsiveness, quick action, and reckless charges on the battlefield; sitting and waiting were pure torture for him after preparing for this battle so long, all his life really. The delay angered him. He was ready to fight. He reviewed the battle plan for the hundredth time, rechecking every detail, the placement of his and d'Estaing's men, the signals to give the French reserves who would hide until they were needed, and even where to secure the prisoners they would take.

Infuriated that the French had still not arrived and the blackness of night was fading to a light gray, he focused his mind on the battle plan.

Just as at Brandywine, I'll surprise the British with a charge they aren't expecting and are too dumb to counter. Nothing will be left but to take prisoners and start clearing Savannah of the last of the British. Savannah will belong to the Americans again and serve as a good base for the Continental Army to protect Charles Town and the southern colonies. I will have defeated the British and won the laurels I deserve.

Leah had rushed to camp, grabbed a lantern, and headed straight to the spot on the river where Bishop attacked her. She saw the dragline of rocks splattered with blood that led into the water. It was clear what had happened. Bishop shot or stabbed Samuel and pushed him into the water to be carried away by the current. This was another secret she must keep from the general.

He can't be grieving for one he loved as a son when he leads the charge, she thought. *And Abe might be so traumatized by Samuel's death he'll forget to stay close to the general. No, for now, I must conceal what Bishop has done to the General's Legion this day. But he will pay, I swear by all that is holy, I will kill him.*

She rode toward the redoubt and took the aide de camp's proper place at Casimir's right side.

"Well, did you find Samuel?" He asked.

"Yes, sir, He slipped on a rock by the river. From the looks of things, he landed pretty hard on another one. Said he was out cold for a couple of hours and then couldn't stand up for the pain in his chest. Looks like he's got some broken ribs. He's not fit for fighting today, so I left him in his tent."

"Good," was all Casimir said, but he was relieved that Samuel was okay and would not be in the battle.

Leah sat, rigid, awaiting his instructions and thought, *I must serve him well today. I have been with him long enough to know that fighting is his life. It comes above all else. I think that is why he rejected me after our lovemaking, and why he is still avoiding me. If I am to be part of his life, and I desperately want to be, I must live the role I have chosen, that of a soldier willing to die in battle. He will not tolerate weakness in anyone, not even a woman, I'll never tell him what Bishop did to me. I will let him know Samuel is dead, but only after the battle, when I have a story ready that doesn't mention Bishop raping me. And by that time I hope I have killed the major so he can't dispute what I say.*

Casimir didn't glance in her direction or speak to her again, although not doing so took a great deal of effort.

He had endured too many hardships and disappointments trying to gain fame and fortune for himself, the Pulaski name, and the first American cavalry, his cavalry — to be distracted by a woman. There would be time for her later.

Sunrise came creeping above the horizon at its usual slow pace, turning the gray sky pink, then red, and finally yellow gold. But it seemed to Casimir that it flew up from behind the marsh grass and trees, rushing into a bright and clear day that eliminated his ability to move undetected.

"Blast the French, where are they?" Casimir hissed between clenched teeth.

Then finally, in broad daylight, they trudged through the tree line behind him, with swamp and marsh mud caked on their uniforms and their horses' bellies and tails.

Their captain, covered in mud, looked no better than his men. He rode up to Casimir, saluted and offered an explanation for their tardiness, "Count Pulaski, we have suffered terribly in these American swamps. Our horses became stuck up to their bellies, the cannons sank to the axles, there was no moonlight to guide us, and we escaped one quagmire only to be trapped by another. When men tripped on the same fallen tree twice, we knew we had circled on the same trail the entire night."

Casimir's anger deepened. What a bedraggled group and what a lame excuse. He felt nothing but disdain for the pathetic array of French troops. Even though he himself had struggled through Southern swamps and knew how difficult they were to get through, he gave them no quarter. A battle had to be fought according to plan. There could be no excuses. But it would do no good to complain to the captain or let his anger show since the damage was done. He would simply have to find another way to win.

"We are together now Captain, we have a good plan, and we can still win if we stick to it," Casimir said, exercising great restraint to keep anger and sarcasm out of his voice.

In sharp contrast to the downtrodden French troops, he saw excitement on the faces of his troops which shone as brightly as the sun glinting on their gold uniform buttons. Young, eager, and proud, they sat as strong and straight in their saddles as the Pulaski lances they carried.

He still couldn't look at Leah. Her bravery and devotion had served him well as his aide de camp and as interpreter with the Indians. Then she gave him sweet gentleness and what he suspected was love between a man and woman. Maybe after this war, when the time was right . . .

His gaze moved down the line of faces. Each one reminded him of lives risked and saved by these stalwart defenders of freedom. They came from the mountains of Vermont, the beaches of South Carolina and the hills of Pennsylvania. A few were aristocrats like Paul, but most were the sons of farmers, merchants, ministers and blacksmiths. They didn't fight for titles or money. They fought for a country where they and their children could be free to build a good life on a foundation of hard work and honesty, a life free of overbearing, opulent monarchs. Others had come from France, Germany and Ireland seeking adventure, but regardless of background or education they were all disciplined and brave. He couldn't be prouder than he was at this moment to be leading them into history.

They had come to him with strong character, bravery and tenacity and he had trained them to be the best at riding, fighting, and shooting. Those were the skills they needed to win, and just as important, he gave them self-esteem and pride. They were the

Pulaski Legion. Their fame grew with each battle. Today, they will become immortal, he thought then remembered, *"You will meet immortal men and become immortal yourself."* Again, Woja's words gave him strength. Today would be his day, the day he would achieve the great glory she spoke of.

The men and their horses were startled as the ground beneath them shook. Thunder roared from the cannons on the French ships, signaling the battle was to start. A flock of frightened doves flew from the edge of the marsh to the safety of the woods. Casimir reached down to give Visner a reassuring pat on the neck whispering, "Steady now. We're going to show them today."

Screams rose from the enemy as exploding cannon balls from the French ships hit their targets. The barrage was the signal for Commander d'Estaing to launch his attack. Casimir wished they had stolen closer to the British during the night, but their superior strategy should overcome this setback.

Freckle-faced, redheaded Tad O'Reilly, Casimir's thirteen-year-old Irish drummer boy, struck up the Pulaski marching beat, fueling the men's excitement. The Legion marched and rode to a very different pace, a loud and rapid staccato Tad had composed just for them. The sound was infectious. Even their well-trained horses felt the electricity in the air but the riders held them steady. The standard bearer with an exact replica of the new American flag first unfurled at Neshaminy Creek, took his position directly behind Casimir, holding the banner high for all to see.

Looking every inch the grand general he was, Casimir raised his Sobieski sword and the sun glinted on the silver blade and gold-plated quillon making it a beacon for the men to follow.

Another day of glory awaited them. He began a canter across the open field toward the redoubt of the British. His dark hair and Visner's white main were easy for his men to follow and just as easy for the red coats to identify. He picked up the pace and led his troop headlong into the British gunfire. His cavalrymen were thrilled by the vision of their general, sword raised, astride his white stallion, yelling like a wild man while cutting and shooting his way through the British musket barrage and grape shot. Everything about him was breathtakingly bold and brave. He looked like a Greek warrior flying across the field, highlighted by the sun as though he were a mythical god.

In the midst of his charge, Casimir saw Commander d'Estaing lurch forward in his saddle and fall, perhaps mortally wounded. The French troops halted when they saw their leader fall.

Attempting to save the commander and rally his men back into action, Casimir charged across the open field toward the fallen d'Estaing until he saw he was conscious and being moved out of harm's way. He then turned back to the battle galloping headlong into the British in an attempt to get Count d'Estaing's Frenchmen to resume their charge. This tactic had worked many times before, just as it did with Washington's guard at Brandy-wine, but today things were different.

D'Estaing's troops were untrained in what to do without their leader, and were soon in disarray. Casimir raised his sword even higher urging them on, yelling, "Frais, vers l'avant, frais," and raced across the open ground urging the Frenchmen to regroup and rejoin the action. They needed a new leader and he was giving them one.

He galloped back and forth, between his and the fallen commander's men encouraging and energizing them to fight against the relentless barrage of British musket and cannon fire. The wild charge was insanity, but brazen courage had prevailed before. Only this time, something was wrong. Nothing was working as it should.

Casimir knew d'Estaing's first mistake was agreeing to give the British a day to consider surrendering which they used instead to reinforce the fort. His second was insisting on starting the battle before General Lincoln arrived with his force of more than 3,000 American troops because of his excessive fear of a hurricane destroying his fleet.

But all that should have been irrelevant. Casimir and his men were almost always outnumbered but rarely outmaneuvered. Fortifications were made to be scaled, toppled or overrun as far as he was concerned. Surprise, superior strategy, and unsurpassed horsemanship had almost always won before.

So, what was wrong? Why weren't things going as he planned?

Casimir finally got the French troops organized and positioned to attack the center. He then led his troops in a charge against the weaker left side of the British defensive line, as he and d'Estaing had planned. But the left flank was strong, not weak. It had been reinforced and was well defended. It seemed the British knew his plan and anticipated his every move.

Casimir could think of only one possible answer. A spy. He thought: A traitor gave the British our attack plan and they reinforced their left flank. Is it the woman? Women are used as spies. No, that's impossible. She has been by my side since joining the Legion. She is always by my side and is here even now in the heat of battle. This woman hates the British and is totally devoted to me. It had to be someone else, but who?

His mind raced through the possibilities.

Elijah George, the freed man Washington used as an agent — could he be a double agent? He easily moved between the British and American lines gathering information. Did the British give him a better deal than Washington? But he wasn't with me when d'Estaing and I created the plan because Washington relied on him too much to risk him in battle. Instead, Washington sent Major Bishop. Bishop. Could it be Bishop? He is full of hate and jealousy. Would General Washington's own aide betray him and the country out of spite? I can't be sure, but when the battle is over, I will find out, he vowed to himself.

But now the battle was raging and it was not going well. Despite the surprise the British had sprung on him, Casimir wouldn't retreat. Instead, he launched another charge. The noise from cannon fire, grape shot, musket blasts, screaming horses, shouting men and clashing lances was deafening. Gunpowder smoke and dust from pounding horses' hooves choked and blinded the men, and the smell of blood and urine clogged their nostrils; but the men pushed on through the hell that burned around them.

"No," screamed Casimir, as he saw a redcoat sink his lance into Tad O'Reilly's chest. A look of disbelief and incomprehension spread across the child's face as his freckles paled and he fell forward driving the lance through his back. There was nothing Casimir could do for him in the midst of the battle but give a quick prayer for his soul and be thankful that Sergeant Wilkes had not witnessed the death.

The British next targeted the flag bearer. He lurched in his saddle and started to slide to the ground after a musket ball hit him in the chest. General Washington's words rang in Sergeant Jasper's head, 'this flag must never fall to the ground.'

He rushed in, grabbed the flag, and kept advancing it toward the enemy for the men to follow. But as rode his horse up the redoubt, holding the flag aloft, he was shot and the flag fell with him.

As if watching from afar, Casimir saw that the battle would be lost, that his plan had gone awry and that he was unable to control the field.

Then he heard the unmistakable whistle of grapeshot loud and close, very close, followed by a blow and a sensation of falling, the world spinning, Visner whinnying wildly and his mind racing.

Something warm is running down my legs, could it be blood? Yes, it is blood, a lot of blood. How can this be? How can this happen to me? I am to win today. But I'm growing weak. I'm sliding from my saddle. I can't give in to this pain and weakness. I must lead my men. I have to be out in front of them. My sword, where is my sword?

He tried to make his voice forceful, but could barely whisper, "Where is Visner? Someone find him and help me to re-mount."

Trying to stand, he stumbled and collapsed onto the very earth he had fought so hard to defend. Aware that it was hard, firm earth, his mind rebelled at the injustice.

Why after swimming the Savannah River and slogging through the soft, sucking black mud and wet salt marsh full of holes and pit-falls waiting to trip even the best horse, have I ended up like this, on a hard-packed dirt hill with a wound pouring out my life's blood?

And as he was lying on the ground, unable to rise, he wondered.

Why, after finally getting to a place where horses can get a footing and charge forward to win this battle am I knocked from Visner's back by grape shot in the groin, the very part of my anatomy I've concealed all my life? It can't be. Others will see me. They'll learn my secret. Why is nothing as it should be in this battle? Wait 'til I get back to camp and find the traitor who caused this. This wound may be different but injuries are not new to me. My bones are scarred and ache from the impact of lances, swords, and musket balls I received in Poland and I survived to fight again.

But, this isn't like the other times. I'm not in control, I can't stand or even speak. Where is Franciszka's medallion, I must pray to the Blessed Mother.

He heard Abe's voice drifting through a fog. "It's a trick men, keep fighting. He will come up under Visner's belly on the other side firing. You'll see. He ain't down, he just ain't."

Then an unfamiliar voice, "We got the horse too. Let's finish them both off."

There were boots and hooves all about him. Would he be trampled? Bayoneted? Shot? Where were his pistol and sword? Visner? Where was Visner? He had to remount or he would surely die ignobly here on the ground, not gloriously leading his men.

Leah had stayed close behind as he ordered, and now she tried to get to him, but he was surrounded by British and Pulaski troops fighting directly over him. She looked around for an escape route, just as he would have done, and was sickened to see Bishop, dressed in a British captain's uniform standing safely inside the British redoubt next to a swivel shot cannon that was still aimed directly at the point where Casimir had fallen. The smirk on his face said it all—he was the traitor, and there was no escape route.

Suddenly the command, "Cease fire. Remove the wounded," came from the British side. A tradition of honoring heroes by allowing them to be carried from the field was being extended to Casimir.

The fighting stopped. Some of the boots walked away and he could see the white trousers of his cavalry uniforms as the Pulaski troops formed a protective circle around him.

The force of the cannon grape shot that hurled Casimir's body from his saddle knocked Visner off balance. A lance intended for Casimir grazed his shoulder and he tripped over the bodies of British soldiers falling to his knees. Now, struggling up, he hobbled to where Casimir lay and pushed his nose against his master like a mare trying to get a new-born colt to stand, neighing softly. But his friend, did not, could not, rise.

Dr. James Lynah's son pushed through the circle of disbelieving soldiers with a slave and Casimir had the sensation of them lifting him onto a stretcher. He heard Visner's whinnying, and knew his horse was following close by.

The jostling of the stretcher as the men walked over uneven turf and rocks brought scorching hot pain that ripped through Casimir's entire body as his blood drained away. Casimir sensed he was far more seriously injured than ever before, and that he might die.

Had the Blessed Virgin abandoned him? Had his pride defeated him? As the Bible said, 'pride goth before a fall.' Had he abandoned his faith to be abandoned by it?' He clasped Franciszka's medallion of the Blessed Virgin Mother hanging from the chain around his neck in his hand and kissed it.

Death was a risk all soldiers faced, he was resigned to it. But there was something he feared far more than death. From somewhere deep within, he found the strength to rise onto one elbow and ordered, "Take me to a ship. Don't leave me on land where the British can find me."

Though the British might torture him, he feared even more that they would turn him or his body over to the Russians for the reward. He would not have Catherine gloating over his head on a pike.

Doctor Lynah had been summoned and was by his side when he made his plea. "Sir, we are out of range of fire here. I can possibly save you if I operate here and now. At the rate you are losing blood, you will either bleed to death on the way to a ship or shortly after you board. There will be nothing I or anyone can do for you if you delay surgery."

He heard the doctor's words, but he remembered the story his father told him of the Russians mutilating his grandfather's body, of the ridicule he had suffered in the French prison because of his anatomy, and the oaths General Drevitz and Ambassador Repnin had sworn to have his head; he could not endure the thought of what they would do to him if he were captured and his anatomy discovered.

"No, a ship, take me to a ship," he muttered before fainting.

Maurice and Leah had followed behind Casimir's stretcher with Maurice leading Visner. They overheard the conversation between Casimir and the doctor.

"I'm going to find the nearest ship and ask for permission to take Casimir aboard," Maurice told Leah.

"But the doctor said he will not survive the trip to a ship, he needs to be treated here, oh Maurice, please don't go, let the doctor save him here," she begged.

"I will not. I know him, and I know his fears. He will die in peace on board a ship where he feels safe from the Russians. If we can get to one soon enough, the doctor may still be able to save him. Now, I must go."

He was back with Captain Bullfinch's permission to take him aboard the Wasp by the time Casimir regained consciousness still murmuring, "No, no . . . take . . . ship . . . "

A hand rested on his shoulder and he heard Maurice say, "It's done Kas. You're going aboard the *Wasp*, a Continental ship that will take you to Charles Town for medical care. Just rest now."

Casimir nodded slightly, then saw Leah with tears streaming down her face. Ah, she was safe and it was good to see her. He tried to lift his head to look at her. He must let her know what he felt. His eyes reached out to hers and his lips formed a soft smile, telling her everything.

That he had acknowledged her and their feeling for each other filled her heart with joy. But she knew she might lose him, and her tears flowed freely. She must be with him and care for him.

Maurice went on board with Casimir, but Leah was turned back when she tried to follow. Maurice protested but the ship's captain refused saying, "We've had enough bad luck today without bringing a woman on board."

He couldn't understand how the captain knew Leah was a woman, until he turned. She was sobbing uncontrollably. Her demeanor and actions were purely female. Her protests that she was the general's aide de camp and needed to attend him would have been met with bawdy laughter if all on board had not respected General Pulaski so much.

Maurice walked down the gangplank to where she and Visner stood. Knowing he was giving her false hope, he handed her Visner's reins, and said, "Take care of Visner for the general until he returns." It was the only way he could think of, to get her to leave.

There was nothing she could do but take the reins. Visner whinnied and looked toward the ship, then back at the field as if he was telling her to finish what his master had fallen trying to do. Her own safety was of no concern to her now, and after suffering through twenty-four hours of unimaginable emotional swings, action was the only thing that could give her any relief.

Leah charged back to the battlefield astride Visner determined to kill Bishop, and then all of the rest of them if she could. But what she found was total undisciplined, confusion. Without d'Estaing or Pulaski, the Colonial and French soldiers were running wildly away from the British looking for any place that might give them cover. To Leah, it was unthinkable that Pulaski troops would dishonor themselves like this. The scent of mangled bodies and blood spilling into the creeks that fed the Savannah River was attracting alligators and ravenous scavengers, now in a feeding frenzy, anticipating fresh meat. The troops were accustomed to fighting enemies who outnumbered them but the threat of being eaten alive was terrifying. They were frantically trying to escape from the British without being forced into the river.

Her hatred for the British magnified Leah's strength. She charged at a Redcoat and shot him. Maurice had taken the

Sobieski sword from the battlefield and sheathed it next to Visner's saddle. Now she waved it over her head just as Casimir would have done while shouting his battle cry, "Forward, forward" and charged into the enemy lines.

The cavalrymen recognized Visner and the sword and many knew the aide de camp. They began following her, thinking the general had instructed his aide to launch one of his famous charges and would be returning to the battle soon.

As she rode into the middle of the fight, she spotted John Bishop still standing alone far out of harm's way, nodding happily as he observed the near annihilation of the Continental forces. When he saw her, he puffed himself up, flicked an imaginary speck of dust from his spotless new British captain's uniform, and smugly turned to leave.

Wild with anger, she kicked Visner harder than she intended, and he sprang forward. Bishop started running but was no match for the stallion. As Visner gained on him, Leah hurled her lance with all the righteous might of her pent-up anger and hatred. It became a high-speed missile that caught him in the left thigh, exactly where she aimed.

He tried to pull it out to rise and run, but the Pulaski-designed hook was imbedded deep in his flesh. In horror, he saw Visner rear up with his mighty hooves flailing the air and realized he would again be trampled by a horse. Visner came down on his face and shoulders and continued striking out with his hooves as Leah rode calmly in the saddle with a cold gaze fixed on Bishop's crumbling body. When she pulled Visner away, Bishop had been pounded into the earth—earth wet with horse and human blood. His new uniform was indistinguishable, it could have been British or American.

To her great satisfaction, Leah saw that he was alive, conscious, and in great pain. She dismounted, and walked to his side. He gasped, "Please. Please help me." She raised Casimir's sword, took quick measure, and thrust it deep into his groin, the same spot where Casimir had been injured.

A shudder ran through his body and he started twitching. His mouth opening and closing like a fish out of water. Leah spat on him and remounted Visner, hoping Bishop's pain would last a long time, as his tormented life left him.

The Pulaski troops continued to search for a way out of the massacre. Because she was one of them, Leah knew that when they saw Casimir carried from the field they lost the sense of invincibility he instilled in them. The difference was they feared death; she did not.

Only a few held their ground, as the rout continued. Leah and a handful of the cavalry troops fought fiercely with pistols, sabers, lances and their horses' crushing hooves. Abe Hawkins in particular, seemed to be everywhere, thrusting his sword, waving it above his head Pulaski-style, and encouraging the others to keep fighting. While they did some damage to the redcoats, who were once again startled by their unexpected ferocity, the situation was hopeless. They were too outnumbered.

Sergeant Wilkes began trying to organize a fighting retreat while Jack Turner helped as best he could, but for the most part, the men paid no attention and continued to run.

In the midst of the melee, Wilkes saw Leah struggling to stay on the general's horse while surrounded by British infantry. She would be killed if something wasn't done quickly. He had seen the tenderness between Leah and Casimir as he was carried off the field and when he saw her tears and sobs as they were separated he realized the aide de camp was a woman. Now he understood why the general had been so brusque to her that morning, and then so tender after he was wounded. She must be saved.

"We ain't doin' no good here," he shouted to Jack. "These stupid idiots just run away. Come on with me. Let's help the ones that are still fightin'." The British were in for yet another surprise from what was left of the Pulaski Cavalry Legion.

Sergeant Billy Wilkes led the way twirling a whip in each hand slashing faces, throats and the hands holding guns, while his big white cross Arabian mare thundered over fallen men and knocked others to the ground.

"Git back," he shouted at Leah. "Fall back." But her answer was to push forward, even more determined to attack the British now that help had arrived. Jack Turner rounded up the mounts of fallen men and drove twenty crazed horses into the battle, wreaking havoc with the British line while Wilkes maneuvered his horse in between Leah and the redcoats shouting again, "Fall back. Git your ass back to the woods. The general needs you there."

That stopped her. Reality was overcome by hope. Could the general have recovered? Did he need her now? She had to find out.

But getting back wouldn't be easy. The British had targeted her and the big white stallion and were blocking her retreat. The old Kentucky horse-tradin' sergeant stampeded the horses Jack brought directly at them scattering the Redcoats like mice running from a hungry cat. Leah and Visner leaped into the opening Wilkes and Turner cleared for her. Wilkes, Turner, and the remaining cavalrymen followed her out.

She rode Visner hard, in her haste to get to the woods, even though Visner was exhausted from battling all day carrying Casimir and then her.

His shoulder and left knee were injured from the lance thrust and the fall, and just as they cleared the battlefield he stumbled on a cannon cart wheel and fell once again, sending Leah flying over his right flank onto a blood slickened log. The fall dislocated her shoulder and cut a deep gash across her forehead.

Her ankle buckled beneath her when she tried to stand and a nearby group of redcoats saw her go down and started zeroing in for a kill. Jack Turner and Sergeant Wilkes held them off by firing directly into them. Jack was able to catch and calm one of their horses. He lifted Leah onto its back and led them into the woods while Wilkes followed, holding Visner's lead rope as the badly limping horse trailed behind him.

When they reached the camp in the woods where most of the Continental Army troops retreated, she learned Wilkes had lied to her. The general wasn't there. But Wilkes insisted that Casimir did need her there, out of harm's way. While Leah was furious, she was too tired and injured to do more than collapse alongside the other exhausted, bloody, and forlorn soldiers.

Wilkes found someone to treat and bandage her wounds then pop her shoulder back into its socket. She refused to acknowledge any pain. Pulaski troops were tough and the general's aide de camp had to be the toughest of all. In her mind, her stoicism was a way to honor him. Her ankle was broken but nothing could be done other than binding it, and using a crutch. She was told it would heal in time. And she knew her body would mend, but her heart never could.

That she hadn't been shot or impaled on a bayonet was one of the small miracles that survivors of this bloody battle would one day tell their grandchildren.

"She rode like the general himself and seemed just as invincible," they would say.

CHAPTER TWENTY-SIX

THE WASP

Savannah River
October 1779

The ship, *Wasp*, was aptly named. The kind of chaos a swarm of angry hornets can create, spread over its deck and poured into the hold below. And, ironically, Casimir had been compared to a wasp while 'stinging' the enemy in night raids and daring day charges with a small force.

Now, soldiers, sailors, and civilians ran up the plank to the deck of the *Wasp* jostling the wounded troops being carried aboard on stretches. Sounds of cannon blasts, musket fire and screaming horses carried across the water to the ship from the still raging land battle. The crew dashed to the rigging, preparing the ship to set sail to a safer area.

Then just before the lines were cast off, freeing the ship from the angry land, Dr. Lynah and Maurice came aboard with two men carrying Casimir on a stretcher. The yelling of the crew ceased, wounded soldiers lying on deck looked at the figure wrapped in the colorful cape and stifled their moaning and cries for water. A path opened for them, marked by respect and silence.

Captain Bullfinch recognized his new passenger. He quietly motioned the men to place the stretcher near his cabin door, away from the other wounded and the hubbub of a beleaguered ship preparing to make a run out to sea.

Casimir was gravely wounded and couldn't speak, although his other senses were intact. In the past, he had always pushed through injuries and moved on. But the agony in his upper thigh and groin was different, hot and searing. It raced from his groin up through his chest, ripping the breath from his lungs. Shock set in and brought bouts of merciful unconsciousness. Each time he came to, the agony began anew. It never ceased or diminished. Unable to speak or move he could only listen helplessly as he heard his fate being decided by others, while he lay unattended on the ship's deck. Finally, the slave who helped carry him aboard pressed a flask of water to his dry lips. But he could not lift his head to drink and the young boy mercifully dribbled a few drops into his open mouth, providing only minor momentary relief from the overwhelming pain that tore at his body and brain.

"Doctor Lynah is there any hope for our brave general?" Captain Bullfinch asked in hushed tones. "Will he be able to return to battle and lead his troops again?"

"Sadly, no, my good captain. I could have performed surgery near the battlefield and possibly saved him, but he insisted on being brought onboard which delayed treatment. He has fought his last fight. The end will come soon. The best we can do for him now is to make him as comfortable as possible."

"Please doctor if there is anything, anything at all you can do to save him, you must try it, I beg of you, oh my God, please," Maurice cried out, breaking the eerie silence that had descended around them.

"I am so sorry, but as I said, there is nothing that can be done."

Regaining his composure Maurice said, "Then we must take him to Charles Town where he has friends who will either care for him during his last struggle or, or . . . take charge of his body and give him the honor he deserves. Captain, you are on a course to Charles Town, will you get us there as quickly as possible?"

Bullfinch sighed, shaking his head, "Sir I will continue on to Charles Town at full sail, but if he dies before we reach port, a sea burial may be necessary. Some crew members are very superstitious and having a corpse on board might panic them into mutiny or jumping ship."

Those words were worse for Casimir than the pain. With every aching fiber in his body he tried to call out against a sea burial but his shout was trapped in his throat and emerged as a gasp. He remembered the viciousness of the sharks, whales and other monstrous sea creatures ripping into bodies thrown overboard from the Massachusetts. But, hard as he tried, he who had crushed so many larger and better armed adversaries didn't have the strength to form three simple words, "No sea burial."

But then he heard Captain Bullfinch, "I promise we will proceed as fast as possible in an effort to save him from the sharks. I know he has fought too valiantly to meet such a fate." And Casimir remembered Woja's prediction, *the sea will challenge you, but the land will claim you.* He knew he would not be buried at sea.

"Indeed, he has!" Maurice exclaimed. "I will not allow a sea burial, for he would abhor that final resting place. No, if the worst happens, he will have a grand funeral in Charles Town with the full honors befitting a hero."

Marshalling his last reserve of strength, he was barely able to whisper "Maurice" to his beloved half-brother.

"Yes brother, I am here," Maurice cradled Casimir's head and asked, "What is it?"

"Jasna Gor . . . " was all he could rasp out, but he knew that Maurice understood his request.

Casimir realized that it was improbable that Maurice could get his body back to Poland, but he had always overcome the odds and accomplished what others thought was impossible. He had no doubt Maurice would do everything he could to make it happen, he was certain of it, and that gave him a small measure of comfort.

'Jasna Gor . . . ' were the last words Casimir would speak, although his mind kept working, trying to analyze what had gone wrong. How could fate have abandoned him so quickly? How many of his cavalrymen remained? What would happen to the Pulaski Legion without his leadership?

Then he remembered John Bishop's face so red with fury as he stormed about camp and the major's shadow through his tent wall sneaking by it as he, Paul, Maurice, and Sergeant Wilkes discussed strategy for the siege of Savannah. The man always seemed to be nearby when they were planning the attack although he was not invited to attend the discussions.

It was hard to believe General Washington's own aide could be a traitor, but he had seen Bishop rushing up the river bank early yesterday as if trying to flee from someone. He had avoided looking at Casimir as if he had something to hide.

And again, as Casimir was being transported to the ship, he had a glimpse of Bishop smirking as he was carried from the battlefield. The thing wrong with the image, which he hadn't noticed at the time, was that the Major wore a British officer's uniform. It had to be Bishop. He was the traitor that had cost so many lives, and possibly the war.

Beware the Bishop, Woja's whispered warning came back to him. Why had he not remembered it earlier or heeded Sergeant Wilkes' advice to have him jailed?

He and his men were betrayed. How could he have been so careless in openly talking of their plans? He had been intent on making his advisors understand what he wanted in his broken English along with some French, when he should have been more concerned about keeping his ideas confidential. Ironically the eavesdropping Bishop, was able to comprehend everything he planned.

How unfair. Just as he was on the threshold of his greatest glory, to be denied life itself. He had fought so hard for the freedom of others, yet had tasted so little of it himself. His father chose his military career and after he started on that path there was room for nothing else. He was losing everything. He would never again see his home, enjoy his friends, lead men, or ride a horse.

Floating in and out of consciousness, he was aware that it was a cool October day, with a gentle breeze pushing the *Wasp* toward Charles Town. The temperature was perfect and the air was dry, finally free of the coastal south's sapping humidity. He could feel the gentle rolling and swaying of the ship beneath him and taste the salty ocean spray.

Overhead, puffy white clouds shaped like his beloved mounts, Pushka, Wolny, and Visner floated by in a lapis blue sky. How many happy days he had spent with them.

Remembering those days somewhat eased the pain, and he drifted off, dreaming about what a disappointment it had been that Pushka couldn't go with him to the court of the Duke of Courland—but what a joy that Franciszka was there and how wonderful when she gave him Pearlina who foaled Visner . . .

A large wave rocked the ship shooting a jolting pain throughout his body that brought him back to the acrid smell of gunpowder, the musk of horse sweat and the warm stickiness of the blood that soaked his trousers. He longed to be clean and dressed in a new uniform, to once more look like the charismatic leader who had won countless battles.

He found comfort remembering the new suit Paul brought to the French prison, and then recalled seeing him in the recent battle when he took his usual position, on the line opposite from Casimir, and charged into the enemy. It was a successful strategy they had used together in Poland. Paul was still fighting when he left the field and Casimir knew his old friend would survive. They had played together throughout childhood, fought wars on two continents side by side, and shared many moments of camaraderie. Yes, Paul would take care of him. He knew Paul would dress him and make sure he was properly honored.

As far as his military career was concerned, Casimir was satisfied the honors he had received in Charles Town, his general's rank, the cease fire the British called to allow him to be removed from the field out of respect for his great heroism, and his splendid Pulaski Legion were all proof he had accomplished his goal of restoring the Pulaski prestige and winning acceptance for his cavalry.

He did regret that he had no children to carry on the great Pulaski name and tradition of responsibility to family and freedom. His father and Frank were gone, and Antonin had made no mention of a woman in his last letter. A great noble line could end with him.

Death's dark curtain began to move over the horses in the sky as voices around him grew faint, and his thoughts turned to the woman. The gentleness of her head on his shoulder after their lovemaking was a tender touch he'd known for only a brief moment. The one knowing look that passed between them on the battlefield, and the tears she shed when she couldn't join him on board, told him they could have had more intimacy and tenderness, the kind that he now realized every man needs. And was it possible . . . could he even hope . . . that his invincibility was not gone from the earth but perhaps flowed into her womb to reemerge in future generations? *A child will bear your name*, Woja had predicted. All her predictions came true and there were no more, except he would become immortal.

A sea gull soared overhead. His pain slipped away. He saw his father's smiling face bending over him once more, as he climbed up the braided tail of a great white stallion and onto its back. It was Pushka. He climbed into the saddle and they rode between twelve knights mounted on white steeds. When they passed through a golden gate his father said, "Your earthly work is done my son. Well done, I am proud of you."

Maurice who was still kneeling by Casimir's side, tenderly closed his eyes. "Good night my brother, peaceful sleep. You are now with Frank and our father and I must keep my promise to you," he whispered as he rose to face Dr. Lynah.

"I am so sorry he couldn't be saved, but his pain is over and he is at peace now, his countenance shows it," Doctor Lynah said. "Now I must tend to the living."

"Thank you, doctor. Casimir is my half-brother. We fought together in many battles. Since I am the only family member present I must ask if it is possible to fulfill his and his family's wishes to have at least part of him interred in the monastery at Jasna Gora. The priests have kept a place waiting for him."

"Good God, man, did you not hear anything the captain said earlier?" asked the doctor. "His body is already rotting with gangrene. The crew will panic when they catch the smell. What you ask is impossible."

"I understand, but I've heard there are ways to preserve body parts and in fact it has been done by monks for some of the saints. Do you know of this process? If so, I ask only for his heart. For that has always been in Poland, and he asked to be buried there. He is Catholic, and Jasna Gora is the holiest shrine in Poland. He once saved it from plunder. He has earned the right to be there."

The doctor looked at him with disbelief, and rubbed the white stubble that days of tending the wounded without sleep or benefit of a razor had created. After a moment, he answered slowly, "Yes, frontier people preserve their winter's supply of meat by salting it down. There are several barrels of salt pork on board the ship. Usually there's a two-inch layer of salt on top that the motion of the ship distributes throughout the meat during the voyage. As the ship was just provisioned two days ago and has been in calm waters, most of that layer should still be at the top of the barrels. It will be easily accessible."

Maurice felt his eyes filling with tears and clasped the doctor's arm. "I beg you, please remove the heart and help me preserve it and get it off the ship. I have others who will see its safe passage to Europe and from there to Jasna Gora."

Dr. Lynah nodded. "I regret I was not able to save the life of one who has made such a difference in the world. So yes, I will do it. But I must work in privacy. If any of the crew sees what I am doing they will think I am practicing witchcraft. And I also have the wounded to attend. Find a strong container at least ten inches square and begin lining it with salt. It would be best if we can seal the box with melted wax and wrap it in a heavy cloth."

Grief stricken, Maurice could only manage to mutter over and over, "Thank you, thank you, thank you, doctor," before cautioning, "We must keep this a secret between us. The British might try to capture his great heart if they knew. And the Russians would pay a handsome price for it. We already know there is a spy among us."

The doctor quickly agreed and said, "Now I have to work fast and unseen. Find a place to move the body to. There is not a moment to waste."

Maurice saw the Captain approaching from across the deck. He rushed over to him, blocking his view of Casimir. "Captain, the general has rallied and the doctor now believes there is a chance to save him if he operates immediately. He needs a private surgery. May we use your quarters?"

"This is astounding news," the Captain said. "The doctor was so sure there was no hope a few minutes ago. Are you sure?"

"Casimir has always overcome the odds, and while there is only a small chance we can save him, I beg you to let the doctor try."

"Well, yes, of course, do you need help moving the general?"

"No, Captain. I will take care of getting him inside. Thank you so much."

Maurice opened the door to the Captain's quarters and saw a long table with maps and charts scattered across the top. He swept it clean with a swift move of his arm and heard something clatter to the floor. It was a square wooden box.

He rushed back outside and helped Doctor Lynah carry Casimir into the Captain's quarters. They placed him on the table where the doctor could perform his work that the battle-seasoned Maurice could not watch.

He picked up the box from the floor, emptied it of the charting tools he found inside, carefully placed them on the Captain's writing desk, and left to find salt and wax.

He carried the box out onto the deck where he found Captain Bullfinch. "Captain, please forgive me for taking you away from your duties," he said, "But I noticed this wooden box on your table. I apologize for my brashness but I took the liberty of removing your compass and charting instruments. I know that was inappropriate and what I am about to ask is also. But General Pulaski was carrying important documents that must be safeguarded until they reach General Washington. I will find a courier to deliver them as soon as possible, but such a wooden box, sealed with wax, would both protect the papers from the weather and also alert the general if the seal were broken that someone had read them. I wonder if I might buy the box and some sealing wax from you for that purpose?"

"Certainly, you may have it. But how is the general?"

"The doctor is operating now. It is too early to tell if he will survive."

Oh, how Maurice wished his words were true.

He felt guilty about the lies he had told the captain about the surgery and why he needed the box. But he could not think of another way to keep his promise to Casimir or a better vessel to protect his heart on its long journey. The fewer people who knew of its true contents the better.

He opened his jacket and withdrew several gold coins from an inside pocket, where he kept them to bribe enemy informers, but now reached out his hand to Captain Bullfinch offering them as payment for what he considered an almost sacred box.

"Sir, please do not insult me, I am a Patriot. It is my fervent hope your brother will recover. I admired his heroism and fighting for our cause. The heroic tales of his exploits that were told about him inspired many of us during some very dark hours. I am humbled by the opportunity to help him and my country. There are candles and matches in my quarters you may use for the sealing wax."

"Thank you, Captain, your words and generosity are comforting. It was always important to Casimir for leaders like you to recognize his great contributions."

When Maurice returned, the doctor was closing the incision in Casimir's chest. A blood-soaked bag the doctor had stitched together from canvas lay next to Casimir's left elbow. Maurice had to steady himself against the table when he saw the fist-sized conical shape of the bag. Totally fatigued, physically and emotionally, he imagined he saw it move in a rhythmic breathing motion. He knew his mind had betrayed him for a moment and then felt a terrible racking sob explode from his chest.

Doctor Lynah straightened, gripped his forearm reassuringly, and walked outside. Maurice appreciated all the doctor had done including giving him time alone to pay respect to his dear brother and to take care of his body. He picked up the bag, cupping both his hands around it for a moment as he prayed, "Oh Blessed Virgin Mother, please accept him into your loving embrace." He then gently placed it in the box, which was coated with the layer of the salt he had taken from one of the barrels below decks, secured the top in place, and wrapped three layers of burlap around the box. He lit a match and dribbled hot wax from the melting candles over the entire surface.

He was interrupted by a knock at the door. It was the captain.

"I saw the doctor. He gave me the grave news. I am so sorry." He glanced at the body in its blood-soaked uniform and said, "He deserves a hero's funeral and his men deserve the opportunity to pay their respects. I'm sure General Washington will want to honor him as well. But we had to commit three other soldiers to the sea since leaving port to keep the crew calm. Some of them believe the spirits of those meeting a violent death hide in the body to take revenge on all around them. The sooner the corpse can be disposed of, the less risk we have of mutiny. It troubles me greatly, but for the safety of all on board, we must bury him at sea."

Maurice was stunned, he would not, could not, let this very thing Casimir feared so much happen. "No," shouted Maurice with fists tight at his sides. "He must be buried on land where mourners can visit the grave. Where monuments can be raised to him. He will not be eaten by sharks and sea scavengers."

"I understand. But, his life is gone and my duty is to the living," the captain said. "The best I can offer is to put in at that point directly ahead so he can be buried there, if the crew do not learn of his death before we get there. Can you accept that?"

"Yes, thank you Captain." Maurice breathed a sigh of relief, at least Casimir's remains would be saved from the sea. "I will carry him off the ship myself to keep others from knowing where he will be laid to rest. There is still a bounty for him dead or alive."

"Yes, that is wise." The captain agreed and then said, "I'm sorry for the loss to both our countries."

"Thank you, Captain, it is a great loss. You have been so gracious already, but I fear I must ask one more thing of you, something that would be important to my brother. You see, he was a proud and meticulous man. The uniform he is wearing is soaked with blood and covered in dirt. Is there some clean clothing on board I can dress him in for a proper burial?"

"I understand, from what I have read in the papers he and his Legion were very colorful. They captured the admiration and lifted the spirits of many of our citizens who grew tired of seeing soldiers in rags. I would gladly offer one of my uniforms but a naval uniform would not be appropriate and it would be much too large for him."

The captain shook his head and let out a sigh but then suddenly snapped his fingers. "I have it. When we sailed from Marble Head several weeks ago, a Mrs. Abbot gave me a uniform she was making for her son, who was serving with General Pulaski. She knew we were providing support to the troops fighting near the coast and hoped I could deliver it to him. Mrs. Abbot said she had received a letter from the general praising her son's dedication and bravery and saying he planned to make her boy, Samuel, an officer. She was so proud she decided to make him a Pulaski Cavalry officer's uniform but it was not quite finished when we set sail.

"I remember now she said she didn't have time to sew the buttons on, but she thought he could find a local seamstress to do that, and she sent buttons matching those on the vest along with the uniform."

He walked over to a chest at the foot of the bed and rummaged through a stack of his own clothing until he found it. "It is quite handsomely done and if the boy was as fond of the general as she said, I believe both he and his mother would be proud to have it used for General Pulaski's burial."

The realization that young Samuel Abbot, the boy who idolized Casimir, would be giving him his final uniform brought another wave of intense emotion for Maurice. After regaining his voice, he said, "Thank you, Captain Bullfinch, that is most appropriate.

Samuel Abbot worshipped Casimir, and the general always kept a watchful eye out for him and his friend, Abe Hawkins.

I know he would be honored to wear Samuel's uniform. If you have a needle and thread, I'll transfer the general's epaulets to it myself," Maurice said, and then not knowing that Samuel was dead, continued, "I won't need the buttons but I'll make sure both Mrs. Abbot and Samuel know and are properly thanked for this great final service they have performed for General Pulaski."

He laid Samuel's uniform on the right side of Casimir a safe distance away from the blood so it would not be stained.

"I will leave you alone then," the captain said, while exiting.

Maurice went back to where Casimir lay and began removing his clothing. He had loved Casimir as a brother and admired him more than any man he had ever known. It would be hard to go on without him. But now he had a mission — to get Casimir's heart back to Jasna Gora. It would be a challenge but one he needed. Action, especially performing such a meaningful final tribute; conceived and carried out in love for a brother, hero, and friend, would help dull his sense of loss.

He was thankful for the privacy afforded Casimir. Years earlier, Maurice had accidently discovered the 'deformity' their father had felt responsible for at Casimir's birth. Back in Poland, he had seen Casimir stand and walk from a bathing pool. After that Maurice was always considerate in avoiding situations that would make Casimir feel uncomfortable. Now, he tenderly undressed Casimir and saw that the mutilation from the grape shot concealed the anatomy he had kept hidden for so long.

The basin of water Doctor Lynah had requested to wash his hands sat close by, and Maurice used it to bathe his brother. He then slid the uniform pants up over Casimir's legs and fastened them at the waist. He gently lifted the body and slipped on the shirt and vest. The gold chain holding Franciszka's medallion dangled to the side, and he placed it over the incision on Casimir's chest. After transferring the general's epaulets from Casimir's soiled uniform to Samuel's new one, he placed the jacket on Casimir. He used a bit of the water and a small amount of the wax to smooth the tousled hair and wax the moustache. He retrieved the red fez that had dropped next to Casimir and sat it atop his head at the suave, rakish angle he loved. He was comforted. Casimir looked like the proud, dashing, and heroic general he was. He would be well-dressed on his final journey.

Maurice left him to go out onto the deck to find Captain Bullfinch and locate some canvas and ropes he could use as a wrap for the body. He walked to the ship's bow where Bullfinch was using a spy glass to scan the horizon looking for British ships. As he walked, he saw the body of a soldier slide from a tilted plank on the railing into the water below. He shivered at the thought of the feast the sharks would have and hurried on, but the incident gave him an idea.

"Captain, is it possible that we could pretend Casimir is buried at sea? It would help keep bounty hunters from searching for his remains. The traitor who caused our defeat and possibly the loss of the war may be on board. He would certainly be open to a bribe if he knew that Casimir's body was taken ashore."

"My good man, as I said before I admired the general. But I have complied with every request you have made of me and I do have other matters to attend to. The British fleet could be upon us at any time. The weather is uncertain. And you want me to take the time to fake a sea burial. Why? When there is such a burial every few minutes anyway. How could one be distinguished from another?"

"Sir, a general's burial at sea, especially for a famous general, would be different. There would be more ceremony and reverence. You no doubt know better than I how that would be done.

I give you my word I will not ask anything more and will not distract you again. We will soon be at the landing site you chose earlier where I will disembark with the general's remains."

"Damn it man. This is becoming a nuisance, but I understand your concern. Apparently, the general preferred to risk his own death rather than be treated on land where his body could be used by the enemy. If the British want it so badly I will be glad to deceive them. Go create a bundle that looks like a body and get it to the railing. You will find some ballast stones below deck near the cattle."

"Thank you, sir. I will have it at the railing in a few minutes."

Maurice rushed below decks and found several large ballast stones and a discarded and bloody blanket, probably from a wounded and now deceased soldier. He took them to where Casimir lay in his clean, new uniform. The soiled one was in a heap next to him. He added the stones and the old uniform to the blanket and wrapped it around them allowing the braided gold tassel at the shoulder of the uniform to fall out. Some of the soldiers were sure to recognize it as the trappings of an officer.

He carried the bundle resembling a shrouded corpse to the railing where Captain Bullfinch stood. The captain looked at the bundle and nodded approval.

"Lower the flag to half-mast," he yelled to a crewman near the flag spar. Then, he ordered, "Man the starboard cannon."

The burial plank lay next to his feet. He looked from it to Maurice who understood and placed the weighted blanket onto it. "Burial brigade." Two sailors stepped forward and began to tilt the board. As the 'body' began to slide, the Captain yelled, "Fire." Then "Fire" and a third time, "Fire."

Those on shore saw the flag lowered and heard the three-cannon salute and they knew the worst had happened.

The captain shook Maurice's hand and walked back to the bow of the ship. When Maurice was alone a man approached him. He wore a workman's apron with tools sticking from pockets along the bottom of it.

"Sir, my name is Joseph Henry. I am sorry for your loss."

"Thank you, Mr. Henry."

"Uh . . . I don't think you saw me but I was below decks when you came for the stones and the blanket."

Maurice was pulled out of his misery by a new fear. How much did this man know?

"I assume sir, that even without a body, people will want to pay their respects and have a memorial service for such a hero." He phrased his thoughts deferentially, and did not seem to be threatening to disclose the truth.

But Maurice was not taking any chances. "That may be true, but what is it to you? Why do you ask?"

"My boy, Joe Junior, fell at Charles Town. Nothing would do but he had to go join the Pulaski Legion after he saw them parade through town. He was raised as my apprentice and could barely get on a horse much less ride and fight in the cavalry. But I guess the general saw the want in his eyes and let him stay on as one of his infantrymen. Just to be with the general and the other Pulaski Legion made him so proud. After I got word telling me that he was killed at the battle outside of Charles Town, I received a letter from General Pulaski himself tellin' me what a fine young man my Joe was and how bravely he fought. He went on to say he took full responsibility for every man lost that day, and he hoped my family could forgive the mistakes he made and be comforted by the knowledge that Joe died doing something that made a difference in the war. You see, even though Joe died, Charles Town was saved from the British. That's worth a whole lot in my mind. And to my way of thinking it took a good man to write that letter. So, if there is anything I can do to help honor him I would like to."

Maurice remembered Casimir sitting at his table writing letters late into the night with von Hessen's record book listing the names and addresses of the family members of his troops next to him. Von Hessen had translated many of them into English, but the families of the German and French troops received the original letters written in elegant script by Casimir. How many of those letters had he written? And how many mothers, fathers, sisters, brothers and sweethearts were comforted by them? If it were possible, his love and respect for his brother grew even more.

"Thank you for letting me know about your connection with the General. I am sorry for your loss. What did you have in mind when you asked about a memorial service?"

"Well, I think in most cases there is a coffin riding on a caisson with mourners following. I am a carpenter and could build a coffin if you wanted to use it, I mean, even though the General was buried at sea . . . as we all saw . . . it would help give the people something to focus on."

Maurice could see the man was earnest and wanted to help, and he liked the idea of Casimir being laid to rest in a coffin rather than in the dirt full of worms.

"Thank you, that is a kind offer. I believe there will be such a service. If you can build it quickly, please do so. I'm leaving the ship soon and would like to take it with me. I am most grateful for your offer and will see you are paid for your work."

"I can have it ready very quickly, coffins are simple things, and in these times of war I have boards already cut to size. And . . . sir . . . I can see you were very close to the general. I am sure whatever you did today, you had a reason for doing, a reason that benefitted him." Joseph Henry walked away and began his work. And Maurice returned to Casimir to keep vigil until the ship docked.

The sunset turned the sky a dried-blood burgundy that evening, but no sailor took delight in it. Its reflection flattened and reddened the water making it seem thick and heavy. Through this motionless and eerie inlet that seemed to be waiting for an ominous event, the captain slowly maneuvered the *Wasp* close to a pier built for loading cotton and lumber onto barges. Once the ship was tied fast, he had the gangplank lowered to the pier, and ordered the crew below decks with the excuse they needed to check that everything was tightly secured before they headed out to sea.

He announced that Captain Beniowksi was going ashore to ensure that fresh horses and provisions were on the way to the troops still engaged in the battle for Savannah, and would return shortly. They would then be on their way again.

Maurice, had wrapped Casimir's body in some canvas he found onboard, concealing the new general's uniform. Once the deck was cleared of the crew's curious eyes, he stepped solemnly but sure footedly down the gangplank carrying Casimir to his resting place. He could not yet bring himself to turn the body over to anyone else. Joseph Henry and a Chinese sailor, who spoke only Mandarin, carried the empty coffin ashore.

A light was swaying down the pathway to the river from the plantation house when Maurice stepped off the pier onto a wagon road. As it drew closer he saw it was a torch carried by a slave escorting a finely dressed lady.

"Good evening sir. I am Jane Bowen, wife of Samuel Bowen, the owner of this plantation. Please tell me, we heard terrible news today that Count Pulaski was wounded and placed on board the ship you just left. We also heard a cannon salute before the ship turned toward shore. Is it true that the heroic Count Pulaski has fallen, never to rise again?"

Maurice saw a wet, crumpled handkerchief in her hand and noticed the redness in her swollen eyes and the anguish in her voice.

"I am so sorry Madam, it is true. I am Captain Maurice Beniowski, his half-brother. I saw him fall and remained with him on board the ship. The doctor and captain insisted on a quick sea burial to avoid unrest among the superstitious crew."

He then shifted his eyes first toward the bundle over his shoulder and then to the coffin. "I have brought the body of his lieutenant, Andrew Jorsky, for burial on land as he died later and the body could be taken from the ship quickly. Is it possible you would allow us to use a small plot on your land for this purpose?"

Jane Bowen blinked and looked into Maurice's eyes. He guessed that she clearly understood the situation when she said, "Yes, of course, there's a perfect spot above the river that looks east, toward Europe. I often go there for solace to meditate when I am troubled. I believe a straight northeasterly line would take you to France and then across the continent to the middle of Poland. I have often thought it would make a fine eternal resting place, but my family insists I be buried in our family cemetery next to the church. I will take you there, it is close."

He followed her to a peaceful, grassy knoll on a promontory above the water. The white plumage of egrets roosting on the tiered branches of a giant cypress tree were points of light in the veil of darkness dropping rapidly around them.

"I appreciate your offering such a beautiful spot," he said, as he directed Henry and the Chinese man to place the coffin on the ground and sent them back to the pier to wait for him. He gently laid the canvas-wrapped body next to the coffin.

Mrs. Bowen turned to her slave. "Jedidiah, go back to the main house and get two shovels from the tool shed, and be quick about it. It will be dark as pitch in a few minutes." When he returned with the shovels she told him to give one to Maurice and to begin digging with the other. Maurice did not know how she guessed he wished to help dig the grave, performing a final service for Casimir, but he was moved by her thoughtfulness as he began shoveling the soft sandy soil.

When they were finished, Jedidiah and Maurice placed the body in the coffin. Maurice asked Jedidiah and Mrs. Bowen if he could have a moment alone. They immediately stepped away leaving the lantern next to the coffin. Maurice folded the canvas back away from Casimir's face and body revealing the well-dressed general and shed a silent tear as he wished his brother farewell. He then placed the lid on the coffin and stood to signal Mrs. Bowen and Jedidiah it was okay to return. He and the slave lowered the casket into the grave.

It seemed so lonely and sad that there was only the three of them to commit his body to the gray sand. Casimir deserved parades, honor guards, bishops and priests with all the church's high sacraments at his interment. Maurice fell to his knees in the fresh spaded dirt and prayed for the acceptance of Casimir's soul into Heaven, there to be reunited with his father and Frank.

When he rose, three glistening white egrets flew across the water to the roosting tree as the last light disappeared in the west. *His soul, joining Frank and Father's,* Maurice fantasized.

It was well after dark when they smoothed the earth and scattered pine straw and cones over the fresh dirt so the grave wouldn't be noticeable either through the trees lining the path to the plantation house or from the river. As a further tribute to Casimir, the *Wasp* waited for Maurice's return.

"May I impose on you once more, Mrs. Bowen?" Maurice asked, reaching into his pocket to pull out a note he had hastily written while on the ship.

"Yes, of course Mr. Beniowski, these are troubling times," she said. "Anything, anything at all that I can do to contribute, I am most anxious to do. My husband's sympathy lies with the British but we both admire bravery and heroism. I know General Pul . . . " She blushed and corrected herself, "I mean Lieutenant

Jorsky was a great freedom fighter if he served with General Pulaski. How may I help you now?"

"Please find a means to get this note to Paul Dobrachek," he urged. "Paul will be with the Pulaski Legion. The Continental Army commanders should know where they are. God grant they are safe."

"I have a most trusted servant I will send to find my husband. We both met General Pulaski in Charles Town. In spite of his political views, my husband was drawn to him. We both admired him greatly. It will be an honor to do this for him, or . . . rather for one of his fallen men. My husband will see that the note is safely delivered, I assure you. And I promise that even though it's location will remain secret; the lieutenant's grave will be cared for with respect."

"Thank you, Madam, I and countless others, here and in Europe, are indebted to you. Now I must return to the ship. Please don't risk your own life. Let your husband carry the note to Paul."

"I will," she promised, "Godspeed," and then embraced him before he turned and walked down the hill toward the pier, leaving Casimir, like his father, on foreign soil.

CHAPTER TWENTY-SEVEN

RETREAT

Savannah River
October 1779

Leah was dazed from her injuries and the trauma of losing Casimir. She could see the Pulaski troops were trapped between the river and the advancing British Army. If they didn't find an escape route during the night, they would face certain death or capture with the first morning light.

Without either Paul, Maurice or Casimir to guide her or the troops, she didn't know what to do. They so needed Casimir's defiance and military genius to save them, and without him they seemed doomed. The Savannah River was their best option but it held its own dangers. Many of the wounded couldn't swim and would be left behind at the mercy of the British while the injured who tried to swim would likely drown. Even the fit would risk being eaten by alligators and sharks. Still, there appeared to be no alternative.

Her spirits lifted when she saw Paul approaching her. She had feared that he was killed in the battle.

"Oh Paul, I am so glad you are alive. We need help. Please tell me if you have heard news of the general. Is he recovering?"

"No, well yes." He looked worse than she had ever seen him. There was none of the usual pride in the set of his shoulders or humor in his eyes. "I was able to make my way through the

British line and I rode to the river's edge. From there I watched the ship Casimir was taken on sail down the river. After a short while, the flag was lowered to half-mast. And then I heard . . . I heard . . . " he went on, "I heard a three-cannon salute. I have lost my dearest friend and the world has lost a true patriot and hero."

He walked away without saying more or taking any interest in helping the troops escape. Leah understood that he was in no condition to help and did not call him back.

She was so distraught that she could not have carried on a conversation with him anyway. She resigned herself to die in this wooded spot. It would be by the hands of the British, but perhaps she could take a few of them with her first. It didn't matter, she had lost everything worth living for.

The sun slipped below the horizon painting a golden walkway across the water. She had always loved sunsets on the water and she drank this one in, knowing it was probably the last one she would ever see. Her thoughts of death and loss were interrupted when her wilderness training alerted her to movement at the opposite shore. She watched as tiny ripples spread out from paddles being silently and skillfully dipped into the muddy water to slowly move three rafts toward her. When they came closer she saw the men who were guiding the awkward wooden craft and recognized Tathtowe on the front of the lead raft. He and the several Cherokee with him had watched the battle and the retreat from a rise on the opposite shore and had organized a rescue.

"God Al'mighty if we didn't have enough trouble already. We now got Indians coming after us," Sergeant Wilkes swore as he walked up next to her and looked out at the approaching rafts. "The damn British must've sent some of their Indian allies to circle around behind us on the river."

"No, Sergeant, those are my friends, they've come to help us."

When they landed, Tathtowe and the others crept close to the ground until they reached them. They directed her, Wilkes, and

Turner to leave on the first raft and the other troops to follow. The rafts were too small to carry all of the men so some would have to risk swimming across with their horses.

"Oh no," said Wilkes, in as much of a whisper as his booming voice allowed. "I ain't about to climb on some piece of driftwood and leave my troops here. I'll have to stay to organize the evacuation, loadin' the men and what equipment they can take onto the rafts and choosin' which ones will have to swim the river with their horses."

Abe Hawkins rushed up to them, interrupting their conversation. "I ain't a goin' until we get Samuel. He's back at camp in the tent and can't walk. The British will kill him if they find him. I gotta go git him. I'll find my way to you later. Sam and I know how to stay in the woods for days at a time and survive on what we find."

Leah thought she had endured as much as could possibly be asked of her in one day. She pulled together the strength to face another wrenching task and said, "Abe, Samuel is not in his tent. I lied to you and the general to relieve both your minds as we went into battle. Samuel was killed by a Redcoat down by the river and his body was dragged into the water. I saw the blood on the rocks and drag marks. It is the reason he never returned from getting water."

"I ain't a believin' it. British in our camp, that don't make sense Lee, your head is all messed up from that fall you got," he protested.

"I wish it were Abe, but I caught a glimpse of the Redcoat running from the river yesterday morning. He was too far away for me to catch or shoot and he was alone so I didn't think it was worth alarming the whole camp when we were getting ready for battle. When you said Samuel went to the river to get water and I saw the blood on the rocks I knew why the Redcoat was running away."

"Which way did he go, I'm goin' after him. He won't be too far away for me to kill," Abe cried out in his anguish as Leah's words penetrated his wall of denial.

"He was at the battle, Abe. He's dead. Visner and I killed him. I swear it is true. Samuel has been avenged. Now, Sergeant Wilkes needs your help getting the men across the river. You can't help Samuel, but you can help the rest of us."

Abe wiped his nose and eyes on his dirty sleeve and nodded. Then he walked over to Sergeant Wilkes, waiting for orders.

Leah knew Wilkes was the right person for the job of organizing the men and told Tathtowe to choose a badly wounded soldier to go in Wilkes' place. Both the soldier and Leah needed help to reach the rafts and Tathtowe motioned to his Indian companions to bring the drag made of hides stretched across willow sapling poles they brought with them and he hooked it to a horse. The wounded soldier was placed on it. Jack mounted the horse. Wilkes and Tathtowe lifted Leah up to him for the slow ride to the river where they were loaded onto a raft and waited for the others.

The rafts quickly and quietly filled with men and a few provisions. They could not risk the British hearing them make their escape. Then the horses and remaining soldiers waded into the water. No one questioned Sergeant Wilkes' decisions about who would board a raft and who would have to swim with the horses. Everyone knew he was not a man to challenge when he was in command, and he had gotten them across the river safely up at Purryburg. The troops had witnessed his use of whips and his gallant rescue of Leah during the bloody battle in Savannah. Those he picked to swim preferred alligators and snakes to the sergeant's anger.

He ordered some men to swim between the horses and the rafts, using both for support if necessary, being careful not to place enough weight on the rafts to sink them. Others were instructed to hold onto the tail of a horse and let it help pull them across. They would be the ones on the outer side, where they were vulnerable to alligators and sharks in the murky water. The biggest risk was sharks. The alligators were not likely to venture far from the river bank, but they were nearer to the sea here where the water was salty and blood from the day's battle had found its way down the creek and into the river. Both factors would attract sharks and gators.

Just before they got underway, the Indians began making an almost inaudible swooshing noise, like heavy breathing, imitating the sound dolphins make when they clear the surface of the water. Soon, great gray dolphins were sighted rhythmically rising and falling above and below the water line. They stayed close as the rafts pushed off from the shoreline and the light from the tiny crescent of a new moon turned their bodies an incandescent silver that bounced the moonbeams back toward the sky. The Indians and Leah knew there would be no shark attacks that night. The Indians believed they were under the protection of the Great Spirit who controlled all animals and had sent the dolphins to protect them. Leah didn't know about the Great Spirit but she did know, and was thankful, that sharks don't venture where dolphins swim.

The still flooding river pushed the overloaded rafts downstream, toward the many small islands that dotted the area. They chose one concealed behind the first two so the British wouldn't hear or see them. Once they reached it, the soldiers stumbled ashore and fell to their knees giving thanks to God that they had been momentarily spared.

Leah watched for Sergeant Wilkes, wishing he hadn't given up his space on the raft to others. Then, after the last of the horses and men scrambled ashore, she spotted Visner's white head just above the water line and, there at his tail, was Wilkes. During the crossing, they had continued swimming from front to back and then to the front again, making sure everyone was safe and moving at a slow, steady pace. She couldn't get up to give him a hug, but rewarded him with a sparkling smile when he approached. It was the first time she smiled that day.

Paul stayed behind when the rafts departed, assuring Leah and Sergeant Wilkes he would follow as soon as he could. He hoped to get a message to Count d'Estaing telling him of their retreat across the river so that they could regroup later. But he had no way to get a dispatch to the French ships offshore where d'Estaing had been taken. And in truth, he did not know what force the Pulaski Legion should now join, if any. Disconsolate and dreading facing the troops who would want answers, he delayed as long as he could. Finally, knowing Sergeant Wilkes and the others needed him, he and his horse swam the river to the island where the remnants of the Pulaski Legion were attempting to set up camp.

Sergeant Wilkes had taken command. When Paul arrived, he saw that Wilkes had given each able man a task to keep a semblance of order and discipline. He guessed that both the stone face Sergeant Wilkes wore and his giving orders to the men was a way for him to keep himself busy and hold his own grief at bay. Paul knew the sergeant would make sure they were all safe before he took private time to grieve.

Sergeant Wilkes walked up to him, saluted with a shaking hand and gave a report on the injured and their overall situation, which was not good. And then with watery eyes the big man said, "I . . . guess that little runt of a drummer boy didn't make it either?"

"I'm so sorry Sarge. He didn't. Casimir and I saw him go down. There was nothing either of us could do."

The Sergeant nodded, blew his nose and sat down on a log. Paul joined him and they talked and reminisced about Casimir for an hour, helping each other accept the unacceptable.

The sergeant finally said, "There's something I think you need to know. That skinny Lee is really a woman. Told me her real name is Leah. I think the general was in love with her and she is for sure in love with him. It will probably make things simpler if we start treating her like a woman, even though she fought harder today than any man I've ever seen, with the exception of the general. But I don't think we should let the troops know, just yet."

Paul agreed. He was only surprised about the relationship between Leah and Casimir. Casimir had never shown interest in any woman other than Franciszka and her marriage to Duke Karl prevented anything more than a distant fondness from developing. As for Lee being a woman, he had figured that out on his own.

It was almost morning when Paul heard, "Halloo." Obviously, someone had found them and didn't want to be shot. Paul walked to him, noted the planter style long coat, vest, and boots and was satisfied that he was neither a Redcoat nor a spy. "What can I do for you, Mr. . . . . "

"Sam Bowen, sir. I have a message for Paul Dobrachek."

Paul's heart leaped. Could it be from Casimir? Had he survived? Were the half-mast and cannon salute for someone else? Or a ruse? Did he want them to join him?

"I am Paul Dobrachek." He said as he thrust his hand forward to take the message.

He ripped it open. Sergeant Wilkes hovered close by in case Paul needed him. He scanned the note quickly. It read:

> He is going home to his church and needs the
> fastest possible transit. He will sail from Charles
> Town. You are the obvious choice to make the trip
> with him as his longest and dearest friend. I believe
> his sword should be with him, if you have it, will you
> bring it? My heart breaks for the two of us and the
> Pulaski Legion.

It was signed simply, 'M'.

Knowing the note might fall into enemy hands, Maurice had deliberately made it vague.

Paul found the note confusing, but the reference to church surely meant Casimir's body was going to Jasna Gora as he had always wished. But he heard the cannon salute for a sea burial. And how could a body be transported that far, when it would take weeks for it to make the crossing? He only knew that Maurice wanted him in Charles Town with the Sobieski Sword. He had to get there quickly, not only to help find 'the fastest transit' possible but to solve the riddle Maurice's note created.

He was concerned that a civilian had found them so easily. He thought that Samuel Bowen must be the Loyalist husband of Mrs. Bowen whom Casimir had mentioned.

"Sir, thank you for this. I know you put yourself at risk to get here and your sympathies lie with the British, increasing the risk even more. Your kindness will not be forgotten. But please tell me how you found us. No one that I am aware of knew of our retreat to this island."

"I travelled these islands as a timber dealer buying logs throughout this section of the Low Country, he replied. "I know that the river is the only way to escape from the battlefield area and it made sense that you would drift downstream in the flooding current toward one of the barrier islands. Most of them have only scrub brush, but this one has heavy vegetation with wagon roads from the sea to the interior. The roads were built by former planters who raised fields of rice until the war drove them to the mainland. It would be easy to set up camp here and transport your supplies inland. You chose your landing site well.

"Obviously, I can't give your position to the British, even though I support them, without disclosing I met with a Continental army officer. That would be a hanging offense and I don't want to hang."

"But why did you take such a risk? Why didn't you refuse to bring the message?"

"I met General Pulaski. I was quite impressed by the dashing count willing to risk his life in a foreign land. Even though we were on opposite sides of this war, I was saddened by his death. My wife sent the note to me saying he had died in battle and that she was asked, as a personal favor to the general's brother, to have the note delivered to you. She assured me it was a family matter and had nothing to do with the war. I find it hard to say no to my wife and this seemed a mission of mercy, so I agreed. Now I must return home as quickly as possible and say nothing to anyone about meeting with a Pulaski Legion officer."

"Thank you, sir. We are most grateful to you and your wife. By the way, I cannot take undeserved credit. It is happenstance that we landed here. We knew nothing of the roads or the island's history. The sergeant over there just thought it was shielded from view of the British and would be a good place to find shelter, to fish, hunt game on horseback, and hide from the redcoats."

"Well sir, it seems you have providence on your side. I can't wish you well in the war, but I hope you have a good, long life." Bowen said as he departed.

In spite of Bowen's promise of secrecy, Paul knew the troops would have to leave this pleasant island. If one person found them so easily, others could also. But meanwhile, he had to find a way to Charles Town to meet Maurice.

CHAPTER TWENTY-EIGHT

CHARLES TOWN

South Carolina
October 1779

aul needed Visner for his ride to Charles Town since most of the other horses were either injured, dead, or traumatized by the roar of cannon and their long swim in the river. His own horse had barely made the crossing. Even with his injuries, Visner was the strongest and fastest horse left. Paul called on all the experience he had with horses, as well as all that Casimir had taught him, but Visner still shied away from him.

He was no ordinary horse. He was an exceptional animal for an extraordinary man and was now as frantic as any person would be who had lost a close friend. Paul could neither control nor console him. Still, Visner was the fastest, most dependable mount in the Pulaski Legion and Paul desperately needed him for the ride to Charles Town, in part because he needed to feel a connection with Casimir. Somehow riding Visner would give him that final camaraderie with his lifelong friend. And, deep down, out of respect for the horse, he thought a final farewell to his master was warranted, if indeed Casimir's remains would be in Charles Town. He had to meet Maurice and he had to get there quickly. If only the horse could understand that they would be performing a great service for Casimir.

Visner's tired and bruised muscles had been soothed and cooled by his extended swim in the brackish river water, and, like his master, he was stronger and quicker to heal than most. But he became highly agitated after arriving at the island. Casimir and he had an exceptionally strong bond and Visner had a special sense about when his master was hurt or needed help.

His agitated actions showed he knew something was terribly wrong. Where was his friend Casimir? Why didn't he get up when he fell off in battle like he always did before? Why did those men carry him away? Why wasn't he here to brush him, talk to him and feed him. It was far later than the normal time for their evening ritual of togetherness. As minutes and then hours passed without his master coming to him, his agitation grew and he broke free of his hobbles to roam the camp looking for Casimir.

Sergeant Wilkes went to the horse and, in a low and soothing voice said, "Now, now, Visner, it'll be okay. Your master is gone, but you still have to help lead the troops and help us win this war. You are the best war horse ever and you need to make your master proud. Now settle down, for ol' Sergeant Wilkes." But Visner pulled away and galloped through the camp, snorting, kicking and whinnying with an almost human wailing.

Paul sent Jack Turner to get Leah and when she arrived, wounded and anxious for word of Casimir, he said quietly, "I need your help. We're returning the general home to Poland. Maurice has asked me to meet him in Charles Town tomorrow morning with the general's sword. I need to ride Visner but he is too agitated. Do you know where the sword is and do you have anything personal of Casimir's I can carry so Visner will accept me? I need to ride him since he's the fastest mount we have and," then choking on his words he swallowed hard and continued, "And . . . he's been such a loyal friend he should be allowed to say good-bye to his master."

Then regaining some of his composure he said, "I thought as his friend and aide de camp you might have some of Casimir's personal items or know where we could find some?"

She stumbled backward and Jack caught her before she fell. Her face had gone white and Paul guessed he had just given her the final and indisputable confirmation that Casimir was dead.

Her face crumbled, and Jack let her sag to the ground and walked away. "He's dead and even his remains will be taken far away." She sobbed. "I never got to see Jimmy's grave and now I won't get to see his either. It's not fair, it's not fair. I want to kill all the British."

"Leah, I understand." She gave him a shocked look. "Yes, I know you are a woman and that Casimir . . . Casimir valued you. So, for him, you must help me fulfill his wish to be returned to Poland."

"I, I . . . I valued him too." She dried her eyes and said, "All his personal belongings were either with him when he entered the battle or back at his headquarters that the British will have ransacked by now." She hesitated, looked even more mournful and said, "I do have something we could try. I will go get it."

"Let me go, you are in no condition to walk."

"No, I have to do it myself. Just help me up and hand me that pole to use as a crutch."

He did as she asked and she hobbled away, a pitifully small and forlorn figure that he felt a great sympathy for. She had given so much and lost so much.

She soon returned dragging the sword in the dirt next to her as she clutched something to her chest. Paul saw that it was the shirt she was wearing a few minutes earlier.

"I wore this shirt when the general and I . . . when . . . we were together. I had planned to always keep it, but if it will help do what he wanted, I am willing to give it up. Visner let me ride him into battle while I was wearing it today.

"I killed John Bishop with the sword during the battle. He was the traitor. I saw him dressed in a British uniform standing next to the swivel shot cannon that killed the general. He also killed Samuel Abbot."

Paul, was not surprised about Bishop. Like Wilkes, he had thought the man dangerous. But it was good to know the traitor was dead. They would not have to worry about being turned into the British by one among them. He was sorry to hear about Samuel. It was another loss to the Legion.

"Thank you, Leah. Under the circumstances, Sergeant Wilkes and I will keep your secret from the troops but we will treat you with the respect you deserve. Not just because you are a woman, but because you have made great sacrifices for the cause and for the general. Now I must hurry."

Paul immediately rubbed the shirt lightly under Visner's nose. After catching the scent, he whinnied pitifully but calmed down and allowed Paul to swing up onto his back and ride away. The long trip to return Casimir to the arms of Jasna Gora had begun.

It was low tide and Paul found a narrow point to cross the inlet to the South Carolina shore. He began a headlong race through a countryside infested with thickets, swamps and British troops, but he arrived at the Charles Town dock early the next morning. The *Wasp*, now a somber ship with its flag hanging lifelessly at half-mast, lumbered slowly into port and tied up beside the city dock. Oppressive heat blanketed the town. Maurice walked down the gangplank carrying the wooden box containing Casimir's heart with great care. Paul met him with a sorrowful look in his eyes and gazed at the box questioningly.

"His heart, it must get to Jasna Gora," said Maurice, passing him the precious box with the same tender touch he would have used to handle the Holy Grail.

Paul walked a few feet away to where Visner stood and retrieved the Sobieski sword from its scabbard. He handed it to

Maurice and said, "He had many friends and admirers here and I'm sure they'll help us find the fastest vessel to Europe. You, as the family representative, must go while I must stay and continue his work."

"But, you were a brother to him longer than I was," Maurice protested. "You knew him since childhood. I met him much later. Your fathers were close. It's just as much your right as mine to accompany him. The honor and privilege should be yours, or we can both go."

"No, Maurice, I loved him like a brother, as he loved me," said Paul. "We would have died for one another but his blood flows in your veins and it's your duty to go. My duty to him is to see that the Pulaski Cavalry survives and is recognized. Just make sure Poland and all of Europe know what a hero he was. They slandered him and refused to recognize him when he fought the Russians. Now let the world know what he did here. He will be famous forever for his fight for freedom in both the Old and New World."

"I'll make sure of that," replied Maurice. "The Pulaski name will be known in school rooms and war rooms for centuries to come. He has earned that honor."

"I know you'll do him justice, Maurice," said Paul, adding "And just one more thing. You should meet with the Duchess of Courland, Franciszka Kransinki. She'll be distraught and will want to hear the details of how he died. She can help plan a proper service for him at Jasna Gora. Tell her he died as courageously as he lived, and he was wearing her gold medallion when he fell. He never took it off."

"Paul, my friend, it will be done," pledged Maurice, reaching out for the wooden box and its precious contents.

Visner saw the two men who were with Casimir more than any others and the sword that his master was never without. He moved over to them and whinnied pitifully, looking at the box held so protectively. Maurice instinctively drew it back, but Paul said, "No, let him sniff it."

Maurice complied and the horse nuzzled the box, then pawed the ground with his front hooves, and rose up on his rear haunches as if Casimir was astride him leading a charge. He then rubbed his warm nostrils against Maurice's neck, as if to say, "take good care of him," and calmly returned to where Paul had dismounted earlier with his head lowered.

Paul and Maurice were moved beyond words. Tears flowed freely down both their cheeks. "You must see that he is taken care of, he should not carry another rider into battle." Maurice told Paul.

"I will, I think I know a horse trader from Kentucky who will give him the care he deserves," Paul promised, and then said, "Now let's find out when the next ship sails."

They wrapped Leah's shirt around the box, Maurice strapped the Sobieski sword around his waist, and they left immediately for the governor's home. They informed the servant who answered the door they were calling on behalf of General Pulaski. They could hear the heavy footsteps of the governor running down the hall to the door. He swung it open, pulling his breakfast napkin from his collar and vest and wiping it across his moustache.

"Gentlemen, how may I assist you? I rushed to the door as soon as I heard our beloved General Pulaski's name, please tell me . . . "

"Governor, we are sorry to disturb you. I am Paul Dobrachek, a lifelong friend of General Pulaski's and this is Maurice Beniowski, his half-brother. You have no doubt heard that he fell at the siege of Savannah yesterday," Paul said in answer to the governor's questioning look.

"Yes, horrible news, we are all saddened," he replied. "He was such a charismatic personage. He lifted all our spirits and his valiant drive against the British saved us. Is there anything I can do to help? Oh, forgive my manners will you come in and join me for breakfast?"

"No thank you sir. We are here on a matter of some urgency and your assistance would be of great help," Maurice said.

"Yes, yes, anything I can do, I am happy to."

"We need to find a ship bound for Europe as soon as possible," Maurice continued.

"You are in luck, gentlemen, *The Freedom*, an American privateer, is leaving for France this afternoon. I know the owners and the captain."

"Thank you, governor, will you book passage on her in my name," Maurice asked.

"Of course, Mr. Beniowski," the governor replied. "*The Freedom* is small, sleek and fast. With a good wind, you can be in France in four weeks. God speed and may General Pulaski rest in peace."

"Thank you, sir, we will let you get back to breakfast now. The general enjoyed knowing you."

"You are quite welcome, I am happy to do what I can. By the way, can you tell me why the haste to get to Europe?"

"I need to notify his family in person and take care of some business matters on his behalf. There will be a memorial service at the monastery where he worshipped and arrangements for that need to be made," Maurice replied being partially truthful.

By late afternoon Maurice had boarded *The Freedom* with the small wooden box, now wrapped in Leah's shirt. Paul went aboard to say a last good-bye and, with more emotion than Maurice had ever seen him display, confessed, "I don't know what I will do, or how I'll do it without either you or Kas."

Gone was the good-natured humor that had always lifted the spirits of everyone around him. All that was left was sadness and fatigue. He was two years older than Casimir and he was ready to give up fighting forever, now that his leader and best friend were gone.

"If we do get that good wind, he will be with the Paulite monks at Jasna Gora in five weeks," Maurice said, obviously trying to console Paul. "As soon as I know the monks' wishes, I'll send word to his mother, brother and sisters so they can attend the service and light candles for him in the church's great nave. Casimir will be with the brave knights who gave their lives for Christianity and what they believed was the right cause. It's fitting, Paul, very fitting. He had the wisdom to know that is where he belongs.

I plan to give Antonin his sword. It has been in the family for generations and should remain with a Pulaski," Maurice said, then continued, "As for me, Paul, I don't plan to return to America. Kas told me Antonin has done quite well for himself so he may need someone good at analyzing things to help manage his estates. If not, I may become a lawyer and represent the less fortunate who don't normally get legal help. I think Casimir and my father would like that."

"Yes, I think Josef would be proud," said Paul. "As for me, as I said, I'm not sure what I'll do. It will be easier for me to leave America without you or Kas here but I don't think his work here is finished so I may stay . . . for a while at least. I want to see that his cavalry is preserved and properly recognized — we may have to fight a few more battles to accomplish that.

"Uh, before I say good-bye, there is one other thing. Do you mind if I take that shirt back with me? Visner is calmer with it nearby and the person who loaned it to me would like to keep it."

"Certainly, Paul, here it is," Maurice said as he unwrapped the shirt from around the box and handed it to Paul.

Thank you, Maurice, write when you can. I'd like to know about the service at Jasna Gora and your new career. Be safe, my friend, and have a long and joyous life."

They embraced and parted, never to see one another again. The circle of the three steadfast friends had been broken and could never be rejoined.

Paul returned to camp and the troops while trying to think what Casimir would do, whether he should continue to fight for the Americans, and what to do about the woman, Leah. Above all, he was driven to make sure Casimir was properly honored in America.

All of Charles Town mourned, especially the ladies. Many wore black arm bands to display their mourning and handkerchiefs and smelling salts were kept handy for those who were overcome by the loss. Meanwhile, the southern ladies kept busy doing what they did best, preparing food and planning an event, the most momentous event of the season, Casimir's funeral. They got Governor Rutledge to agree that the entire town would turn out, all shops would be closed, and bands would play Polish and American songs.

A cortege with a rider-less horse carrying a boot turned backward in the stirrup led the Pulaski Legion through the main square. Leah, dressed in her aide de camp's uniform for the last time, rode between Paul and Sergeant. Wilkes in the front line. Abe Hawkins followed close behind, too distraught to focus on the dignitaries who saluted them as they rode by the viewing stand. Ministers, members of Congress, and army officers followed on foot. Red and white flowers, Poland's colors, decorated every doorway and all flags flew at half-mast on this and the following thirty days. The Marquis de Lafayette attended to pay his respects and to represent General George Washington.

General "Lighthorse" Harry Lee, the famous horseman and Low Country Revolutionary leader, delivered a brief eulogy.

"His name is dear to me. He was sober, diligent, and intrepid, gentlemanly in his manners, and amiable in heart. He was very reserved,

and when alone, betrayed strong evidence of melancholy. Those who knew him intimately spoke highly of the sublimity of his virtue, and the consistency of his friendship. Commanding his heterogeneous corps, badly equipped and worse mounted, this brave Pole encountered difficulty and sought danger. Nor have I the smallest doubt if he had been conversant in our language and better acquainted with our customs and country, but that he would have become one of our most conspicuous and useful officers."

The absence of Mrs. Samuel Bowen was noted. She chose to spend the day in silent meditation, reading verses from her Bible while seated on a bench she ordered set up on the grassy knoll overlooking the river.

CHAPTER TWENTY-NINE

PULASKI LEGION CAMP

Near Savannah
October 1779

ack and Sergeant Wilkes stopped pretending Leah was a man. They hid her from the prying eyes of the other soldiers, in a small tent, claiming the general's aide contracted yellow-fever and was quarantined. After two weeks, her energy had not fully returned and she began getting sick each morning.

Only Leah knew why she had symptoms not common to war wounds and her life suddenly changed. All her crushing losses were bearable, and she was filled with happiness and wonderment. She had been right in her conviction that conception occurred when she and Casimir made love. What a child this would be. It would grow up in a free country with the kind of education her mamma had wanted for her. It could achieve anything it wanted through good character and hard work. This child had to be protected at all costs.

She never allowed the thought that the child could be Bishop's to enter her mind. She knew this child was conceived in love, tenderness and beauty, not some ugly and vengeful assault.

She found Sergeant Wilkes squatting at the water's edge. He had been recalling the spontaneous handshake he enjoyed with Casimir as they were readying for the crossing of the river to march to Savannah. Leah could see his big shoulders shaking, and waited until she saw him blow his nose in his handkerchief before calling to him from a distance so as not to embarrass him.

Recognizing her voice, he rose immediately, wiping a sleeve across his eyes and saying, "Damn 'no see'um gnats got in my eyes. They sting like turpentine on a cut."

"Sergeant, I have news that will make those damn gnats fly away," she said with a broad smile. He didn't understand, since no one was smiling these days, especially Leah, and replied, "I don't get your drift, Laddie . . . I mean Leah. 'Cuse me Ma'am, I know you're a woman, and a mighty fine one, but sometimes this ol' mind of mine just slips back to better times."

"Well, Sergeant, I guess you'll have to give that Laddie idea up. I'm going to have a baby. *HIS* baby," she said, almost bursting with pride and happiness.

While it was pretty hard to knock the wind out of Sergeant Wilkes' sails, Leah had done it. He looked unbelievingly at her, but the joy on her face convinced him she was telling the truth. Grabbing her and lifting her to the sky, he shouted, "Well blast my worthless hide. Oh, Lordy, I didn't hurt you, did I? Here, do you need to sit down? Let me get you some water . . ."

"Sergeant Wilkes, everything is fine, wonderful in fact," she said. "I don't need to sit down. Matter of fact I feel like dancin'."

"Well we got to tell the others," he hollered. "Do they know? When . . . oh, don't tell me. I don't need to know nothin' else." The sergeant's belly danced for both of them as he turned in circles, throwing his hat in the air, and doing a little jig.

"Whoa, Sergeant, you're going to trip and hurt yourself if you're not careful," she warned. "We can't let that happen because this baby's gonna' need a strong uncle to help him or her grow up the right way. I reckon you're the right man for the job." Her words stopped him dead in his tracks. Then, pausing to scratch his head, he said, "Me, I can't be the little Countski's uncle. I never had young'uns around. I wouldn't know what to do for him if he got hurt or asked tough questions, and he's likely to be smart, real smart given who his mammy and pappy are.

"I think you're just perfect for the job and I know his father would agree," she assured him.

"Mam, that's more than I could've hoped for," he stammered, "all them others would be willin' to fight for the job."

"Well, Sergeant, he or she can have more than one uncle, but you'll always be Uncle Number One and I'm sure you can learn to deal with all his questions," she laughed.

"Let me get the others," he yelled. "I still can't believe it. Finally, we've got somethin' to celebrate." Then he ran off to find Abe, Jack and Paul.

When they returned, she gave them the joyous news and everyone agreed to help with the child. Abe became an honorary brother, Jack another uncle and Paul became the Godfather.

They all agreed she must leave immediately for the safety of the north Georgia mountains, far away from the battlefields. Since both she and her husband, Jimmy, were war heroes, they were sure she would be awarded some land there where she could raise the child in the peaceful solitude and beauty that only mountains can provide.

By week's end, Tathtowe had arrived to accompany her and Paul started arranging the trip. "Sergeant Wilkes and I will see you through the Redcoat territory between here and Charles Town," he said, then interrupted himself to share his secret.

"Before leaving for Europe, Maurice told me about the kindness of the Bowens at Greenwich Plantation outside of Charles Town, particularly Mrs. Bowen," he said, glancing from Wilkes to Leah, before lowering his voice to just above a whisper. Knowing they could be trusted, he continued, "You see, Kas wasn't really buried at sea and only his heart went to Poland. His body is in a hidden grave on the Bowen's plantation. I think we have a pilgrimage to make. It's an opportunity for us to say thank you to Mrs. Bowen and a final farewell to Casimir. Leah, if you agree, I'll send a messenger ahead to alert Mrs. Bowen of our visit."

Thrilled by his information, she responded breathlessly, "Oh yes, Paul, please. I need to see his grave. Yes, oh yes please. I'm so relieved that he's buried on land."

Following Paul's orders, the Pulaski troops had moved to another hiding spot, closer to the South Carolina mainland, several days earlier. Now, the three friends waited for nightfall to ride across a narrow inlet and then overland to the Greenwich plantation. Travelling slowly, due to Leah's injuries and pregnancy and to evade the British patrols now roaming the countryside, they headed north along the South Carolina coast toward Charles Town which, thanks to Casimir, was still under the Continental Army's control. The light of a full moon and the reassuring bird calls of Tathtowe's friends guided them to the loading dock at Greenwich plantation where Jane Bowen was waiting.

The sun had made its journey across Poland, France and the Atlantic Ocean and now rose up out of the river in the east, causing fresh dew to glisten on the grass as Mrs. Bowen led the way to the grassy point.

A pelican seemed suspended between sky and water as he started his search for breakfast among the mullet and shrimp in the stream. Silently, the group dismounted and walked near the edge of the promontory. Tathtowe pointed to a spot where the pine cones were arranged too neatly to have been blown there by the wind. Leah stepped forward, bowed her head and fell to her knees at the site. The others kept a respectful distance for a few moments before Paul knelt beside her, crossing himself and saying a prayer as he pulled a rosary from his vest pocket.

Paul, Leah, and Wilkes were joined by Mrs. Bowen in holding hands to form a circle around the grave. Bowing their heads, they prayed for the soul of their beloved comrade and then each, in turn, read his favorite verse from the Bible Mrs. Bowen had brought with her. Leah read about the birth of the Baby Jesus and when Paul's turn came, he read the story of David who slew the giant, Goliath, with his slingshot. Wilkes smiled, thinking how appropriate that seemed for one who had encountered and overcome so many giants in his brief life.

After the reading, Leah walked over to a holly bush decorated with bright red berries and broke off a small forked branch. A bough of mistletoe with white berries lay close by. She carried both back and laid them on Casimir's grave. Her beloved, always the colorful hero, needed some decoration at his resting place and the red and white berries symbolizing Poland's colors were perfect.

EPILOGUE

eneral Provost lost no time in locating Casimir's island headquarters and ransacking it. He hoped to find intelligence about plans General Washington had for the Southern campaign following the siege of Savannah, and other information about troop strength and caches of gunpowder and ammunition. Instead, he found a few maps of the area, and what appeared to be a diary and a journal, all in Polish, a language he considered gibberish. In disgust and anger, he threw them all in the river assuring that Casimir's secret specialness would remain a secret.

A similar fate had already befallen Dr. Borloff's labor of love: his meticulous journals. The professors at St. Petersburg Medical School discounted them because they were in Polish, not a language that fell into the 'enlightened' category at the time. They used them for kindling in the massive fireplaces that heated their offices. Thus, the world remained ignorant and intolerant of these gifted people for many years

In December, a courier brought a letter from Maurice which read:

My dear Paul,

Our brother is finally at peace. The service at Jana Gora was held in mid-November. Father Stephen from Warka and Bishops Trosky and

Luckowski officiated at a high mass in the grand nave. Kas' mother, sisters, and Antonin, as well as the Duchess of Courland, attended. The priests swung orbs with burning incense spreading scented smoke as they marched from the main church to the Hall of Knights. An old priest from Skawina Valley requested and was granted the honor of leading the processional. Kas' mother and Antonin placed the box containing his heart in a vault behind one of the wooden panels that line the wall. Marianna asked that our father's small prayer book be added and it was. Three lines of lighted prayer candles sat atop tables in front of every wall of the grand Knight's Hall. They burn for father, Frank, and Casimir and will remain lit until next Easter.

The old priest from Skawina brought with him a girl named Roksana who took me to the grave of Wolny a few days later. A stone marker with the name Darius Pruneski carved in scrolling script sat above what appeared to be the grave of a local parishioner. It was well tended and the only unusual thing about it was the clumps of oats that grew on each side of the marker. I believe Kas is pleased.

Antonin has changed greatly. He seems more loyal to Russia than Poland. For that reason, I donated the Sobieski sword to the knights' weapon room at Jasna Gora and I have decided to reopen father's law practice. I am reading all his law books and studying cases to prepare myself. I have kept my heritage secret from the family so as not to hurt anyone. Again, I believe Kas is pleased.

Please keep in touch,
Maurice

Mrs. Samuel Abbot was shocked to also receive a letter from Poland written by Maurice Beniowski. She recognized the name as the trusted adviser of General Pulaski who Samuel had talked about. It read:

Dear Mrs. Abbot,

I would like to extend my deepest condolences to you and Mr. Abbot on the death of Samuel.

He was a brave and loyal Pulaski Legionnaire who performed valiantly while riding with General Pulaski. On the day of his and the General's deaths, he discovered the traitor among us and tried to apprehend him. Unfortunately, he was killed in this brave attempt.

You may recall how proud all the Pulaski troops were and how smartly they dressed. The uniform you made for Samuel was one of the most handsomely made I ever saw. I hope you will not mind, and will instead consider it an honor, that General Pulaski was buried in it. It was impossible to ask permission at the time. The general was very fond and devoted to both Abe and Samuel. I have no doubt that he is proud to be wearing Samuel's uniform and that they now ride together in a better world.

May God Bless and smile upon your family. The Pulaski Legion and America owe it a great debt of gratitude.

Yours,
Maurice Beniowski

Paul took temporary command of the Pulaski Legion, making sure the discipline, pride and horsemanship Casimir valued were maintained. Abe was his second-in-command and he was even more driven than Paul to maintain the Pulaski aura.

Paul and Maurice never saw each other again, but remained close friends by corresponding frequently. Three years after Casimir's death, Maurice wrote to Paul:

> Father is now at Jasna Gora with Casimir. A sergeant Casimir left behind in Istanbul to recruit troops and buy supplies with money sent by Prince Radziwill squandered the funds on whiskey, women, and opium.
>
> After he heard of Casimir's death, he tried to extort money from the family by offering to show them where Josef was buried. Apparently, he accompanied Frank with the body as far as the Polish border but turned back after helping Frank bury father when they encountered a large force of Russians.
>
> I insisted he show me the grave before getting any money, which he did. I took several men with me, and after we had the remains properly loaded onto a wagon, we captured the sergeant and brought him to Warka where I prosecuted him for blackmail. He is serving a long sentence in prison.
>
> The grateful monks complied with Josef's lifelong wish to be buried in one of the side chapels of the great cathedral. I have no doubt he is with Frank and Casimir in heaven where Kas is designing gowns for the angels.
>
> Leah's baby girl was born near a place called Marthasville, Georgia. She named her Marianna Ellen Pulaski, for both Casimir's and her own mother. Mary, as she was called, grew up learning about nature, horsemanship and history from her Indian friends, Uncle 'Wilkie', half-brother Abe and her very special, Papa Paul, as she called them.

Leah asked Paul to write a letter to Casimir's mother in Polish, telling her that she had a granddaughter named for her. Paul wrote the letter and made arrangements to have it delivered to Marianna. There was never a reply from any member of the family.

When Mary was four years old, Paul brought Leah a letter from someone else in Poland, the Duchess of Courland. Leah was astonished that it was addressed to her. It read:

My dear Leah,

I know you are a special woman because you captured the heart of my hero and the hero of two countries. Miraculously, his leather pouch was found buried in the sand at his last headquarters by a member of General Lafayette's staff after Savannah was retaken from the British.

The Marquis made sure that a letter Casimir wrote on the day before his last battle was forwarded to me. In it he told me of your brief relationship and his hope that it could be resumed after the war was won.

While others may deny his child, I will not. God Bless you for continuing the noble Pulaski line and much good fortune to you and the child. I would love to hear of her progress if you will be kind enough to keep in touch with me.

Leah, put the letter away in the Bible Mrs. Bowen had given them after the service at Casimir's grave.

The Bible became the family Bible and was passed down through generations. The letter from the Duchess disappeared, but another Leah wrote disclosing Mary as the daughter of General Casimir Pulaski survived through the ages.

Mary was smarter than the other boys and girls her age and displayed an uncanny ability to train, ride, and identify with horses. Her favorite was Pushka II, son of Visner and the mare Sergeant Wilkes stole from the British officer. All Mary's descendants have been involved with special horses, training, riding, racing, performing challenging feats, and loving them.